'Cain is among a new breed of women writers stepping way out of the stereotypical female comfort zones . . . serving up meatier and more gruesome stories. . . . Cain knows how to keep readers fortified with psychological drama'

Chicago Sun Times

'Cain continues to display her remarkable ability to probe the psyches of her characters . . . Popular entertainment—the kind that mixes crime, horror, and even a little black comedy—just doesn't get much better than this'

Booklist (starred review)

ALSO BY CHELSEA CAIN

CHELSEA CAIN
LET ME GO

SIMON &
SCHUSTER

London · New York · Sydney · Toronto · New Delhi

A CBS COMPANY

First published in the USA by St. Martin's Press, 2013
This paperback edition published by Simon & Schuster UK Ltd, 2014
A CBS COMPANY

1 3 5 7 9 10 8 6 4 2

Simon & Schuster UK Ltd
1st Floor
222 Gray's Inn Road
London WC1X 8HB

www.simonandschuster.co.uk

Simon & Schuster Australia, Sydney
Simon & Schuster India, New Delhi

A CIP catalogue record for this book is available from the British Library

Paperback ISBN: 978-1-47113-428-9
Trade Paperback ISBN: 978-1-47113-427-2
eBook ISBN: 978-1-47113-429-6

Typeset by Hewer Text UK Ltd, Edinburgh
Printed and bound by CPI Group (UK) Ltd, Croydon, CR0 4YY

For Kelley Ragland, Andrew Martin,
and George Witte. Thank you.

CHAPTER

1

Archie Sheridan had a paper birthday hat on his head and six bullets in his front pocket. The bullets rattled when he moved, making a clinking sound that no one else seemed able to hear. The hat's tight elastic band dug at his neck. He pulled at it, feeling the imprint of a ligature mark forming.

"How was the bridge traffic?" Doug asked. Archie guessed that Debbie had sent him over. *Go make small talk with the awkward guest.* That's what he was now, a guest. It still took some getting used to.

"Fine," Archie said. He rolled the bullets between his fingers. It was a lie; the bridge had been backed up for miles.

Archie saw Doug's face light up and then turned to see Debbie coming toward them from the kitchen. She was wearing a white chef's apron and licking frosting off her thumb. Her hair was dark and very short and her body was strong and lean, though Archie supposed he wasn't supposed to notice that anymore. Doug reached to put his arm around her waist as she stepped next to them, but she gave him a quick look and he pretended to do something else with his arm. *No public displays of affection in front of the guest. He might feel bad.*

"Archie says the bridge was clear," Doug said. He was tall and long-limbed, with light brown hair and a wispy beard that made him look like a graduate student. He looked ten years younger than Archie even though they were the same age.

Debbie gave Archie a knowing smile. "Really?" she said. "At this time of day? That would be a first."

Archie shrugged. He'd grown a beard once, but it had just made him look like a rabbi.

He could hear the kids in the kitchen, but he couldn't see them. They had stationed him in front of a window in the far corner of the living room, while they frosted the cake. The apartment still smelled like the lasagna Debbie had made for dinner. There were dirty dishes on the table.

The window looked south, over downtown Vancouver. Archie could see the red taillights of airplanes lining up to land at the Portland airport, a barge making its way east down the river, the lights of the new Vancouver library, Fort Vancouver, a movie theater, a digital bank tower clock. Oregon was just on the other side of the Columbia River, a distant, indistinct horizon. Archie lived in Portland. He knew its topography, its skyline, its bridges and landmarks. But the view from Debbie's window was an unfamiliar landscape.

"It's not as far as people think," Debbie said. "If you can avoid rush hour."

"I know," Archie said. But the truth was, he wondered sometimes if she had moved far enough. He missed his family, but he knew that the farther away from him they were, the safer he could keep them.

Debbie's condo was on the tenth floor of a secure building. The kids didn't have a yard anymore, but no one got in or out of the building without being buzzed in. The elevators required a keycard to operate. Security cameras monitored the hallways. Two security guards were on duty in the building around the clock.

The kids could live without a yard.

"Sara wants to be Gretchen Lowell for Halloween," Debbie said.

Archie inhaled quickly and coughed.

Debbie patted him on the back. "I already said no," she said with a glance toward Doug, who was staring at his shoes. "I just wanted to give you a heads-up. In case she brings it up."

Archie's fingers tightened around the slick brass cartridges in his pocket. "She's seven years old," he said.

"She wants to be something scary," Debbie said. "It has nothing to do with you. Most of her friends don't even know."

It had been over a year since Archie and Debbie had split for good and she had enrolled the kids in school in Washington under her last name. It made sense for security reasons. It also required fewer explanations. Archie had been a public figure during the years he ran the Beauty Killer Task Force, but after Gretchen Lowell had kidnapped him and tortured him for ten days, he had reached a new infamy. Since her escape ten weeks before, the media had been revisiting every horrific detail.

Doug's eyes darted around for something to say. "I hear you got a dog."

"Sort of," Archie said, not wanting to explain.

"The kids are excited," Doug said.

Archie didn't need Doug to tell him anything about his kids, but he decided that now maybe wasn't the time to broach that particular topic.

"We're ready," Ben hollered from the kitchen.

Debbie pressed some matches into Doug's hand. "Can you help the kids with the candles?" she asked him.

He smiled, happy to have been given something to do, and pattered off to the kitchen.

"He's nice," Archie said. He was making an effort to be pleasant, but he also meant it. Doug was dependable, good with the kids, kind to Debbie. Doug engineered wind turbines, a profession with limited exposure to serial killers. Archie liked him. When he could force himself to forget that Doug was having sex with his ex-wife and spending quality time with his children.

"Are you seeing anybody?" Debbie asked gently.

Archie's fingers tightened around the bullets, and for a moment he thought that Henry might have told her about Rachel. But when he looked at Debbie's face, he saw only tentative concern. The question wasn't loaded.

"Not really," Archie said.

She frowned skeptically. "What does that mean?" she asked.

Archie opened his hand and let the bullets drop back to the deep corner of his pocket. "It means I'm seeing some-one," he said. "But I don't want to talk about it yet."

Debbie's face brightened with pleasure. "Is it Susan?" she asked.

"No," Archie said. "Seriously?"

Debbie narrowed her eyes. "Does Henry like her?"

Archie hesitated.

"Tell me she's not blond," Debbie said.

Before Archie could come up with an answer, singing filled the living room and Archie's children appeared, faces bathed in the glow of lit birthday candles. Doug stood be-hind them, guiding them forward, protective hands on their shoulders. Sara held one side of the cake plate and Ben had the other. They were dark-haired and freckled, baby teeth giving way to changed smiles. Every time Archie saw them, they looked more like their mother.

They finished singing, and Archie blew out the candles.

As he stepped back from the cake, he felt his phone vibrate.

"Make a wish, Daddy," Sara said.

He didn't make wishes anymore. But he pretended. He closed his eyes. When he opened them, Sara was beaming at him. "What did you wish for?" she asked.

"I can't tell you," Archie said. He pulled a candle from the cake, and handed it to her to lick the frosting off.

The phone was still vibrating in his pocket.

Archie glanced at the caller ID. It was Henry.

He turned away from the cake, and answered the phone. "Yeah," he said.

"I'm at the Gold Dust Meridian," Henry said. "Homicide. You'll want to see this."

Archie turned back toward the cake. Sara and Ben were plucking candles off and sucking them clean. Debbie had threaded her hand into Doug's.

Forty-two candles. Six bullets. Two kids, every other weekend.

"Okay," Archie said.

He slid the phone back in his pocket and looked over at Debbie. He didn't have to explain. She knew the drill.

"Do you have to leave?" she asked.

Archie nodded.

"One slice of birthday cake to go," Debbie said. "Coming up."

CHAPTER

2

The man lying on the bathroom floor of the Gold Dust Meridian looked to be in his mid-fifties, but it was hard to tell because part of his head had been blown off and was dripping down the wall over the toilet. The killer had used a high-caliber weapon at close range. The wall was spattered with a stew of flesh, hair, and bone. The toilet seat was down, stained with a fine mist of sticky red. The bathroom was small. No window. One toilet and a sink. The body took up three-quarters of the floor space. The crime scene techs had a long night ahead of them.

Archie and Henry stood in the hall, studying the scene over the crime tape across the open door, their gold shields clipped visibly to their belts. The bar was closed. The patrons had been assembled in the seating area, and were waiting to be interviewed. The lights had been turned up and the music turned off, and the place was uncomfortably bright and quiet.

"You know you have a birthday hat on, right?" Henry said. He had a day's growth of salt-and-pepper stubble on his shaved head, and with his hulking physique he looked more like the bar's bouncer than a homicide detective.

Archie reached up and touched the conical paper hat on his head, then pulled the hat off and pushed it in the pocket of his blazer. He could hear the toilet in the bathroom running, the hollow sound of water moving through pipes. The blood on the floor gleamed in the fluorescent light.

"Why am I here?" Archie asked Henry. It was an ugly crime scene, but didn't look like something for the Major Case Task Force.

Henry glanced back down the hall where two uniformed officers stood talking. "You knew him," he said quietly.

Archie didn't let himself react. Not emotionally. But he consciously waited a beat before he let his eyes move back to the corpse on the floor. He could make out the man's jaw and neck, half of an ear, but the face was too damaged. He didn't recognize him.

Henry pulled an evidence bag with a Visa card in it out of his pocket. "He had a tab open at the bar," Henry said.

Archie took the bag and examined the name on the card. This time his spine stiffened despite himself. He looked back at the body. Then back at the card. "Shit," he said.

"What do we do?" Henry asked.

Archie rubbed the back of his neck and tried to think. The cops in the hallway were still talking. Someone from the ME's office would be here any minute.

"Let's go for a walk," Archie said.

Over the years, Archie had gotten good at projecting calm. He'd developed that skill first as head of the Beauty Killer Task Force, dealing with relatives of victims, his bosses, other cops. Then, after he finally went home from the hospital, after Gretchen Lowell had held him captive for ten days while she tortured him, he had again come to rely on that particular expertise, so he could pretend to be normal for his family. Two years later, when he'd come back to work after medical leave, addicted to pain pills, he pretended every day. He could look anyone in the eye and assure that person, with absolute confidence, that he was fine. He had learned to lie.

That skill had come in handy. He had Gretchen to thank for that.

Now Archie forced himself not to hurry. He relaxed his limbs. Henry transferred the evidence bag to one of the patrol cops and Archie and Henry exited through the side door. Archie searched for anyone watching, anyone out of place. It was almost eight P.M. on Friday night. Four patrol cars were parked in front of the Meridian on Hawthorne Boulevard. If Portland was hipster central, then the Meridian was Portland condensed down to its hipster nucleus. The vibe was midcentury, but the zeitgeist was 1970s cocktail lounge. An oil portrait of a topless pinup girl hung just inside the door. There was a crowd out on the sidewalk most nights. But tonight's crowd was different. The patrons who'd been interviewed and released were now milling around out front. Many were in costume. A man dressed like Jesus Christ was hitting on a young woman in braids and a brass breastplate. Thor was arguing with a woman whose costume of strategically placed green fabric led Archie to presume that she was either a superhero or some kind of saucy leprechaun. Cleopatra was taking video with her cell phone. Three zombies stood chain-smoking on the sidewalk. The bar had clearly been hosting some sort of Halloween event. Then there were the array of pedestrians who'd stumbled upon the scene— people with take-out boxes, cyclists, dog-walkers, and diners from nearby restaurants who'd wandered out to rubberneck. Some of them had cell phones out and were taking pictures. Cars slowed as they passed.

Archie and Henry walked around the corner past a Lebanese restaurant housed in a restored Queen Anne Victorian. In the restaurant's yard, stainless steel patio heaters glowed dark orange over the outside dining area.

As they rounded the corner, the street turned residential. There were fewer people around. Maybe someone was watching; maybe someone wasn't. But Archie didn't want to take chances. He unlocked his car, and they got in. He didn't turn on the car. He didn't want the dash lights to illuminate their faces.

The dead man in the bathroom was Carl Richmond. He was a DEA agent.

"We can't blow his cover," Archie said.

"I'm guessing it was already blown," Henry said.

Archie rubbed his face with his hands. "We don't know that."

"This was an assassination, Archie," Henry said. "The bartender saw him. Says he was alone. He met someone in that bathroom. The toilet lid was down. He wasn't in there pissing. He met someone, and that someone shot him in the head. No one heard anything, so I'm guessing our killer used a silencer. No one saw anything. Body was discovered by the next guy who went in there to expel some Miller Lite. This was planned. It was a hit."

Henry was right. But it didn't change anything. Richmond had been running a deep cover operation. Drugs. Dirty cops. It had been years in the making. Henry didn't know the half of it. "We don't do anything," Archie said. "We follow DEA's lead on this." If they didn't know Richmond was dead, they'd know soon enough. "We let this play out," Archie said. He peered out the car window. An upstairs light was on in the house across the street.

"You think they're watching?" Henry asked. He wasn't talking about the DEA.

"If I imported massive amounts of heroin," Archie said, "and I suspected someone was a cop, and I had him killed, that's what I'd do." A woman walked by the car with a black Lab. "I'd wait for twenty guys in DEA jackets to show up. Because if they do, I know for sure that I was right."

"Either way, everyone your buddy worked with is in danger."

"He wasn't my buddy," Archie said. He'd known Carl for fifteen years. But he had never liked him. Carl put his investigations ahead of everything, and he was willing to sacrifice anyone to make the case. A decade before, Archie had delivered Carl an intelligence jackpot—Leo Reynolds, the twenty-one-year-old heir apparent of the family that had controlled the drug business in the Pacific Northwest for the last quarter century. Leo had come to Archie for help getting away from his father; instead Archie and Carl had sent

Leo back to operate under deep cover for the DEA. Ten years later, Leo Reynolds was still living a lie. If Archie had it to do over, he would have told the twenty-one-year-old Leo Reynolds to change his name and walk away.

Leo.

"Carl was Leo's only contact," Archie said, feeling his stomach tighten. If they had gone after Carl, Leo might be next. Archie fished his phone out of his jacket pocket and started to punch in Leo's number. But halfway through pressing the digits, Archie stopped, his fingers hovering uncertainly over the phone's keypad.

A couple walked past the car, holding hands. She was already a little tipsy, and stumbled and then laughed.

It gave Archie an idea. He deleted the partial number he'd entered, and called a different telephone number instead.

Susan Ward picked up right away.

"Hey," she said. "You never call me. Have you noticed that? I am always calling you. But you never call me. Is that weird?"

"Is Leo with you?" Archie asked.

"Seriously?" Susan said. "You're calling my phone and it's not even to talk to me? Do you know how strange that is?"

"Is he with you?" Archie asked again. He glanced over at Henry, who was sitting in the passenger seat, watching him. It was chilly. The car was dark. The windows were fogging up.

"Yeah," Susan said. "Why?"

Archie could hear her reporter's instincts kicking in and knew he had to get off the phone before she got too interested. The last thing he wanted was Susan getting involved in this.

"I need you to tell him that I have to cancel lunch, okay?" Archie said. "Tell him that exactly. Archie needs to cancel lunch."

"He has a phone," Susan said. "Call him and tell yourself."

"Susan," Archie said. "Please."

He needed Susan to do this for him, and he needed her not to ask questions.

Susan groaned. "Fine," she said.

"Thank you," Archie said, trying not to let her hear the relief in his voice. He ended the call and started the car.

Henry had found the piece of birthday cake on the dash and had unwrapped the tinfoil and was eating it with his fingers. "Tell me that's code," Henry said, his mouth full, "and that you really didn't just call to cancel lunch."

Archie wiped some condensation off the windshield with his forearm. "We need to go celebrate my birthday," he said.

"Your birthday isn't until tomorrow," Henry said.

"Do you have cash?" Archie asked, eyes on the rearview mirror as he put the car in reverse. "Small bills?"

"For what?"

Archie allowed himself a smile as he pulled away from the curb. "The strippers," he said.

CHAPTER

3

Why Leo suddenly wanted to go to the Dancin' Bare, Susan didn't know, but she wasn't happy about it.

She was dressed for the opera.

They weren't going to the opera. They were supposed to be going to a musical stage adaptation of the Patrick Swayze eighties movie *Road House,* but she had just bought an embroidered silk cape at a thrift store and she was determined to wear it. It was silver, with a red lining and a rhinestone clip at the neck, and it grazed the back of her knees when she walked. She had paired it with a black sleeveless shift, hot pink tights, and her silver twenty-eight-eye Doc Martens. She had recently dyed her hair black with a white skunk stripe down the middle, and the whole look was very Cruella De Vil meets Daphne Guinness. It was perfect for a fringe theater performance. It was not ideal for a strip club.

Leo breezed past the doorman, while Susan stalked sullenly behind him, through the wood-paneled entryway into the dark bar. Posters on the way in advertised the chance to meet girls "up close."

She did not like to go to strip clubs with Leo. It wasn't that she had anything against strip clubs per se. She just didn't like the way that everyone at the strip clubs seemed to know her boyfriend. Leo's father owned some of those clubs. Leo did business at some of them. But there was more to it than that. Leo liked these clubs. He liked them in a way that Susan knew she could never fully understand.

It certainly had nothing to do with the decor.

You couldn't smoke in bars in Portland anymore, but the club still reeked of stale cigarette smoke, and no one had bothered to collect the black plastic ashtrays that were still stationed on every surface. Candles flickered, Italian-restaurant-style, in red glass jars on the tables. Colored Christmas lights festooned the ceiling, some blinking, some not, every string a different style from the last, seemingly hung at random, as if the whole mess had been left behind by a rowdy bachelor party of drunken elves. Rope lights outlined the bar and the stages, the PVC tubing affixed with a staple gun. All that gaudy lighting, and the place was still too dark to see properly. Leo knew where he was going, though. He led Susan around the line to play Keno, past the first stage, toward the main stage at the center of the room. The club was bustling with the usual suspects. A dozen testosterone-fueled frat boys gathered around two tables and chanted encouragement to a poor asshole wearing a candy bra over his shirt and pounding a beer. Men in suits hunched over cocktails, ties loosened, wedding rings in their pockets. A few couples leaned close, giggling. Some Portland Timbers fans were so drunk that one of them nearly tripped over his scarf. And then there were the creepy guys, the ones who sat along the stage racks, their caps pulled low, nursing beers and clutching cash in their hands.

Susan could tell that Leo was looking for someone. He wasn't obvious about it, but she noticed his eyes scanning the room. He must have settled on someone, because he bee-lined for a table at the far side of the main stage. A birthday boy, apparently—Susan could see the dorky paper birthday hat he was wearing. As Leo and she sidled past the stage, behind the creepy guys, Leo nodded at the stripper who was performing. She had dark hair and melon-sized breasts and a star tattooed over the pelvic bone she was swiveling. The stripper mouthed the words *Hi, Leo.* She was wearing a red headband with devil horns on it. Susan wondered if she always wore it, or if it was supposed to be some sort of Halloween costume. Maybe she'd started out in a full Satan ensemble and had slowly stripped it all away.

They got to the table and Leo put his hand on the birthday boy's back. The birthday boy turned and looked up.

"Archie?" Susan said, the sound of his name swallowed by the music.

Henry appeared then, with two beers in plastic cups, and he set the cups on the table and sat down in the chair next to Archie.

Susan looked from Henry to Archie, expecting some sort of explanation, but she didn't get one. Henry avoided her eyes.

Archie took one of the cups and lifted it in a toasting motion in her direction, and some of the beer slopped out of the cup onto the table.

Was he drunk? Was Archie Sheridan drunk in a strip club wearing a child's birthday hat?

Susan wasn't sure what to say. It was like the time she went to get her eyebrows waxed and one of her editors from back when she'd worked at the *Herald* was there making an appointment for an anal wax. She couldn't get through an editorial meeting after that without picturing his smooth, hairless sphincter. There were things about people you just weren't supposed to know.

Her face must have communicated her bafflement, because Archie pointed to the birthday hat. And then at Henry. "His idea," Archie yelled over the music.

Susan tightened her fingers around Leo's arm. She wanted out of here. She had fled the brow wax and never gone back to that salon again. Archie could get drunk and go to strip clubs. That didn't mean she had to watch it.

Archie motioned for Leo to lean in close and then Archie said something to him.

Leo stood up and laughed and clapped Archie on the

shoulder. "Let's get you a birthday present," he said loudly. He looked up at the busty brunette humping the stripper pole and beckoned her with his finger and she smiled and slid off the stage. Archie picked up his drink and stood up next to Leo.

Everyone else around the stage jeered and wolf-whistled.

"What's going on?" Susan asked.

Leo said, "I'll be right back."

Susan was confused. They were leaving her? "No," Susan said. "I'll come with you guys."

Leo leaned close to her and took her gloved hand. "I just bought Archie a lap dance," he said. He nodded at the girl, who was now pressing her bare chest against Archie. "I think he'd be more comfortable if you stayed here."

Susan laughed. Leo was insane. A lap dance? Archie didn't want a lap dance. Archie Sheridan didn't do lap dances. There was no way. This was some sort of miscommunication. Susan looked over at Archie, waiting for him to honorably reject the offer. The girl had her arm around Archie's waist. He didn't seem to mind. He was smiling. Susan felt her face get hot. "Oh," she said.

She stood there stiffly, while Leo walked Archie and the girl off to one of the private rooms down the back hall, and all the creepy guys seated around the stage clapped.

Then she sank down in Archie's empty seat and peeled off her purple elbow-length gloves. She could feel herself starting to sweat, the silk cape sticking to her skin.

"You changed your hair," Henry said.

"Don't talk to me," Susan said.

A new song started, and another mostly naked girl climbed up on the stage and started wiggling. Susan took a sip of Archie's abandoned beer. She didn't know what it was, but it tasted terrible.

CHAPTER

4

Leo led Archie and the dancer into one of the club's private rooms. It was the size of a walk-in closet with a built-in bench on all sides, and mirrored paneling custom-fitted to the walls and ceiling. The effect was disorienting—Archie's reflection stared back at him from every surface. The dancer took his hand and he allowed her to guide him to the bench and sit him down. Leo grinned and took a seat next to him on the bench. Then Leo poured some of the Glenlivet he'd acquired as they had passed the bar into two glasses and handed one to Archie. There was a brass pole at the center of the room. Electronic dance music played through speakers that Archie couldn't see. The dancer leaned forward and blinked at Archie with her heavily made-up eyes. Her breasts swung. Her chest was beaded with sweat. She was wearing devil horns. "Happy birthday," she said in a breathy voice.

"Thanks," Archie said. "But it's actually not until tomorrow." He looked over at Leo, who was already topping off his drink. "I don't really want a lap dance," Archie said.

Leo reached his arm out and turned a dial on the wall and the music lowered to a tolerable background beat. Then he settled casually back onto the bench, the glass of whiskey resting on his thigh. His eyes moved to the dancer. "There's a camera," Leo said under his breath. He took a sip of whiskey and glanced at the far corner of the ceiling. "They can't hear us. But they can see us." His gaze flicked over to Archie. "What's going on?"

The dancer stepped back and reached for the pole. As soon as her fingers found it, she dropped into a spin, her body moving effortlessly around the pole, legs crossed at the ankles, her feet wedged into five-inch-high heels. Her face was blank, her eyes focused on the middle distance. Archie hesitated.

"She's okay," Leo said. "She's a friend."

"You can't trust people just because you've slept with them," Archie said.

"I didn't say I trusted her," Leo said. He took a sip of whiskey and smiled. "I said she wouldn't say anything."

The dancer continued to twirl around the pole, her hair grazing the floor. Her black thong matched the color of her shoes.

"Carl Richmond was killed tonight," Archie said in a low voice. "Someone shot him in the head in the bathroom at the Gold Dust Meridian. Happened about two hours ago."

Leo nodded. He didn't say anything, but Archie saw the corners of his mouth tighten. Carl had recruited Leo. He'd trained him, and mentored him. He had been, for years, Leo's only lifeline to his alternate identity.

"You okay?" Archie asked.

Leo finished off the remaining whiskey in his glass in one swallow, his eyes on the camera. "They know someone's inside," he said. "I don't know if they think it's me. But they know enough to be paying attention."

"So get out of there," Archie said. "Come with me right now. Walk away."

"I've been doing this for ten years," Leo said. "It's not an assignment. It's my life."

"They'll kill you," Archie said. Leo had always been in danger, but if they were actively onto him, he was in serious jeopardy. And if Leo got himself killed, Archie knew that

Susan would never forgive him. "Your father will kill you if he finds out who you are," Archie said. "You know that, right?"

"I'm close," Leo said. There was a gravity in his eyes that Archie had never seen before. "Richmond was right. About corruption. But my father isn't just paying people off. He has partners, Archie. People high up in law enforcement."

It was what Richmond had always suspected—the reason why Jack Reynolds's shipments always made it through. If it was true, and Leo could identify the corrupt officials involved, it would be a game-changer. This was why Richmond had been willing to risk so much. "And you can get names?" Archie asked.

"He's grooming me," Leo said. "It's a family business. He wants his kid to run the store. The man is loath to give anything up. But he knows he has to."

"What kind of law enforcement?" Archie asked.

Leo poured more whiskey in his glass. "I don't know."

"DEA?" If Jack had someone in the DEA, Leo was in even greater danger. Richmond had protected him as a source all these years. But with Richmond dead, Leo would get a new contact.

Leo chuckled and lifted the glass to his mouth. "Probably," he said. "Richmond worried about that. He always told me that if anything ever happened to him, to assume DEA was compromised. He said the Bureau would step in. They've been running their own investigation, but they don't have anyone inside."

There were only a handful of people who knew Leo was working against his father. If the FBI was taking over, Archie knew there was only one person Richmond would have trusted to run the operation.

Leo lifted an eyebrow. "You know who my new contact is, don't you," he said.

Someone banged on the door. Archie and Leo barely had a chance to exchange a glance before the person on the other side pushed the door open a crack. "Leo?" a gruff voice called through the opening. Leo signaled the dancer with his hand

and she spun off the pole and moved in front of Archie just as a man pushed through the door. Archie kept his eyes on the dancer in front of him, but he could see the man's reflection in the mirrored walls. He was tall and broad, with a face that had seen too many fists up close. Scar tissue had left his flesh lumpy and his features lopsided. His cheekbones and nose looked like they had been broken and reset more than once by someone who had no future in otolaryngology. His hair was a thick graying tangle that hung in wisps against his shoulders. His upper arms were the size of Archie's thighs. No, Archie thought. Bigger. The dancer rotated her hips in low slow circles, her eyes leveled at Archie. Archie swallowed hard.

The man took in the scene with barely a flicker of eyeball movement, and Archie had the feeling that he'd been watching on a monitor somewhere, and that he knew exactly what he'd find.

"What are you doing?" the man asked Leo.

"Celebrating with a friend," Leo said, lifting his glass. "Are you following me, Cooper?"

"He's a cop," Cooper said with an almost imperceptible nod in Archie's direction.

The dancer was still writhing in front of Archie. She traced her fingers around her nipples and moaned.

"He's a family friend," Leo said. "My sister, as you may recall, was murdered by Gretchen Lowell." Archie had scooted back on the bench as far as he could go. The dancer was caressing her abdomen with her hands. Leo chuckled. "This is Archie Sheridan."

"Nice to meet you," Archie said.

Cooper grinned at Archie from every mirrored surface in the room. His teeth were stained gray from old fillings. "The hero cop," Cooper said. He crossed the room in four steps and stood with his arms crossed, behind the dancer, who appeared not to have noticed that Cooper had entered the room, or was pretending that she hadn't. "I know who you are," Cooper said. He regarded Archie with head-cocked suspicion. The dancer ran one of her hands along her inner thigh. Cooper sat down on the other side of Leo. The bench shook. "He almost gets himself killed going after your sister's killer," Cooper said to Leo, "and all you get him is a lap dance?"

"You're right," Leo said. Archie glanced over at Leo as Leo poured himself another drink and lifted it to his mouth. Then Leo turned to Archie and said casually, "You can fuck her, if you want to."

Archie coughed. The dancer kept moving her hips. The star inked over her pelvic bone was black, about the size of a nickel. "Maybe I'll play that by ear," Archie said.

The conviviality left Cooper's face. "What's your problem?" he said. He leaned forward, toward the dancer. "Is he hard?" Cooper asked her.

Her expression didn't shift. For a moment Archie hoped she hadn't registered the question. Then she squatted in front of him and pushed his knees apart. Archie glanced at Leo for help, and got only a faint shrug. Cooper reached under his jacket and made a movement like he was unsnapping a shoulder holster. The dancer slid her hands slowly up Archie's thighs. Her eyes were still fixed on his, that dead stare, both seeing and not seeing, and Archie let himself look back. Her mouth was open a little, her head between his knees. She licked her bottom lip and arched her back a little so that her breasts lifted. She let her fingers dance over his zipper. She smiled at what she found.

"So is he a eunuch, or what?" Cooper asked.

"He's hard," she said. Her thick lashes fluttered in Cooper's direction. "Want to feel?"

Cooper stood up, and for a moment Archie thought he was going to take her up on the offer. But Cooper just stood looking at Archie. "So fuck him," Cooper said.

The dancer glanced at Leo.

"Wait," Archie said.

"Do you want to get off or not?" Cooper asked.

Archie grasped for something to say, some way to get out of this without compromising Leo. The dancer was still between his legs, a hand on each of his thighs. "I'm a little drunk," he said.

"Maybe he wants some privacy," Leo said. "Turn off the camera."

Cooper's eyes went to the corner of the ceiling. Then back to Archie. The room refracted all of their faces. Cooper. Leo. Archie. The dancer. It made Archie dizzy.

Cooper studied Archie for another minute and then seemed to make a decision about him. He reached into his pants pocket, got out a clip of cash, peeled off three hundred-dollar bills and laid them on the bench between Archie and Leo.

"It's on me," Cooper said. Then he pointed at Leo. "Walk with me," he said. "We need to talk."

Leo gave Archie a weary look. "Have fun," he said.

The dancer climbed back to her feet, tucked herself between Archie's open legs, and began rocking back and forth against his groin. Archie was going to kill Leo for this. "Thanks," Archie said.

The door closed behind Cooper and Leo, and Archie was left in the mirrored room with the girl. The rocking turned into slow circles. Archie could feel his face flush.

"What's your name?" Archie asked.

"Star," she said.

"Will we know when the camera's off?"

"You'll see the red light go out," she said.

"Okay," Archie said. He kept his eyes fixed on the camera. "We'll just play along a little longer."

She had lifted herself off of him now, but only by centimeters. Her elbows were above her head, her hands holding her dark hair up. He could see the sides of her breasts as they swung while she writhed. The edges of his vision were going black. He tried to think of something else besides the nearly nude girl with her ass in his lap. But he couldn't avoid it. He saw her in every surface, every angle of her.

"Touch me," she said.

A trickle of sweat crawled down Archie's neck. "I'm okay, thanks," he said.

"Guys don't just sit there," she said. "Put your hands on my hips."

Archie studied the camera. He had no doubt they were being watched. Probably by Cooper. Archie lifted his hands from where he had been gripping the bench and placed them on the curve of Star's hips. His palms were damp. His fingers grazed the waist of her thong.

"You haven't done this before, have you?" she asked.

Her shoulder blades seemed to crawl under her skin; her spine undulated. Strands of her loose hair feathered against his face. "Not really," Archie said.

The camera's light went off. Archie exhaled and lifted his hands from her body. "It's off," he said.

Star climbed off of him and sat down on the bench at his side. She had instantly transformed. The parted lips, the heavy eyelids, the blank expression—all vanished. With a natural expression, her features looked different. She looked younger. She lifted a foot up and started unbuckling a shoe. "My feet are killing me," she said.

Archie's groin throbbed.

He looked at his watch. They needed to stay in here long enough to sell it.

"How long does this usually take?" he asked her.

"With someone like you?" she said with a smile. "Not long."

CHAPTER

5

It was Saturday morning and Archie had retrieved his newspaper and was sitting in his living room reading it over a cup of coffee. Ginger was stretched out on her side on the floor, her foxlike head resting on Archie's bare foot. Every so often she lifted it and looked at him with her plaintive brown corgi eyes and then, when she wasn't invited up onto the couch, exhaled loudly and lowered her chin back on his foot.

Richmond's death was on the inside page of the Metro section. He was described as the owner of a pawnshop and his death by gunshot was characterized as possibly drug-related. The entire incident had warranted one paragraph of coverage. No photo. This was good. Archie leafed through the rest of the paper. The quality of the *Herald* had gone downhill since Susan had been fired, but he hadn't gotten around to canceling his subscription. These days, most of the front section was dedicated to the manhunt for Gretchen Lowell. It had been ten weeks since she'd escaped the state mental hospital, and she was probably halfway around the world, but the breathless stories continued at a frantic pace. The Beauty Killer industry was back in full force. The Dead

Body Bus Tour. The T-shirts. Salons had started offering Beauty Killer manicures again. At least some people were happy that she was at large. Portland's cottage industry around the Beauty Killer dropped off considerably when she was locked up. Now they seemed to be making up for lost time. And with Halloween just two days away, it would only get worse.

Archie closed the paper and saw his own photo on the back page of the front section. It was part of a story about the history of the task force. The photo was a younger version of himself—back when he'd first taken over the Beauty Killer Task Force, when he was still married, before the gray in his hair, and the scars that Gretchen Lowell had left on his chest. He had never been handsome. His nose was crooked from a car accident when he was a teenager. His features were just asymmetrical enough to appear off-kilter for no identifiable reason. His eyes were dark and deep-set, so that he never really looked happy even when he was.

Archie felt Ginger lift her head from his foot and he glanced down to see that her triangular ears were upright and angled toward the door. He was putting down the newspaper when he heard the first knock.

It was Susan. She always knocked the same way: two short knocks, with a pause, followed by three short knocks.

"I know you're in there," she called through the door.

Ginger stood up and trotted to the door and then stopped and looked expectantly back at Archie.

Archie tightened the belt around his terry-cloth robe, got to his feet, and followed Ginger to the door.

He hadn't planned on letting Susan in. He was going to stand his ground, and explain that it was Saturday morning and no one had been disemboweled or beheaded and he wasn't working. But she had a way of circumventing the best of his intentions.

She pushed past him and headed for the kitchen. She was wearing a silver skirt that looked like it was made from tinfoil, black tights, black Converse sneakers, and a red hooded sweatshirt, unzipped, over a black tank top. Ginger, whom Susan sometimes walked, pranced along at her feet, panting happily. "Do you have any coffee?" Susan asked.

Archie closed the door behind her. Susan was already getting a mug out of the cupboard. "Help yourself," he said.

Susan's clothes smelled like cigarettes. Archie had noticed it the moment he'd opened the door. Susan smoking cigarettes this early in the morning was never a good indicator.

He watched as she poured herself the last cup of coffee from the pot and then stooped down to pat Ginger on the head.

"Happy birthday," she said in Archie's direction. "I forgot your present."

"You didn't have to get me anything," Archie said.

Susan straightened up and looked at him. She held the mug between her hands and blew on the coffee. Her eyes were red and her mascara was smeared. She looked like she'd slept in her makeup. "Leo's not answering his phone," she said. "We had an argument last night. He left. This morning I went by his place. He didn't answer the buzzer. And I fucking *leaned* on it," she added. "If he'd been home, he would have answered."

Archie wanted to ask what the argument was about, but he didn't. "Do you have a key?" he asked.

She glanced away. "No."

Archie took a deep breath. He didn't want to overreact. It was true that Leo might be in danger, but it was also true that Leo had his demons. Before Leo and Susan had started seeing each other, Leo had been linked with every exotic dancer and party girl in town. He was at clubs every night. He was not given to monogamy. For all Archie knew, Leo had spent last night with Star. Archie searched for a kind way to phrase it: "He stays out sometimes, right? Maybe he found somewhere else to crash."

"We had a fight," Susan said. "Outside the club. He would have called. To make up." She gave Archie a meaningful look. "Trust me," she said.

Archie checked his watch. It wasn't even ten A.M. The way Leo had been drinking last night, he was probably hungover. "Give him time," Archie said to himself as much as Susan.

Susan twisted a piece of black hair around her finger. "I have a bad feeling," she said. Her eyes darted toward the floor. "Has he said anything?" She glanced up. "I mean, about me?"

Archie struggled to grasp the situation. No one had ever accused him of being savvy about relationships, but it was beginning to dawn on him that he had misunderstood. Susan wasn't worried that Leo was dead. "You're afraid he's going to break up with you," Archie said slowly.

"He's so distracted," Susan said. "Something's going on with him, isn't it? I'm concerned about him. I know he's DE—"

Archie lifted his hand to cut her off. "Shh," he said. He looked at the bedroom. The bedroom door was open. He didn't hear any movement. Rachel was probably still asleep.

Susan's brow furrowed. "What?" she said. She peered toward the back of the apartment. "Is Henry here?"

"No."

"Who is it?"

Archie scratched the back of his neck. "I have a guest."

She looked at him, still not getting it.

"A *female* guest," said Archie.

Susan's eyes widened with alarm. "The stripper?" she said.

"No," Archie said, incredulous.

Susan took a tiny step back. "You're dating someone?" she asked. He could see her trying to hide her distress, her mouth getting small. "How long have you been dating someone?"

"Not long," Archie said. "When was the last time you saw Leo?"

"You said you didn't want to date anyone," she said.

They both knew what she meant. He had said he didn't want to date her. Rachel was different. He couldn't have sex with Susan and not feel something. Rachel didn't want anything from him. At least nothing emotionally.

He was trying to figure out how to begin to explain this when Rachel sauntered into the room. She was in the black tank sundress and sandals that she'd had on when she'd come over late last night, and even without a shower or makeup, she was a knockout. At that moment, Archie wished she was ugly. Rachel was Susan's physical opposite. Even Archie had not seen that until now, with the two of them in the same room. Where Susan was pale and freckled, Rachel's skin was a solid golden tan. Where Susan's figure was boyish, Rachel was curvy. Rachel was blond. Susan was . . . whatever color she happened to be that week. Rachel's beauty was obvious. Susan's was exotic.

Even worse, Rachel was two years younger than Susan. Since Archie had used his age difference with Susan as one of his go-to excuses for why he couldn't be with her, this made him look like even more of a heel.

Archie fumbled for words. Susan didn't move. Her eyes were fixed on Rachel. Her coffee cup had slipped forward at a perilous angle.

Rachel looked as surprised to see Susan as Susan was to see her. "Hi," Rachel said.

Ginger glanced back and forth from one woman to the other.

Archie lifted a hand to his head.

"I have to go," Susan said quickly.

"Susan, wait," Archie said. He went after her, and she turned around and faced him at the door.

"It's fine," she said. "You don't have to explain. You're an adult."

Archie mentally kicked himself. He shouldn't have let her in. But there was nothing he could say that would undo it. "I'll see if I can check up on our friend," he said. *Our friend.* He hadn't wanted to say Leo's name in front of Rachel, but it came off as some weird platitude.

He wanted to tell Susan that she was not the reason why

Leo was "distracted." He wanted to tell her that he would make sure that Leo was safe, and that someone, somewhere, was looking out for him. Archie wanted to tell her, but again, he couldn't.

Susan's eyes were green and hard. She handed him her mug. It had a red ring of lipstick on it. "Thanks for the coffee," she said.

She left, and Archie walked back into the living room and sat down in a chair. He set the lipstick-stained mug on top of the newspaper on the coffee table and looked at it.

Ginger had flopped in front of the door that Susan had just exited through, and was eyeing Archie accusingly. Archie called her, but she refused to come.

"Sorry," Rachel said.

"It's okay," Archie said. "It's complicated." He didn't offer any further explanation. He didn't talk to Rachel about Susan, or Henry, or his work. They didn't really talk about anything. She had come into his life suddenly, moving into the apartment a floor below his in the middle of the night. What little he knew about her was fraught with inconsistencies. It intrigued him. But it wasn't until that moment that he realized this was the very thing that attracted him to her. He could have sex with her because he couldn't trust her.

"I have to go to class," Rachel said. "But I'll see you tonight."

"Okay," Archie said. He was glad she had to leave but he tried not to show it. He was already thinking about how he could track down Leo.

Rachel seemed to sense that he was distracted and she leaned forward and put her hand on his chest, and kissed him on the mouth. As the heat of their mouths met, her hand slid inside his robe to the sensitive scar tissue over his heart. She dug her fingernails into the delicate skin, and Archie's breath caught in his throat.

By the time she stood up, they were both breathing heavily.

Rachel wiped the shine of saliva from the corner of her

lip. "Do you want anything special for your birthday?" she asked.

The scar on Archie's chest stung and he felt a buzz of anticipation in his groin. He smiled. "Do you know how to do a lap dance?" he asked.

CHAPTER

6

As far as your average incognito rendezvous went, the East-bank Esplanade was as good a place as any. Archie stood facing the river, looking across to the west side, where the downtown Portland skyline rose prettily behind the green band of Tom McCall Waterfront Park. The pavement at his feet was new. The only signs of the flood that had wreaked havoc downtown last winter were some spindly saplings and a plaque the city had installed explaining it all to tourists.

On the other side of the river, the verdant west side esplanade was bustling with active Portlanders exercising in every manner imaginable, from roller skates to unicycles. It was the lunch hour and the benches facing the river were hosting the usual array of people eating food-cart quinoa veggie bowls, loitering teenage transients, and schizophrenics feeding seagulls. Kids played in the fountains. Canada geese sunned themselves in the park. October was all Portland saw of fall—a month of clear, high skies, leaves just starting to turn, a fresh coolness to the air. By November all the fountains would be turned off, the leaves would be gone from the trees, and the sky would be low and gray until mid-July.

The Eastbank Esplanade, where Archie stood, was skinnier and less colorful than the west side, and shoehorned between Interstate 5 and a riverbank choked with blackberries. The air tasted like exhaust, and the constant din of traffic blurred all other sound. Even the geese stayed away. But Archie liked it. There were fewer people, and more historical plaques.

Ginger tugged on her leash at a passing cyclist and Archie reeled her in closer to him. She plunked down at his feet and quickly became absorbed by a couple of seagulls paddling by in the river. The water sparkled in the midday sun, and looked deceptively clean and blue. Archie knew better. They pulled a corpse from the Willamette once a week.

"Nice watchdog you have there," Raul Sanchez said with a grin. He stepped beside Archie and Ginger, who didn't even look up. Sanchez was a compact man, with thick dark hair and rough-hewn features made rougher by the pockmark scars that peppered his face. Whether the scars were a result of childhood acne or a close encounter with gravel, Archie had never asked. Some people didn't like to talk about their scars.

"She's monitoring those dangerous gulls," Archie said. "And I saw you coming as soon as you crossed the Hawthorne Bridge," he added. "I almost didn't recognize you without your FBI windbreaker."

"You should see my FBI pj's," Sanchez said. He started to say something else, then stopped and fiddled with a button on his tan jacket. "Obviously, you know I can't talk to you about the Beauty Killer thing," he said.

Sanchez was the FBI liaison on the task force charged with hunting down Gretchen Lowell. Archie heard updates through the grapevine. He read the headlines. He knew she'd supposedly been seen in six countries so far. But there was never any solid evidence. No trail. They had all agreed, back in August, that the best thing for Archie's mental health was not to be involved. Nothing had changed. Archie had been the one who'd lobbied for Sanchez to take the lead.

"I just want to know when she's dead," Archie said.

One of the gulls squawked and flapped off, flying low above the water.

"Let's talk about Leo, then," Sanchez said.

Archie glanced over his shoulder at the interstate behind them. "Somewhere quieter," he said. The two men headed north, toward the Steel Bridge. Archie had to give Ginger's leash an extra tug to get her to leave gull duty, but soon she was trotting happily ahead of them. A cyclist pedaled past pulling a small boy in a three-wheeled netted trailer. The boy smiled at Archie. He was probably high on exhaust fumes.

Archie and Sanchez followed the concrete path along the river until it diverged from the interstate and the din of traffic waned. The Willamette gleamed serenely. A nearby sign warned that fish caught in the river might be toxic. "Leo's not answering his phone," Archie said.

Sanchez turned his collar up against the chill. "I know," Sanchez said.

"Everything okay?" Archie asked.

Sanchez stopped walking, so Archie knew it was bad.

"He's on the island," Sanchez said. "They took him there last night. We have surveillance outside. I have no idea what's going on inside."

"Does he know you're his contact?" Archie asked.

"If he read the note I sent with the flowers," Sanchez said. He squinted out across the river. "He's cut off. We can't contact him. There's no way to get a message through."

If anything happened to Leo, Archie knew that Susan would never forgive him. "You need to extract him," Archie said.

Sanchez peered at Archie, worry lines creasing his craggy forehead. "This isn't your problem, friend," he said. "You're too close."

In the distance, Archie could hear the pedestrian alert bells of the Steel Bridge readying to lift. "Are we still talking about Leo?" he asked.

"What do you think we're talking about?" Sanchez asked carefully.

Archie had worked the Beauty Killer case for thirteen years. She had cost him everything. Gretchen would always be his problem. They could take him off the case, but she would always be his.

A brisk wind rippled the surface of the river. A jogger, still thumb-sized, was heading south on the esplanade toward them.

"We're talking about Leo," Archie said. "I brought him to you guys," he added. "I'm the one who convinced him that he could do more good by staying in his goddamn family than by leaving. He came to me because he wanted my help getting away from his father. He trusted me. And I wrapped him up in a bow and delivered him to Carl."

Sanchez nodded and looked out, stone-faced, at the Willamette. Up river, the center of the Steel Bridge had started to raise, lifting the old wooden machinery shack affixed to the upper deck along with it. "I need to determine his status," Sanchez said.

"So do it," Archie said.

Ginger barked excitedly. The jogger was almost upon them.

"There's no way in," Sanchez said. "Our resources are limited here by necessity. If we ask the wrong people to help, it could get him killed."

Archie lifted his finger and they waited as the jogger passed, although he couldn't have overheard anything with the ruckus Ginger was making. He was wearing lightweight shorts and a "Life is Good" T-shirt with the sleeves cut off. Every inch of his bare flesh glowed bright pink from exertion. His face looked pained. He didn't give them a second look as he went past. Ginger, disappointed, quieted and began snuffling in the grass.

When the jogger was thirty feet south of them, Archie asked, "How many people know Leo is the source?"

Sanchez scratched the back of his neck. "Besides me and you and"—he looked at Archie questioningly—"I'm guessing Henry? That's it."

"Henry's my partner," Archie said. "I don't keep him in the dark." That hadn't always been true, but Archie didn't mention that.

"Anyone else come to mind?" Sanchez asked.

In fact there was another person who knew Leo was DEA, a person Sanchez had not mentioned. Archie knew that Leo had told Susan his secret a few months ago. Protocol required Leo to report that to his superiors. Clearly, he hadn't.

"I wouldn't know," Archie said.

A barge loaded with construction equipment cleared the Steel Bridge, nudged along by an old tugboat. Men with construction hats stood on board, gazing at the shore.

"This operation is new to me," Sanchez said. "I was the safeguard. Carl briefed me years ago, so that if anything happened to him, I could step in and Leo wouldn't get left in the wind."

"You mean like if Carl got his head blown off in the john, for instance?" Archie said.

"That would fit the criteria," Sanchez said. "In the meantime, I'm trying to coordinate the search for a dangerous escaped serial killer."

"I think I read something about that," Archie said.

Sanchez caught himself. "Sorry," he said with a grimace. "I've just got a lot on my plate. I can't get Leo out without revealing his identity. But if I reveal his identity it could get him killed before I can get him out."

Archie wasn't buying it. This had been an important operation for the feds. A lot was riding on it. It was a career-maker. "You don't want him out until he has the names," Archie said.

Sanchez rubbed the side of his nose. "Okay, no bullshit," he said. "This operation has taken ten years. If Leo can get us the names of Jack Reynolds's partners, then yeah, I think that's worth not rushing into anything. I have bosses whose names are on that list. So do you. That's why we have to keep this close."

The Burnside Bridge yawned open to let the barge through.

"Someone else knows," Archie said.

"The girlfriend," Sanchez said with a heavy sigh.

"He shot someone in front of her," Archie said. "He kind of had to explain. She doesn't know anything. Just that he's DEA."

Sanchez's jaw starting working and his lips tightened. He mulled for a few moments, and then his face lit up.

Archie knew where he was headed.

"You think she would go in for us?" Sanchez asked.

"No," Archie said quickly.

But he hadn't convinced Sanchez. Archie could see it in the way his jaw kept working, the way Sanchez kept clenching his teeth. Sanchez's gaze was on the river, but Archie knew that his mind was playing out the op. Sending Susan in would be the most logical step. It made sense. She had a relationship with Leo. She would be the perfect conduit for passing information.

"Use me," Archie said.

"News flash," Sanchez said with a grunt. "Jack knows you're a cop."

"Jack and I are friendly," Archie persisted.

"Jack Reynolds is nice to you," Sanchez said. "That doesn't mean he won't kill you."

"I said we're friendly. Not friends. He knows about the pills. I can make that work for me. Convince him I have something to lose."

Sanchez reached into the inside pocket of his jacket, extracted an envelope, and handed it to Archie.

"What's this?" Archie asked.

Sanchez smiled. "It's an invitation to a party at his house tonight."

Archie looked down at the envelope. His name was printed on it. "You little fucker," Archie said. "You knew I'd do it."

"Go in," Sanchez said matter-of-factly. "Determine Leo's status, and then get the hell out."

Archie looked up at the cloudless sky. It had seemed like such a nice day when it had started. "Do you want me to wear a wire?" he asked.

"If you wear a wire they'll shoot you," Sanchez said.

Archie turned to Sanchez. "Maybe I'll skip the wire, then."

"I have people outside," Sanchez said. "Basic surveillance. We'll be watching everyone who goes into that party. If you can get to the bridge, we'll see you, and we'll come for you. But once you're inside, you're on your own. So don't do anything heroic. I know you feel responsible for this kid. But he knew what he was getting into. And he's not exactly an innocent flower." The barge had cleared the Burnside Bridge and now the Hawthorne Bridge had started to open. Traffic downtown was fucked.

"What if he's already dead?" Archie asked.

"Then there's no one to protect," Sanchez said. "You scream like a girl and we send in the cavalry. But if he's alive and he's okay, you leave him there. If he's alive and he's not okay, you leave him there. No heroics. I just need to know his status. Then we make a plan." Sanchez glanced at his watch. "I have to get back across the river," he said.

"Can I expense the tuxedo rental?" Archie asked.

"No," Sanchez said. He leveled his gaze at Archie. "We clear on this?"

"No heroics. I determine Leo's status." Archie raised his eyebrows at Sanchez. "And you stay away from Susan."

Sanchez smiled, and Archie gave Ginger a tug and started back north along the trail. He only made it a few steps before Sanchez called his name. "Yeah?" Archie said, turning back.

"Happy birthday, buddy," Sanchez said.

"I had plans tonight, you know," Archie said.

Sanchez chuckled. "She'll wait."

CHAPTER

7

Archie poured himself a drink to calm his nerves.

The morning's blue skies had given way to cloud cover that had come in over the West Hills and hung low over the city.

The tuxedo he was wearing had a black single-breasted two-button jacket with a peaked lapel, and flat-fronted pants. At least that's what the woman who'd helped him at the tuxedo rental shop had said. He must have looked helpless, because she'd taken him under her wing right away, outfitting him with the appropriate jacket, pants, shirt, shoes, and bow tie. He'd taken a pass on the cummerbund.

Archie lifted the hem of his pants and studied his socks—the only thing he was wearing, besides his underwear, that was his. They were black. He usually wore them to funerals.

The last time he'd had a tuxedo on had been at his own wedding.

He heard Henry and Claire in the hallway before they knocked. Specifically, he heard Claire's laugh. It was girlish and merry, and always sounded wrong coming from her mouth. Archie had canceled the dinner out that the three of them had planned for his birthday. The fact that they had decided to stop by anyway did not surprise him.

Archie opened the door reluctantly. Claire was dressed to the nines in a black long-sleeved dress that hugged her growing maternity bump, and Henry was as formal as he got, in black jeans, his black leather jacket, a gray T-shirt, and cowboy boots. Their faces were beaming—apparently in the midst of a shared joke. Archie felt a surprising swell of jealousy. He missed that level of intimacy with another person. Whatever he and Rachel had, it was not a relationship in the traditional sense.

Claire looked Archie up and down. "Did you get a catering gig?" she asked with a grin.

Archie glanced down at his tux. "I thought I looked like James Bond," he said.

Claire laughed again. Archie couldn't remember ever having seen her in a dress before. With her very short dark hair, boyish frame, and penchant for jeans and T-shirts, Claire Masland was pretty and feisty and smart, but few would describe her as ladylike. Her pregnancy had brought out her latent femininity. She was in her second trimester, and Henry had told Archie that last week he'd found her crying over a bowl of cake batter. This from a woman who had once left a witness handcuffed to a park bench next to a flooding river. Estrogen. It was a powerful thing. Claire produced a small, sweetly wrapped gift and put it in Archie's hand. "We wanted to drop off your present," she said. Then she bit her lip and gazed past him, into his apartment. "I have to pee," she added.

Archie stepped aside. "You know where to go," he said.

She hustled past him toward the bathroom, her black high heels tapping against the fir floorboards.

Henry walked in and closed the door behind him. "She's been peeing every fifteen minutes," Henry said. "I don't know where it's all coming from."

Archie flashed back to his ex-wife's two pregnancies. "It'll pass," he said.

Henry took the drink from Archie's hand and sipped from it.

"Do you want one?" Archie asked.

"I don't want to be any trouble," Henry said. He lifted Archie's glass to his mouth again and grinned. "I'll just take yours."

Archie examined his now-empty hand. "I find that I am suddenly thirsty," he said. He walked to the kitchen and got another glass and then set it on the bar that separated the kitchen from the rest of the main living space, and poured another drink. Henry leaned against the bar next to him. Archie saw him glance across the living room at the closed bathroom door. "You're getting mixed up in this whole thing with Leo, aren't you?" Henry asked in a low voice.

Archie recorked the whiskey. "No comment."

Henry ran his hand over his face and then smoothed his mustache with his thumb and forefinger. "Who's running it?" he asked.

Archie took a drink and then set the glass on the bar. He looked at Henry with a helpless shrug.

"Jesus, Archie," Henry said, his face reddening. "What if something happens to you? You don't turn up, who am I supposed to call?"

"I'll be fine," Archie said. "But I need you to stop by tonight and take the dog out, okay? Use your key."

"At what point do I start to worry?" Henry asked.

Archie glanced outside at the darkening sky. "Twenty-four hours," he said. He picked a pen up off the counter and wrote a telephone number on a piece of notebook paper, tore the paper out, folded it in half, and handed it to Henry. "If you don't hear from me by this time tomorrow, open this."

Henry looked down at the folded piece of paper between his fingers. "Is this your will?"

Archie heard the toilet flush and water running.

"It's my Visa number," Archie said. "Run up as much as you can before they find out I'm dead."

Claire came out of the bathroom and started toward them.

"That's not funny," Henry said, putting the folded paper in his jacket pocket.

Claire stepped next to them. "Did you open it?" she asked, her eyes shining.

Archie exchanged a glance with Henry, thinking she meant the paper he'd just passed him.

"The gift," Claire said, looking at the two of them like they were idiots. "Do it quick, before I have to pee again."

Archie pulled the present from his jacket pocket and unwrapped a white cardboard box. He lifted the lid. Inside was a round brass object, about the size of a Kennedy dollar but thicker, with a small knob on the side. It looked like an old-fashioned man's pocket watch, but without a watch face. It appeared to be solid brass on both sides.

"It's a compass," Claire said. She took it from Archie's hands and flipped a latch at the bottom and the top opened to reveal a compass face underneath. The compass arrow trembled and then swung to point north.

"Claire thought you'd like it," Henry explained.

Archie did like it. Though he wasn't sure what he was supposed to do with it exactly.

Claire gave Archie a teasing poke in the ribs. "So what did your girlfriend get you?" she asked.

Archie's mind went to the promised lap dance and he felt himself blush. He pulled at the collar of his shirt. "She's not my girlfriend," he said.

"Whatever," Claire said. "It's been two months. Have I met her? No. If Henry hadn't seen her with his own eyes, I'd wonder if she was your imaginary friend."

"Susan met her this morning," Archie said.

"How'd that go?" Henry asked, lifting his glass to his lips.

"Could have gone better," Archie said.

"Susan hated her, didn't she?" Claire asked, beaming.

Archie picked up his glass and took a drink from it. He wondered how long Susan would be pissed at him. Probably weeks. "Yep," he said.

"I want to meet her anyway," Claire said. She didn't wait for a response, which was good because Archie wasn't prepared to make any promises. Claire picked up Henry's wrist and looked at his watch. Her eyes widened. "We have reservations," she said to Archie. Even with the high heels she had to lift herself up on her toes to kiss him on the cheek. "Happy birthday," she said. "We love you. Despite all your obvious problems and weird proclivities."

"Thanks a lot," Archie said.

She dragged Henry out the door. Henry caught Archie's eye as Claire pulled the door shut behind them. "Call me tomorrow," Henry said. "Twenty-four hours."

Archie stood in his apartment alone. The cloud cover out the window was the color of ash. The Willamette River looked like molten silver. Archie finished his drink and then called Rachel. He got her voice mail.

"Something's come up," Archie said. "I have to work." With someone else he might have had to apologize or explain more, but he and Rachel had different rules. "But," Archie added, "I'm hoping I can get a rain check on that birthday present."

He ended the call and put the phone in his pocket. Then he loaded his gun and clipped the holster to the waistband of his pants. He smiled to himself. *Now* he looked like James Bond.

Lastly, Archie headed into the bathroom. He opened his medicine chest and pulled out a large amber prescription bottle marked PRILOSEC and tapped out ten Vicodin into his palm. He'd been clean, more or less, for a year, and while he'd been in rehab, Henry had done a banner job rooting through Archie's apartment and disposing of every pain pill he could find. But the one place that people never looked was right in plain sight. All Archie had done was switch out the pills. If his stomach ever started burning and he needed a Prilosec he was screwed.

He didn't use the pills. He just liked knowing they were there. Now he gently transferred the Vicodin into his old brass pillbox. It had been a long time since he'd carried that thing around in his pocket, but if he was going to play the role of the self-destructive detective, he needed the right props.

Archie gave the pillbox a shake. The familiar sound of

the pills rattling against the metal confines of the box made his mouth water. But he swallowed hard and tucked the pill-box in the pocket of his tux.

He glanced at his watch. He'd been forty-two years old for seven minutes now.

So far, so good.

CHAPTER

8

Susan's mother didn't allow her to smoke in the house. Marijuana was fine. Bliss kept her bong right out in the open on the coffee table like a decorative sculpture. Incense? No problem. Bliss bought it by the case, filling the whole house with a thick cherry-flavored smog. But when Susan wanted to smoke a cigarette, she had to do it on the porch.

Susan got it. Weed was natural; cigarettes were cancer. Incense smelled nice; cigarettes didn't. Plus, it was Bliss's house, so she got to make the rules. Susan may have grown up in the dilapidated Victorian, but it wasn't like her name was on the mortgage. She had moved back in with her mother while she was saving up to buy a place, then she had lost her job at the *Herald*. The freelancing gigs were too unpredictable to sign any kind of lease. And her credit report wasn't exactly star renter material.

So here she was. Getting cancer on her mother's porch. Bliss was at work, dyeing someone's Mohawk pink or something. Only in Portland, Oregon, did punk rockers go in for a root touch-up and a blow-out. Bliss was the go-to stylist for the rage-against-the-machine set. It made for interesting hours.

Susan tapped her cigarette ash into the jack-o'-lantern on the top porch step. The jack-o'-lantern had squinty eyes and a round, surprised mouth. Susan's jack-o'-lanterns never turned out as spooky as she intended. She pulled the hood of her sweatshirt up and checked her phone to see if Leo had texted her back yet. He hadn't.

She heard the car pull in front of the house and looked up. It was black and sleek and official-looking, like one of those town cars rich people hire to take them to the airport instead of just getting a cab like everyone else.

The car sat there for a minute. The windows were tinted and Susan couldn't see inside. She stared at it anyway. Maybe Johnny Depp was inside.

Finally, the driver's-side door opened and a huge man climbed out and started up the walk toward Susan. He was carrying a bouquet of pink roses, and was very definitely not Johnny Depp.

Susan continued to stare. He led with his chest when he walked, and moved at a quick, confident clip, his huge arms at his side. His long dark gray hair flapped at the shoulders of his dark leather jacket.

She recognized him. She didn't know him. She had never been introduced to him. But she had seen him around. He was one of several men who always seemed at the periphery when she went out with Leo. He'd be at a nearby table, or at a club. Occasionally he'd appear and say something in Leo's ear and the two of them would vanish for a while.

She didn't know who he was. But she didn't like him.

She took a drag of her cigarette and didn't stand up.

The man got to the porch steps and proffered the bouquet like it was the head of a dragon he'd just slain for her pleasure. Susan took the flowers, but was careful not to look too enthusiastic about it. She gave them a brief inspection and then laid them next to her on the porch. There wasn't a note. "Did Leo send you?" she asked skeptically. Leo had wooed her with flowers back when she'd worked at the *Herald*. But these weren't his style.

Up close the man's face was thickened with scars. They

made his pale features blurry and uneven. "He'd like you to come to a party," he said. His voice was hoarse, like he had a cold, but Susan had the feeling it always sounded that way. He made a florid gesture like a footman welcoming someone on board a carriage.

Mr. Gallant.

Susan looked at the town car and then at him. "When?" she asked. "Now?" She laughed nervously and shook her head. "No. No way. He can't just ignore me all day and then send me flowers and expect me to drop everything at his beck and call."

The man swallowed and his jaw tightened. She could tell he was someone who was not used to being told no. The corners of his mouth turned up, revealing a set of stained crowded teeth. "It would really mean a lot to him if you could come," he said.

"What's your name?" Susan asked, flicking ash from her cigarette into the herb garden.

"Cooper," the man said.

"Let me tell you something, Cooper." She picked up the bouquet and looked down at the plump pink blooms. "The chemicals they use on roses are some of the worst in the world," she said, holding the flowers out so Cooper could see them. "Twenty percent of the pesticides they use on roses in Colombia are illegal in the U.S. Roses require a lot of fertilization. Do you know how much fossil fuel is needed to make fertilizer?" Cooper stared back blankly. "One kilogram of nitrogen-containing fertilizer takes two liters of oil," Susan said. "Irrigation puts pressure on local water supplies, and results in salinization of local farmlands. That's not even getting into the wage inequality endemic to most of the large corporations that dominate the global rose market." Susan shook her head. "Don't get my mother started on roses," she said. She put the bouquet down and leveled her gaze at Cooper. "Leo knows my mother. And Leo would never send roses to me at her house, because he knows he would never hear the end of it. So I'm thinking Leo didn't send these flowers, and he didn't send you."

Cooper's smile was gone. It was probably for the best. It definitely didn't make him look friendlier. "His old man sent me," Cooper said. "He's hosting a rather extravagant fete this evening. Leo will be there, and his father would like you to join them."

Susan *did* want to see Leo. "Like a Halloween party?" she asked.

"More like a masquerade ball," Cooper said.

"Seriously?"

Cooper shrugged. "Rich people," he said.

Susan considered her options. Jack Reynolds was a criminal—a wealthy and socially prominent criminal, granted. She had met him once, through Archie, the same day she had met Leo. Jack had been rather charming, considering they were there to grill him about a murder. He had a private island. He probably had really good parties. Then there was her supposed boyfriend. Leo had gone off the grid before, but this was different. She hadn't been entirely honest with Archie. The truth was that she had been the one to storm off last night, outside the club. She had blown up at Leo for making them miss the musical production of *Road House* and she'd called a cab. But really she'd just been mad about the lap dance he'd bought Archie. Now she was pissed that he wasn't returning her calls. She wanted to see him, if only to read him the riot act. Susan stubbed her cigarette out, dropped it into the jack-o'-lantern, and stood up to go into the house. Cooper was up the stairs in one step. He didn't touch her, but she stopped cold.

"I need to change," she explained. She pulled at her hoodie. Her black tights had a hole in the knee. "I don't have anything to wear. I need makeup." That was all true. But she also wanted to go inside and call Archie.

"We'll take care of all that," Cooper said. "What are you? A size four?"

Susan nodded, and fidgeted some more with her hoodie. She didn't like that he was looking at her that closely.

Cooper studied her for a moment and then something seemed to dawn on him. "You're scared," he said. "You're scared of me." His eyebrows lifted awkwardly, like he was trying to seem amiable. "If Jack Reynolds ever wants you dead, lady, he won't send me and a car to get you," he said. "Too many neighbors. People see shit. They remember more than you'd think. Look behind me," he said.

Susan looked over his shoulder and saw their across-the-street neighbor, Bill, standing in the street by the curb with a rake.

"You see that guy pulling leaves out of the storm drain?" Cooper asked. He turned and gave Bill a friendly wave. Bill waved back. Cooper turned back to Susan. "That guy's a witness," he said. "The lady who passed us with the dog?" Susan hadn't even seen a woman with a dog. "She lives in the neighborhood," Cooper said. "So she knows you. The cops come by later, start asking questions, she's seen me and the car—she's a witness." Cooper nodded at her. "If Jack Reynolds ever wants you dead, you won't see me. *They* won't see me." He smiled at her, seemingly pleased at the excellence of his explanation. "This isn't how we do it. So you've got nothing to be afraid of."

Susan's spine was as rigid as a board. "Is that supposed to make me feel better?" she asked.

"It's a party," Cooper said, his eyes pleading. "You want me to put a glass slipper on your foot?"

Susan didn't know what to do. She looked across the street at Bill. He was wearing rubber rain boots and jabbing the wrong end of the rake into the sludge of dead leaves that filled the storm drain. "Hey, Bill!" she shouted. Bill looked up. Cooper was right about one thing, Bill noticed everything that went on in that neighborhood—she had no doubt he'd made note of her visitor and his car. So she'd just make sure it stuck. "I'm going to a party at my boyfriend's house!" Susan called. "His dad sent this guy Cooper to drive me! Tell my mom, okay?" Bill flashed her a peace sign.

Susan looked at Cooper. He appeared vexed again.

"Let's go," Susan said. She left the flowers on the porch next to the jack-o'-lantern and started down the porch steps for the car. "Do you have a minibar in that thing?"

CHAPTER

9

Pay attention. It was one of the tenets of journalism. Susan fixed her gaze out the tinted window as the car went over the gated stone bridge to Jack Reynolds's island and tried to take in as much as she could. The bridge was lined with lit torches that sent threads of black smoke snaking into the dusky sky. Traffic was already backed up, awaiting instruction from men in suits wearing earpieces and carrying clipboards and barking orders at hired valets in red jackets. Cooper ignored the line and went over the bridge in the wrong lane. Once they'd made it the two hundred feet to the other side, he bypassed what appeared to be the main drop-off point. Susan could see partygoers up ahead, people in tuxedos and evening gowns, walking up the trails through the manicured grounds to Jack Reynolds's neo-Tudor estate. They were all wearing masks—some elaborately festooned with feathers and gems, some basic black. Cooper hadn't been kidding. This wasn't just a ball; it was a masked ball. As social anxiety instigators went, masked balls were pretty near the top of Susan's list, right after playing team sports and giving speeches to old people (the old people always fell asleep and Susan never knew if it was the speech or just their normal nap cycle). But people in masks were always assholes. It was a scientific law. Give someone anonymity and all social niceties break down. The Internet had proven that. By ten o'clock the couples would be fighting and the single people would be hooking up with people they wouldn't be able to recognize in the morning. This was how masked balls went. This was what made them dangerous. Susan sank glumly in her seat as Cooper continued winding along a private lane that led around the side of the main house.

Susan had been to the island before. Once. Archie had gone to Jack for help on an investigation, and Susan had tagged along. That's how she had met Leo. Leo had introduced himself as Jack's attorney. He'd conveniently left out the part about being Jack's son.

She hadn't even known there were any islands in Lake Oswego before Archie had driven her over the bridge that first time. Lake Oswego was a large private lake run by the Lake Oswego Corporation and ringed by tony lakeside residences. The city of Lake Oswego, where the lake was, was a wealthy suburb of Portland, a place where Trail Blazer players lived, and people waited twenty minutes in line for a croissant. Most of the Portlanders Susan knew didn't even know that Lake Oswego had a lake.

Susan hadn't gotten to see much of the five-and-a-half-acre island that first trip. They hadn't been invited inside the 1929 nine-thousand-square-foot Tudor mansion at the center of the island. Instead she and Archie had talked to Jack and Leo near the castlelike stone boathouse on the private dock next to Jack's sailboat. Susan had Googled the island several times since then, and through old real estate records and Google Earth she had put together a pretty complete mental picture of what she had missed the first time—namely, the helipad, formal rose garden, guesthouse, waterfalls, lakeside pool, sauna, and the nearly one mile of walking trails.

She and Leo had been dating for nine months and he had yet to invite her to the family compound. She got it. His father was a drug lord and Leo was secretly working for the DEA. There were a lot of secrets to keep straight. He was probably afraid that she'd blurt out something she shouldn't over canapés with dear old Dad.

Cooper parked the car next to a smaller Tudor structure, built out of the same old-growth timber and basalt as the main house. This was the guesthouse. Susan had seen pictures of it online in an old issue of *Oregon Home* magazine. Apparently Jack Reynolds entertained a lot of guests—his guesthouse looked twice as big as her mother's place.

Cooper got out of the car and came around and opened the backseat passenger-side door for her.

"This way," he said, lifting his chin toward the guesthouse. She followed him without question. It wasn't that she didn't have questions; just that she had so many that she didn't know where to begin. Activity swarmed around them. The guesthouse was situated behind the main house, and was clearly being used as a staging area for the party. A caterer's truck parked next to a florist's truck parked next to an event supply truck. Men wearing windbreakers with the word SECURITY across the back muttered into walkie-talkies. Caterers in black pants and white shirts and black ties unloaded cases of wine.

"When can I see Leo?" Susan asked.

They had reached the guesthouse. The entry was an enormous arched oak door, framed with stone. Wrought-iron lamps hung on either side of the door under gargoyles that had been carved into the stone. It all seemed a little ostentatious for a guesthouse, even an obnoxious one.

Cooper turned the knob and went inside and Susan scuttled in after him. The door opened into a cavernous room with a half-timber-and-stucco ceiling and walls paneled with gleaming dark wood. Arched leaded glass windows looked out on the lake. Twilight was giving way to bona fide evening. Susan could see the lights of the houses along the shore. The lake was black and empty, like a patch of starless sky.

"You were right about her size," she heard Cooper say.

Susan redirected her attention inside the room. It was the living room, or parlor, or whatever the very wealthy called places where they came together and drank sherry after eating escargot. The furniture was all dark wood and worn velvet and cracked leather. Oriental rugs blanketed the floor at carefully quirky angles. Antique books lined the built-in shelves. A young woman with long wavy dark hair rose from a chair and walked toward Susan. She paused at a portable garment rack, on which several evening gowns hung, and pulled one from its hanger. Susan saw the professional-looking makeup box on the coffee table—a tackle box full of blush and oily sticks of foundation. The woman strolling toward her with the gown looked familiar. She was tall and fit, in her early twenties but with the effortless confidence of someone older. Her black pants and black T-shirt were non-descript, but still showed off her curves. Her makeup was natural, her hair was loose, but there was something about the way she moved—she had the self-possession of someone used to people watching her. Maybe it was the way she flipped her hair, or the sway of her hips—but something clicked. Susan recognized her. And as soon as she did, Susan felt her cheeks burn. She was the stripper from the night before, the one who had given Archie a lap dance.

The hussy.

Susan had tried not to wonder what had gone on in that room. What, exactly, the woman had done to get Archie off, and if he'd liked it. Susan had tried, but she couldn't get it out of her head. Archie had seen this woman almost naked. She had rubbed herself against him. Had he put his hands on her? Had Leo?

Susan took a long breath, willed her face to cool, and smiled.

The hussy stuck her hand out and smiled back. "Hi," she said. "I'm Star."

CHAPTER

10

A valet had taken Archie's city-issued Taurus. He often felt the need to apologize when valets took his car. They always looked so disappointed. He wanted to explain that it wasn't his car; that it belonged to the city—but the truth was, if he ever bought his own car, he'd probably end up with something just as boring.

The invitation had gotten him over the bridge.

Now a thick-necked man wearing a dark suit and an earpiece looked Archie up and down. He had a broad chest and deep-set, watchful eyes, and his hair was shaved down to a stiff bristle. He looked like a cop—though Archie didn't recognize him—or maybe ex-military. "Name," he demanded.

"Archie Sheridan," Archie said.

Archie produced the invitation Sanchez had given him but the man waved it away, and instead scanned a printed list he had on a clipboard. Archie could see the bulge under his suit where he was wearing a gun. That kind of thing could be hidden, but he wasn't trying. "I don't see you," the man said. Archie saw his body language shift. He straightened up, his chest expanded. He rotated a finger in the air, and two other men in suits looked up and started to make a beeline for them.

"I'm a friend of Leo's," Archie said quickly. "Maybe you should check with him."

Archie had a brief fantasy of the man with the clipboard calling Leo down from the house and then Archie and Leo jumping into a car and driving away together. Could it be that easy?

The other two suits arrived on either side of Archie. They looked like they'd come out of the same Humvee that the first guy had—same body type, same general facial structure, same military bearing.

"Stay with him," the first suit told the other two, and he gave Archie a skeptical look and stepped back, already lifting a cell phone to his ear.

The two new suits crossed their arms in unison. Party guests streamed past them, jewelry glinting in the torchlight. They were all wearing masks. Archie was pretty sure his tux hadn't come with one. Maybe he could cut two holes in his sock and tie it around his head. He thought about making that joke out loud, but he had the feeling it would go unappreciated.

"So," Archie said. "Nice place, huh?" The island was over five acres. Archie wondered how many bodies were buried on it.

They didn't answer.

"Have you seen Leo around?" Archie asked. Just an old friend, dropping by for a visit.

Nothing.

The first suit returned. "You're wanted inside," he said.

Jack Reynolds was waiting in his office for them, wearing a tuxedo and puffing on a cigar. Music from the party was a distant thrum through the textured stucco walls.

It had been over a year since Archie had seen Jack. When they'd first met, almost fourteen years before, Jack had been leaner, almost hawkish. He was one of those men who seemed to get better-looking as they aged. Though he was sixty-five, the lines around his eyes and mouth, the silver in his dark hair, only made him look more dashing. He looked like one of those grinning silver-haired men in Viagra commercials who were always getting off motorcycles and heading inside to get it on with their waiting wives.

Now Jack sat on the edge of his desk, the desk lamp behind him the only light on in the room. Cigar smoke hung like a cloud over his head.

Archie had been in this room before. It was a masculine lair, the stucco walls hung with photographs of Jack's sailboats. A built-in bar sparkled with crystal glassware and expensive liquor bottles. Leather chairs and a leather sofa created a sitting area in the middle of the room under a massive wrought-iron light fixture. Behind Jack's desk, the room's leaded glass windows looked out into darkness.

Jack grinned and rolled the cigar between his fingers. "Do you know who this guy is, Karim?" he asked. He wasn't talking to Archie. He was talking to the caramel-skinned man sitting next to Archie.

"No, sir, I do not," Karim said in a British boarding school accent.

Archie eyed Karim. He had a knife-cut part in his dark hair and perfectly erect posture. His tuxedo fit him well. He didn't look like Jack's usual muscle. Archie had a feeling that he did something more important.

Jack stood up and walked over to them. "This is Archie-fucking-Sheridan," he said. "He ran the Beauty Killer Task Force. That bitch took him hostage and tortured him for ten days. Took his fucking spleen out and sent it to his partner. So Archie here is strapped to a gurney in a basement in Gresham and he convinces Gretchen Lowell to let him go. She calls 911 and turns herself in. Saves his life."

Archie wished it had been that simple. "That's not exactly how it happened," he said.

Jack put his arm around Archie's shoulders, like a proud father showing off his son. "A few years later the bitch escapes from prison, and you know what this motherfucker does?" Jack asked Karim. "He catches her again!" Jack clapped Archie so hard on the back that he lurched forward. Archie coughed and straightened up. "So they send her to the nuthouse the next time," Jack continued. "And a year later, damned if she doesn't slaughter a nurse and saunter the fuck out of there."

Karim caught Archie's eye. "Next time you catch her, you should consider shooting her," he said.

"Thanks for the tip," Archie said.

Jack took a puff off his cigar and grinned.

Archie wondered if it would be impolite to ask for a drink.

The music seemed to be getting louder.

"So why are you here?" Jack asked, settling back on the edge of his desk.

Archie didn't miss a beat. "Leo invited me," he said. Archie fished the invitation from Sanchez out of his tuxedo pocket and handed it to Jack.

Jack smiled and tossed the invitation aside. A circle of his cigar smoke floated past Archie's face and then dissipated. "You working Vice now, Archie?" Jack asked.

Archie waved the smoke away, out of his eyes. "I don't care about your business, Jack," he said. It was true enough. All the years that Archie had come to this house, updating Jack on the investigation into his daughter's death, he had always treated him like any other bereaved family member. It didn't matter to Archie what Jack did for a living. Jack had lost his daughter. So Archie overlooked the rest of it.

Jack nodded to himself. "Leo invited you," he repeated skeptically.

Archie played his ace card. "It's my birthday."

Jack studied his cigar for a moment. Then he nodded at Karim, and Karim stood up and took a step toward Archie.

"May I?" Karim asked pleasantly.

Archie stood as well and lifted his arms. "Inside left pocket," Archie said.

Karim reached inside Archie's jacket and pulled out his wallet. He opened it and extracted Archie's driver's license and then took it to the desk lamp to study it. After a minute he returned the wallet and the license to Archie. "Happy birthday," he said to Archie.

"He must have forgotten to put you on the list," Jack said.

"Must have," Archie said.

"You'll need a mask," Jack said. He reached around and picked a mask off his desk and handed it to Archie. It was a shiny black plastic oval, with two holes for the eyes and a curved mold over the nose. A white elastic band was stapled to each side. Archie took the mask, but he didn't put it on.

"If he's not on the list, he hasn't been vetted," Karim pointed out.

"He's a cop," Jack said. "I think we can trust him not to steal the silverware."

"I don't like it," Karim said. He glanced at Archie. "No offense."

"He caught my daughter's killer," Jack said. "I think he's earned access to the no-host bar."

No mention of Jeremy, Archie noticed. Jack had edited out that part of the story. Archie couldn't help himself. "She killed your son, too," Archie said.

"I owe her for that one," Jack said. He said it easily, like it was something he said all the time. Then he directed a shrug in Karim's direction. "My waste-of-space youngest went apeshit last year," he explained without emotion. "Tried to kill our friend here with an ax. Turns out he was harboring an unhealthy fascination with the Beauty Killer."

Aren't we all? thought Archie.

"The shrinks blamed his sister's murder," Jack continued, "said he never got over it. But he always had a weak mind."

Archie had no doubt that Isabel's murder had fucked Jeremy up; but his father had played a role in Jeremy's deterioration, as well. "I guess that explains why I didn't see you at the funeral," Archie said.

"That's your problem, my friend," Jack said, reaching forward to straighten Archie's bow tie. "You don't know when to give up on people."

Karim produced a small black electronic gadget about

the size of a deck of cards. It had a dial on it and a small red light. He held it in front of Archie. "Any wires you want to tell us about?" he asked.

"I told you," Archie said. "I'm invited."

Karim scanned the gadget up and down Archie's body, front and back. "He's clean," he said to Jack. "I hope you're not offended," Karim added to Archie with a shrug. "Can't be too careful."

"Of course," Archie said.

Karim pocketed the gadget and then held out his hand in front of Archie, palm up. Archie knew what he wanted. He set the mask on the desk, opened his tuxedo jacket, pulled his weapon from his holster, ejected the magazine, put the magazine in his pocket, and then laid the gun in Karim's open hand. "I'm going to need that back," Archie said. It was his personal weapon, registered under his name. Leaving it out of his sight was an insane proposition. Karim would know that. Which was exactly why Archie needed to allow it. It was a gesture of trust. Or recklessness.

"Of course," Karim said. He put the gun on the desk behind him. "Now I just need you to empty your pockets," he said.

Archie reached into his pockets and emptied out the contents on the desk. The compass. The brass pillbox. His wallet. Cell phone. Badge. Karim picked each up and inspected it. He came to the pillbox and opened it. "What are these?" he asked, looking at the white pills.

"Painkillers," Archie said.

"I thought you went to rehab for those," Jack said.

Archie picked the mask up off the desk and put it on, snapping the elastic band around his head. "I did," he said.

Karim held the pillbox out and laid it in Archie's palm. "Enjoy the party," he said.

Archie closed his hand around the box and slipped it back into his pants pocket. "So where's Leo?" he asked.

Cigar smoke veiled Jack's face. "He's around," he said.

CHAPTER

11

Susan pulled at the hips of her dress. She'd chosen a strapless maxi number with pockets and a tight structured bodice. The dress was gold silk, and the lining was just a hint too snug. It was possible that she was a six and not a four, but she sure as hell wasn't going to admit it now. Star had presented her with ten pairs of shoes in several sizes. She had picked out a pair of gold ballet flats, all the better if she had to make a run for it. Star had done her makeup and managed to slick Susan's shoulder-length bob into something resembling an updo. Once Susan was deemed properly gussied up, Star had presented her with a rhinestone-encrusted mask at the end of a long black wand. It was a female fantasy cliché: being whisked off to a ball and dressed up like Cinderella. In reality, it just felt creepy.

But now, as Susan held the sparkly mask up and peered through it, she had to admit, Jack Reynolds knew how to throw a party. The grounds had been transformed into a wonderland. White paper lanterns glowed in the darkened trees. Torch-lined paths wound through gardens to hidden bars and musical quartets. There was a surprise around every corner: a fire juggler, a trapeze artist, women clad only in body-paint tuxedos serving salmon tartines off silver trays. A Charlie Chaplin movie projected onto strips of muslin stretched between two massive Douglas firs. Susan guessed there were five hundred guests, at least. Everyone was wearing masks, but she still thought she recognized a few of them. The scions of old Portland families; people whose ancestors had made a mint clear-cutting old-growth forest, or running whorehouses for sailors down by the river. Their last names were on buildings downtown, on wings at the museum; they served on boards and went through acrimonious divorces. She hadn't seen so many of them in one place since she'd covered the opera one year when she'd worked at the *Herald*.

She probably knew other people there, too, but who could tell with all the masks? Portland was a small city, and if you knew anyone at all, chances were you knew some of the people they knew. It was the kind of town where you could show up at a party thinking you'd know no one, and end up seeing five of your closest friends and a few people you'd been hoping never to see again.

It was kind of a relief to be wearing a mask. She didn't have to pretend to know anyone. She didn't have to make small talk. She was anonymous.

Susan took a tartine from a painted lady and huddled next to one of the propane outdoor heaters that were stationed throughout the yard. Her elbow was getting stiff from holding the mask in place. She still hadn't seen Leo. She'd texted him four more times since she'd gotten to the party, and he had yet to respond.

She took another tartine from a passing tray, stuffed it in her mouth, and negotiated sideways past an approaching group of laughing couples. It was still early, but everyone seemed a little drunk already. The paths were clotted with slow-moving guests, too caught up in the ambience or their own conversation to remember if they had a destination. The masks with feathers shed, and the feathers floated in the air like maple keys and colored the path with splashes of black and purple and green. Susan darted past the other guests, beads of gravel crunching under her feet. She navigated around everyone expertly, pivoting and dodging and skittering, occasionally offering an apologetic shrug or a half-swallowed "Excuse me." She pretended she was trying to get somewhere, to find someone; that she was late. She pretended she was hurrying along a subway platform. All the while, she kept the mask in place, her elbow crooked at a ninety-degree angle, the wand in her fist. She zigged and zagged down the crowded path, past another bar, behind the Charlie Chaplin movie, and down some slate stairs that led to a pool. The pool was a dark green luminous rectangle carved into a stone patio that opened onto the river. LED orbs the size of softballs floated on the pool's surface, pulsing through a rainbow of colors. The stairs were lit with discreet accent lights, and lampposts stood sentry around the pool and lake embankment, but the landscaping around the patio was dark.

Susan took the stairs two at a time and ran across the stone pool deck to where the paving stones gave way to a wall of trees. She stopped short as she glanced up at one of the bronze lampposts. Squatted on top of the lamp, wings outstretched, was a grinning bronze gargoyle. The cognac-like glow of the lamp's antiqued glass gave the gargoyle's eyes a mad gleam. Susan stepped off the patio and backed against the trees into the darkness. She was alone. She could hear the lake lapping against the shore, and, farther away, up the hill, the sounds of music and laughter. Across a half mile of black water, she could see the lights of other houses, just visible through the conifers that surrounded the lake. The night sky was high and hard, like even the stars wanted to keep their distance. Gargoyles squatted on lampposts all around her, like a murder of crows.

It was cold by the lake, and Susan's skin hummed from the chill. A few fall leaves, caught in the wind, scratched along the patio, and then finally flitted into the pool and were still. Susan lowered her mask and pressed herself against a tree trunk, hoping it would hide her silhouette.

She kept her eyes on the stairs.

Sure enough, he came.

He had been following her through the party, always at the edges of her peripheral vision. Someone else might not have noticed. It was crowded, the men were all in tuxedos, wearing masks; it was dark. But Susan wasn't just anyone—she was a reporter. She paid attention. She noticed people. Especially when they were wrestler-sized tough guys who had recently kidnapped her.

Cooper took the stairs casually, with the easy gait of someone not in a hurry, not bothered, not stalking someone. He had changed into a tuxedo—nothing fancy, and a decade out of date—and he was wearing a simple black mask, like a comic-book henchman. When he got to the bottom of the stairs he stopped. Susan didn't move. The bark was rough against her shoulder blades. She could feel Cooper's gaze searching for her in the darkness.

Suddenly the boisterousness of the party seemed very far away.

"Watch out for snakes," Cooper called.

Susan had to bite her lip to keep from whimpering. She stood on her tiptoes and scanned the dark ground around her for any sign of movement.

"Leo's brother Jeremy liberated two pet Burmese pythons a few years ago, and no one's seen them since," Cooper called.

Susan thought she heard a slithering in the dark. She tightened her grip on the wand of the mask, and wondered if it could be used to fend off a python.

"Pythons will wind around tree branches and drop right on top of you," Cooper said.

It was too much. Susan leapt forward, away from the trees, and stumbled out of the foliage onto the paving-stone pool deck. Cooper chuckled, the silver in his teeth glinting in the lamplight.

Susan quickly checked behind her for snakes, saw none, and then turned back to Cooper. "Why are you following me?" she demanded.

He was still fifteen feet away, and he didn't make an effort to get closer.

"It's a big island," he said pleasantly. "I didn't want you to get lost."

"I want to see Leo," Susan said. She brushed at some of the tiny bits of leaves that were stuck to her dress. "Or I'm leaving."

"Okay," Cooper agreed.

That was too easy. "Right now," Susan said, to be clear.

Cooper produced a cell phone and lifted it to his ear. He said something into it, but Susan couldn't make it out. She was too far away. She took a few uneasy steps toward him across the stone patio, but by the time she was close enough to hear, he had already put the cell phone back in his pocket.

He didn't say anything. She hated that. He made her ask.

"Now what?" she asked.

"Want to skinny-dip?" he asked.

"No," she said.

He shrugged. "Then I guess we wait."

"I know Archie Sheridan," Susan said. "He's a personal friend of mine. He's caught serial killers. So he could catch you guys, if something happened to me. I've called him and told him I'm here."

Cooper crossed his arms and gave her an amused look. "Have you, really?"

"Yes."

"Why don't you check and see if he's called back?" Cooper said. He gave her a nod. "Go ahead. We have a minute. Check. You might have a voice mail."

Susan tucked the bejeweled mask under her arm, and got her phone out of her evening bag and checked it. No voice mails. She scrolled through her texts to see if Leo had gotten back to her, but saw only red exclamation marks next to the texts she had sent him. She tried to hide her growing alarm. None of them had gone through.

"The elder Mr. Reynolds is not a fan of cell phones," Cooper said. "He finds them rude. If you ask me, he's fighting a losing battle, but he's the boss, right? He's had cell phone blockers installed. You can't get reception anywhere on the island."

He held up the cell phone he had been talking on and Susan realized that it wasn't a cell phone at all—it was a walkie-talkie.

She was on an island with a bunch of masked criminals and no way to call for help. The lake was very black and very cold and the lights on the other side were very far away. The gravity of the situation was dawning on her. "I shouldn't have come, should I?" she asked.

Cooper's face looked grave in the lamplight.

There was a noise at the top of the stairs and Susan found herself hurrying to Cooper's side. As she stepped beside him, two male shapes appeared side-by-side at the top of the stairs she had descended minutes before. The men were both in tuxedos, their faces shadowed and masked, but Susan knew Leo right away. She wanted to run to him, but she felt Cooper's hand tighten around her shoulder. Leo didn't see her, or at least didn't recognize her. Susan could tell by the way his attention was fixed on the other man. The second man was older, the same height as Leo, but a bit thicker, and accompanied by the orange glow of a lit cigar. Jack Reynolds, Leo's father. Susan could smell the cigar from ten feet away.

Jack had his hand on the back of Leo's neck as they walked. With another father and son, it might be an intimate paternal gesture, but Susan could tell by Leo's stiff gait that there was nothing paternal about this. Jack wasn't so much guiding Leo as he was steering him.

Leo stopped on the stairs and Susan saw his posture harden. He'd seen her. She lifted her mask and waved it meekly at him. She couldn't make out his face—it was too dark up there. Jack laughed and slapped Leo on the back and then left him and jogged down the last few stairs and over to where Cooper and Susan were standing in the lamplight.

"There's our surprise guest," Jack said cheerily to Susan. He put his hands on her shoulders and kissed her on both cheeks. He stank of cigars and liquor. She could feel the heat of the cigar in his hand against her arm. "A vision of loveliness," Jack said. "I knew Star could put something together for you. She wants to be a stylist. Such a waste. She fucks like a jackrabbit. We've all wet our dicks in her. Hey, Leo," he called back toward the stairs, "did you ever think you'd share a fuck with Archie Sheridan?"

She flinched when he said it. Jack must have seen it, because he smiled. He looked like one of the gargoyles. Susan had seen Gretchen Lowell smile like that, too. It was the pleasure that came from causing people pain.

"What is she doing here, Jack?" Leo asked from the stairs. His voice was firm but strained, and it made Susan feel even worse for coming, because Leo so clearly had no idea she would be here.

Jack stepped beside Susan and put his arm around her and gave her a squeeze. "The social event of the season, and you don't invite your girlfriend?" he called up to Leo. "You've been banging this one since what, January? And you've yet to bring her out to the house. I was starting to think you were embarrassed by me."

Leo didn't move. "She's not my girlfriend."

There was that gargoyle smile again. "She thinks she is," Jack said.

Susan's eyes burned. *She's not my girlfriend.* She told herself that this was part of Leo's act. He lied for a living, didn't he? He'd told her he was working for the DEA. He was probably trying to protect her. So why wasn't he coming down the stairs to get his father off her?

"I don't want her here," Leo said.

"It does make fucking Star later awkward," Jack said. Susan forced herself not to react to his goading. She wasn't going to give Jack the satisfaction. She just wanted to get out of here.

"I want her taken home," Leo said.

Finally.

But Jack's fingers tightened over her shoulders. "She's all dolled up," Jack said. The playfulness had left his voice. "She's here, and she's staying the night."

Susan couldn't stand the smell of him, the cigars, the cologne, the brandy. "I can't spend the night," she said. She had plans. She had to wax her legs and watch *Law & Order.*

Jack's blue eyes settled on hers. "I wasn't asking," he said. She was chilly, but his touch wasn't making her warm—it was more like he was sucking the heat right out of her. He gave her another smile, this one more shark than gargoyle. "If everything goes well, you'll be home tomorrow in time for brunch. In the meantime, enjoy the party. Have you tried the mini-quiches?"

Susan looked up the stairs, searching for some sort of guidance from Leo, but he remained a silhouette in the dark.

"We should get back to our friends," Jack said to her. "Let Cooper know if you need anything." He turned and climbed up the first part of the stairs to where Leo was standing. When he reached his son, Jack settled his hand around the back of Leo's neck. The gesture made Susan shiver. She didn't know what sort of fucked-up game Leo and his father were playing, but she was pretty sure that Jack had just tossed her on the table and raised the stakes.

"Susan," Leo said. "Don't do anything stupid, okay?"

"Can I come with you?" she called.

Jack Reynolds chuckled in the dark. "She's a hoot," he said.

"Yeah," Leo said quietly.

She watched as Jack steered Leo around and then escorted him up the rest of the stairs. She was on an island. Without cell reception. Dressed like a Mardi Gras Christmas ornament. And her boyfriend was acting like the Manchurian Candidate. This was so fucked.

A gust of wind blew off the river, and dried leaves rained from the trees. She wondered if Cooper had been telling the truth about the pythons.

The party sounded louder, like people were drunker, but she could still hear the sound of Cooper breathing.

"So which is it?" Susan asked him. "Is he using me to make sure Leo does something, or doesn't do something?"

Cooper put his hands in his pockets. "You want to know what I would do if I were you?" he asked.

Susan gazed out at the cold black water. "Swim for it?" she said. It had been less than a year since she'd almost drowned in the flood. Technically, she *had* drowned. She had been clinically dead when Archie had pulled her from the river. Even the thought of her body in that lake made her squirm.

"It's nine P.M.," Cooper said. "The party will go on until four in the morning. There's food, music, scintillating conversation. Relax. Have a drink."

Was he serious? "Because a champagne cocktail is exactly what I need right now," Susan said.

Cooper leaned close to her. He was a foot taller than she was, and three times as wide. The weird thing was, the gesture didn't feel threatening—just the opposite. He made Susan feel safe. She had thought he was following her in order to scare her. Now she wondered if he was actually trying to protect her.

"It will be better for him if he thinks you're not afraid," Cooper said.

CHAPTER

12

Archie had never liked crowds. He depended on his ability to absorb detail, to notice what was out of place, and too many people softened the lens. Everyone blended together.

He had been patrolling the party for the better part of an hour. He hoped it looked like mingling. Every once in a while he would set a drink on a tray and pick up another one, so that to anyone watching it would look like he was drinking more than he actually was.

There was no good vantage point. The grounds were a maze of horticultural nooks and crannies.

The island was crawling with guests. Everyone looked sweaty from alcohol, and glowing with their own importance. Most of the tuxedos looked custom. Most of the women had hair that cost more to maintain than Archie brought home in salary. The valets had stopped parking cars. The gates at the end of the bridge were closed. None of the guests seemed to mind that they were all essentially now trapped on the island.

Archie hovered near the house, scanning for signs of Leo. Some people had given up on their masks, abandoning them for the sake of comfort or conversation, or maybe because they were tired of looking like idiots, but Archie kept his mask firmly in place. He liked it. For the first time in three years, he could move among a crowd without worrying about someone recognizing him as the man who survived ten days with Gretchen Lowell.

A bar was set up near a hedge maze in the left quadrant of the front yard, and people waited in line for drinks. Others streamed in and out of the house. The music had transitioned from instrumental to electronic dance music. It pounded through speakers erected in the trees, and vibrated the leaves on the branches.

The main house was three stories of winsome Tudor architecture. Archie could see lights on throughout the house. The exterior walls were either stone, or stucco crossed with decorative half-timbering. The roof was pitched and accounted for two-thirds of the house's surface. Getting an idea of the interior layout from looking at it was impossible. It looked like someone had taken fifteen storybook cottages and smashed them together.

Archie grabbed a new drink off a server's passing tray and headed for the front door. The first floor of the house was technically open to guests, except for a few rooms, like Jack's office, which were locked. Most people who came inside to look around quickly left. Archie didn't have a reason to be there. There wasn't a bar or a table of food, so he did what people trying to get away with poking around had done for millennia—he pretended to look for a bathroom.

He was within a yard of the bottom stair when he felt a hand tighten on his shoulder. Archie turned around and found himself face-to-face with another one of Jack Reynolds's private security detail. This one didn't have the same military bearing as the others, and his suit was cheaper. He was wearing a black mask like Archie's, probably given to him by the same person. Archie could see the tiny pricks of razor burn where he'd shaved with a dull blade or rushed the job. You could tell a lot about a man by how he shaved: if he cared about using the right tools; if he lacked patience. "Upstairs is closed," Razor Burn said.

"I'm looking for a bathroom," Archie said.

Razor Burn scratched at his sideburn. "Didn't you just use that bathroom a half hour ago?"

For someone with a bad shave, he was very observant.

"Prostate issues," Archie said.

Razor Burn lifted his hand off Archie's shoulder and jabbed a finger down the hallway to the left of the stairs. "Second door down the hallway to your left," he said. "Same place it was thirty minutes ago."

"Thanks so much," Archie said.

Archie backed away and headed down the hall where Razor Burn had directed him. A very young-looking woman had her ear against the bathroom door. She was skinny in an unformed way, like she'd just had a growth spurt and hadn't gotten used to her longer limbs yet. She looked like she should be wearing jeans and a backpack, on her way to high school, but instead she was wearing a royal blue slip dress and carrying a pair of stiletto heels in her hand. A mask coated in purple glitter was pushed up on her forehead in a tangle of blond hair. When Archie got close, she looked up at him and laughed. Her face was pink. The whites of her eyes were bloodshot. She reeked of alcohol. Most cops didn't need a sobriety test to tell if someone was drunk. The sobriety test was for the courts. Cops could tell the moment you rolled down the window. It was all in the eyes.

"Are you okay?" Archie asked.

"My friend's a little wasted," she said. She held up another mask—this one coated in gold glitter—which Archie assumed belonged to the friend. She laughed again, and Archie could hear, underneath her giggles, the distinct sound of someone violently vomiting on the other side of the bathroom door.

"Do you want me to get help?" Archie asked.

The young woman had her hand on the door, holding herself upright. Her silver nail polish was chipped, like she'd chewed at it. "She's fine," she said with a hiccup. "She said so."

"Get her some water, okay?" Archie said. She nodded vigorously and Archie started to turn away, but then turned back. "How old are you?" he asked.

She paused—probably longer than she thought she did. "Twenty-two."

There was no way she was more than nineteen. "Listen," Archie started to say. But his concentration was broken by the sound of Jack Reynolds's voice behind him. Archie turned to look down the hall and saw Jack leading two men in tuxedos through the foyer in the direction of his office. Jack was between them, a step behind—a hand on each of their shoulders. Archie couldn't see the men's faces, only Jack's. But as they stepped out of Archie's view, Jack looked up, right at Archie, and smiled.

Archie hurried forward down the hall, leaving the underage girl, but when he reached the foyer, Jack and the men were gone. The door to the hall that led to Jack's office was closed, and a new goon was standing in front of it. The goon had his arms crossed over his chest and was staring, heavy lidded, into the middle distance. He wasn't wearing an earpiece and he wasn't wearing a mask. He also wasn't wearing a suit. He had big hands and a broad nose and a leather jacket that looked like it weighed twenty pounds.

Archie looked down at his drink. It was half empty. He drained it. Then he held it up in front of the goon. "Do you know where I should put this?" he asked him. The goon didn't respond. Archie held the glass between them and then opened his hand and let the glass drop. It hit the floor with an explosion of splintered glass shrapnel.

"Dolboeb," the goon snapped under his breath. He stepped back a few inches and kicked the broken glass off his shoes.

Russian?

Archie smiled.

The Russian straightened up again, his dead gaze fixed over Archie's shoulder. He didn't make a move to clean up the glass.

"Sorry," Archie said. "I'm a little drunk."

Archie waited. The Russian didn't move. He didn't leave the door. He didn't call for someone to clean up the glass. Archie turned his head and glanced back at Razor Burn, across the foyer, still leaning against the wall at the bottom of the stairs. He wasn't in any hurry to help. These two didn't work together. They had different bosses. The Russian had come with whoever was in the office with Jack.

Archie was considering the pros and cons of dropping another glass, when a woman appeared at the top of the stairs. It was hard to miss her. She was wearing a black dress that was made out of some sparkly gauze material. A triangular piece of fabric harnessed each breast and then attached behind her neck. Her back was bare all the way to her waist. Her dark curly hair was twisted up loosely on top of her head. She was carrying a reusable grocery bag. Her head was turned so that Archie couldn't see her face, but he recognized her body.

Star. His lap dancer.

Razor Burn saw her, too. He'd lifted his shoulders off the wall and pulled his hands out of his pockets. It was a predatory move. His posture shifted forward to put his weight on the balls of his feet. He was leering at Star as she descended to him. She kept her head down, a classic ploy to avoid interaction. But she had to pass him, and when she did, Razor Burn caught her by the waist.

The Russian across the hall unfolded his arms.

A caterer hurried through the foyer with a tray of small bites from the kitchen, and exited through the front door.

Razor Burn pulled Star to his chest. She smiled and straightened up and said something to him and Archie saw her move the bag she was carrying behind her hip. Whatever was in it, she didn't want it drawing Razor Burn's attention.

Razor Burn's lips were shiny with saliva. He wrapped his hand around Star's wrist and moved her hand to the front of his pants. He was either oblivious to anyone else's presence, or he didn't care. No heroics, Sanchez had said.

"Star," Archie said loudly.

Razor Burn and Star both snapped their heads in Archie's direction. Archie strolled toward them, feeling the Russian's gaze on the back of his neck.

Star didn't pull away from Razor Burn. She was smart. Men like Razor Burn needed to feel in control. If she disentangled too soon, he might react violently.

"You remember me," Archie said, lifting his mask above his eyebrows. "*Detective* Sheridan."

Archie saw a trace of a smile cross Star's lips. "The birthday boy," she said.

"That's right," Archie said.

"You're Leo's friend," Star said with a glance in Razor Burn's direction. Archie saw what she was doing. She was spelling it out for him, but letting him put it together himself. Razor Burn might be dumb, but he knew enough not to do something stupid in front of a friend of the boss's son. Sure enough, Razor Burn retracted his arm. "I'll find you later," Archie heard him snarl.

Star adjusted the strap of her dress and stepped forward, out of Razor Burn's reach. Her wrist was red where he had grabbed her and Archie could see the pulse in her throat throbbing. She had been afraid, even if she'd done a nice job not showing it. Her knuckles were white where she clutched the straps of the grocery bag. It was one of those polypropylene grocery totes that the stores guilted people into buying instead of using paper or plastic bags. This one had a recycling symbol on the side of it and a sad-looking polar bear. Archie had five similar bags in his trunk right now. His bags were all empty. The bag Star was carrying was not. She saw him looking at it, and moved the straps up her arm and onto her shoulder.

"Can I buy you a drink?" Archie asked.

"The drinks here are free," Star said.

"Even better," said Archie.

"Well, come on, then," she said, and Archie followed her toward the front door.

Star's legs were bare and her dress showed them off. She was wearing black strappy high-heeled sandals, which didn't slow her down at all. Her polypropylene bag was secured under her arm like a top-secret diplomatic pouch.

"Good luck with your prostate," Razor Burn called after Archie.

Archie ignored him, but did glance back one more time at the Russian as they left the house. He had recrossed his arms and was looking straight ahead, where Razor Burn had settled back against the wall, directly in the Russian's field of vision. The broken glass was still at his feet.

Then Archie followed Star through the door and out into the night.

She was several feet ahead, and Archie had to hurry to catch up with her. She navigated the grounds easily—she had clearly spent some time here. They passed other guests, but everyone was drunk and no one seemed to notice them as they went by, moving off the main path to a smaller one and then around the left side of the house along the border of one of the waist-high hedge mazes that Jack had installed throughout the grounds. Archie wondered how many decomposing bodies of lost guests turned up in those things. Star led him around the back side of the hedge. The path was gravel and their steps made a grinding noise as they walked. Tiny rocks spit out from under Star's heels, but it didn't slow her down. There wasn't a bar on this side of the house, and it wasn't well lit. Archie couldn't see any other guests now. The electronic music still pounded but they were far away enough from any speakers that it was background din.

Star stopped, hugging her arms for warmth as late evening set in. A lone torch flickered nearby, casting her face in a jittery tangerine glow. It was the first time Archie realized that she didn't have a mask. Her glittery black dress winked and sparkled. Something glinted in her hair. At first Archie thought it was a barrette.

"Thanks for the graceful exit," Star said.

It was a kiss-off. Archie had served his purpose. She was in a rush. And it had something to do with whatever was in the bag.

"What are you doing here?" Archie asked her. He was trying to stall her. It wasn't a barrette; it was something wet.

Archie peered at Star's hairline, attempting to puzzle out what had briefly caught the torchlight.

"Look," she said. "You're sweet. But I have to go."

Archie reached his hand up and touched her hair. She didn't pull away. She didn't even look surprised. She was used to men hitting on her. She took it like a pro.

Archie moved his fingers away from her head and showed them to her. The torchlight bathed them both in uncertain dark shadows that quivered with the flame. Archie could smell the citronella torch oil burning, a pungent chemical lemon mixed with sulfur. He held his hand nearer to the torch so she could see the stain of red on his fingertip.

"It's blood," he said. "It's called transfer splatter. That means that someone touched blood and then touched you."

She was trembling. Her hand shot up to the spot where Archie had touched her hair and she started to claw at it, pulling the hair loose.

"It's okay," Archie said. "I got it." He could feel the wet on his fingertips, a coolness on his skin.

She had allowed a crack in her façade and now the wall was crumbling. Her hands tightened into fists. Her face tensed with fear. The skin of her neck and chest was rough with goose bumps. It's what happened to people after car accidents, after the adrenaline surge dropped and the body indulged in all that repressed panic.

Archie had to refocus her, keep her calm. "I can help you," Archie said. Leo had talked to Archie freely with Star in the room. Archie didn't know how much she knew, but Leo clearly trusted her with his life. Whatever their relationship was, Leo relied on her. If he was in trouble, he'd go to her for help. Archie tilted his head at the bag. "Is that for Leo?"

She nodded, swallowing hard.

"Where is he?" Archie asked.

"In the guesthouse," she said in a voice barely above a whisper.

"Can you get me in there?" he asked.

She seemed to consider it, taking several long breaths. She was gathering herself, rebuilding the emotional wall. He watched it happen. Her bearing changed. She set her shoulders back. She lifted her chin. Her expression settled into a mask of pretty/neutrality. Finally she gave him a nod. "Maybe. If they think I'm taking you there for a party."

"A party?"

Her eyes were hard now, her irises reflecting the orange flame. "I'm not here as a guest," she said. "I'm working."

Archie digested this. So Star did more than dance. It made sense considering their introduction. But he had hoped, for her sake, that their interaction had been an anomaly. He measured his response, searching for the right level of nonchalance. "Oh," he said. "Right."

Archie heard voices approaching. Star leaned forward and swiftly pulled the shirttails from Archie's pants and then reached up to pull his tie loose. She fumbled with it for a moment and then Archie whispered, "It's a clip-on."

He thought he saw her roll her eyes. But she unclipped it and opened his shirt collar.

The voices were closer and Archie looked over Star's shoulder to see two of Jack Reynolds's security detail rounding the corner. Star pressed against him, the black bag between them, touching but not touching. Whatever was inside the bag, it was soft.

The men looked at Archie and sniggered, but kept walking, and soon disappeared around the house.

"All clear," Archie said.

Star stepped back, creating space between them. "If we run into anyone else, I may kiss you, so try not to freak out or cry or anything," she said.

"Sure," Archie said, wondering what it was about him that made her think he'd cry if he was kissed. She took his hand and they continued along the hedge maze away from the light of the torch and back into the darkness.

Her hand was cold, and as it warmed in his, Archie searched for something to say. He barely knew this woman, but they had shared an intimate moment. He had seen her barely clothed. He'd been turned on by her. But then, it probably hadn't seemed intimate to her at all. She'd just been working. She'd figured him for a prude. If only she knew. "So is Star your real name?" he asked, the question sounding stupid even as it left his mouth.

"Star's my stripper name," she said. The dark side yard opened up to a brightly lit gravel driveway filled with catering vehicles. Across the driveway was a vine-covered Tudor cottage straight out of a fairy tale.

"My real name is Destiny."

Archie thought he saw Star wink when she said it, but he couldn't be sure.

CHAPTER

13

The door to the guesthouse was unlocked. But Archie noticed that Star opened it slowly, peering cautiously inside before she quickly stepped over the threshold, and pulled him in behind her, past the stone gargoyles that stood sentry on either side of the front door. No one had questioned them. Two men in catering uniforms with masks around their necks were leaning against a van smoking cigarettes, but they had barely glanced up as Star and Archie had walked by. Archie didn't spot any of Jack's security detail stationed at the back of the house, but that didn't mean they weren't there.

"There are cameras," Star said, closing the door. "All over the island."

Archie didn't know if she knew that for a fact, or if she was just being paranoid. But if she was being paranoid, it was contagious, and he found himself scanning the corners for telltale red lights.

Inside, the house looked bigger than it did on the outside. The Tudor architecture carried over, with dark exposed wood beams and arched doorways, and stucco walls that had been expensively and laboriously distressed for authenticity. The lights in the room were on a dimmer switch and had been dialed down to the perfectly calibrated ambient glow of a high-end restaurant—barely light enough to see your food, but not light enough to read the menu.

There was a selection of gowns spread out in the living room, and what looked like a makeup kit on a table, as if someone had used the space as a makeshift dressing room. Archie noted a red hooded sweatshirt cast over the back of a sofa, and a pair of black sneakers kicked under a chair. Susan had a sweatshirt like that. But so did half the people on the east side.

"Upstairs," Star whispered.

Archie nodded and followed her out of the living room and up a flight of carpeted stairs. Their footsteps were soundless on the carpet and the house felt still and empty. But as they headed down the second-story hall, Archie could make out the faint sound of water running. Star stopped at a closed door and put her ear to it and listened. The water sounded like it was coming from the other side. "It's me," Star said. She turned the doorknob and pushed the door in.

Archie followed her inside to a large guest bedroom suite.

The door to the private bath was open, and Leo Reynolds stood in front of the sink, with the faucet running. He was wearing a tuxedo, but the jacket and tie were gone. His shirt was unbuttoned and open, and his sleeves were rolled up. The white fabric of the shirt was soaked with blood—arterial spray, low-velocity. The water in the sink was pink. He was cleaning up.

Leo froze when he saw Archie. His eyes were bloodshot. His hands shook. Whatever had happened, it had been bad.

"Are you okay?" Archie asked.

Leo exhaled roughly and stared at Archie with dismay. Then his eyes went to Star. "What have you done?" he asked. "Bringing him here?"

"He can help," Star said.

"We were worried about you," Archie said. "What's going on? Tell me what happened."

"They'll be back any minute," Leo said. "Jesus Christ." He looked fixedly at Archie. "We have a problem," he said.

He walked toward Archie and put his arm around Archie's shoulder. Archie could smell the soap Leo had used, an astringent, eye-watering odor; he'd known to use something strong, something that would obliterate any trace of blood that Luminol might pick up. "Listen to me," Leo said. "We don't have much time. Susan is on the island." Archie felt something deep inside him go cold. "They're using her to control me," Leo said. "You have to find her and get her out of here."

"Susan?" Archie said. His mind went back to the red hooded sweatshirt downstairs. "What?"

Archie felt Leo's arm tighten around his shoulder. "I'm sorry," Leo said, as he stepped behind Archie. Leo's elbow hooked under Archie's chin and the hand of his opposite arm palmed the back of Archie's head. Archie tried to step away, but Leo pressed against him, his thigh secured against the back of Archie's leg. Leo's grip on Archie's neck was firm and Archie struggled to get a breath. He could already feel the black fog of unconsciousness closing in on him as his brain screamed for oxygen. The carotid artery traveled up the side of the neck. When blood flow was interrupted, you had maybe a minute before you blacked out.

Archie clawed at Leo's arm, but he was already losing strength.

"I don't know how to do this very well, so don't fight me," Leo whispered into Archie's ear. "I don't want to break your neck."

Archie's hands were tingling. His lips and tongue were going numb. He felt his hands drop to his sides and his body relax as Leo lowered him to the floor. Leo's arm was still tight around Archie's neck, his hand still pressing hard against Archie's skull. Archie saw his feet out in front of him, twitching on the floor, his stupid rented shoes. And he saw Star inching forward into his vision. Her hand was over her mouth. Her dress shimmered. And then she blurred, and when she came into focus again, she was gone, and Gretchen was there.

Gretchen didn't look like she had the last time he'd seen

her, when she'd freshly escaped from the mental hospital and her hair was dark, her body still showing signs of the medication they'd pumped into her. She looked like she had before, in all her homicidal glory. Her thick blond hair fell in glossy waves to her shoulders. Her features—those famous blue eyes, her regal nose, that beauty queen smile—were almost blindingly attractive. She was just a hallucination. The mind did funny things when it thought it might be dying. But Archie was still aware enough to find it interesting that of all the people his brain decided to conjure at this moment, it chose her.

She smiled at him and took his hand in hers and lifted it to her cheek. He felt her imaginary touch all the way to his groin.

"There, there, darling," she whispered. "You didn't think I'd let you celebrate your birthday without me?"

CHAPTER

14

The bedroom window is open and a cool breeze blows through, tickling Archie's chest and arms. In the heat of sex he hadn't noticed it, but now he is cold. He pulls the sheets up to his waist. Gretchen is lying on her side next to him, but he doesn't cover her. Her cheeks are still flushed and she doesn't look chilly. Also, Archie likes to see her naked.

"What did you tell Henry?" she asks.

She has one arm supporting her head and the other draped along her side, her elbow resting in the deep dip of her waist, her forearm curved along her hips, her hand on her bare thigh. Her hair is tousled, and her skin glows with perspiration. He can look at her body all day long—the fullness of her breasts, her smooth thighs, every angle and curve.

"I might have mentioned that I had a counseling appointment," Archie says. Gretchen's relationship with the task force has made coming up with excuses easy. She had offered them her services free of charge. Archie had been one of the first to sign up for sessions. He told himself at the time that he was leading by example, but in retrospect his intentions might have been baser.

"Do you think you'll ever tell him?" Gretchen asks.

She brings this up a lot. She seems to worry that Archie and Henry will go out for beers one day and Archie will spill his guts. She doesn't understand Archie's relationship with Henry at all. There is no way Archie will ever tell his partner anything about this. He has already let himself down. He doesn't want to let Henry down, too. "God, no," Archie says. "No offense."

Gretchen looks skeptical. "Many men brag about their conquests."

"I'm not proud of this," Archie says. "It's not something I would ever brag about. And believe me, Henry would not be impressed."

He's seen the way that Henry looks at Gretchen. He knows Henry doesn't like her.

Gretchen sighs deeply, and looks away. The room is painted pale yellow and the light from the brass and crystal chandelier overhead gives everything a buttery glow. When she turns back to him, her eyes seem sad.

"I'm sorry I cause you so much pain," she says.

"I'm here, aren't I?" Archie says. Just looking at her makes his heart rate increase. The attraction he feels toward her is unlike anything he has ever experienced before. He reaches for her hips and pulls her closer to him on the bed. "I have free will," he says. "I'm the one who's cheating. You're not doing anything wrong."

"I think your wife might disagree," Gretchen says.

"Probably," Archie says. "But I'm the one she'd hate."

"For a detective, you're not very smart about women," Gretchen says.

Her body is warm under his hands and he feels the physical pull he always does when they are this close.

He has memorized her. He knows her intimately. Even after their first sexual encounter he could conjure her in his mind like a photograph. "I can't get you out of my head," he tells her. "I spent all day at a crime scene, and all I could think about was you."

She leans closer to him. "Tell me about it," she says.

Archie hesitates. She'll get the file tomorrow, anyway,

and it hardly seems like bedroom talk. "It'll all be in the file," he says.

"I want to hear about it from you," Gretchen says, laying her head on his chest, her cheek over his heart. Her blond hair rises and falls as he breathes.

Archie doesn't talk about his work with Debbie. Even when Debbie presses, he refuses to talk to her about the murders. He tells himself that she doesn't really want to know. He doesn't want to scare her.

But Gretchen is a consultant on the case. She's seen all the crime scene files. She's read all the notes. She's viewed all the crime scene photographs and autopsy reports. For the first time, Archie can tell someone about his day. He can unload. It makes him regret not being able to share that with his wife.

"She was young," he tells Gretchen quietly. "Twenty-two. Graduated from Cornish up in Seattle in the spring. Lidia Hays. The Beauty Killer murdered her at her apartment in North Portland. She lived off of Alberta, in a house that had been subdivided into four units. She didn't lock her door. We think he entered early in the day and waited for her to come home from work. She was a server at a brewpub downtown. She got off at ten and told her coworkers that she was headed straight home. He kept her alive most of the night. She was tied spread-eagled and naked to her bed. She had duct tape over her mouth, or the neighbors would have heard her screaming."

"The killings aren't usually sexual," Gretchen says. Her hair is over one shoulder, revealing the curve of her neck.

"It doesn't look like she was sexually assaulted," Archie says. "But the scene was definitely staged to make a point." The chandelier throws a large shadow on the ceiling above the bed, like a giant spider. "Maybe she reminded him of someone," Archie says.

"What did she look like?" Gretchen asks.

Archie hesitates, not sure she wants to hear the answer. "You, actually," he says. "Blond, blue eyes. A beauty."

He feels Gretchen shiver.

Archie touches the back of her neck. "Do you want me to close the window?" he asks.

"It's not that," she says.

His finger finds the small hollow at the base of her skull. "We don't have to talk about this."

"I want to know," she says firmly. "I want to try to understand the killer."

"The killer." Never "him." Never "he." Gretchen is always gender-neutral. "You're avoiding pronouns again," Archie says.

"You don't know it's a man," Gretchen chides him. "That's your assumption."

The spider on the ceiling seems to crawl as the crystals on the chandelier tremble gently in the breeze. "Women don't kill like this," he says.

She rolls over, so the back of her head is now resting on his chest, and she looks at him. "What did he do?" she asks.

"He poisoned her," Archie says. "We found a half-empty bottle of drain cleaner and a spoon on the bedside table. And she was cut. All over. With a scalpel, it looks like. Superficial. Just enough to hurt and to make her bleed a little, but not enough to kill her. He must have cut her a thousand times. Working up one leg, then the other. She would have anticipated each incision." That would be the worst part, knowing it was coming, knowing it would go on and on.

"It must have taken hours," Gretchen says.

Each cut had been deliberate. "There was a pattern to it," he says. It was as if her flesh had been decorated, each incision a new detail in a grisly textile. "He carved column after column of curved slices that intersected like segments of a chain." Archie curls his hands and hooks them together in front of Gretchen to illustrate.

Gretchen frowns. "Like pieces of a heart?"

"Maybe," Archie says. "The incisions covered every inch of her, except for an area right here"—he places his palm lightly at the base of Gretchen's throat—"about the size of my hand." That area of the body had been clean, except for one delicate incision in the shape of a heart. He can feel the pulse of Gretchen's carotid artery under his touch. "That's where he carved his signature," he says.

Gretchen threads her fingers through his hand and lifts it from her throat.

"She had a poster of Multnomah Falls on the wall of her bedroom," Archie continues. "You can buy them at the gift store." How many times had he and Debbie taken out-of-town guests to Multnomah Falls, and then the gift store at the base of the waterfall? How many of them had bought that very poster? "And a lot of books," Archie says. "She snowboarded. That's what her mother told me. She just moved here two months ago. Her mother said she spent all her tip money on a season pass for Mount Hood."

"You'll catch the Beauty Killer," Gretchen says. She says it with so much conviction that Archie almost laughs. But her expression is completely serious. "I know you will," she says.

These days, Archie isn't so sure. He feels farther from the killer than he's ever been, and the murders are only accelerating. Each new killing weighs heavier than the last. "Why didn't she scream?" he asks. It has been bothering him all day. "Her upstairs neighbors were home the whole time, and didn't hear anything. He would have had to take off the tape to feed it to her. Did he hold the blade to her throat and force her to drink the drain cleaner? Or did she do it willingly? Was she just done?"

Gretchen squeezes his hand. "The killer had been terrorizing her for hours by then. It was probably something of a relief."

Archie isn't sure which is worse—the idea that the drain cleaner had been forced down the victim's throat, or the idea that she'd been driven to take it without threat or force, as a means to end her own suffering. "She should have screamed," he says.

They are quiet. The curtains on the window move a little. The spider on the ceiling dances. Otherwise, the room is still.

"Is that why you thought of me today?" Gretchen asks. "Because she looked like me?"

The truth is more shameful. "I thought of you because she was naked on a bed," Archie says.

"It turned you on," Gretchen says softly.

He looks away. Lidia had been a beautiful woman, even bloodied and cold, and she'd been sexually staged, splayed open and tied to a bed. He's male. He has reactions. Lizard-brain reactions. He can't be blamed for that.

"It's okay," Gretchen tells him.

Archie swings his feet onto the floor and sits up. "I have to go home."

Gretchen crawls behind him and puts her arms around his waist. "It's an understandable biological response," she says. She lifts a hand and runs it through his hair along the back of his scalp. "Look at me," she says.

She has perfect blue eyes.

"It was nothing. Don't let it get to you." A smile plays on her lips. "Some people like to be tied up," she says, eyes twinkling. She moves her face near his cheek and nuzzles at his ear. "If I asked you to tie me up, would you?"

Archie pulls away and looks at her, unsure if he's heard correctly.

She raises an eyebrow at him and smiles.

"I don't want to tie you up," he says.

"You've done a lot of things recently you never thought you'd do," she points out. She lowers her chin and gives him a flirty look. "It's fun. I would make it fun. It's fantasy. It's completely normal. A lot of people play games in bed."

"I'm going now before you pull out a latex mask," Archie says.

"You'll think about it, though, won't you?" she asks. She lies back on the bed and wraps her hands around the bedposts. It is eerily similar to how the latest victim had been secured to her bed, but Gretchen couldn't know that. She arches her back and moans, and Archie feels a twinge of heat in his groin.

"Good-bye," he says, looking for his socks.

She lets go of the bedposts and wriggles toward him on the bed. "Stay longer," she purrs.

"I can't," Archie says. "I have to get home. They're waiting for me." He sighs and pulls on his pants, already feeling the knot of guilt and shame that tightens in his chest every time he leaves her house. "It's my birthday."

CHAPTER

15

Archie awoke to the sound of birds. He opened his eyes, squinted in the light, and saw water. It lapped gently below him, shimmering with dawn. His whole body hurt. He lay there for a few minutes without moving, trying to piece together where he was and what had happened to him. Then he slowly took in his surroundings. He was splayed on his side on a muddy bank, surrounded by ferns. He could see across the lake, to the docks and houses hedged in by conifers. He was still on the island. He wrestled his wrist forward with a groan and looked at his watch. It was almost five-thirty in the morning. He felt cold to the bone and his hands felt numb and clumsy. He tried to sit up and felt a stabbing pain in his head. He took a few slow breaths and then gently eased himself to a sitting position. His shirt was grimy and stained with dirt. His jacket and tie were gone. His mask was gone. He had mud under his fingernails. His hands smelled strangely of lavender. He felt an irritation in his throat like he'd swallowed something and it had gotten caught halfway down. Archie coughed, trying to dislodge it, but couldn't bring it up. He swallowed hard a few times, trying to get it down the other way, but it remained firmly in place, a small itch behind his Adam's apple. He emptied his pockets. His phone still said no service. He still had the compass from Henry and Claire. He still had the magazine of bullets that he'd ejected from the gun. He still had the brass pillbox. He opened it. There were only two pills. He stared at them, perplexed. There had been ten when he'd started the evening, and he didn't remember taking any. He touched his throat, wondering if that's what he was feeling—a pill. He pinched the remaining two between his dirty fingers, tossed them on his tongue, and chewed them. The bitter taste pulled at the corners of his mouth as the pills broke apart between his teeth. He swallowed the last of the chalky residue and looked at the water. Then he tried to stand.

The sudden change in elevation drove a blade of pain through his head again. He reached up and touched his skull and his fingers found dried blood. He searched his memory for any clues to what had happened and came up with nothing. He remembered Star. He remembered finding Leo in the bedroom. And then . . . nothing.

He stumbled to the edge of the water and looked at his reflection. His face was smeared with mud. Blood clotted his hair. He coughed again, trying to clear his throat.

What had happened to him?

Archie saw splinters of images. Star coming down the stairs. A gargoyle on top of a lamppost. Leo washing blood off his hands. Then he had a flash of body memory—Leo's arm around his neck, the pressure of Leo's palm pressed against the back of his skull. Leo had choked him.

Archie worked backward. Trying to puzzle it out. He saw Leo's face, talking to him; the urgency in his eyes. He was trying to tell him something important.

Susan.

Susan was on the island.

Archie turned and started clawing his way up the mud embankment.

CHAPTER

16

Susan yawned and turned the page of the *Town & Country* magazine that she was reading for the fourth time. She didn't feel so elegant anymore. Her makeup had dried to a cakey mask that felt like it cracked when she smiled. The fabric of the gold dress stuck to the stubble on her legs, and her armpits were sore where the bodice had chafed her raw. She snuck a glance at Jack Reynolds. He was sitting behind his desk with his tie unknotted and a cup of coffee next to him, reading that day's *New York Times* and looking like the cover of *Cigar Aficionado* magazine. A housekeeper had brought the paper a half hour ago, along with a copy of *The Wall Street Journal* and a cup of coffee. No *Herald,* Susan couldn't help but notice. He probably read it online.

He hadn't said a word to her for the last hour. He hadn't even offered her a section of the paper.

The coffee smelled good.

Cooper was sitting in one of the chairs that faced Jack's desk, not really doing anything. He hadn't been doing anything for hours, which made Susan bored even to watch, but seemed to suit Cooper just fine. Susan, meanwhile, had read *The Economist,* two issues of *Palm Beach Illustrated,* and something called the *Robb Report*. The *Town & Country* wasn't actually that bad. Who knew that Christie Brinkley's Hamptons remodel had been such a trial? Susan felt bad for her.

The phone on Jack Reynolds's desk rang. Susan noticed that he let it ring exactly twice, even though he was sitting right there. He picked it up, listened, and then said, "Let him in."

Susan put the magazine down. She had been in that room waiting for Leo to take her home for over four hours. It was about fucking time. The truth was she didn't feel bad for Christie Brinkley at all. She felt bad for Leo, whose boyfriend stock was currently tanking, and to whom she planned to give the talking-to of a lifetime. She searched the floor for her shoes and put them on, and picked up the paper shopping bag that held her street clothes and purse.

When the door to the office opened, she was ready to go.

But it wasn't Leo who walked in.

It was Archie.

He was coated in filth. Disheveled. Begrimed. Grubby. *Dirty* didn't even begin to describe it. His clothes were creased and crumpled. His hair was a catastrophe. He had soil smeared on his face. Bits of vegetation clung to every part of him. He gave her a nod. "It's time to go home," he said.

Susan looked at Jack and Cooper. They didn't look back. They were staring at Archie.

"Now," he said.

Susan gulped and nodded. She didn't know what he knew or didn't know or what had happened or how long he'd been there, but she knew now was not the time to ask any of those questions. She hopped up off the chair and hurried to him, clutching the paper shopping bag to her chest.

Jack had laid the newspaper down on his desk and was looking up at them calmly. "You're tracking dirt on my Persian rug," he said to Archie.

"Where's Leo?" Archie asked.

Up close, Susan could see blood in his hair. It had collected and congealed, leaving the top of his head matted with dark red. A trail of red traveled along his hairline and disappeared behind his ear. Susan took his hand. It was freezing.

Jack picked up his cup of coffee and lifted it to his lips and took a sip. Then he set it down. "Leo's gone," he said.

"Wait," Susan said. "What?" If Leo was gone, why had she been sitting here for four hours waiting for him? She leaned close to Archie. "I saw him last night," she said, "down by the pool. They said he'd meet me here and take me home in the morning." Archie smelled like mud. Underneath all the dirt, she could see that he was wearing a tuxedo. He'd been at the party. Had he come looking for her, or for Leo? A small brown leaf unstuck itself from his shoulder and fluttered to the floor. "What are you doing here?" she asked. "Did you come because of me?"

Archie didn't answer. His eyes were still fixed on Jack. "Give me my fucking gun," Archie said.

Gun? Susan's stomach did a somersault. She could feel the tension in Archie's hand, every muscle tightening.

Jack got a key out of a box on his desk and he unlocked one of his desk drawers and slid it open and reached in and pulled out a gun. Susan scrutinized Archie's face, searching for some clue as to what the hell was going on.

Cooper walked the gun over, and Archie let go of her hand and took the gun from him, and then Cooper stepped away, and leaned up against the wall next to a framed photograph of a sailboat named *Isabel*.

Susan wanted to get out of here. She hovered at Archie's elbow, tightening her grip on the paper bag as if she might turn and dash away at any time. But Archie's attention was on the gun in his hand. He lifted it to his face and inhaled deeply, smelling it. Then he reached into the pocket of his pants and produced a magazine of bullets and loaded the weapon. He did it like he did it all the time, though Susan realized that she'd never seen Archie fire his weapon the entire time she'd known him.

"I heard you had too many pills and passed out, my friend," Jack said from the desk. "I thought you'd left."

Susan glanced anxiously at Archie. It was no secret that Archie had struggled with a pill addiction, and Jack was probably full of shit, but she still wanted Archie to deny it. Archie met Susan's gaze silently, and she looked away, embarrassed.

"Where's Star?" Archie asked Jack.

Star? Susan practically coughed. That's why Archie had come? To find the stripper? She adjusted her grip on the bag. "Please," she said. "Let's go."

Archie just stood there, his gun in his hand at his side.

Jack's grin widened slowly. "You want another crack at her?" he asked.

"Where is she?" Archie repeated.

"She's working," Jack said, and he made a humping motion with his hips to illustrate.

Susan waited for Archie to respond. Jack's comment hadn't registered on Archie's face at all, but she knew that it had bothered him. Archie didn't like men who talked disrespectfully about women. He didn't even like men who talked disrespectfully about Gretchen Lowell, and she murdered people for sport.

"I'll be right back," Archie said to Jack, and then he turned and put his hand on Susan's back and shepherded her toward the door.

"Wait," Susan said, pulling away from him. She wanted to go, but she did not want to be herded, and she certainly was not going to leave without Archie. "Tell me what's going on."

Archie glared at her. His brown eyes looked bleary. He had that look, that look that said, *Don't ask me questions—just follow my lead.* "You're going home," he said.

Cooper was still leaning up against the wall. He cleared his throat. Susan looked over at him. He said one word: "Go." She didn't even see his lips move. It was hard to know for sure he'd even spoken.

Susan's skin itched.

She had the feeling then that everyone in the room knew something that she didn't. She adjusted the bodice of the dress, feeling the tender heat of the rising welts under her armpits. She was tired. She wanted to go home. She looked at Archie and nodded reluctantly.

He took her by the elbow again, keeping the gun drawn. He kept his hand on her elbow the whole time as he escorted her out of the office and down the hall, the paper bag crinkling in her arms. They followed the muddy footprints he'd left on the way in. Susan was aware of people behind them, eyes on her back, footsteps in tandem with theirs. But she never turned to look, so she didn't know how many it was, or who. Archie held the door open for her and they stepped outside into the light. The white vinyl tents shimmered with dew, the gas heaters had been collected together and the gold chairs stacked. The sky was tinged with the apricot glow of dawn. Archie led Susan down the wide path through the manicured front lawn. The torches on either side had all been extinguished. Here and there, napkins littered the ground. A lone wineglass sat empty, abandoned on the grass. They followed the path to the curved driveway and then walked along the private road over the bridge to the gate. They stood there for a moment, waiting. There was a security camera mounted on a gatepost and Susan and Archie looked at it looking at them. After a moment, there was a metallic hissing sound and then the gates yawned open.

"Get on the main road and then keep walking," Archie said.

Susan looked at him, incredulous. "By myself? What about you?"

"Someone will pick you up," Archie said. "Don't talk to anyone about Leo except for Henry and someone named Sanchez."

"What are you going to do?"

"I'm going back to check on some things," Archie said.

Susan saw through his evasiveness. "You're going back to check on Leo and that stripper," she said. She knew the stripper's name; she just didn't use it. "I'll go with you," Susan added. "Leo's my boyfriend." Archie flinched when she said it. He always did. It's why she'd used the word—*boy-friend*.

Archie pressed his lips together. "Leo needs to know you're safe."

The road beyond the gates was quiet. No traffic. The morning air was crisp and cold. Susan hugged her arms. *Boyfriend*. Now she felt bad. Her eyes went to the blood along Archie's hairline. "Does it hurt?" she asked.

"*I* need to know you're safe, Susan," Archie said. "I have to go back. Please go now."

Susan nodded numbly. She didn't know what to say. *See you soon? Call me later? Don't get yourself killed?* So she didn't say anything. She cradled her paper bag of clothes and walked through the gate. She heard the mechanical gears of the gate closing the moment she'd cleared the property line, and she looked back, but Archie had already turned and was walking back over the bridge to the island. *Sanchez. San-chez.* She was suddenly very cold and she dropped the bag and dug out her red sweatshirt and put it on over the gold dress and zipped it up and put up the hood. She got her phone out of her purse and checked for reception. One bar. She picked up the bag again and started down the road, her eyes fixed on the phone screen in her hand. Two bars, and she'd call Henry. The road didn't have sidewalks, so she shuffled along the edge, her ballet flats scuffing against the pavement. There was no one around. Newspapers, safely en-sconced in plastic bags, poked out of the mailboxes that lined the road. The dried leaves that had fallen during the night blanketed the grass, waiting for the leaf blower. Crows squawked in the fir trees. Two bars.

She didn't hear the car until it was right upon her. She stepped onto the grass as it rolled past her on the right. A black, industrial-looking van. No markings. It pulled over to the side of the road just ahead of her and waited. Susan froze. Archie had said that someone would pick her up, but he didn't say it was going to be Ted Bundy. She would call for a cab if she had to, thank you very much. She was scanning her phone contacts for Henry's number when she heard the van backing up. It was rolling in reverse right toward her. She didn't have time to react. She was too startled. Too sleep-deprived. Too flummoxed. When the van got so close she could have kicked it, it stopped, and the back door opened. A man in jeans and a sweatshirt and a day's worth of beard held out his hand to her.

"FBI," he said. "Get in."

CHAPTER

17

Archie sat on the stone steps of the Tudor mansion, feeling pleasantly high. He remembered this now. The shudder of warmth under his skin; the way his bones seemed to soften; that feeling of wet cotton lining his skull. All the small discomforts to which he'd grown accustomed—the stiffness in his ribs, the prickly sensations of his scars, the burn of acid in his throat, the stab of pain when he inhaled deeply—all melted away to something peripheral. He didn't even mind the itch in his throat anymore. It was amazing what two little pills could do. A few years ago, it would have taken a handful to reach the same effect. His tolerance had changed.

He reached up and touched his head, winced, and then looked at the gritty dry blood on his dirty fingertips. Too late for stitches. He'd have another scar.

Now he just had to find out how he'd gotten it.

The front door opened and Jack Reynolds came out and sat down next to Archie on the step. Jack had a round red ceramic mug of coffee in each hand, and he held one out to Archie. Archie took it. The hot mug reminded him how cold he was. He took a sip and let the steam coming off the coffee warm his face. The Vicodin made his tongue feel thick.

"I remembered that you take it black," Jack said.

"Yep," Archie said.

The orange glow of daybreak had given way to a blindingly blue morning. Archie liked the sound of dawn, the way that every noise seemed bright after the hush that had settled overnight. The grass glistened with dew. The trees were ablaze with fall colors.

"Are you planning on spending all day on my stoop?" Jack asked.

Archie took another sip of coffee. "I'm not leaving until I see Leo."

Jack frowned over his coffee cup. "I have houseguests."

The Russians. Archie had been counting on that.

"I know," Archie said.

Jack looked at Archie for a long time. His eyes were attentive, thoughtful, but beyond that Archie had a hard time reading them. Jack was a handsome man. Even Archie, who knew he could be obtuse about such things, couldn't miss that. As Archie aged, he saw himself fade and slacken in the mirror. As Jack aged, he only got better-looking—distinguished, people called it. His face was chiseled, his temples gray; he had that square-jawed sitcom father from the fifties look. Just your friendly drug kingpin next door.

Archie felt a ripple of relaxation move up his spine to that wet cotton in his skull.

Jack took a sip of coffee. He squinted at Archie, the picture of conviviality. If he knew something violent had happened at his house, he was doing a good job of hiding it.

"Take a shower," Jack said. "You can join us for breakfast."

CHAPTER

18

Archie leaned into the steaming water, letting it run over his head and down his back, rinsing the blood out of his hair. The shower was the size of his entire kitchen, with slick black granite walls, and a built-in granite bench on one side. Archie didn't know what the bench was for—maybe some people got tired while they took showers and had to sit down. There were three polished nickel spigots. A large one, about the size of a hubcap, over the center of the shower, a hand spigot on a metal hose looped on the wall, and another spigot installed into the granite at knee level, that Archie could only imagine was for washing feet, although why someone would get into a shower just to wash their feet escaped him.

There was no shower curtain or glass divider—the shower had granite slabs on three sides and was entirely open to the rest of the room on the fourth. Rich people liked to let it all hang out, apparently. Somehow this seemed to work. So far, as far as Archie could see, no water had splashed beyond the imaginary shower border onto the marble bathroom floor.

Archie studied the expensive-looking products arrayed on the granite shelf at elbow level: shampoos and conditioners in fancy bottles, body washes, soap in a wrapper with

French writing on it, and two black washcloths rolled up like burritos.

If this was the guest bathroom, Archie couldn't help but wonder what the master bathrooms were like. Solid gold fixtures? The hardware alone looked like it cost more than what he made in a year. The Tudor theme of the rest of the house ended at the threshold—this bathroom was entirely twenty-first century, with automatic faucets, recessed lights, a marble floor, and a gas fireplace. It had taken Archie ten minutes to figure out how to operate the Japanese toilet seat.

Archie picked up one of the soaps and unwrapped it. The soap inside was black. He'd never seen black soap before. He lifted it to his nose. It smelled faintly like whiskey. Archie rubbed it around in his hands and then lathered his chest. The suds were thick and creamy and as he moved them around his chest the rough, tender tissue of his scars tingled under his touch. He moved his fingers over each one. He knew the topography of every scar—the soft pearly ones that were long and surgical, the tough lumps where she'd driven nails into his chest, and the smaller gouges that marked where she'd just cut him for fun. The combination of the heat of the shower, the pleasant musky odor of the soap, and the pills in his system left him feeling more relaxed than he had been in months. Endorphins pulsed in his brain. He moved his hand down, tracing the length of the scar that ran from his xyphoid process to his solar plexus. The surgeons at Emanuel had given him that one when they'd opened him up to repair the hack job she'd done taking out his spleen. That scar was hard and thick, the flesh faded to a pale seashell-pink. He moved his hand lower.

"Archie," he heard someone hiss.

Archie dropped the soap and spun around. Through the steam, Archie could make out Leo entering the room, just closing the bathroom door behind him. Archie stood there flustered for a moment, and then fumbled to turn off the faucet.

"Let it run," Leo said, walking over. "I don't know if they're listening." He came to a stop on the other side of where the shower curtain should be and then just stood there, casually, as if it were perfectly normal to be having a conversation while one person was naked and lathered with soap.

Did Leo really think that Jack Reynolds bugged his bathrooms, or did he just think someone might have their ear to the door? Archie didn't pursue it. But he left the shower on.

"Are you okay?" Leo asked.

Archie had stepped out of the downpour coming from the hubcap spigot, but stayed in the shower. Blood-tinged water was splattered on his feet. Steam rose around him. Soapsuds slid down his chest. He waited for Leo to toss him a towel, but he didn't. "I woke up an hour ago near your boathouse with a concussion," Archie said. "What do you think?"

Leo was standing in front of the towel rack, blocking Archie's access to it.

"The Russians were coming back," Leo said. "I didn't want them to kill you. I didn't have time to explain. I used the choke hold to knock you out. I told them you didn't see anything. We left you in the bedroom. That was the last time I saw you. You were supposed to come to in a few minutes."

They were really going to do this. They were going to have a conversation while Archie was completely naked. The soap on Archie's chest traveled down the inside of his legs in foamy clumps. He stepped back under the shower stream to rinse it off.

"What do you mean, you told them I didn't see anything?" Archie called through the water. "What didn't I see exactly?" He eyed Leo through the water and steam. Leo had changed out of his bloody shirt, but otherwise appeared still to be wearing his clothes from the night before. His tux pants were wrinkled. His shirtsleeves were rolled up. The collar of the new shirt was open and the pits were slightly stained. He hadn't slept. He seemed agitated.

"The guy that was bleeding in the bathtub," Leo said.

The walls of the granite shower stall were starting to sweat. Archie inhaled the heat. The pills made his head feel heavy, like his brain was marbled with fat, and he had to fight for clarity. "Go on," Archie said. He'd washed the soap off and was hell-bent on getting a towel. He moved out from under the shower stream, but Leo was still blocking the towel rack. Archie had to reach around him to get to it, his bare flesh grazing Leo's body. Still, Leo didn't move. Archie pulled the towel into the shower with him and started to dry off.

"One of the Russians," Leo continued. "They think he was informing to the FSB. He walked in on something he wasn't supposed to see. They brought him to me. Jack doesn't trust me, Archie. He was about to walk into a meeting. I had to prove I could handle it."

Archie wrapped the towel around his waist, relieved to finally have some coverage. "What happened to him?" he asked.

"I shot him," Leo said matter-of-factly.

The words sank in. Now the towel seemed trivial. Archie sat down on the granite bench. Water flowed around his feet. "He's dead," Archie said.

"He was dead the moment they suspected him," Leo insisted. "If I hadn't done it, someone else would have." He looked at Archie pleadingly through the thin wall of steam that divided them. His eyes were red. A slick film of mucus lined one nostril. Leo wiped at it with his hand.

None of this made sense. "Where's the body?" Archie asked.

"I don't know," Leo said, shaking his head. "I helped them get it downstairs into a catering van. When I came back up, you were gone. I assumed you woke up and got out of there. I hoped you had."

Archie tightened the towel around his waist and stood up and walked over to Leo at the edge of the shower. "You're done here," Archie said. "You know that, right? You're walking out of here with me, today."

"I've given ten years of my life to this," Leo said. "In a few days I can bring down the Russian connection and Jack's partners in law enforcement. I could do time for murder."

"Ya think?"

"I'm not doing it alone," Leo said. "I'm taking them with me."

Archie couldn't believe they were having this conversation, Archie in a towel, a deluge of water going down the drain behind him. Leo had killed someone. He was compromised. He was clearly high on coke. And Archie was the one who'd gotten him involved in the first place. "You need to talk to Sanchez," Archie said.

The color drained from Leo's face.

"What?" Archie asked.

Leo took a small step back, like an invisible hand had suddenly given him a hard shove. "Sanchez is dirty," he said.

Acid burned in Archie's throat. No. That couldn't be true. Archie had sent Susan to Sanchez. He'd told her she could trust him. But if Sanchez was dirty, why had he sent Archie to the party to begin with? "He came to me," Archie said. "He sent me here last night to check on you."

Leo's eyes widened. "Sanchez knows I'm undercover?"

Archie nodded, seeing where Leo's mind was going.

"Then Jack knows," Leo said. The torrent of water in the shower was the only noise. It sounded like a rainstorm. Then Leo laughed—a hard, mirthless chuckle. "He's fucking with us," he said. His eyes were desperate. "I killed a man, for nothing."

"Are you sure he's dirty?" Archie asked. "There's no doubt?"

The bathroom door opened again, and Jack Reynolds walked in. Archie made a mental note to lock the door if he ever took a shower here again.

Leo turned his face toward the wall, clearly fighting for composure.

"You people have some interesting notions of boundaries in this house," Archie called.

"I brought you some clothes," Jack said, holding up a neat stack of clothing and a pair of shoes. He set the stack next to a potted orchid on the marble vanity and then sauntered over to join them near the shower. Archie tried to act like there was nothing strange about the fact that he was standing there wet and wearing a towel talking to Leo while the shower continued to run behind them.

Leo still had his head turned, but his color was better, and his expression had formed into something close to neutral.

"Am I interrupting something?" Jack asked, looking from one of them to the other. "This is quite the intimate little picture. You two seem to like the same women. Maybe you should cut out the middleman and just fuck each other."

Leo met his father's gaze and smirked. "What makes you think we haven't?" he asked.

The comment hung in the air.

Archie coughed.

Leo crossed in front of Archie, and stepped directly in front of Jack. For a second Archie thought Leo might take his father by the neck. Maybe try out that choke hold again. Archie might not even have stopped him. But Leo's body was relaxed, his shoulders loose. He had been undercover so long that he could drop into character just like that. Leo grinned at Jack. They were nose to nose, Jack refusing to give ground. "I had his cock so far down my throat," Leo said, "I thought I'd choke." He ran his thumb along the corner of his mouth and licked it.

Archie couldn't think of anything to say to that, even if he'd wanted to. He wasn't going to get into this pissing match. Not that anyone was looking to him to say anything anyway.

Jack smiled, though he didn't look amused. "Clean yourself up," Jack told Leo. "Our guests are awake."

Leo shot Archie a quick look, and under his mask of libertine bemusement Archie thought he saw another emotion: fear. Then Leo reached out and straightened Jack's tie. It was an odd little display, rich with both intimacy and malice. When he was done, Leo stepped around Jack and strolled out of the room. Archie watched him go. The door closed silently behind him. If it had been Archie, he would have slammed it.

Jack stayed where he was. He looked Archie up and down, his eyes lingering on Archie's torso, his chest and abdomen, where he had the most scars. If Leo had noticed the ravaged state of Archie's body he hadn't shown it.

"I'd really like to finish my shower without an audience," Archie said, fighting an instinct to re-secure his towel.

Jack's eyes stayed on Archie's abdomen, traveling up the thick scar along his midline that marked where Gretchen had split him open for his spleen. "She worked you over, didn't she?" he said.

"She tortured me," Archie said.

"Yeah," Jack said. He lifted his gaze and met Archie's. There was something lascivious in Jack's eyes and Archie was certain that Jack had meant for him to see it. Jack chuckled. "I left you something in the clothes," he said. "Consider it a free sample." Then he turned around and left the bathroom.

As soon as the door closed, Archie stepped back into the shower, turned off the water and then stood watching as the last of the water streamed around his feet and circled the silver drain. His pulse throbbed in his fingers. His throat itched. The shower spigot dripped.

Archie coughed, and felt something come up his throat a millimeter. He coughed again. The tickling sensation intensified, scratching at his larynx. He cleared his throat and spat in the shower and coughed again. His head pounded. He gagged and his throat constricted and the itch became a raw sting. He was bent over, a string of saliva dangling from his lips, when he finally managed to dislodge it. He reached into his mouth to the back of his tongue, gagged once, and pulled out a small, light-colored hair.

He held the hair between two fingers. It was thicker than scalp hair, and shorter, coarser, with a slight curl.

Archie felt a vise tightening at the back of his neck.

He left the shower and walked, dripping, to where his grimy tux lay in a heap on the floor. He dug the brass pillbox from his pants pocket, opened it, and gingerly laid the little hair inside, his fingers clumsy and wrinkled from the shower. Then he snapped the pillbox shut, set it on the marble vanity, and backed away.

There were explanations.

The pain in his neck spread forward, up behind his ears.

The hair might have been in something he'd eaten. He might have inhaled it. It could be a facial hair.

Archie rubbed the back of his neck. He was losing his mind. This was ridiculous. It was a hair. It could have come from anywhere. Hadn't a few of the caterers had beards? It could have come off a beard, fallen into a drink Archie was served, and then lodged in his throat.

He had dreamed about Gretchen, that's all. She was on his mind, and he was high, and he was being paranoid.

He needed to get dressed and get off the island. Sober, after some sleep, things would start to make sense.

Archie dried off and pulled on Jack Reynolds's satin boxers and tweed pants. The pants were lined with silk. They looked like they cost more than Archie's car. As he pulled them to his waist, something knocked against his leg. When he reached into the front pocket he found an amber plastic pill bottle. The pills inside were small and round. Oxycodone. There had to be two hundred. There was no label, no prescription. *Consider it a sample.*

Archie rolled the bottle in his hand, listening to the music the pills made as they cascaded over each other. He could feel the physical anticipation in his body, his Pavlovian response.

He set the bottle on the vanity while he finished getting dressed.

A cashmere sweater. A pair of cashmere socks. A pair of handcrafted leather shoes. He examined his reflection in the mirror. Archie had never looked more in his life like he was wearing someone else's clothes.

Archie picked his filthy tux pants off the floor and transferred his phone and the compass into Jack's pockets, and then tucked his gun in his waistband.

Finally, he picked up the brass pillbox with the hair in it.

The pillbox was small, about the size of a child's palm. The brass lid shone under the bathroom lights. Archie held it in his hand for a long moment—such a perfect pretty object in his imperfect hand—and then he slipped the box into his pocket. There were many explanations, but that didn't mean it would hurt to run a DNA analysis, if only for his peace of mind. There was nothing to do about the rented tuxedo and shoes. They were ruined. Archie picked up the dirty clothes and eased them into the bathroom trash. As the tux fell from his hands the image of the gargoyle flashed in his mind again. His throat burned and he rubbed his eyes. Then he snatched the bottle of pills off the vanity. He pocketed the bottle as he headed downstairs. The pills made a satisfying rattle every time he took a step.

CHAPTER

19

The van was small and dark and crowded and it smelled like BO and stale peanut butter and mildew and cigarettes. The cop with the five o'clock shadow sat in front of a bank of monitors, switches, and dials. Susan had to sit on the carpet, which was gray and stained with spilled coffee. Inside, the van didn't look like a van at all, but more like a recording studio in a submarine. The cop with the stubble was named Richard. He was sitting in a gray velour chair with armrests that looked like it had been salvaged from the driver's side of an RV. Richard's partner called himself Bear. He had a Vandyke beard and dark oval wire sunglasses pushed up on top of his head, and a stool to sit on that wasn't as comfortable as the chair, but still better than the carpet.

"I can call a cab," Susan said, twisting her legs around in an effort to get comfortable.

"Sanchez will be here in a few minutes," Bear said.

She'd been waiting for Sanchez for an hour now. Richard and Bear couldn't leave their post, apparently. But they also wouldn't let her leave until she was debriefed. She wondered if getting debriefed by the FBI involved waterboarding. She hoped it involved a bubble bath and an expensive hotel suite.

"Someone's on the move," Richard said, his narrow eyes on one of the monitors.

Susan scooted forward on her knees and peered at the image on the monitor. A man was walking over the bridge, approaching the gate.

"Is that Jack?" Bear asked Richard.

"Can't tell yet," Richard answered.

"It's Archie," Susan said.

He was wearing different clothes, but it was Archie—she was positive. She knew his hunched shoulders and the way he kept his elbows bent, hands in his pockets, when he walked. He stopped at the gate and waited as it swung open. Then he stepped through it and got something out of his pocket and held it up.

"What's he doing?" Richard asked.

"Looking for a signal," Bear said.

He seemed to find one, because he bent his head over his phone for a minute.

"He's sending a text," Bear said.

"Should we pick him up?" Richard asked.

"Give him a minute," Bear said. "See what he does."

Archie got his car keys out of his pocket and held them loosely in his hand.

"He's walking to his car," Richard said. "The valets parked along the road last night."

"It's the Taurus," Bear said. "It's a quarter mile back."

Susan heard the sound of tires on gravel. Someone had just pulled up behind the van. Sanchez, probably. It was about time.

Susan's phone buzzed. Her bag was behind her so she was the only one who heard it.

She reached around and pulled her phone out and looked at it.

One new text from Archie Sheridan.

She opened it.

It read, *Don't talk to Sanchez.*

Susan's mouth felt dry.

There was a knock on the back of the van.

Bear reached back to unlock the door. "There's your ride," he said to Susan as he threw the door open.

Susan blinked into the sudden brightness. A short Latino man stared back at her. He had rough-hewn skin and thick dark hair, and features that looked like they'd been whittled by someone who didn't really know how to whittle but had decided to take a stab at it anyway. He smiled at her and lifted his eyebrows. "Susan," he said. "I've heard so much about you."

"Um, hi?" she said.

Sanchez held out a hand. "Let's go," he said. "We can talk in the car."

How was she supposed to get out of this one? Susan glanced down at her phone and, in one quick motion, deleted the text.

Then she took Sanchez's hand and stepped out of the van.

CHAPTER

20

Sanchez had taken Susan to the FBI's Portland Field Office. Archie had arranged to meet them there. In the meantime, he could only hope that Susan had gotten his text.

The FBI's Portland office was in the Crown Plaza building downtown, within walking distance of the Willamette. It wasn't a pretty building, or really notable in any way. Just a concrete gray box filled mostly with law offices, except for the fourth floor, which housed the FBI.

Since it was Sunday, most of the building's other tenants were closed, and the place was empty except for a uniformed security guard whom Archie had passed smoking outside in front of the massive revolving doors of the main entrance, and who had waved Archie by with barely a glance.

Archie walked through the lobby, past the shuttered café, to one of the banks of elevators, and then punched a security code into the elevator keypad. When the elevator doors opened on the fourth floor, Sanchez was waiting for him. Compared to most government facilities, the Portland FBI offices were rather stately. There were marble floors, orange and gold hall carpet runners, and glossy maple doors. But scratch the surface and it was just like any other office: steel drinking fountains in the hallway, emergency floodlights mounted on the walls, a paneled drop ceiling cluttered with fluorescent lights and fire sprinkler heads. Archie could hear the drinking fountain humming.

Sanchez looked alarmed.

"She's sick," he said. "She said she's having a really bad period. In the car on the way over she said her cramps hurt so bad she couldn't even talk. I found her some Midol. But now she says she feels like she might vomit." Sanchez's eyes flashed with concern. He was a man who only had sons. "Is this normal?"

Archie had to work hard to suppress a smile. "Where is she?" he asked.

Sanchez led Archie down the orange and gold carpet, through a pair of maple double doors with gold letters that spelled out FEDERAL BUREAU OF INVESTIGATION, past an American flag planted in a floor stand, to a door with a women's restroom symbol on it.

"I'll check on her," Archie said.

He approached the door. Sanchez hung back, pacing. Archie knocked. "Susan?" he called.

"Um, I'm really bleeding a lot," Susan's voice called through the door. "And throwing up. You don't want to come in here. It's like *The Exorcist*."

Archie opened the door a crack. "It's me," he said. He could smell cigarette smoke and quickly entered the bathroom before Sanchez caught a whiff of it.

The bathroom had one sink and three metal stalls. Two of the stall doors were open. The other one creaked open as Archie walked in. He could see Susan's feet under the partition, two dirty Converse All Stars.

As Archie came around the open stall he saw that Susan was sitting on the toilet, fully clothed, a cigarette dangling between her fingers. The gold dress was stuffed in an open brown paper grocery bag and she was back in her street clothes—tights, the silver skirt, a tank top with the red hooded sweatshirt over it. The hood was up. She'd scrubbed all her makeup off. There was still pink liquid bathroom soap around her hairline. Her sweatshirt had dark spots where water from the sink had splattered on it.

"What took you so long?" Susan asked, ashing her cigarette into the toilet.

"I had to make a call," Archie said. He didn't add, *or Henry would have rushed the island with a SWAT team.*

"I did what you said," Susan said. "I've barely said two words to him."

"He's ready to call an ambulance," Archie said. "I think you've traumatized him."

"Men really can't handle menstruation," Susan said, rolling her eyes. "It freaks you guys out." Her gaze landed on his shoes. She looked impressed. "Are those Italian?"

Archie looked down at his feet. "I don't know."

Susan took a drag off her cigarette. "Now what?" she asked, grinning.

She liked this, Archie realized. She was enjoying herself. He'd created a monster. "Now we talk to Sanchez," Archie said.

"But you said—"

"We talk to him," Archie said. "But we're careful about what we say."

"Why?" Susan asked, pulling at a hole in the knee of her black tights.

"It's probably nothing," Archie said. He tried to be diplomatic in how he put it. "But Leo had some reservations about how much Sanchez could be trusted." Archie gave Susan a serious look. "Can you follow my lead?"

Susan dropped her cigarette butt into the toilet water between her legs and brought a hand to her forehead in an exaggerated salute.

Archie suspected that Susan Ward had never followed anyone's lead in her life, but he didn't see a lot of options. "I need you to lie to the FBI," he said. "Can you do that?"

CHAPTER

21

Archie glanced over at Susan. She was chewing on her fingernails, sleeves pulled over her palms, hood up, reeking of stale cigarette smoke and hair spray. They were sitting across from Sanchez in a small, windowless room that had all the maneuverability and ambience of a storage closet. Sanchez was sitting ramrod-straight, eyeballing Susan like she might burst into flame.

"What's this space used for?" Archie asked Sanchez. Archie had been in the FBI interview rooms, and this wasn't one of them. That was good. It meant that the room probably wasn't equipped with a surveillance system, though with the FBI you never knew.

"It's clean," Sanchez said. "No surveillance. We had a bunch of junior agents in here sorting paperwork for a big case." He slipped a hand into his pocket, pulled out a tin of mints, and snapped it open. "We can talk," he said. He held the open tin across the table like a peace pipe. Neither Susan nor Archie took a mint. Sanchez closed the box and dropped it back in his pocket without taking one, either. The mints left a lingering fine dust of white peppermint-smelling powder floating in the air.

Archie had known Sanchez for almost as long as Archie had known Henry. Sanchez had been the FBI liaison on the Beauty Killer case. He had put in as many hours as anyone on the task force. Now Archie found himself searching his memory for any signs that Sanchez might be corrupt. But he couldn't come up with anything. No exotic vacations. No extravagant purchases. The man drove a twenty-year-old Honda Accord with a dented fender. Archie was the one trussed up in ridiculous, expensive clothes. Sanchez was wearing pale blue jeans and a tan jacket over a golf shirt. The jacket was khaki, with patch pockets and epaulets that made him look a little like a safari guide or zookeeper. Archie had seen Sanchez wear it dozens of times. The guy wasn't exactly a clotheshorse. His parents still lived in Mexico. There was nothing flashy about him. Which just meant that if he was corrupt, he was careful. In the meantime, Carl Richmond was dead, and Raul Sanchez was now essentially running Leo's undercover operation. If he wasn't dirty, Leo needed him. If he was dirty, Leo was in serious danger. Either way, Archie had the feeling that he needed to parse what he told Sanchez right now very carefully. Leo's life might depend on it.

"I saw Leo," Archie said. "Last night and again this morning." He looked Sanchez in the eye, trying to communicate the seriousness of the situation without frightening Susan. "You need to get him out of there."

Sanchez sat up a little and uncrossed his arms. "He wants out?"

"No," Archie said, with a glance in Susan's direction.

Sanchez looked at Susan. "Give us a minute," he said.

Susan hesitated. Archie put a hand out, motioning for her to stay where she was. "She's a part of this whether she wants to be or not," Archie said. "And she already knows too much." That was all true. But he also needed her here. He needed a witness. If Sanchez was dirty, then the conversation they were about to have might become important.

Sanchez nodded and Susan relaxed back into her chair.

"The party was a cover," Archie said. "To get people on

the island. They know they're under surveillance, so they invited five hundred guests and hoped the more important ones would get lost in the shuffle." Nice plan. Apparently it had worked.

"What kind of meeting?" Sanchez asked.

"Leo says they're working on some deal with the Russians," Archie said.

Sanchez's eyes widened almost imperceptibly. The expression of surprise seemed authentic. "Did you see any of them? Can you identify players?"

"It was a *masquerade* ball," Susan said with an exasperated roll of her eyes. "As in, *masks*."

"It wouldn't hurt to look at pictures," Archie said. He thought of the Russian outside Jack's office. "Not everyone was wearing masks."

Sanchez fixed his attention on Susan. "Are you sure you didn't see any of these people?" he asked. "Maybe you heard someone speaking Russian?"

Susan nibbled on a cuticle.

"Answer him," Archie told her.

"I didn't see or hear any Russians," Susan said. "Were they wearing fur hats?"

"Fur hats?" Sanchez said.

Susan sighed. "I'm kidding," she said.

"Tell him how you came to be there," Archie said, leading her.

Susan peeled something off her fingertip and chewed it. "Someone named Cooper came to my house," she said. "He told me Leo wanted me to come to a party. He was insistent. He drove me out there. They got me all dressed up. But Leo didn't know anything about it. Not until I saw him out there last night."

"They used her as leverage," Archie said.

"They wanted to ensure that Leo would do something for them," Susan added.

"And they let you go this morning," Sanchez said. Archie could see him thinking, his eyes roving. After a few moments, Sanchez came to the inevitable conclusion. "Leo must have done what they wanted," Sanchez said. His eyebrows knitted. "Any idea what it was?" he asked them.

Actually, Archie had a pretty good idea. But he wasn't going to tell Sanchez that. "No," Archie said.

"No," Susan said. She frowned. "But it might have had something to do with the letter."

This got Sanchez's attention. He fingered the flap of one of his safari jacket pockets. "The letter?" he said.

Susan shrugged. "Last week. Leo gave it to me to mail. He seemed really nervous about it."

"Where is it?" Sanchez asked. "Do you have it?"

"Have what?" Susan asked.

Sanchez's face was scarlet. "The letter," he said.

Susan looked from Sanchez to Archie, a picture of innocence. "I mailed it," she said.

Susan had delivered it perfectly, exactly as Archie had instructed her in the bathroom. If Sanchez was corrupt, he was bound to be paranoid. He would worry that Leo had learned Sanchez was dirty and that the letter incriminated him. At the very least it might buy Leo some time.

Sanchez swallowed a few times. His forehead glowed. He touched the tips of his fingers to his mouth. "Do you remember the address on the letter?" he asked Susan.

Susan offered an uncertain smile. "I think it was Oregon," she said. Then she made a pained face and laid a hand on her lower abdomen. "Ouch," she said. "There's that uterine cramping again."

Sanchez's roughcast features seemed to spasm. He glanced away, cleared his throat, and then put his palms on the tabletop. His gaze was steady now, his expression uncompromising. It was the expression that FBI agents practiced in the mirror. "I need to know everyone who was there," Sanchez said. "I need you both to look at mug shots." He cast a meaningful glance at Archie. "We can leave Leo out of it," he said. He directed his attention at Susan. "I'll get my assistant in here to walk you through the database. She won't ask too many questions, and she can help you with your . . . female issues." He raised his eyebrows at Susan. "Now, can Archie and I have the room for a minute?"

"You want me to wait in the hall?" Susan asked. She was looking at Archie.

"Just for a few moments," Sanchez said.

Susan was still looking at Archie.

"It's okay," Archie said.

She relented and pushed her chair back from the table, yanked the wrinkled paper bag of clothes from under her seat, and stalked out of the room into the hall. She didn't close the door behind her and Sanchez had to get up and shut it and then sit back down.

Archie pulled the compass out of his pocket and turned it in his hand under the table.

Sanchez still had the G-man face on. "Suppose you tell me what's going on," he said.

Archie lifted an eyebrow, but didn't speak. He could feel the bottle of pills in his pants pocket, pressing into his leg like a hand on his thigh.

"You know I'm an FBI agent, right?" Sanchez asked. "A trained investigator. Went to Quantico and everything." He leaned forward slightly. "So, you want to tell me why you walked off that island wearing different clothes than the ones you had on when you arrived?"

Archie met Sanchez's unblinking gaze. "I got dirty," he said.

The two men looked at each other for a minute, and then Sanchez shook his head. "I told you not to get involved," he said.

Archie couldn't respond, not without telling Sanchez everything, and there was no way he was going to do that until he knew he could trust him.

"These people are not your friends, man," Sanchez said. "They don't owe you anything. You think Jack's daughter's murder makes him like other grieving fathers? He counts on that. He's preyed off public sympathy since her funeral. His daughter's murder was the best thing to ever happen to his business. We gave him a walk for years after that. Then his freaky son Jeremy goes and gets himself murdered? Jack must have pinched himself, he was so happy."

Sanchez had a point. But right now Archie couldn't entertain it.

"Are you going to pull Leo out of there or not?" Archie asked. He spun the compass in slow circles on his palm.

"It's an active investigation," Sanchez said. "I can't comment."

"I see," Archie said.

Sanchez started to say something else, but hesitated. Archie wondered if he was thinking about the letter. "Thank you for your help," Sanchez said.

"Sure thing," Archie said. He slid the compass back in his pocket as he stood. "By the way, you owe me three hundred and twenty-eight bucks for the tux."

"Wait," Sanchez said. He rubbed his forehead. He looked conflicted, like he was struggling with something. Archie had a feeling this wasn't about the tux. "Wait," Sanchez said again. He exhaled slowly and then reached into the inside pocket of his khaki jacket and pulled out a folded piece of printer paper. "I shouldn't be showing this to you," he said. "But I think you have the right to know."

Archie took the paper and sat back down.

"Gretchen was spotted crossing the border in Blaine two days ago," Sanchez said.

Archie stiffened. Blaine was just south of the border between Canada and Washington State, just a five-hour drive north on Interstate 5.

"Gretchen is spotted everywhere," Archie said, fingering the still-folded paper. "She's like Elvis."

"It's a still from a security camera," Sanchez said. He snapped the paper from Archie's hands, unfolded it, and returned it to the table. "Look at it," he said, tapping the printout.

Archie looked down. The image showed a close-up of the driver's side of a car, probably taken from a camera mounted to a customs booth. The vehicle was a white SUV, though Archie couldn't see enough of it to determine the make or model. The woman behind the wheel had her blond hair pulled back and was wearing a white blouse. The car window was rolled down and her arm was outstretched, a passport in her hand. She was smiling, apparently at the customs agent who was about to receive the passport. The passport was blue, but a blacker blue than the U.S. passport. The woman was reaching toward the customs agent, but she was looking right up into the camera. There was no doubt in Archie's mind that it was Gretchen.

"How did she get through?" Archie asked hoarsely.

"She had a Canadian passport in a different name," Sanchez said. "A fake, obviously, but a good one. It didn't raise any flags. The car was registered in the same fake name as the passport. We have the plates, but she's probably dumped it by now."

Archie's pulse throbbed in his throat. He swallowed hard. "The entire world is looking for her, and she manages to drive over a border? She's not even wearing a disguise."

"Exactly," Sanchez said.

Of course. It was the smartest move she could make. Everyone expected her to have altered her appearance. No one was expecting Gretchen Lowell to look like Gretchen Lowell.

"The customs agent had just finished training," Sanchez continued. "She'd probably been watching. It was the kid's first solo shift. He's on leave now. I suspect he won't be going back on the job anytime soon."

"What name did she use?" Archie asked. "On the passport?"

"Isabel Stevens," Sanchez said. "Does that mean anything to you?"

Archie's head stung. He reached up and scratched at the fresh scab. "Isabel was the name of Jack Reynolds's dead daughter," he said quietly. He chuckled darkly. He had only learned about the name Stevens a few months before. It was the closest he had ever gotten to Gretchen's past, and still he knew only what she had allowed him to discover. She was always one step ahead. And she was reminding him of that.

"And Stevens was the last name Gretchen used when she was a teenager in the foster system." He glanced up at Sanchez. "But you knew that."

"Why would she use Isabel?" Sanchez asked. "Of all the people she killed?"

"It means something to me," Archie said. He touched his pants, making sure that the brass pillbox was still there.

"You want to share?" Sanchez asked

Gretchen had maintained that she hadn't, in fact, killed Isabel Reynolds, that it had been Isabel's brother Jeremy. Jeremy had been a spoon short of a full drawer and he'd sure as hell had an unhealthy obsession with the Beauty Killer. Archie half believed Gretchen was telling the truth. Then again, Gretchen never told the whole truth. But Jeremy was dead, and that was a hornet's nest that Archie didn't feel like kicking. "It won't help you," he said.

They were quiet for a few moments, the photo between them on the table. Sanchez fished the tin of mints out of his pocket again, and put one in his mouth. This time he didn't offer one to Archie. "You want to change your mind about protection?" Sanchez asked.

"No point." Archie was still studying the image. It was the same with every picture of Gretchen—he had trouble tearing his eyes away. But there was something about her expression in this one—the way she was looking at the camera—that made him feel like she was looking right at him, into him. He reached for it, his throat dry. "Can I keep this?" he asked.

"Knock yourself out," Sanchez said.

Archie pulled the photo toward him and stood up. The pills rattled in his pocket. The plastic bottle knocked against the brass pillbox.

Sanchez stood up as well, and the two walked around the table and met at the door. "You need to figure out who your friends are," Sanchez said.

"You have no idea," Archie said.

Gretchen had been Archie's friend. Until she had drugged him, strapped him to a gurney, and started cutting him into small pieces. This was one of the things Gretchen had taught him—his instincts, always so reliable when it came to crime, could fail him when it came to people. It was why Archie had so few people in his life—he was never sure when someone was going to slip him a paralytic and start torturing him—and that sort of uncertainty tended to put a strain on relationships.

Sanchez leaned close to Archie. It was an intimate gesture, as if he were about to share a confidence, even though they were the only people in the room. Archie could smell the peppermint on his breath. "Take care of yourself," Sanchez said.

The caution implied danger. But what was Archie supposed to be in danger from? Gretchen? Jack Reynolds? The pills in his pocket? And were Sanchez's words a warning, or a threat?

"I always take care of myself," Archie said.

The statement was such an obvious lie that it made both men grin.

CHAPTER

22

Archie drove Susan home. The roses Cooper had brought were still on the porch, limp and wilted. Her mother had probably walked right by them. Susan stooped to pick them up, noticed that Archie was waiting for her to get inside before he drove away, gave him a wave, and opened the front door. She was greeted by the smell of warm caramel and the sound of Jefferson Starship blasting on the turntable. She found her mother in the kitchen. Bliss's platinum dreadlocks were separated into two long braids and she was wearing a T-shirt with an image of a marijuana leaf on it and the word LEGALIZE, along with red and orange tie-dyed yoga pants. There was a pot of melted caramel on the stove and several dozen blushing green apples sitting on the counter.

Clearly, her mother had not been exactly panic-stricken about Susan's disappearance. "Seriously?" Susan said. She stalked to the sink and began stuffing the roses in the compost bin.

"I'm making caramel apples for Halloween," Bliss explained.

"Not that," Susan said. That was pretty evident. "Didn't you wonder where I was?" The roses were long stemmed and Susan had to use a dish towel to protect her hands as she folded and smashed down the bouquet on top of decomposing orange peels and tea leaves.

Bliss paused, the wooden spoon in her hand hovering over the pot of caramel. "You called me two hours ago," she said.

"I mean before that," Susan said. She jammed the lid on the compost bin and tossed the dish towel aside. "After I disappeared yesterday."

"Don't put those roses in the compost," Bliss said. "They're soaked in pesticides."

Aha! So her mother had noticed the roses on the porch. She just hadn't wanted to pick them up without a Hazmat suit. Susan snatched up the compost bin and emptied the entire contents into the trash.

"Bill told me you'd gone to a party at Leo's father's house," Bliss said, stirring the caramel. "I assumed you'd spent the night."

"Did he tell you the part about the big man and the black car and me acting strangely?" Susan asked.

Bliss set the spoon down. "Honey, you always act strangely."

"I was kidnapped, Mom. Held against my will. Like the Lindbergh baby."

"I thought you were on the island," Bliss said. She picked up a wooden Popsicle stick and jammed it into the bottom of an apple. Juice bubbled out where the stick separated the flesh.

"I was on the island," Susan said.

Bliss licked the juice off her fingers. "They wouldn't let you leave?"

"Not really," Susan said. "I mean, it was implied that I shouldn't leave. Leo was supposed to bring me home this morning. But then Archie showed up in a mud-covered tuxedo with blood on his head." Susan knew this was sounding ridiculous, but she continued. "He got me out of there. Then an FBI surveillance van picked me up. And I had to go to FBI HQ downtown. I've spent the last hour trying to identify mug shots of Russian gangsters. They wouldn't even let me draw masks on any of them, even though I told them that was the only way I'd ever recognize anyone."

Bliss picked up the apple that was now firmly secured on a Popsicle stick and, holding it by the stick, dipped the apple into the pot of hot caramel. "Was the party fun?"

It was all the yoga and meditation, Susan decided. Her mother had thrown herself into both since Pearl had been killed. It was possible she had actually meditated her blood pressure down to a permanent semiconscious state. Susan threw a glance at the caramel apples Bliss had already finished and laid out on wax paper. "No one eats those, you know. Their moms make them throw them away. It's got to be store-bought, or it might be poisoned or filled with razor blades."

Bliss lifted the apple and held it above the pot, letting the extra caramel drizzle off in thick ribbons back into the pan. "I know," she said. "But I've been making Halloween treats for twenty years, and I'm not going to stop because some people are paranoid," she said. She set the apple down on the wax paper with the others, and stabbed another Fuji with a Popsicle stick. "That's when the police state wins," she added.

Pearl had only lived with them a few days. She was a seventeen-year-old runaway who had once Tasered Archie to the point of unconsciousness, but Bliss had always had a soft spot for anyone with an anti-authority streak. It had been more than two months since Pearl had been dragged from their house and murdered. Bliss still wouldn't talk about it.

Still, you'd have thought with all they had been through that her mother would be a little more concerned about Susan's welfare. Gretchen Lowell was on the loose. A psycho had snuck in their back door with a machete last summer. Pearl had been murdered.

"I'm going to lay down," Susan announced huffily.

"*Lie* down."

"Whatever."

"Susan?" her mother said.

Bliss was standing over the caramel pot, an apple in her hand. The Jefferson Starship album hit a scratch and skipped.

For the first time, Susan noticed how pale her mother was, the circles under her eyes. She hadn't gotten a good night's sleep since Pearl had died. Bliss looked down and jammed another Popsicle stick into an apple. "What are you doing, sweetie?" she asked.

"Excuse me?" Susan said.

Bliss wiped her hands on a dishrag, came around the counter, put her palms on Susan's cheeks, and stared deep into her eyes. Her hands smelled like marijuana and caramel and coconut-scented lotion. Susan didn't like where this was going. "You have all these story ideas," Bliss said gently. "These book concepts. You can live here, rent-free. But you have to *do* something."

A thread of panic pulled tight in Susan's stomach. "I free-lance," she protested.

Bliss smoothed Susan's hair. "You haven't written anything in two months," she pointed out.

"I've been doing a lot of thinking," Susan said, voice rising. "Did I mention that I was kidnapped?"

"You can't wait for life to fall into place, sweetie," Bliss said, squeezing Susan's head between her hands. "Don't worry about the direction. Just move."

Susan stammered, not knowing how to respond. This was all she needed, new age wisdom from her mother. This was a woman whose pubic hair was currently waxed in the shape of a pot leaf and who had once woken up to find a tattoo of Salvador Dalí's mustache on her hip with no memory of how it had gotten there. "Just move? Did you see that on a bumper sticker?" Susan asked.

Bliss let go of Susan's face. "Your father said it once to me," she said. "We were high on psilocybin and wandered away from a Rainbow Gathering into a national forest and got lost."

Susan didn't point out the fact that most likely her father hadn't meant those words to be some big metaphor—he was just trying to get them out of the woods. She didn't want to quibble. Her mother wasn't wrong. Susan didn't exactly have a five-year plan. The *Herald* would certainly never take her back. Susan looked down at her pale, hairy knee poking through the hole she'd pulled apart in the black opaque fabric of her tights. It had started out the size of her pinkie, but she'd worried it and worried it and now it was big enough to put her arm though. How could she take care of herself? She couldn't even take care of a pair of tights. She couldn't even remember to shave her legs. "Don't worry about the direction," Susan repeated. "Just move. Got it."

"And sweetie?" Bliss said, walking back around the counter.

"Yeah?" Susan said with a sigh.

Bliss's smile vanished and she gave the caramel pot a determined stir. "Everyone loves my caramel apples," she said. She picked up a Popsicle stick and stabbed another apple.

"I know," Susan said.

Bliss gave her a satisfied nod.

"I'm going to *lie* down," Susan said, turning for the stairs.

"Pigs can't look up," Bliss said.

"Excuse me?" Susan said.

"Pigs can't look up," Bliss said. "They can't see the sky." Bliss gave Susan a helpful smile. "We all have problems."

"Thanks," Susan said slowly. Bliss's smile widened. Susan jabbed a thumb at the stairway. "I'm going to *just move* to my room now," she said. Then she swiveled around and marched upstairs, the wooden stairs creaking under her feet. The smell of caramel followed her down the hall all the way to her bedroom. She thought of it that way now—her bedroom. When she'd first moved back in with her mother she had thought of it as her childhood room, or the guest room, or the room in which she was staying, or her mother's meditation room. But it had been over a year since she'd moved back home, and more than seven months since she'd been fired from the *Herald,* and it wasn't feeling so temporary anymore.

She didn't even bother to kick off her shoes before she flopped down on her futon. Her hair-spray-coated hair crunched as it hit the pillow.

Halloween. Susan wasn't sure she could take it. All those

people acting like it was fun to splatter fake blood on their clothes and savage innocent pumpkins. If any kids came to their house dressed like Gretchen Lowell, Susan was going to pepper-spray them.

Then there was Leo. Had Susan really thought he'd choose her over his obsession to put his father in jail? Was he supposed to drop everything and get her off the island? He'd allowed her to be used as some sort of bargaining chip. And then he hadn't even shown up the next morning to make sure she got home. That had been Archie, as usual.

The light of the late-morning sky poured through Susan's sheer curtains. Downstairs, Bliss flipped the record over and side B of Jefferson Starship's *Knee Deep in the Hoopla* drifted through the floorboards. Susan knew that album by heart. Every word. It had been her father's album. When she was ten, he had taught her how to play "We Built This City" on the kazoo. She'd sounded good, too. It had only occurred to her later that her father's enthusiasm for the song was ironic.

She rolled over on her side and put a pillow over her head, and then practically choked on the trapped hair-spray fumes. This wasn't even Jefferson Starship's best album. She threw the pillow on the floor and sat up.

It was useless. She was too wound up to sleep.

Susan got out of bed, pulled her laptop off her desk, got back under the covers, and started to write.

CHAPTER

23

A cheerful sign on Rachel's front door spelled out HAPPY HALLOWEEN in silver glitter. A small black cat made out of tinsel and wire sat on the hall floor just to the left of the door. Archie nearly tripped on it. He took a minute, before he knocked, to recover some composure. He ran his hands through his hair and wiped the grit from his eyes. He touched the scab at his hairline to make sure it wasn't actively bleeding. It wasn't. This was as good as it was going to get. He knocked.

Rachel opened the door within moments. Her face lit up when she saw him and her smile widened into a huge grin. She was radiant. He had never seen her look happier. She lifted her arms as if she were going to throw them around him, but then her eyes filled with tears and she lifted her shaking hands over her mouth. Her shoulders trembled. "Sorry," she said. She gulped back a small sob. He could see the lines of worry on her face now, the tension in her arms. She glanced at him, and there was a flicker of terror in her eyes. "I thought you were dead," she said.

Archie stood in the doorway, confused. The pills were wearing off, and he felt headachy and tired. He had not expected Rachel to burst into tears at the sight of him. If his brain had been working faster, he might have been quicker on the uptake. But it took him a long moment, standing there dumbly as she sniffled, to put it together.

She had been worried about him.

Archie had not seen that coming. He'd been an idiot. It simply had not occurred to him that she would worry, not like Debbie had. It just wasn't their dynamic. "I got your messages," he said. She had left four messages last night, and another three that morning. He had not called her back. The texts had been casual, just checking in. He had missed the signals.

Their dynamic, apparently, had changed, when he wasn't looking.

For a detective, he wasn't very good at noticing these things.

Rachel wiped the tears off her cheeks. She was still sniffling. She could barely look at him.

"I had bad cell reception," Archie said. He reached a hand and touched her wet cheek. "I'm not dead," he said.

Her eyes moved up his face and stopped at his hairline. She swept a forelock of his hair to the side and studied his head wound, the line between her eyebrows deepening.

"You should put some ice on that," she said. Then she stepped back. It was an invitation.

Archie slid past her into the apartment. She was wearing tight white jeans tucked into brown boots, and a fitted white T-shirt and vest. Her blond hair was tied back into a ponytail. He caught a whiff of vanilla and coconut and could feel his body respond. He tried to distract himself.

Rachel's apartment was the same layout as Archie's, but less depressing. The furniture matched. The walls were painted. She had cork floors and granite countertops and stainless steel appliances. There were always fresh flowers on the glass coffee table. Halloween decorations were tucked here and there—a ceramic jack-o'-lantern on an end table, a spider constructed out of the same black tinsel and wire as the cat in the hall sat on the kitchen bar.

"Sit down," Rachel told him.

Archie walked to her butter-yellow leather sofa and sat down. He watched her in the kitchen getting the ice, the daylight blazed through her factory windows and made his skin warm. He worried that if he blinked too long, he'd fall asleep.

"I didn't have cell reception until this morning," Archie explained again. "And then"—he considered name-dropping the FBI, but knew he couldn't—"I had a meeting."

She walked across the room to him, carrying a gel ice pack wrapped in a dish towel. Then held the gel pack out, one hand on her hip. Her brown leather belt had a shiny gold buckle shaped like a lion.

"I'm sorry," he added, taking the ice pack, eyes on the lion. "That you were worried. I should have prepared you more . . . for this." Archie placed the ice pack against his forehead and flinched from the cold. It woke him up a little.

"I want to talk," Rachel said.

Now he'd done it. He looked up at her. She had her other hand on her hip now, too.

They were going to have a conversation, he realized. Archie didn't know a lot about women, but he had been married and he knew when a conversation was coming, and he knew that when a woman wanted to have one, the best thing you could do was get it over with.

"Right," he said.

Rachel placed her hand on the gel pack and held it against Archie's head until he let his own hand fall away. Then she stepped around his knees. He expected her to take a seat next to him on the sofa, but instead she lowered herself onto his lap.

Archie didn't know how to respond. He kept his hands at his sides, unsure what level of affection he should exhibit in this situation. Rachel was sitting across his thighs, her legs stretched out on the sofa, her back resting against the sofa arm, holding the gel back against his skull. He was fully awake now.

"Why haven't you introduced me to your kids?" Rachel asked.

Archie had hoped she'd start with something easier.

She looked at him, waiting.

Archie chose his words carefully. "I didn't know you wanted to meet my kids," he said.

Rachel frowned. She tilted her head slightly. He could feel her shift against his groin. The pill bottle in his pocket pressed into his thigh. He hoped she didn't think it was an erection.

He cleared his throat, and tried to explain. "I don't want to confuse them," he said.

Rachel sat forward, her weight off the pills, and put her free arm around his neck. "How am I confusing?" she asked.

Archie sighed. "How do I introduce you, Rachel? As my downstairs neighbor?"

She glanced at him hesitantly. "You could try girlfriend."

This was the opposite direction that Archie thought this conversation would go. His discomfort must have been obvious.

"Okay," Rachel said quickly. "Then tell them I'm your sweetpatootie. Or special friend. Or sex kitten. Whatever. I don't care. Just introduce me. I don't want to be a secret."

"Okay."

She dabbed the gel pack at his forehead. "Does Debbie know about me?"

"Yes."

She smiled. "Good."

Rachel curled happily in his lap. Archie's body struggled between the need for sex and the need to sleep. She shifted her weight again, positioning herself in a place that made his arms tingle.

"Would someone call me?" Rachel asked. "If you were really hurt or killed. Would anyone know to call me?"

"Henry would," Archie assured her. He was getting self-conscious about his arousal. The condensation from the gel pack had soaked through the dish towel and was cold and wet against his skin.

"Can you write it down somewhere?" Rachel asked. "Can

you make it official? So that if something happens, I know. I don't want to hear about it on the news."

Archie hesitated. He already had an emergency contact.

"They'd call Debbie first, wouldn't they?" Rachel said, almost to herself. "That's important. Because of the kids."

"I can see if I can add you," Archie offered.

"It's okay." Rachel rolled her eyes and laughed. "I'm being paranoid. I was just overanxious last night. I had a bad feeling. Isn't that silly? I had this feeling you were in danger. And when you didn't return my calls, I started to get nervous. I don't have Henry's number. I called the nonemergency number, but they said they couldn't tell me anything and they wouldn't put me through to anyone who could." She looked away, and when she looked back, her eyes were wet. She gave him a helpless shrug. "And then I realized something," she said. Her lip trembled. "I realized that I want to be the person you spend the night with on your birthday."

Archie had spent last night unconscious in the mud. But he knew she meant it more metaphorically. Now she sat on his lap, eyes fixed on his. Waiting. Archie still wasn't sure how exactly this had happened. But it appeared he had a girlfriend.

"How about next weekend?" he said. "I have the kids next weekend. We can all do something together."

Rachel's face flushed with pleasure. "Okay."

"I'm sorry I'm not better at this."

She removed the gel pack and rewrapped it in the dish towel. "Your divorce really did a number on you, didn't it?" she said softly, as she placed the gel pack back on his forehead.

Archie moved his hand along the length of her ponytail, the thick blond hair slick beneath his fingers. "It wasn't Debbie."

"You know," Rachel said, lifting her eyes to his, "people with girlfriends tell their girlfriends about their lives. Just FYI. It sort of comes with the package."

"I guess I have a lot to learn about girlfriends," Archie said.

"We also get a shelf in the bathroom."

"You already have a shelf in the bathroom," Archie said. "I noticed that you also took over half a drawer in my dresser."

"Did I?" Rachel asked with a grin.

He could feel her against him again, the heat of desire.

"It's getting warm," she said.

Archie cleared his throat.

"The gel pack," Rachel said. She took it from his skull, unwrapped it, and fingered the soft incandescent-blue gel trapped under the plastic. Then she put it and the dish towel behind her on the end table and returned her body to his. Archie's forehead was numb and damp. Rachel ran her hand over his chest. He wanted her hand to go lower.

"I know you're taking your kids trick-or-treating tomorrow," Rachel said, "but Halloween is my absolute favorite holiday, and I've been planning a special costume that I think you'll enjoy." She gave him a hopeful look. "Maybe we can get together after?"

"We won't trick-or-treat much past dark," Archie said. But he was careful not to commit to anything specific. He knew better than that. In his line of work, things came up.

Rachel nuzzled against his shoulder. "You look nice," she said.

Archie looked down at his clothes reflexively. Rachel's cheek was pressed against Jack Reynolds's cashmere sweater. It seemed too complicated to explain. "Thanks," Archie said.

Rachel raised her head and lifted her chin toward the bedroom. "Do you want to stay?" she asked.

"Yes," Archie said immediately. He wanted to stay very badly. But he couldn't. "But I need to sleep," he said.

"Good," Rachel said with a grin.

She climbed off his lap and stood, and Archie felt a strong, naked urge to pull her back to him.

"I have to go to class," she explained. She looked him up and down, a tiny line of concern between her eyebrows. Then she extended a hand for him to take. "I'll walk you upstairs first."

"Do I really look that bad?" Archie asked.

She turned her hand palm up and beckoned him. "Take my hand," she instructed.

Archie took hold of her hand and let her pull him up into a standing position. They held hands—almost like boyfriend and girlfriend—as she retrieved her shoulder bag of books, and then all the way out her door, to the elevator, and down his hall. As they neared his apartment door, Archie saw her sneak a peek at her phone, and realized that she was checking the time. He didn't want her to be late for class.

"I can take it from here," Archie told her.

She looked worriedly at his head wound. "You sure?"

"I just have to make it to the couch," Archie said.

She kissed him gently on the mouth and looked at him for a long moment, like she was seeing him for the first or last time. "Sweet dreams," she said. Then she turned and headed for the elevator. He watched her go. He liked watching her from behind, the way her ponytail swung as she walked, the way her hips moved.

He wondered how much a cashmere sweater was, and whether Jack would miss his if Archie kept it.

"Give me a hint," Archie called after her. "About the costume."

Rachel threw him a flirty look over her shoulder. "It comes with a lap dance," she said. She beamed at him and then, with a toss of her ponytail, continued down the hallway.

Archie smiled to himself and pushed open his door. He could already hear Ginger on the other side, scrambling to greet him.

Maybe he could have a normal relationship after all.

CHAPTER

24

Gretchen holds back as Archie opens the door to Lidia Hays's apartment. It has been sealed with crime-scene tape and as he cuts through it the yellow plastic flutters to either side, like ribbons snipped open on a present. He uses a key to unlock the door and then pushes it open and steps back to allow Gretchen to enter. She hesitates, and he realizes that the courtesy of holding the door for a lady is probably not the best rule of thumb when entering crime scenes. She doesn't want to go first.

"Sorry," he says. "Wasn't thinking."

He ducks under the remaining piece of tape and enters the apartment. It has been sealed for two days and the smell of decomp still sours the air. The lights are off. Archie reaches and flicks on a light switch as Gretchen enters behind him. It is her idea to be here. She is usually content to see photographs of the scene, but she says this is part of some new approach to get closer to the murders. They have FBI profilers for that, but Archie figures at this point they need all the help they can get.

"Crime Scene finished up yesterday," Archie says as Gretchen walks past him. "The apartment manager still needs to get someone in here to clean. Then we'll let the family in to collect her things."

The living room, where they are standing, is unremarkable. The action has happened in the bedroom. Gretchen is walking around the room, her attention drifting from item to item. A thrift store sectional takes up much of the space. Posters for bands Archie has never heard of are tacked on the walls, along with a few posters of snowboarders captured frozen upside down in midair. It is the little things that get to Archie—the cold half cup of coffee left on the coffee table the morning of the murder, the toothpaste stains on the bathroom sink, a book on the bedside table—evidence of daily life. Gretchen's eyes keep moving, never pausing, taking everything in. She is wearing a form-fitting skirt and a blouse with a bra just dark enough that Archie can see its shadow beneath the fabric. He wonders if she's worn that for him.

"Where do you think the killer hid?" she asks.

"In the bedroom closet," Archie says. The closet door had been found ajar, and clothing had been pushed to the side and some of the shoes on the floor had been disturbed.

Gretchen points toward the door to the bedroom and raises her eyebrows questioningly.

"Are you sure you want to go in there?" Archie asks.

"I've seen the photographs," Gretchen says.

"It's not like the photographs," Archie says.

"I want to see it."

Archie shrugs.

She hesitates before she touches the doorknob.

"It's okay," Archie says. "CSU is done."

Gretchen pushes the door open. He can see the fear in her neck and arms, and he is impressed that she is going forward despite it. She turns back and gives him a pleading, vulnerable look, and he steps beside her, happy to be her protector. He enters the bedroom and turns on the light.

The smell is stronger in here.

The bed frame is dark wood, an antique by the looks of it, maybe something from the family, an heirloom to get her started out on her own. The mattress has been removed since Archie's last visit to the apartment, but Lidia Hays had bled enough that a faint person-shaped dark red stain is visible on the box spring below. The blood spatter around the bed makes the gray carpet look like it has been scattered with rose petals.

Archie leans against the wall just inside the bedroom door as Gretchen takes a few tentative steps toward the bed. He doesn't talk to Debbie about his work. He lets her think it's because reliving his day is too upsetting for him, but the truth is he is rarely upset by what he sees anymore. The crime scenes haven't bothered him for years. But he doesn't want Debbie to know that. He worries it will scare her. It scares him sometimes.

"It doesn't bother you, does it?" Gretchen asks, looking back at him.

He is only mildly startled by the question. He is used to Gretchen's ability to read his mind. She's a psychologist, after all. "I've seen a lot of this kind of thing," Archie says. He chooses his words carefully. "The death bothers me. But not the mess."

It strikes Archie how quiet the apartment is, without the presence of the crime scene techs and cops. He doesn't hear any sounds of neighbors. There's no traffic.

Gretchen takes a step toward him, her back to the bed. "I didn't see you yesterday."

"I couldn't get away," he says.

"You work too much," she says matter-of-factly.

"That's what everyone says."

She is facing him. They are eye-to-eye. He is just a few inches taller than she is, and when she wears heels they are the same height. She tucks her fingers between the buttons of his shirt and touches his abdomen above the waist of his pants. Her fingers move, caressing his belly, and he feels waves of heat radiate down his legs. She brings her lips to his and he accepts her mouth hungrily. He loses himself when they kiss. He has from the first time. The things he usually finds important drift to the background until only she remains.

She pulls her mouth away and smiles. "I've decided that you need to let go of your inhibitions," she says.

"Are you calling me uptight?"

She keeps her eyes fixed on his as she digs his shirttails out and then starts to unbutton his pants. He is already hard from the kiss and he wants to let her continue. He needs this. He's spent the last two days interviewing Lidia Hays's neighbors and friends, he's watched the ME slice her open and catalog her wounds, he's worked through the night reviewing crime scene evidence and photos. Gretchen's eyes are still on him, those perfect blue eyes, as she unzips his pants and moves her hand inside. But a glimpse of the bloodstained bed over her shoulder pulls Archie out of the moment and he puts his hand on her wrist. "This is a crime scene," he reminds her.

He fumbles to zip up his pants, trying to fight his ache for her.

Her fingers play with a button on his shirt. "You said they were finished," she says.

He looks at her incredulously. "I'm not worried about evidence," he says. "A woman was murdered in this room. It's a crime scene. It's not right." She drops her hands and he finishes tucking in his shirt. He glances at his watch. If he leaves now, he can get home in time to see his kids before bed.

When he looks up, Gretchen is slithering out of her skirt. It drops around her ankles and she steps out of it, one stiletto at a time. Her legs are bare and her flesh-colored underwear utilizes a minimal amount of fabric. Archie can feel sweat beading on his upper lip. She lifts the blouse over her head and lets it settle in a gauzy pile on top of the skirt. Then she reaches behind her back, unhooks her bra, and lets it drop to the floor. She smiles at him as she slips out of her underwear and kicks it aside.

She is naked. Archie hasn't stopped her.

His breaths come heavily. It is suddenly very warm in this room. His skull is sweating.

Gretchen stands completely nude, the grisly tableau of the murder bed behind her.

"I'm not afraid of this," she says.

Archie's mouth feels like sandpaper. The heat in his groin is almost overwhelming.

"It's going to be the best sex you've ever had," Gretchen tells him. "Then you can go back to work, relaxed and ready to focus." She glances at the box spring and arches an eyebrow at him. "Do you want me to lie down?"

Archie's eyes move down her body. "Not on the bed," he says. "Against the wall."

She gives him a wicked grin and then saunters to the wall and puts her back to it. He walks over to her quickly, already unbuttoning his pants. By the time he reaches her, he has his cock in his hand.

She glances down at him approvingly. "It looks like you're ready to go," she says.

He kisses her, all the while acutely aware of the bed behind him, of the fact that he isn't the only one with a key to the crime scene and that anyone can walk in at any time, of the smell of decomp that still permeates everything. He knows that he will still stink of it when he gets home, and that the smell will remind him now of this, of Gretchen.

He can feel Gretchen's breathing quicken and her nipples harden under his hands. She lifts one knee and tucks her hips forward and he slides into her, and they both groan. He can feel her clinging to him as he begins to thrust.

"I want to try something," she says breathlessly in his ear. "I think you're going to like it. Will you let me?"

He nods. He would agree to anything in exchange for this.

She reaches behind his head and a moment later he feels a stinging pain at the base of his skull. He reaches up and tries to pull away, but she has her hand in his hair, and her foot hooked behind him, holding him inside her. "What the fuck?" Archie says, his cock softening. His hand touches blood.

"Stay inside me," she tells him. "Breathe."

It hurts.

"Do you feel it?" she asks him. "The endorphins from the

pain. They heighten sensual pleasure. It's just a nail. I've got it pressed into your skull. It won't go in any farther."

A nail?

"Feel it?" Her eyes are shining.

She is rocking against him, and he can feel it. She's right. Everything is amplified. He can feel himself hardening inside her again, and he can't help himself, he has to push deeper, to keep thrusting. He lifts her knee higher.

The pain is still there, but it is diluted by his mounting arousal. He shudders, almost dizzy, pleasure coursing through him.

"Can I stab you again?" she asks, out of breath.

He kisses her hard, pressing her against the wall, and she pushes her tongue deep into his mouth, just as hungrily. He tastes blood. He doesn't know whose. Then he remembers his wife. "Don't leave any marks," he says.

CHAPTER

25

Archie woke up from a hard nap on the sofa, disoriented and sore, his body slimy with cold sweat and a bag of melted ice next to his head. Ginger was snoring gently on the floor below him, one ear twitching. He glanced at his watch. It was almost three. He'd been asleep for hours. His headache had settled into a throbbing pain behind his eyes. Archie moved the melted ice to the coffee table and touched the scabbed lump on his scalp. He'd changed out of Jack Reynolds's clothes and into a pair of sweats and an old T-shirt. Now the T-shirt was damp with sweat. He could smell it on himself. But his head felt clearer. He'd sweated out the painkillers.

He was still on the couch a few minutes later, imagining what Rachel's Halloween costume might be, when someone knocked on the door.

Ginger lifted her head.

"Come in, Henry," Archie called.

The door opened and Henry walked in. Ginger, seeing it was Henry, laid her head back down and closed her eyes.

Archie put his socked feet on the floor and sat up stiffly. That was the thing with painkillers, when they wore off they only reminded you how much pain you were in without them.

Henry sank down in the chair across from the sofa and put his feet up on Archie's coffee table. There was a dead leaf stuck to the heel of his black cowboy boot. There were dead leaves stuck to everything in Portland in the fall. They had a way of appearing in the most unexpected places. Henry smoothed his mustache and then crossed his arms and looked at Archie like he was waiting for him to say something.

"Thanks for looking after the dog," Archie said.

"I don't like it," Henry said, glancing at Ginger.

"Her," Archie said. "You don't like *her.*"

"She's Gretchen's dog," Henry said.

"She's my dog," Archie said. "Gretchen only had her for a night before she gave her to me. I don't think it was long enough to train her as an assassin."

"When I was a SEAL," Henry said, "I'm telling you, we worked on shit like that." Henry's blue eyes narrowed and he looked Archie up and down. "You sick?"

"No," Archie said. "I was asleep."

Henry shifted forward, anchored his elbows on his knees, and folded his hands. "You thinking about her again?"

Archie's stomach knotted. He could feel a faint burn on his cheeks as he turned his head, eyes on the floor. "No."

Henry didn't press it. It was rare for Henry even to breathe Gretchen's name these days. The more the media brought her up, the more TV specials and exposés, the less they talked about her. They both knew she could make you deranged if you let her. The only defense was denial.

Henry nodded at the bag of melted ice on the table and cleared his throat. "How was your birthday?"

Archie smiled thinly. "I have a headache, so it must have been fun, right?"

Henry lifted his bushy gray eyebrows at Archie. "Are you okay?" he asked.

"Yeah," Archie said, wincing as he touched the goose egg on his head.

"Is it over?" Henry asked.

Archie rubbed his eyes. "Leo's still out there."

"Can you talk about it?"

Archie hesitated. Technically, Henry wasn't cleared to be briefed on Archie's little extracurricular op for the FBI, but Henry already knew everything up until the party. He knew that Leo was working for the DEA. He knew how Jack Reynolds made his money. Henry had known Leo as long as Archie had. Archie needed to talk it through with someone, and he still wasn't sure how much he could trust Sanchez. "Jack's working on some deal with the Russians," Archie told Henry. "The party was just a cover for the meeting. Leo's on his own. He thinks Sanchez is dirty. He doesn't trust anybody. I don't know what to think."

"Do you trust Leo?" Henry asked.

That was the question, wasn't it? But Archie couldn't trust his gut when it came to Leo, because his instincts were clouded by Leo's relationship with Susan.

"I trust you," Archie said. He reached into the pocket of his sweats, retrieved the brass pillbox, and held it out to Henry. "There's a strand of hair in here," Archie said. "Can you run the DNA?"

"Who do you think it belongs to?" Henry asked, taking the box.

"You're going to think I've gone crazy."

"I already think you're crazy."

Archie exhaled slowly. "I walked in on Leo cleaning up last night." He glanced up at Henry. Henry was watching him intently. "He was covered in blood," Archie continued. "He used a choke hold on me. I lost consciousness. He said the Russians were coming back, that he was trying to protect me. He killed someone last night, Henry. He told me this morning. An FSB agent who'd infiltrated the group. He said he had to do it to maintain his cover, that Jack suspects him. I woke up outside on a bank near the boathouse five hours later with a head wound and no memory of how I got there. Leo claims they left me in the bedroom and when he came back ten minutes later I was gone. I don't remember."

Archie glanced at the pillbox in Henry's hand. "But this morning, when I got out of the shower, I found a blond hair," he said. Archie cleared his throat, clarifying. "I coughed it up."

Henry rubbed his palm over his face and then paused, as if considering his response. "You should have a tox screen," he said finally.

If he'd been drugged, a tox screen might show it, but it would also show opiates in his system, and Archie didn't want to have to explain that. "It's been too long," Archie said. "It's probably out of my system."

Ginger whined in her sleep and rolled over on her back and Archie stroked her belly with his foot.

"I've been thinking about her," Archie said. "I had a dream about her last night"—he watched Henry, looking for his reaction—"while I was unconscious. Before I found the hair. It seemed real. Like she was there."

Henry's face was expressionless. "That doesn't mean she was," he said. "So you think you found a hair in your mouth. A lot of people have blond hair. It was a party. You could have picked it up anywhere, off of anyone. I don't have to tell you that. Have you considered the possibility that it belongs to Rachel? You know, the other blond you occasionally sleep with?"

Rachel's private bits were waxed to a prepubescent shine, though Archie was in no mood to get into that level of detail with Henry. Besides, this wasn't about Rachel. Archie bent forward, retrieved the image from Sanchez from the coffee table, and began to unfold it.

Henry glanced at the picture and then waved it away. "I've seen it," he said.

So Henry was more involved in the pursuit of Gretchen than he'd led Archie to believe.

"Maybe that's her," Henry said, flicking a hand at the picture. "Maybe she's in the country. It's a lot of maybes. The plan was not to bother you with this shit, remember? You can't get involved every time there's a sighting."

"I feel her, Henry." Archie had to look away as he said it,

but he still needed to say it aloud, and Henry was the only person he could tell. "I think she's here. I think she was on the island last night."

Archie had stopped petting Ginger with his foot and she flopped back over and sat staring at him, waiting for an invitation up on the couch.

"Now you're sounding like a nut job," Henry said. He held the brass pillbox up between two fingers. "You just happened to have this pillbox with you when you found the hair? You were just carrying it around in your pocket in case you needed an evidence container?" The blood vessels on Henry's cheekbones and around his nose brightened. "How many did you take?"

"Two," Archie said. "Maybe more."

"*Maybe* more?"

"I don't remember," Archie said truthfully. "Some were missing, but I don't remember taking them. I haven't had anything since this morning. It's out of my system."

Henry stood up quickly. Archie thought it was out of frustration, until he saw Henry digging for the phone in his pocket and realized that he must have gotten a call. Henry answered it and then listened, his eyes on Archie.

"No, I'm standing next to him right now," Henry said into the phone. "I'll tell him."

Archie's mind was still on Gretchen, and his stomach tightened, anticipating news of another sighting. "What's going on?"

"A dead body just washed up not far from Jack Reynolds's place."

There it was. The surge of adrenaline that always came with a report of a murder. Archie sat up. His mind felt clear and sharp. He sat forward. "Leo's Russian?"

"You said the Russian was a man, right?" Henry said.

"Yeah."

"Well, it's definitely not him."

"A woman," Archie said.

"So says the LOPD," Henry said.

Archie looked down at his damp T-shirt and sweatpants.

He couldn't go to a crime scene looking like this. "Give me a few minutes," he said.

"Maybe you should sit this one out," Henry suggested. "Go in for that tox screen. Get your head checked."

His head, Archie wondered, or his mind?

"It's a concussion," Archie said. "I've been through worse."

No one could argue with that.

"Where's the rest of the Vicodin?" Henry asked.

Archie only hesitated for a second. "Medicine cabinet," Archie said. "In the Prilosec container."

Henry turned and headed for the bathroom. "I'm flushing them," he grumbled. "Happy fucking birthday."

"Okay." Archie stood and headed for the bedroom to change, Ginger at his heels. As he walked he put his hands in the pockets of his sweats, his fingers grazing the bottle of Oxycodone. Henry hadn't asked about those.

CHAPTER

26

The air had that stillness of fall to it—Archie could almost hear individual leaves falling and settling on the grass. He and Henry had parked behind the four Lake Oswego police patrol cars that were neatly parallel-parked along the road in front of a Cape Cod–style home a half mile past Jack Reynolds's place. There was no activity in the front yard. The house's shingles were stained gray, and its trim was painted white, though the New England theme seemed to end at the yard, which was planted with Japanese maples, neatly trimmed evergreen shrubbery, and variegated grasses. A four-foot-tall stone pagoda rose from a bed of chartreuse hostas. A small man-made pond with a bamboo fountain was lined with round stones and filled with fat orange koi. Ugly metal fencing had been erected around the pond in a desperate effort, no doubt, to keep the raccoons at bay.

Archie could see a man staring through the front window. The glass reflected the sky and the grass, and the man was a ghost behind it, but Archie was able to make out a few details. He was light-skinned, clean-shaven, with glasses, tall and thin, with sloped shoulders and long face, and he was standing next to a large dark dog. Both were looking through the glass at Archie and Henry with the same wary expression. But they didn't open the front door, and Archie and Henry didn't knock. Instead, he and Henry followed a path of paving stones around the side of the house toward the lake.

The house's backyard sloped down to a residential dock that extended into the lake like an accusatory finger. The day had warmed into the high fifties and Archie could feel the heat of the sun on his face, but the lake looked dark and cold. The backyard and the dock were peppered with fall leaves. Not the pretty red and yellow ones—these were brown and dead and shredded by the wind. There was no crime scene tape, no flash of crime scene photography. Only several people standing around on the dock who at first glance might be preparing for a rowboat outing, but in this instance were probably more interested in the corpse at their feet.

People drowned in Oregon all the time. Most of them drowned in rivers. Some drowned in the Pacific. Some drowned in lakes. A lot of the fatalities were due to unpredictable accidents—floods, capsized boats, sneaker waves—but there were also a good twenty people every summer who just went out for a swim and never made it back to shore.

So a report of a drowning in Lake Oswego did not generate the sort of media excitement of a bona fide homicide. There were no helicopters. No news vans. No telephoto lenses aimed from passing boats. Just two LO cops, in their head-to-toe navy-blue uniforms, and someone in street clothes Archie assumed was a crime tech or medical examiner hunched over the corpse.

The two LO cops headed over toward them.

"Major Case," Henry said, showing them his badge. Archie didn't move to show his badge. In situations like this, he let Henry do the talking.

The two cops were both men. They recognized Archie. He could always tell. There was that jerk of surprise and the awkward half attempt at hiding it. The cops were both in their early thirties, a decade younger than Archie, and still swaggering with the confidence of youth. Their silver shirt pins read E. LEONARD and S. VITELLO.

"What's Major Case want with this?" Leonard asked.

"Maybe nothing," Henry said with an impatient smile. He pocketed his badge and he and Archie bypassed the two cops and started down the grassy slope to the lake.

"Careful of the dock," Leonard called. "The leaves are slippery."

He was right. The leaves had coated the dock and begun the process of entropy, forming a primordial sludge. Archie walked with Henry, moving along the wooden slats gingerly, like an old man, aware of the cops standing in the yard watching him. He wondered fleetingly if he had disappointed them. In the flesh, Archie had the feeling that he was not so heroic-seeming as the papers sometimes made him out to be.

The woman kneeling next to the body didn't glance up. She was a decade older than Archie, and had her shoulder-length strawberry blond hair in a ponytail, tucked under a black watch cap. She was wearing jeans and rubber-soled duck-hunting boots and a wool red-checked lumberjack shirt over a thick cable-knit sweater. Dr. L.L.Bean.

The body she was kneeling over looked bloodless by comparison. Archie had seen a lot of carnage in the Beauty Killer days. He had seen bodies that had been gutted and electrocuted and dismembered. He'd seen the remains of people who had been eaten alive by rats. He had smelled burned flesh, and putrid flesh, bleached flesh, broiled flesh, and bodies that had been skinned and baked and boiled. This girl had no smell. The frigid lake had slowed decomposition. Even dead, she looked cold. It appeared as if she'd been submerged, but had been out of the water long enough that she was no longer soaking wet. Her blue dress was damp and stained with lake muck, but the hem had dried enough that it moved in the breeze off the lake, and her wet hair had dried to the point that thin wisps of bright blond were visible. Her arms were at her sides, palms up, her fingers curled just enough that Archie could make out the silver glittery polish on her nails. Her feet were bare. Her toenail polish matched her fingernails. She seemed peaceful, her eyes closed and faintly sunken, a hint of gray where her lips closed in something close to a smile. Yet her death had been far from peaceful. Ugly red gashes cut across her neck and chest, creating open fissures of flesh. The blue slip dress she had on was a wet second skin, revealing every bony notch on her, every cleft and joint. Bodies floated with the head and arms down, backside up, and could get fairly battered, caught in boat propellers, knocked against debris. But this girl hadn't been a floater. She was too fresh. A corpse in water took a week to bloom enough bacteria in the gut to gas up sufficiently to float, longer in frigid water like this. Besides, Archie had seen this girl just last night.

Archie looked over at Henry. "I know her," he said.

Henry's mouth opened.

"Who the hell are you?" Dr. L.L.Bean asked them both before Henry could speak. The ID clipped to the pocket of her plaid wood shirt said she was the Clackamas County ME and that her name was Belinda Green.

"Major Case out of Portland," Henry said, his eyes still on Archie.

Archie said it again, his stomach tightening, emphasizing every word: "I know her." He saw her in his mind's eye, her hand on the bathroom door, face flushed from alcohol. Twenty-two, she'd said, though he hadn't believed her. She looked older now. "She was at the party," he said. "She was with a friend. They'd both been drinking. I only saw her for a few minutes. Her friend was in the bathroom, sick. This girl was standing outside. We spoke briefly. But I don't know her name."

Green twisted around and Archie could see what she was looking at. Jack's island was clearly visible offshore. The house was hidden behind the conifers that ringed the island. But he could make out part of the road, and the dock. Green arched an eyebrow at Archie. "You were at the party on the island?" She gave Archie a once-over and snorted. "I'm impressed."

Henry's eyes were still on Archie. His face was impenetrable. "What time did you see her?" Henry asked.

Archie thought about it, piecing together the sequence of events. "A little after midnight," he said. "About fifteen minutes before I ran into Leo." The rest was implied. A few minutes after running into Leo, Archie was unconscious. Archie's head ached. He had no idea what went on after that.

Green lifted her chin back toward the faux–Cape Cod. "The man of the house let his dog out the back door this afternoon," she said. "Heard Lassie barking its head off. Came down to investigate and found our girl here dead on his dock. Called the cops. He doesn't know how long she was out here. But it looks to me like she's been out of the water for at least a few hours."

"She didn't drown," Archie said.

"Doesn't look like it," Green agreed.

"How much would she have bled out from the wounds?" Henry asked.

Archie knew what he was thinking. The wounds looked deep. They might cause the sort of arterial spray that Leo was washing off in the bathroom. But Archie had seen the girl alive moments before Star came downstairs with the bag, blood already in her hair. Whoever Leo had killed, it hadn't been this girl. The timing didn't fit.

"If they were premortem, she would have bled a lot," Green said. "Maybe enough to kill her. Of course, I can't say for sure one way or another at this point, but if I had to guess, she was cut up before she went into the water. She's not a floater. She's too fresh. But she spent some time in the lake. Probably after she died. I'll know more at autopsy."

Henry ran his hand over the back of his head. "What's to say she didn't have a few too many, decide to go for a swim, or fall in, get cut up in the fall, and then pull herself out here? Where she collapsed and died. Dry-drowning. That's a thing, right? We don't even know that this is a homicide."

Green peeled the wet fabric of the dead girl's dress up over the girl's hips. She wasn't wearing underwear and her genitals were waxed. Exposed like that, she looked so bare and vulnerable that Archie had to resist the urge to take his jacket off and cover her. Green indicated the girl's waist. Archie and Henry peered forward to look. Above her bony hips, carved into her cold pale flesh, a purple line encircled her midsection like a belt. A ligature mark. Like she had been bound. "My guess is she was weighed down with something tied around her midsection," Green said. "Thrown in the lake. Then maybe came loose, or someone had a change of heart." She pulled the blue fabric back down over the girl's legs.

"Was she sexually assaulted?" Henry asked.

Green looked at him hard. "What do you think?"

Archie glanced over at Henry. Major Case had a lot of discretion. The task force could claim almost any case they wanted. That had been the deal. Archie had given up his health and his sanity in pursuit of the Beauty Killer, and in exchange his team got the pick of the litter moving forward. "I want this one," Archie said.

Henry looked neither especially surprised nor especially enthusiastic. "You think that's a good idea?" he asked.

Green's eyes widened at something behind them, and Archie turned to see Raul Sanchez heading down the dock. He had changed out of the safari jacket into an FBI windbreaker and FBI cap, the white lettering bright against blue.

"Oh, goodie, more cops," Green said grudgingly.

Sanchez had his badge out, which seemed redundant considering what he was wearing. "Raul Sanchez," he announced to Green, as he stepped between Archie and Henry. "FBI."

"I can see that," she said. She didn't sound impressed.

"So?" Sanchez asked Archie. "What do we have here?"

Henry gave Archie a look.

"One of the party guests from last night turned up dead," Archie said. "Major Case is taking over the investigation. We're going to need any surveillance footage you have of guests arriving or leaving last night."

Sanchez squinted. Archie could see him considering his options. If they had footage of the girl coming onto the island,

and no footage of her leaving, that was probable cause. They could get a warrant to search the entire island.

Sanchez groped for a phone that was clipped to the waistband of his pants. "I'm going to have to make some calls," he said. He turned and took a step on the dock, almost lost his footing, recovered, and then continued gingerly toward the yard.

Green stood up. "I better go tell the others what we're dealing with. Get some crime scene techs out here."

"We've got this," Henry told her. "We'll have her transferred to our morgue."

Green gave Archie and Henry a long look. "You have kids?" she asked.

"I do," Archie said, knowing where she was going. "A boy and a girl."

Green pulled off a blue latex glove with a snap. "Good," she said. Archie got the subtext: *Don't fuck this up.*

"How old is she?" Archie asked the ME.

Green looked down at the dead girl, pulling off her other glove. "Early twenties," she said.

The girl hadn't lied to Archie after all.

"She's all yours, gentlemen," Green said, hoisting up her ME's kit. Then, with a nod, she headed up the dock back toward the house, passing Sanchez, who was still on the phone.

A breeze blew over the lake, rippling the water. Leaves blew off the trees and settled on the lake's bleak surface, floating for a few moments, and then silently slipping beneath the surface.

Archie stared at the island. If he squinted, he could just make out the boathouse near where he had spent much of the night unconscious. Maybe his blond hadn't been Gretchen after all.

"Where did you say you found that blond hair?" Henry asked.

"Let's just say I had clear chain of custody," Archie said.

CHAPTER

27

Jack Reynolds answered the door dressed like he was going yachting—white pants, a white V-neck sweater with navy piping at the neck, and white canvas deck shoes, no socks.

Archie threw a glance at Henry, who was dressed entirely in black, and hoped this would go better than he was anticipating.

The island was tranquil and muted. The stacks of rented chairs and piles of torches were gone. The bars had been disassembled and loaded into trucks and carted off. The propane heaters that Archie had seen collected together in the yard that morning were now just faint impressions in the grass. It hadn't taken them long to get rid of any evidence that the bacchanalia had occurred. Even the dead leaves had been bagged and hauled away. This was how it went if you had a hundred people working for you. The last time Archie could remember having a party, it had taken Debbie and him three days to do the dishes.

Jack didn't invite them in.

"Nice outfit, skipper," Henry said.

"Did you come to return my Ralph Lauren?" Jack asked Archie.

Just three hundred yards away, back on the mainland, Archie's Major Case team was working the crime scene at the Cape Cod. The dock had been cordoned off with crime tape. Crime scene techs were combing the yard. He had divers looking in the lake around the dock. The road was lined with law enforcement vehicles. There was no way that Jack didn't know that. This was a man who employed men with earpieces. He had surveillance cameras in trees.

Archie nodded at Henry and Henry dialed up a crime scene photograph on his phone. They'd downloaded it before they'd crossed the bridge, anticipating the reception issue, so all he had to do was tap the screen. The picture filled the screen—an image of the dead girl's face and shoulders. Henry handed Archie the phone and Archie showed it to Jack. "I need to know who this girl is," Archie said.

Jack barely glanced at the photo. "I don't know her," Jack said.

"She was at your party last night," Archie insisted. "I saw her, right inside there." Archie indicated the foyer behind Jack.

"As established by your presence," Jack said pointedly, "I was less than familiar with the guest list."

"She's dead," Henry said.

Jack smiled thinly. "I got that."

"We think she was murdered," Archie said. "Possibly here on your property." Jack was a lot of things, but he was also the father of two murdered children, and that counted for something. Archie could use it. It was his way in.

"I don't know who she is," Jack said, his tone softening. "I'd tell you if I did. Maybe she came with someone."

"Who would know?" Archie asked.

"We used a private security company last night," Jack said. "Echo Corp."

"They're military contractors," Henry said.

"Heavy security for a garden party," Archie said to Jack.

"I like my guests to feel secure," Jack said with a shark-like smile.

"They're not exactly local," Henry said.

"They have some local contractors," Jack said. "We flew in a few others."

"Those guys are all ex-military," Henry said to Archie. "They would have had a command hierarchy."

"Who was in charge?" Archie asked Jack.

"He goes by Ronin," Jack said. "Charming, right? I'm guessing that's not his real name."

"He's one of the guys you flew in?" Henry asked.

"Yes," Jack said.

"Where is he?" Archie asked.

"The guesthouse," Jack said. "For all I know, he's still asleep."

Archie stepped closer to Jack. He could smell him—his black soap, his expensive cologne. "Let's wake him up, shall we?" Archie said.

The guesthouse was locked, but Jack produced a heavy ring of keys, sorted through it, and opened the door. The air in the house was thick with the smell of freshly brewed coffee. Three well-muscled men with thick necks and buzz cuts were sitting at the round kitchen table, along with Karim, whose thicket of black hair and slight build left him looking a little out of place. There was a large serving bowl of scrambled eggs on the table and another bowl of sausage links and plates that the men had just begun to heap with food. It was early evening. But this fact seemed to escape everyone at the table.

Jack jabbed a thumb toward the living room. "Karim and Ronin stay," he said. "The rest of you give us a minute."

Two of the buzz cuts looked to a third for permission before they followed Jack's orders. When Ronin nodded, they stood up and carried their plates into the living room.

Karim stayed where he was. Whereas the buzz cuts were all wearing varying versions of exercise pants or shorts paired with tank tops, Karim was impeccably dressed in a well-cut gray suit and a canary-yellow bow tie. Not a clip-on, Archie noticed—this bow tie was the real deal. It had been complexly knotted and was only very slightly askew. Karim picked up a cherry red electric kettle in front of his plate and poured hot water into a dainty cup with a tea bag in it. Steam rose from the cup.

Ronin lifted a forkful of eggs to his mouth and chewed, his eyes darting around the room. His close-cropped hair was a shadow of dark stubble and his eyes were a light brown that looked almost gold. His features and skin color were so multiethnic as to be difficult to pinpoint. He looked like he was from everywhere, and nowhere.

Archie recognized him from last night. He'd been the one with the headset and the clipboard.

"I want you to tell him who the girl is," Jack instructed Ronin. There were empty chairs at the table, but Jack didn't sit. He stood with his arms crossed, behind Karim, like a captain on the bridge of his ship.

Henry held his phone in front of Ronin and Ronin studied the image of the dead girl. He didn't react at all to the fact that he was looking at a corpse. His meaty face didn't change. He did not appear disturbed. But he also did not appear overly cavalier or self-conscious, the way he might if he had something to prove or was overcompensating. It took looking at a lot of dead bodies before you could look at the face of a dead young girl like that without showing even a flicker of emotion. Archie knew that from experience.

"I don't know her name," Ronin said finally, shoveling another bite of eggs into his mouth. "She wasn't on the list."

"Nice," Jack said. "She wasn't on the list, but apparently she *was* at the party. Excellent security. Clearly I'm getting my money's worth."

Archie slipped into one of the empty wooden chairs next to Ronin.

Ronin didn't know her name. She wasn't on the list. But that didn't mean Ronin hadn't seen her.

"You remember her?" Archie asked quietly.

Karim stirred his tea with a spoon, and the spoon knocked against the side of the porcelain cup as he circled it. He was wearing square silver cuff links, each with a small blue gem at its center that matched the fine blue stripes on his white shirt.

Ronin was wearing a black tank top, and shorts that had an elastic waist. His legs were smooth and hairless. He swallowed some eggs and nodded. "She showed up by herself," Ronin said. "Said she'd grown up around here, that she'd always wanted to see the island up close. She looked hot. I figured an attractive woman at the party alone—that was good. She promised not to eat much." He slurped the eggs down with some coffee.

"You hire class acts," Henry said to Jack.

Archie stayed focused on Ronin, tripped up by something he'd said. *She showed up by herself.* But that wasn't right. She hadn't been by herself. "What about her friend?" Archie asked him.

"She didn't have a friend," Ronin said, shoveling some more eggs in his mouth. "She was alone."

"She was with another woman," Archie insisted. "I saw them later in the evening. They'd been drinking." A young woman crashing a party by herself? It seemed unlikely to Archie. But two women together, that he could buy.

Ronin thought for a minute. It looked like it hurt. Bright yellow bits of egg clung to the corner of his mouth. His tongue was stained brown with coffee. "What did she look like?" Ronin asked. "Hot?"

Archie mentally stumbled. He hadn't actually *seen* the friend. She was in the bathroom. He'd heard her throwing up. Or at least what sounded like someone throwing up. "I don't know," he admitted.

Ronin shrugged. "Maybe she met someone at the party, but I'm telling you, she arrived solo. And she was the only person we let in who wasn't on the list." He glanced at Archie. "I mean, besides you."

Karim lifted the spoon out of his cup, tapped it on the cup's lip, then licked the spoon and laid it carefully on the saucer. There was something about him that Archie found unsettling. He was too calm. Too controlled. His cuff links sparkled. The gems were probably sapphires.

Archie turned his attention back to Ronin. Ronin took care of himself—he shaved his legs, for Christ's sake. He considered himself a player. He would have flirted with a pretty girl. And when men flirted with women, they asked their names. It was instant intimacy. Use the first name as often as possible. It was the same technique Archie used in interrogations. Ronin would have asked her name. Which meant that he was lying.

"What was her name, Ronin?" Archie asked.

Ronin's mouth fell open. Archie could see chewed-up egg inside.

Karim lifted his teacup to his mouth. The teacup was a fragile little thing, bone china. A blue stamp on the bottom of the cup claimed it had been made in England. Archie watched as Ronin gave Karim a questioning look, and Karim responded with an almost imperceptible nod.

The command hierarchy.

Ronin's shoulders sagged and he scratched at a ruddy patch on his cheek. "Lisa," he said. "Said she grew up here. Said she graduated from Lake Oswego High. Said she'd always wanted to get on the island." He leaned forward a little and lowered his voice. "But if you ask me, I think she was just interested in hooking up with someone important. Some girls? You can smell their desperation."

"I paid to have the list vetted," Jack said, shaking his head in disgust. "I paid for the headsets, the earpieces. And you let her in because she batted her eyelashes at you?" He looked down at Karim. "Did you know about this?"

Karim returned his cup soundlessly to its saucer. "No," he said.

Archie studied Ronin. Ronin wasn't exactly the sharpest tool in the shed, and yet he'd managed to gather a lot about the victim from a very brief encounter. Archie wasn't convinced that Ronin's powers of observation were that potent.

"You'd met her before last night," Archie said.

Ronin's mouth twitched. "Outside the grocery store, in town," he said. "We talked a little. She was a flirt. I told her

I was in town for a job on the island. She said that thing about always wanting to see the place."

Archie felt a stab of pain, as a father. "You invited her to the party," he said, shaking his head.

Ronin drew his head back defensively. "Hey, I didn't think she'd show up."

"And when she did?" Archie asked.

"I had a job to do," Ronin said, glancing at Karim. "She thought it was some kind of date." He grunted and flashed a world-class asshole smirk. "That little bitch was lucky she got into the party at all."

Archie could imagine Ronin's surprise when the girl he'd talked up in town had shown up in her pretty dress, flush with excitement at the prospective evening. She would have wanted to avoid the humiliation of him sending her away. She would have seen the dazzling guests streaming up the path, the torches lighting their way, seen the tuxedos, the magical landscape, the Tudor mansion, straight from a storybook. It was the kind of party little girls dreamed of. At that point, she would have done anything to get past the metaphorical velvet rope. Archie had seen enough to know what that meant. "You made her pay for her ticket, though, didn't you?" Archie asked Ronin.

Ronin stabbed at some eggs with his fork. Without a commander to order him in no uncertain terms to reveal what he knew, he'd hem and haw all day about this. Men like him were incapable of taking responsibility unless someone with more power told them to. Archie had to force the situation. He put his hand on Ronin's shoulder and gripped it hard. "What did you do?" Archie demanded.

The room went still and silent.

Ronin's shoulder was warm meat under Archie's palm. Archie could see the veins in Ronin's biceps rise as they engorged with blood. Ronin's fist tightened around the fork. Archie had a brief vision of the fork going into his neck. He did not doubt for a moment that Ronin could do it if he wanted to. Archie wondered what it would feel like.

"You don't want to do that," Karim said softly in his British accent.

In the same instant that Ronin's shoulder relaxed slightly, Henry went for his weapon. He leveled it, two-handed, at Ronin's head. "Drop it," Henry said.

No one flinched. Jack looked on, detached. Karim was watchful. Apparently someone drawing a gun at breakfast was not all that extraordinary.

"Drop it," Karim said, picking up his cup.

Ronin's hand opened. The fork stood for half a second, balanced on its tines, and then toppled over onto the plate, splattering fragments of scrambled egg onto the table.

Archie kept his hand on Ronin's shoulder, the ribbed black tank top under his fingers. "She's dead," Archie said between his teeth. "She was sexually assaulted. Are we going to find your sperm on her?"

Ronin met Archie's gaze with his golden eyes. "I guess so."

Archie shook his head in disgust. "Where?" he asked.

Ronin's mouth turned up in a smile. "In her stomach."

Archie let go of Ronin and sat back in his chair. His head was pounding. His hand had left a red print on Ronin's shoulder. Next to him, Henry holstered his weapon, his face flushed. Jack was still standing behind Karim's chair with his arms crossed. Karim was sipping his tea. "We're going to need a DNA sample," Archie said.

Henry lifted a small black case out of his pocket, opened it, and pulled out a long Q-tip. "Open up, Romeo," he said to Ronin. Ronin looked again to Karim, and Karim nodded and Ronin opened his mouth. Henry swabbed the inside of Ronin's cheek and bagged the Q-tip.

"When was the last time you saw her?" Archie asked.

Ronin crossed his arms. "I let her in around nine-thirty. Didn't see her after that," he said.

"So you didn't see her leave?" Archie said.

"No," Ronin said.

Archie looked over at Jack. "I want to review the footage from your surveillance cameras," Archie said.

Jack smiled indulgently, like Archie had suggested that they strip down to their socks and cannonball into the lake. "That's not going to happen," Jack said.

Archie rubbed his hands over his face. He knew there was very little chance of talking Jack into going along with his request, but he had to give it a shot. "I talked to this girl last night. In your house. And today she was found dead on your neighbor's dock. Whatever else you were up to here last night, it doesn't concern me."

"It sounds like it's my neighbor you should be interrogating," Jack said. "A dead girl on his dock? That sounds suspicious. You know, I've never trusted that man. He doesn't pick up after his dog."

"She was here," Archie said. "I need to look at the security footage. See the people she talked to—see if she had any altercations with anyone. For all we know, one of your cameras might have filmed the murder."

Jack leaned forward, reached over Karim's shoulder, and picked a piece of toast off Karim's plate. *The hierarchy of command.* Jack took a bite off the corner of the toast and chewed on it a few times. "Get a warrant and we'll talk," he said.

"I don't suppose you'd consent to allowing us to interview the rest of your staff?" Archie asked. "Maybe check some backgrounds for priors? There was a goon guarding the bottom of the first-floor stairs in the main house that could use a women's studies class, and I wouldn't mind asking him about his movements last night."

"I think I've given you enough time today, Detective," Jack said.

Archie stood up and pushed his chair in. "Say hi to Leo for me," Archie said.

Jack didn't blink. "Leo isn't here."

"Where is he?" Archie asked.

Jack shrugged. "Call him. Leave a message. If he wants to talk to you, I'm sure he'll return it."

"Can I take a piece of toast to go?" Archie asked, surveying the food on the table.

Jack sighed. "Help yourself," he said.

"Want one?" Archie asked Henry.

Henry squinted at him. "No, thanks," he said.

There was a paper napkin dispenser on the table next to the bowl of eggs. The paper napkins were for the help— Archie would have bet money that they used cloth napkins in the big house. He pulled a paper napkin out and picked up a piece of toast and spread some peanut butter on it. As he reached to put the knife back in the peanut butter jar, his elbow caught the edge of Karim's teacup.

The teacup tipped over, rolled off its saucer, and then came to a stop, spilling its entire contents.

Karim jumped back, swearing in Hindi, as hot tea poured over the side of the table onto his lap. His chair clattered, upended, on the kitchen floor and Karim stood pulling at his trousers to keep the scalding liquid off his legs.

Archie handed Karim the dispenser of paper nāpkins. "Sorry," he said.

Jack didn't come to Karim's aid as he frantically dabbed at his slacks with napkin after napkin. He didn't move. His eyes were on Archie. "You should go now," Jack said.

Archie leaned toward Karim. "If you need a shower," he said, "I suggest the second-floor guest bathroom in the main house." Archie gave Jack a wink. "Just be sure to lock it."

Archie felt Henry's hand close around his arm.

"Let's go," Henry said firmly.

"Sure," Archie said. But first he turned back to Jack. "One thing," he said.

Jack raised his eyebrows, waiting.

Archie was struck with a sudden urge to take a swing at him, but he felt Henry's hand tighten on his arm again and he let it pass. "Stay away from Susan Ward," Archie said.

Jack arched an eyebrow and smirked. "Funny," he said. "I think that little stunt bothered you more than it did my son."

"We'll be in touch," Henry said quickly.

Archie tossed his piece of toast back onto the table and then let Henry steer him out of the kitchen.

Archie and Henry didn't speak again until they were off

the island, on the other side of the bridge, through the gates, and beyond the reach of the surveillance cameras. Only at that point did Archie retrieve the folded napkin out of his jacket pocket and hold it out to Henry.

"What?" Henry asked, touching his chin. "Do I have something on my face?"

Archie opened the napkin, revealing the silver teaspoon he'd swiped off the table after he'd spilled the tea. "Karim's teaspoon," Archie said. "Have his DNA checked, too."

CHAPTER

28

When Susan woke up, the light outside the window had faded and dark shadows crept across the wood floor. She listened for a minute. The house was quiet. Susan's laptop was beside her on the bed, and she reached over and touched the keyboard to wake it up. The screen came to life, the Word document she'd been writing still open. The clock on the screen read 6:13 P.M. She blinked groggily, and realized that she had slept most of the afternoon away.

She didn't even feel that rested. She had a faint headache and the pimple on her forehead hurt. She turned on her bedside light, sat up, wrenched off her sneakers, tossed them toward her closet, and then struggled out of her sweaty tights. She had peeled off all her clothes, and was walking naked across the room to retrieve the old kimono she used as a robe, when she noticed the puddle of green velvet on the floor—the cape she'd worn on her last date with Leo. It was right where Susan had left it after she'd thrown it off in frustration. Susan picked up the cape, gave it a shake, and carefully draped it around a hanger. Then she slipped on the kimono and went across the hall into the bathroom to run a bath. She sat on the toilet seat while she poured some eucalyptus bath salts into the water, and then lit as many candles along the lip of the tub as she could without standing up. The bright scent of eucalyptus filled the room. She watched the bathtub fill, steam rising, clouding the bathroom window and beading the medicine cabinet mirror with sweat. When the water was knee-high, Susan dropped the kimono on the floor and stepped into the tub.

The bathroom had a new door. Bliss had bought it at the ReBuilding Center, a house parts salvage yard, and painted it to look like the old one. Susan's mother had tried to match the paint, but it had ended up the wrong color blue. Susan still saw Ryan Motley's hand reaching through the splintered wood, feeling for the doorknob, the fear on Pearl's face. The bathroom had been Susan's idea—she had led Pearl there, a step ahead of the intruder. Until that night, the bathroom had always been Susan's sanctuary.

Susan closed her eyes and sank back in the water. Her face felt hot. She let the water envelop her, until just her chin was above the waterline and the hair spray from the night before leached away, forming a dirty film on the surface. When she came up her skin was the color of coral. She poured a quarter-sized dollop of Dr. Bronner's peppermint all-purpose liquid soap into her palm and washed her hair. Susan's mother bought Dr. Bronner's in a two-gallon jug and meted it out into containers throughout the house. They used it for everything—to brush their teeth, wash their hair, do dishes, wash their hands; Bliss even dabbed a little behind each ear in the morning as some sort of aromatherapy.

Susan finished scrubbing her scalp clean and then leaned back under the water and ran her hands through her hair. When she sat up the bathwater was blanketed with peppermint soapsuds. Susan lathered up her legs with more Bronner's, shaved them without cutting herself once, and then leaned her head on the back of the tub and closed her eyes. Her stomach growled. It was the peppermint. It made her hungry. Susan inspected her hands. They were pale and pruned. She stood up, grabbed a towel, and stepped out of the tub.

She stood on the bath mat as she dried off and the tub drained noisily behind her. The bathroom floor was fir, and a hundred years of water stains had left the area around the tub so blackened with water damage that Susan was sure that one day the floor was going to give way and that heavy claw-foot tub was going to end up in the kitchen. She just hoped she wasn't in it when it happened.

Once Susan had slipped the kimono back on and combed out her wet hair, she wiped up some water on the floor with the towel. Then she walked the length of the tub, humming a Jefferson Starship song, and blew out each candle. The candles were still emitting thin snakes of smoke as she headed across the hall back to her bedroom, starving, and already thinking about the caramel apples downstairs. She flipped on her bedroom light, went to her dresser, and dug a pair of red wool socks out of the sock drawer, and then sat down on the bed to pull them on. As she did, she noticed that something was strange about her computer.

The screen was still lit up. She could see the blue glow emanating from it.

It should have been asleep. She had it set so that if she went four minutes without typing, the screen would go dark.

Susan sighed. Great. It must be frozen. A computer glitch—that was just what she needed. Naturally she hadn't backed anything up in ages.

She reached for the computer and turned it to face her, and groaned as she saw the screen.

Shit. The document she'd been working on had been deleted.

The file that she had left open had been filled with writing. The page that was up now was just a single sentence. Her computer had eaten everything else. Her entire account of the evening before had vanished. The fact that it hadn't been for a story, that there was no editor waiting for it, that Susan had written it all down just for the sake of it—that somehow made it worse. She wanted to pick the laptop up and hurl it across the room. What had happened? She tapped a key on the keyboard. The cursor blinked obediently. There was no frozen rainbow ball. The computer appeared to be working just fine. What the . . . ?

Susan read the sentence on her screen, bile rising in her throat. Seven words. They made her go cold all the way to the bone.

HELLO, PIGEON. DID ARCHIE LIKE HIS BIRTHDAY PRESENT?

Susan leapt up and backed away from the bed like she'd been burned. Her heart was pounding in her ears. *Pigeon.* Gretchen had been the only person who'd ever called Susan that. Susan glanced around frantically. Gretchen had been here—in Susan's bedroom. She'd typed that sentence on Susan's computer. Susan forced herself to turn, openmouthed and terrified, inspecting every shadow. But she was alone. Her darting eyes confirmed it. The closet was open and empty. There was no room for anyone to hide under the futon.

Gretchen wasn't in her room. Dread gripped Susan by the stomach as her eyes turned to her laptop. Gretchen was in her computer.

Susan stared at the laptop. She could see the patches at the bottom of the keyboard where her palms had worn away the metallic surface. The computer keys were coated with her oily grime. The screen was smudged with her fingerprints. Each sticker and decal had been carefully chosen and applied. Susan knew every scratch and speck on that computer like she knew the freckles and scars on her own flesh.

And Gretchen had found a way inside it.

Susan inched forward in her socked feet, peering at the tiny black eye of the camera lens installed above the laptop's screen. She clutched her robe closed. You could take over someone's computer remotely if you loaded the right malware. Susan had done a story about that once. You could even use the computer's own camera to spy on someone.

A trickle of bathwater dripped down the back of Susan's neck. Her MacBook was her life. She wrote everything on it—every story, every half-assed attempt at a novel, every e-mail, every personal thought she'd ever cared enough about to write down. Now she approached it grimacing, arm outstretched, like the computer was something alive, something dangerous, something infected. When she got close enough, she stretched her trembling hand across the bed and slammed the laptop closed. The Apple logo on the back glowed white for a few seconds and then went dark.

CHAPTER

29

It didn't take long to find the yearbook photo. Lake Oswego High had uploaded the last ten years' worth of yearbooks into a digital archive on their Web site. All Archie needed was a password and there she was. The Clackamas County ME's age estimate had been right on the money. The victim had been twenty-two. The senior photograph—jauntily posed with a tennis racket under one arm—was four years old. Her hair was cut bluntly at her chin, her face was fuller, and her skin was Photoshopped to a dewy plastic sheen, but even on the screen of Henry's phone, Archie still recognized her from their encounter outside Jack Reynolds's first-floor half bath.

Her name was Lisa Katherine Watson and she had been voted "most likely to marry a millionaire."

Lisa Watson's parents lived in a hundred-year-old house on a quiet street in the old part of Lake Oswego where the streets didn't have sidewalks and the houses all had gardens.

The same photograph Archie and Henry had seen online was framed on the mantel in the living room. Other photographs were displayed as well: Lisa Watson as a small child with a tennis racket, several of Lisa Watson as a young teenager with a tennis racket, Lisa Watson as an older teenager with a tennis racket. There were no photographs of her parents or any other sibling.

"She was nationally ranked," Peter Watson said. "Before she started partying." He was tall and lean and moved gingerly, like an athlete whose joints had paid the price.

Archie nodded. He dreaded this part, the families. Sometimes he felt like the angel of death swooping in to destroy lives. He had to remind himself that he was only the messenger.

"Can I get either of you a glass of water?" Lynn Watson asked hesitantly. She looked like her daughter—the slight overbite and pug nose, her face nearly as pale as a corpse. Archie thought of Lisa Watson on that dock, the ligature marks across her abdomen. She had not died peacefully. But her mother did not want to know that.

"Yes, ma'am," Henry said, glancing at Archie. "Thank you."

This was what you did. If the family offered you water, you drank it. It helped sometimes to do something, to have a task. There was a delicate balance to family notification. At first, it was important to be clear, to avoid misunderstandings, hope. *Your daughter was found dead. It appears to be a homicide.* But once that devastating reality had been established, once it sank in, you did everything you could to avoid referring to the deceased as a body. "She's at the morgue," Archie had told the Watsons after delivering the brutal news, "she'll be released to you as soon as possible."

You tried to be gentle. You tried not to make any sudden movements. You avoided using the past tense. "Is there anyone you can think of who might want to hurt Lisa?" Archie asked her father.

Peter Watson winced, and his forehead creased. He had aged ten years since they'd walked through the door. "She didn't have a boyfriend, if that's what you mean," he said.

"An ex-boyfriend?" Henry asked. "Anyone she might have run into at the party?"

Watson sank onto the arm of a wingback chair. Its sunflower yellow upholstery seemed inappropriately cheerful, considering. Most of the furniture in the room was the same aggressive shade of yellow as the chair. Embroidered yellow throw cushions on the sofa matched the formal drapes that hung over the windows. The walls were the color of ballpark mustard. Archie wondered if they would redecorate now.

"Honestly, I don't know," Watson said with a defeated sigh. "We didn't even know she was going to that party. She hasn't had a boyfriend since high school. More like"—he looked pained and his eyes drifted to the floor—"encounters."

Lynn Watson reentered the room. She had cleaned herself up a little, Archie noticed. Her face was still haggard with grief, her eyes swollen with tears. But she had applied a careful layer of plum-colored lipstick. The color brought out the blotchiness in her cheeks.

She handed Henry and Archie each a lime-green plastic cup of water, no ice. The cups were printed with a State Tennis Finals Championship logo.

"Thank you," Archie and Henry both said.

Archie noticed that the lip of his cup was dusty, like it had been sitting on a shelf for a few years. He lifted it to his mouth and took a sip of tepid tap water. "Mm," he said.

"They want to know if she could have run into anyone she knew, anyone dangerous, at the party out on that island," Peter Watson told his wife.

"Lisa is very popular," Lynn Watson said, nodding. "She knows a lot of people."

No one said anything for a moment. Archie could hear a dog barking in the backyard.

"Anyone who lived around the lake?" Archie asked her, thinking of the dock where Lisa's body had been found. Archie flipped through his notebook for the name of the property owner. "Wally Swinton?"

The two Watsons looked at each other blankly.

"Swinton have any kids?" Archie asked Henry.

"No," Henry said. "He's a bachelor."

"A bachelor?" Archie said.

"He's gay," Henry said.

"Just say that, then," Archie said.

"I thought I did," Henry said.

The Watsons were both looking at them.

Archie wasn't sure what more could be gained from them. He was growing more and more certain that Lisa Watson had met someone at that party who had killed her. And that meant that the answers weren't here. They were on that island.

"Do you know who she might have gone to the party with?" Archie asked the Watsons. "A female friend?"

"Lisa didn't really have girlfriends," her father said.

"She has a lot of friends," Lynn Watson corrected him. She glanced at her husband sharply and then her face softened. "She just isn't exclusive," she explained to Archie and Henry. "She doesn't have *best* friends. So she doesn't talk about them much. We haven't met them. But she is very popular."

"She moved home last year," her father said. Archie saw him steal a look at his wife, and knew that this fact had been a bone of contention between the two.

"She's a junior at PSU," her mother said. "She took a few years off, but now she's studying physical education." She caught herself and lifted a hand over her mouth. "She *was* studying."

"She went out a lot," Peter Watson said. "But usually alone. I can give you the names of some of the people she knew in high school if that might help."

"We'd appreciate that," Archie said.

"You pressured her too much," Lynn Watson said to her husband.

Peter Watson's face colored.

Parents blamed themselves. The cause of death didn't matter. They always blamed themselves, or each other. Archie had seen it before.

"All your stupid tennis dreams," Lynn Watson said to her husband. "He gave her a racket when she was two," she said, looking from Henry and Archie. "By the time she was six he made her practice every day. Camps all summer. She couldn't take the stress. She'd started partying by senior year. They caught her drinking on campus and kicked her off the team. She couldn't cope." She glanced back at her husband again. She was rambling, not even pausing for a breath. "We shouldn't have let her move home. If she hadn't moved back home, she wouldn't have even known about the party."

"She was nationally ranked," Peter Watson said again, his voice catching.

Lynn Watson stumbled toward Archie, her eyes glassy—lipstick staining her front teeth. Her breathing was rapid and shallow. "You find who did this," she said.

Her eyes went back in her head and Archie just had time to get an arm around her before her knees gave out. Water slopped out of his cup and onto the floor. "Breathe," he told her. "Long, deep breaths." She nodded, and put her weight into his shoulder, and he held her as the hyperventilation passed, while Peter Watson sat motionless on the yellow chair. "Promise me," she said to Archie, clutching him. "Promise me you'll find who did this."

She trembled against his body. The barking in the backyard had grown frantic. "I promise you," Archie said.

Henry cleared his throat.

Archie glanced over at his partner. "I promise you that we'll do everything we can," Archie clarified.

CHAPTER

30

When Archie stepped off the elevator on the sixth floor of his apartment building, he inhaled a lungful of lingering cigarette smoke and he knew that someone was waiting for him. He unsnapped his holster and walked down the hall toward his apartment door, alert for any movement. The building manager had hung glittery white paper skeletons on the walls. They were the size of children, with brass grommets at their joints that allowed their limbs to splay out at unnatural angles. There were four of them between the elevator and Archie's apartment door, affixed to the walls with thumbtacks. They grinned at him as he walked past, with wide unblinking eyes. Skeletons didn't have eyes. Soft tissue, bulging with maggots, they were one of the first things to rot on a corpse. But no one seemed to remember that at Halloween.

Archie's apartment was at the end of the hall, near a corner that led to a fire exit, and Archie was almost to his door when he saw a shadow move on the floor. Then Leo stepped around the corner, the cigarette still in his hand, half burned down, a thread of smoke wafting from the orange tip.

Archie exhaled and put his key in the lock. "Did I keep you waiting long?" he asked.

"About twenty minutes," Leo said. He had something in his hand and he tossed it to Archie. Archie just managed to snatch it from the air. He turned it over in his hand and looked at it. It was a flash drive.

"I didn't want to just leave this in front of your door," Leo said. He moved to step beside Archie and Archie instinctively turned slightly, so Leo couldn't get behind him. Leo raised his palms. "No choke hold," he said. "Scout's honor."

Leo didn't look any better than he had that morning. He clearly hadn't spent the afternoon catching up on sleep. His white button-down shirt was fresh from the dry cleaner's. His hair was molded to perfection. But he still looked like shit. His face was pallid and there was something leaden in his gaze. The rims of his eyes were the color of raw steak.

"Who's the lucky lady?" Leo asked, indicating the shoulder of Archie's blazer.

Archie glanced down at the plum-colored lipstick smeared on the tan corduroy. "It's not what you think," he said, pushing his apartment door open. If Leo tried anything, Archie could always shoot him. He heard a scrambling from inside the apartment, and then Ginger appeared. She pranced eagerly at Archie's feet and Archie felt the familiar swell of well-being that came with coming home, now that he had a dog to greet him. He reached down to pet Ginger with one hand, while turning the flash drive over in the other. "Is this what I think it is?" he asked Leo.

Leo had followed him inside. "The surveillance footage from last night," he said.

Jack had refused Archie to his face when he'd asked for this just hours ago. Archie wondered what had changed his mind. "Does Jack know you brought it?" Archie asked.

"Does it matter?" Leo said.

Archie straightened up and brushed the corgi hair from his pants.

Leo's cigarette ash fell onto Archie's floor. Ginger nosed at it and then lapped it up.

"You can put that out in the sink," Archie said.

Leo looked down at his hand and seemed startled to find

the burning cigarette between his fingers. "Sorry," he said, and he walked over to the kitchen sink and ran the faucet over the cigarette butt and then washed it down the drain. Archie walked to the kitchen counter, got one of Ginger's treats from a box, and held it out to her. She sat and looked at him with her head cocked. Then he nodded at her and she dropped flat and rolled over. He held the treat out and she took it gently from his hand and trotted off with it into the living room.

"Nice dog," Leo said.

"Do you want a beer?" Archie asked, setting the flash drive on the counter.

"I can't stay," Leo said.

Archie opened the fridge and got a beer out and opened it.

"But I'll take one to go," Leo said.

Archie handed Leo the beer and got another one out for himself. They drank silently together, standing in the kitchen. Most of the lights were still off and the apartment seemed dark and empty. Archie heard a train. "Do you know what happened to the girl?" Archie asked.

Leo put his beer down on the counter. "No," he said. He looked Archie in the eye. "I swear," he said. "It had nothing to do with me. I'll try to find out what I can from the inside, but so far no one seems to know anything."

Archie wanted to believe him. "I saw Sanchez today," Archie said.

Leo's back straightened and he put two fingers to his lips. His eyes moved slowly around the room.

Archie followed his gaze. This was ridiculous. Leo couldn't really think that his apartment was bugged, could he? But Leo appeared dead serious. This was looking less like caution and more like paranoia.

Leo cleared his throat. "How's Susan?" he asked.

Archie took a pull of beer. "Annoyed. Tired."

Leo nodded. "I'm going to give us some space," he said. "While I'm out there. For her own protection."

That may have been the smartest thing Leo had said since he had arrived at Archie's apartment.

Leo's eyes went to the dull green light of the microwave's digital clock. "I should get back," he said. But he lingered there in the kitchen, the beer in his hand, like there was something more he wanted to say.

"Thanks for this," Archie said, touching the flash drive on the counter.

Leo drew back the last swallow of his beer and sat the empty bottle down next to the flash drive. "Before you turn it over," he said, "you might want to take a look at the boat-house camera footage." He wiped his mouth and turned away before Archie could read his face.

Archie picked up the flash drive and looked at it. What the hell?

Leo was opening the door, already on his way out of the apartment.

"Wait," Archie said, coming after him.

Leo jumped back, but it wasn't because of Archie. The door opened and Susan stepped through. She was clearly as surprised as Leo was. She had probably been just about to knock when Leo opened the door. Her wet black and white hair was plastered to her head and she was wearing black jeans and an orange T-shirt with the words WORST HALLOW-EEN COSTUME EVER emblazoned across the chest. Her Con-verse sneakers were neon-yellow today. No socks. The shirt was wrinkled. She had dressed in a hurry.

"Hi," Leo said.

Susan frowned, hugging to her chest the laptop she was carrying. Her eyes scanned the apartment, until they landed on Archie. "I just needed to see Archie," she said.

Leo glanced over his shoulder at Archie. "Me, too," he said. Then he looked at Susan, waiting.

It was Archie's apartment, but for some reason he felt like he was intruding. Ginger came out from under the coffee table to investigate. Even she seemed to sense the tension. She looked up at Archie fretfully.

"What?" Susan asked Leo.

"I'm on my way out," Leo said. "You're standing in the doorway."

Susan's eyebrows raised in understanding and her face reddened. She stepped inside the apartment, out of the doorway, to let Leo pass. "Sorry," she said.

Leo moved past Susan. Susan glanced over at Archie. The hall light was bright behind her, and her face was in shadow, but Archie could see the hesitation in her body language. She put her arm out and touched Leo, stopping him. "Will you call me later?" she asked him.

Archie watched as Leo pulled away. "I'll try," he said.

Leo closed the door behind him, leaving Archie and Susan alone in the dark apartment. Archie walked over to the standing lamp in the living room and turned it on. He wanted to give Susan a moment to recover from the interaction with Leo before he asked her what the hell she was doing at his apartment.

But she didn't need it.

When he turned back she was right behind him with her laptop cradled in her arms. Her eyes burned with intensity. "I need to show you something," she said.

Ginger was standing at her feet, waiting to get petted. But Susan didn't bend over.

"Is it the Internet?" Archie asked. "Because I've seen that."

She ignored him and opened the laptop.

He glanced down at the screen. The only open item on the desktop was a Word document with a single line of type on it.

"Read it," Susan urged him.

He did.

HELLO, PIGEON. DID ARCHIE LIKE HIS BIRTHDAY PRESENT?

Archie's skin got hot. He looked up at Susan, perplexed. Her eyebrows jumped impatiently. "It just showed up on my screen this afternoon," she said. "Don't you get it?" She held the screen next to her face, her wet black hair combed back over her ears so that the pink of her skull was visible behind the white skunk stripe. Her nail-bitten fingers gripped the computer so hard they were white. "She hacked into my computer, Archie," she said. "I don't know how, but she did. I had started writing about last night. I wrote two pages. Then I fell asleep. And when I woke up, I took a bath, and when I came back to my room the story I'd written was gone, and this was there instead." Her cheeks were pink, every freckle on fire.

"I don't understand," Archie said, stepping back.

Ginger gave up on Susan and trotted over to Archie.

"It's her," Susan whispered.

Archie's eyes went back to the screen. He could feel his body going cold.

"Gretchen hacked into your computer and wrote that?" Archie said.

"Yes!" Susan said.

Archie lifted his hands and rubbed his face, as if he could scrub what he was seeing from his vision.

HELLO, PIGEON. DID ARCHIE LIKE HIS BIRTHDAY PRESENT?

It didn't make sense. She was trying to distract them with some meaningless riddle. He hadn't gotten a birthday present from Gretchen. He had spent the better part of his birthday alone, unconscious in the mud.

Hadn't he?

Archie got the flash drive that Leo had given him out of his pocket and looked at it. "Give me a second," he mumbled to Susan, and he made himself walk over to where his own laptop hummed on the kitchen bar. Ginger thought he was going for another treat and scurried past him into the kitchen. He was out of his body now, willing himself to put one foot in front of the other, to slide the flash drive into the USB port. He waited for something to happen, an icon to appear on the screen, a window to open, but nothing did. His outer-space screen saver looked vast and empty, billions of stars floating in a black void.

Ginger came around the corner, looking disappointed, and flopped down at his feet.

Susan stepped beside him. "What are you doing?" she asked.

Archie indicated the flash drive, his eyes still on the screen. "This is footage from the security cameras on the island last night," he said. "A young woman was found dead this afternoon on a dock at a nearby property." There was still no flash drive icon on the desktop—the laptop wasn't recognizing it. Archie tapped the return key a few times, squinting at the starry landscape. "I saw her at the party last night," he continued. "Before I blacked out." He stopped there, deciding to leave Leo out of that particular part of the story. "I woke up this morning on the embankment outside the boathouse," he said. He touched the wound on his head. "With this." Maybe the flash drive didn't work. Maybe it was corrupted. "There's a boathouse camera," Archie said, remembering what Leo had said. "I want to see that footage." He scanned the keys helplessly, trying to figure out what more to do to get it to work.

Susan closed her computer and set it on the kitchen bar next to his. "Here," she said, moving his hand away from the keyboard. "Let me." He stepped away from the computer gratefully, and allowed her to take his place.

He watched as she studied his laptop. Then she reached out and wiggled the flash drive in the USB port and the flash drive icon instantly appeared. Apparently, he hadn't inserted the flash drive correctly. Susan glanced over at him with a slight smile, but didn't comment.

"Click on it," Archie said.

Susan clicked on the icon and a window opened with dozens of thumbnails, each with a different label. *SE Garden*. *Pool*. *Dock*. Archie scanned them until he found the one called *Boathouse*.

"Here," he said, pointing at it.

Susan moved the cursor over it and clicked.

Another box opened on the screen and the video started loading.

"Can you make it go faster?" Archie asked.

"Maybe if you had updated your video player in the last three years," Susan said.

The status bar ticked forward at a glacial pace.

"Is that how you hurt your head?" Susan asked.

Archie stayed focused on the screen. "I don't know how I hurt my head," he said.

"So what's the last thing you remember?" Susan asked.

A face flashed in Archie's mind. "Leo," Archie said numbly.

Susan turned to him, eyebrow arched. "What did he do?"

The status bar was at 60 percent.

"Can we agree to let that go for now?" Archie asked.

Susan pressed a key with her thumb and the status bar stopped moving. She had paused it.

"What are you doing?" Archie demanded.

Susan crossed her arms and faced him. "Tell me what happened."

Archie looked at the screen and then back at her. Susan was a snoop by nature. She needed to know everything, especially if it concerned her even in the most tangential sense. Most of the time Archie found that rather charming, but right now it was not charming at all. He needed to see that footage. She had no idea what was at stake.

"Leo used a choke hold on me," Archie explained. "He had his reasons. Which he shared with me later."

"A choke hold?" Susan asked, arms still crossed.

Archie sighed. *Fine.* "He stepped next to me," Archie said, pivoting slightly behind Susan. "Close, like this. I thought he was going to tell me something he didn't want overheard, but instead he put his arm around my neck and pressed his forearm here." Archie reached around Susan, hooking his elbow lightly under her neck, and anchoring his wrist with his other hand. The move required him to tuck his body against hers, as he pulled her back into his arms. He could

feel her pulse on the inside of his elbow, but she didn't pro-
test. "It compresses the carotid artery," Archie explained,
his arm pressing ever so gently against her neck. "Your
brain can't get enough oxygen." His mouth was next to her
ear, just as Leo's had been next to Archie's when he'd told
him not to struggle. "This warm blackness just sort of
overwhelms you," Archie told her. Her hair smelled like
peppermint. He could taste it in the air. Her lashes fluttered,
her eyes straining to access her peripheral vision. "When it's
done right, it just takes a few seconds before everything
shuts down. Your arms and legs go numb, and you black out."
She was very still. She did not move out of his arms. Instead
she leaned back into him, releasing her weight into his arms,
the back of her head resting in the hollow of his shoulder.
"He left me on the floor," Archie continued. "Blackouts
from a choke hold usually last a few minutes. Assuming
you don't break someone's neck. But when Leo came back,
I was gone. He assumed I had come to, and gotten out of
there."

"But you hadn't," Susan said. She was pressed against
him. Had he pulled her that close, or had she backed into him
more tightly? He could feel the heat between them, clouding
his head. Archie dropped his arms and stepped back. "I didn't
come to until shortly before I saw you this morning," he said.
"About five hours later."

Susan's cheeks were pink. She reached a hand to her neck.
"So how did you get to the boathouse?" she asked, looking
sideways at him.

Archie pointed at the screen.

"Okay, okay." Susan started the video loading again.

They stood together in awkward silence, watching the
status bar.

Seventy-five percent loaded.

Eighty-two percent loaded.

Ninety percent loaded.

An image appeared in the black box. It took a moment
for Archie to orient himself. The footage was at night and in
black-and-white. But the center of the image was well lit by

an outdoor post light, the shadow of a gargoyle, wings out-stretched, alighted on its top. Archie could make out the embankment, part of the dock, the edge of the lake. He could even visualize which corner of the boathouse the camera was mounted to. It was not where he'd awoken that morning, but it was close.

Susan hit the play arrow.

Nothing happened.

"It's not working," Archie said.

"Yes, it is," Susan said. "Nothing's happening, so nothing's happening."

She was right. If he looked closely, he could see the tree branches moving, sequins of light reflected on the lake.

They watched for a few minutes, and then Archie said, "Fast forward."

Susan clicked on the progress arrow and dragged it to the right and the image blinked by faster. Then Archie saw the jerky motions of bodies moving into the frame.

"Stop," he said.

But Susan had already stopped.

They both stared at the frozen image on the screen. Archie tasted something salty and metallic in his mouth. Blood. He had bitten the inside of his cheek. He swallowed and cleared his throat. "Back it up," he said.

The figures on the screen stepped backward out of the frame.

"Hit play again," Archie said.

Susan looked over at him.

"Do it," Archie said.

Susan hit a key.

For a long moment, there was just more nothing. The ferns moved in the night air. The lake sat cold. The dark ground was hard and silent. Archie wasn't sure if the video had sound, but if it did there wasn't any to hear anyway. He kept his eyes fixed on the screen. And then Archie stumbled into the frame. He recognized himself immediately. His head was down, chin knocking against his chest. He had his arm slung around a woman.

Archie's chest tightened. He was only half aware of grabbing the edge of the countertop with his hand to steady himself.

The woman was supporting him, guiding him along, keeping him upright, like someone escorting a drunk home after a bender. She had her arm circled around his waist. Her hair was dark and fell past her shoulders. She was wearing a body-hugging evening gown with a deep V that cut down her chest almost to her navel and a slit that reached halfway up her thigh. Even though the video was in black-and-white, Archie knew that dress was red. The woman led him to the embankment and then lowered him to his knees. He teetered there, kneeling before her, leaning against her legs, until she knelt beside him and guided him gently onto his back on the ground.

She looked up at the camera then. And like a magician revealing a trick, she reached her fingers under the scalp above her forehead and peeled off the dark wig. Her light hair fell to her shoulders and there she was. *Voilà.* Gretchen Lowell.

Archie heard Susan's sharp intake of breath, but he couldn't take his eyes off the screen.

Gretchen said something directly into the camera. Archie could see her lips move.

"Jesus Christ," he heard Susan say. It was muffled, like she'd said it through her hands, like she was covering her mouth.

On the video, Gretchen curled over Archie. The red dress was cut low in the back, and he could see the shadows of her vertebrae coiled over his lifeless body. Gretchen had always had a beautiful back. Elegant. Like a dancer's.

She lowered her head next to his, her hair falling like a blond curtain, swallowing his face. She was talking to him, Archie realized. She was whispering something in his ear. As she did, she walked one hand down his chest and over his groin.

Standing there, in his kitchen, he felt her touch, the flow of blood and warmth as he got hard despite himself. He shifted his position, hoping that Susan wouldn't notice.

Gretchen lay beside him on the ground and moved her hand along the inside of her own leg and up under her dress.

Her hips rocked. An uncomfortable heat swelled in Archie's chest.

Her head was still beside his, as if immersed in their private conversation, but she was clinging to him now, her body wrapped around his like a snake, her hips grinding against the hand she had pinned between her body and his thigh. The tent of his erection as he lay there on the ground was clearly visible. But he couldn't be blamed for how his body responded. Susan must know that.

Archie could hear Susan breathing beside him.

He still couldn't look over at her. He couldn't bear to see her face.

Then Gretchen stood. She hitched her dress up around her waist and kept her eyes on the camera as she stepped around his body and put a high-heeled foot on either side of his head.

She wasn't wearing underwear. Archie could see a thin shadow of pubic hair on her pelvis as she lowered herself down and sat on top of his face. She started grinding herself against him, keeping her own hand working in hard circles, the dress pooled around her waist. Her mouth was open. Her eyes were slits. Her head was tilted back. It didn't take long. Gretchen always came easily. She was like a raw nerve.

Her shoulders jerked forward and her head dropped. She kept rubbing at herself, harder and faster, and then her shoulders heaved again and she drove her fingers up inside between her legs and rolled her head back. He heard Gretchen gasp.

But the video didn't have any sound. It had been Susan's gasp.

Gretchen lifted her head and gazed at the camera with a serene smile. Then she stood up, and let the dress fall around her legs as she stepped away from Archie's body, leaving him unconscious on the ground.

Archie heard Susan moving away from the kitchen bar, stumbling backward. He couldn't move, couldn't turn his head after her. He stared at the screen, the impact of what he was seeing too overwhelming for him to respond.

Susan gasped again, although now Archie recognized the sound for what it was—a retch.

He closed his eyes, blocking it all out. This wasn't happening.

"I'm going to throw up," Susan said.

CHAPTER

31

Henry was pacing. His broad face was tense, jaw muscles bulging, his cheeks flushed. Archie sat on the couch, his legs and arms crossed, wishing he could be somewhere else. Susan sat curled up on the opposite end. The space between them felt impenetrable.

Their laptops, in contrast, sat snugly next to each other on the kitchen bar—Susan's sleek silver Mac, covered in old stickers, and Archie's stoic department-issue black PC. The image on Archie's laptop screen was paused at the point where Gretchen had left the frame and Archie's body lay prone on the ground. Henry had watched the footage when he'd arrived, while Archie and Susan sat on the couch not talking. Susan's green eyes were wide and her lips were half their normal size. She sat cross-legged, her yellow sneakers on the couch, her arms around a red throw pillow she'd pulled onto her lap. She had worried a loose thread at the corner of the pillow until it had formed a puddle of string in her palm, and the pillow's piping had come completely off one side. Archie had liked that pillow, but he hadn't asked her to stop.

Henry stopped pacing and turned to Archie. "Are you sure it's her?" Henry asked.

Archie gave him a tired look.

Henry lowered his head and returned to pacing. "Okay, it's her." He glanced back at Archie. "I guess we know where that hair came from."

"She was on the island," Archie said. He'd known it. He'd said as much to Henry, but he decided that now might not be a good I-told-you-so moment.

Henry put his hands together. "We have all the video files?" he asked.

"I don't know," Archie said. "I think so." He tried to catch Susan's eye, but she remained focused on deconstructing his throw pillow.

"We'll get Ngyun to review them all," Henry said. "See if she appears on any of the others. See if there's any footage of Lisa Watson in there, while we're at it."

Archie nodded, but he didn't think they'd find Gretchen in any of the other footage. Leo or someone on the island had reviewed all the video files before they turned them over, and Leo had only mentioned the boathouse camera.

"This was all for you," Susan said stiffly. Her eyes were on the pillow in her lap. Her fingers were still tugging at the thread. "She risked coming back here, risked getting caught, because it was your birthday," she said.

Henry had stopped pacing. The air in the room felt cold and still.

Archie didn't know what she wanted him to say. It was true. He should have seen it coming. He should have known that Gretchen would use the occasion to make a point. He should have been prepared.

"But it wasn't enough for her to see you," Susan said, pulling out another thread. "She wanted you to know. That's why she sent me that message. That's why she let herself be filmed by the security camera. Why she probably murdered that girl. She wanted you to know that she came back on your birthday." She fixed her gaze on him, eyes like green glass. "She wanted you to see her"—her mouth twisted in disgust—"all over you."

Archie tried to meet her eyes, but found it physically

painful. He searched for something else to look at, anything but her. His hands. The coffee table. Of all the people in the world, Susan was the last Archie would have chosen to see that video, though he would never tell her that. Even Ginger had abandoned him, retreating under the coffee table and staring up at him with abject disappointment. Henry had gotten very interested in something out the window.

"How was this supposed to go, Archie?" Susan demanded. "Did she think you'd like the performance? Are you flattered? Does it turn you on?"

"No," Archie said, his voice cracking. He cleared his throat and took a breath. "No," he said again. He needed to make her understand. His body might betray him when it came to Gretchen, but his mind was clear. But it wasn't enough for Susan. That was evident. She was looking at him with tears in her eyes. He'd seen the same wounded frustration on Debbie's face. That was Gretchen's weapon. He could recover physically, he could give up pills, but he would never be better. "I don't get to have a life without her," he said to Susan. He shrugged helplessly. He couldn't fight the truth anymore. He was too worn-out. "She can find me anytime. She is there. Even when I think I'm alone. She'll never let me go." The words hung in the room. "That's what this was about. That's what she wanted me to know." He said it again: "She will never let me go." He forced himself to hold Susan's gaze, hoping she understood what he was trying to say. "And she sent you that message because she wanted to make sure you knew it, too."

Didn't Susan see it? Gretchen had figured out what Archie had worked so hard to keep from Susan. She knew how much he cared for Susan, and she was taking proactive measures to eliminate the possibility of anything happening between them.

Susan balled up the thread in her hands and flung it on the couch cushion. "You know what I think?" she asked. "I think you cheated on your wife. It ended up blowing up in your face. And you're still beating yourself up for it."

Archie's head hurt. "I think I've paid for that," he said.

"You're not still punishing yourself?" Susan asked.

"For that?" Archie said. "No."

"Then why don't you tell people about the affair?" Susan asked. "You're divorced. I'm not talking about sending out a press release. I mean tell the people on your team. Tell the people running the manhunt. Tell them you had an affair with Gretchen Lowell and that it was a mistake and you regret it. It's part of the story, isn't it? It colors her motivations. Maybe you can help them understand her better so they can catch her. You didn't know she was the Beauty Killer. She seduced you. Everyone would understand that."

Would understand what? That he was a heel? That he'd lied to all of them, then and now? That he'd deserved everything that had happened to him? Archie lifted a hand to his temple.

"That's insane," Henry said from the window. "You don't have to do that," he added to Archie.

"I don't think he can move on until it's out in the open," Susan said.

Archie looked at his hands, hands that had held his children, hands that had moved over every part of Gretchen's body. "It's personal," he said.

"Well, your personal issues affect other people personally," Susan said. "Like Lisa Watson, for instance."

Archie looked up. "Gretchen didn't kill Lisa Watson," he said.

Susan sighed audibly and threw up her hands.

Henry pursed his lips and stood silently for a moment, and then came over and sat down in the chair next to Archie. He scooted the chair close and folded his hands under his chin. "They were both on that island," Henry said. "You said you talked to the victim." He peered over his knuckles at Archie. "Maybe Gretchen saw you and got jealous."

"Gretchen doesn't kill when she gets jealous," Archie said, frustration edging into his voice. He rubbed his face, searching for the words to explain it. "She sees it as a challenge. She wants to win. She wants me to choose her." He thought of how carefully Gretchen had laid the groundwork for the collapse of his marriage. "In Gretchen's mind, killing the competition would be cheating." The more Archie thought about it, the more he was convinced that he was right. "It's been fourteen months since she killed recreationally," he added.

Henry lifted his salt-and-pepper eyebrows. "So we're not counting the serial killer she dismembered two months ago after her escape from the nuthouse?"

"Or the nurse she slaughtered on her way out of that nuthouse?" Susan said.

Archie shook his head. They didn't understand. "Those weren't recreational kills for her. She didn't kill those people for fun; she did it because she had to."

"So it's just, what, a crazy coincidence that Gretchen shows up at a party shortly before one of the guests turns up dead?" Henry asked.

"Think about it," Archie said wearily. "Think of all the Beauty Killer victims we've seen over the years. Remember Sarah Jesudason?"

"The librarian," Henry said.

They had found Jesudason's decapitated body in the back of her 1997 Subaru Outback, and her head in the central library drop box a week later, with a note apologizing for it being overdue.

"Gretchen enjoys killing," Archie said. "She stretches it out. She makes an art out of it. This didn't have any of Gretchen's creativity. Lisa Watson was stabbed and thrown in a lake. No. Gretchen would consider that crass. Below her pay grade."

"She's a murderer," Susan said. "She murders people. She doesn't need a reason. You talk about her like she has rules. Let's not forget that she's a psycho bitch. She made that little tape to prove to you, to all of us, that she can get to you. Anytime she wants. Even on an island crawling with private security guards and cameras mounted everywhere and an FBI surveillance van parked out front. Maybe she wanted to kill someone, and instead of killing you, she killed the first person she came across. It's called bloodlust. She was horny for it." Susan's cheeks were scarlet. "You made her horny. So she murdered Lisa Watson. Maybe she didn't have time to make it"—she paused and her eyes darkened—"fancy. She didn't have time to get creative. Maybe she just wasn't feeling her artistic muse that day. So she just killed her." Susan looked from Archie to Henry. "In the end it doesn't matter how she did it, does it? Lisa Watson is still dead."

"I didn't mean it like that," Archie said. He had put Susan through enough; he didn't want to argue with her about this.

"What did you do after we watched that tape?" Susan asked evenly. "You called Henry. He dropped everything and came right over. You showed him the footage. And you two have been wringing your hands ever since."

"So?" Archie said.

"There's a task force out there hunting Gretchen," Susan asked. "Why didn't you call them?"

Archie fumbled for an answer. "I wanted Henry's take on this first."

"It's been forty minutes since we saw proof that she was on that island last night," Susan said. "That's forty minutes that the cops trying to catch her won't have. Maybe she's long gone by now, I don't know. But I do know that when you see a deranged escaped criminal, you call the police. So they can start looking. So they can set up roadblocks. So they can warn the public. You don't call your friend. You don't sit there like an idiot." Susan peered at him intently. "You do want her caught, right, Archie?"

Archie looked to Henry for support. Henry's eyes went from Susan to Archie. He smoothed his mustache and raised his eyebrows at Archie.

Archie sank back in the sofa. "The video *is* sort of compromising," he said.

"The serial killer humping your face?" Susan said. "Yeah, I'd say so. But you're already compromised, if you hadn't noticed. Now you need to decide what you're going to do about it."

"Do you want to make the call, or should I?" Henry asked Archie.

The truth was Archie didn't think they had a chance of catching Gretchen. She was smarter than all of them. But he wasn't going to admit it.

"I'll do it," Archie said with a sigh, and he pulled his phone out of his pocket and dialed.

CHAPTER

32

The crime scene investigator was named Gary. He was in his thirties, Archie guessed, with a slight build and thick dark hair that would have fallen just above his shoulders if it hadn't been pulled back in a ponytail. A feathering of dark hair on his chin appeared to mark the early stages of a goatee.

Archie shifted his weight and the plastic sheeting under his bare feet crinkled.

"Will this take much longer?" Archie asked, clearing his throat.

"If you keep squirming," Gary said.

On the other side of the bedroom door, Archie could hear the others having a hushed, heated discussion, but Gary seemed impervious. Archie couldn't make out many words, but he recognized Sanchez's voice as one of the loudest.

At first it had been a relief when Gary had shown up. At least Archie got to leave the room.

Gary ran a latex-clad finger over the back of Archie's bare thigh and Archie felt his gluteal muscle reflexively tense.

He had been picked clean by CSU before. Just two months ago, after a bomb strapped to a man had gone off, splattering Archie with a pink soup of flesh and bone, Archie had spent an hour being culled for evidence.

But this was different.

He was naked, standing on a plastic sheet, while a fully clothed man knelt in front of him. It was, to put it mildly, a bit more invasive.

Gary touched a mole on Archie's thigh and then peered at it through a magnifying glass like it might be a clue.

"That's me," Archie said with a sigh. "I've had that my whole life."

Gary nodded. His prominent nose was offset with deep-set large dark eyes and eyelashes like Elizabeth Taylor's. If he managed to grow the goatee, it would look good.

Archie stole a glance at his bedside clock. It was after nine. He shifted his weight again.

"I took a shower this morning," Archie said.

"You already said that," Gary said. "And then I said it was still worth harvesting evidence, and then you objected to my use of the word *harvesting*."

Archie remembered that now.

"Are you uncomfortable?" Gary asked.

"I'm naked," Archie said. He was finding himself in this situation a little too regularly for comfort.

"It won't be much longer," Gary said. He got to his feet and focused his attention on Archie's neck. The stray fine hairs at Gary's hairline fluttered every time Archie exhaled. Archie tried to remain perfectly still. It was hard to be still. Every one of Archie's knuckles suddenly needed cracking. His nose itched. He wanted to stretch. He was cold. Gary produced a pair of tweezers and plucked something off Archie's skin and deposited it in a plastic bag. Gary had done that four times so far, and each time the item he'd pulled off Archie had been so minuscule that Archie couldn't see it at all.

"What's that?" Archie asked.

Gary shrugged. "Probably nothing," he said. He tucked the bag into his crime scene kit and returned with a small black plastic comb and then settled onto his heels in front of Archie. "I'm going to comb your pubic hair," he said.

Archie wasn't sure how to respond to that, so he tried to remain stoic as Gary drew the comb through Archie's pubic hair in short swift strokes, stopping after each stroke to examine the comb for any errant hairs. When Gary saw hairs on the comb he eased them into an evidence bag. After thirty or so strokes, he sealed the bag, wrote something on it, and stowed it in his crime scene kit.

When Gary turned back to Archie he was holding what looked like a six-inch-long Q-tip.

Archie had a bad feeling about this. He took a small step back.

"We use this to perform two tests," Gary said, wiggling the Q-tip. "We use it to swab the shaft and glans of the penis to search for traces of vaginal mucus, and we also insert it into the urethra to collect a sample for STD testing."

"Excuse me?" Archie said. His mouth felt very dry.

"It's protocol," Gary said. "For a full examination."

"It's unnecessary," Archie said emphatically. "Because I did not have sex with her."

Gary pursed his lips. "It's my understanding you don't remember much of last night, yes?" he said. "So you can't be sure, can you?"

Archie drew his hands through his hair. He hadn't considered the possibility that he'd had sex with Gretchen last night or that there had been anything more to the evening than what the tape showed. But he had lost five hours, and the tape only accounted for two minutes of that. He was barely conscious in the boathouse footage, but who's to say what state he'd been in before that? He wanted to believe he hadn't had sex with her. But at the same time he couldn't put it past himself, not with their history. He knew himself well enough to know that.

Archie eyed the Q-tip pinched between Gary's latex-clad fingers. "We have to do both tests?" he asked.

Gary considered the Q-tip. "It's possible we could get away with just the one," he said.

"Which one?" Archie asked quickly.

"Do you have a preference?" Gary asked.

Archie raised an eyebrow. Wasn't it obvious?

"Are you concerned about STDs?" Gary asked.

"Right now?" Archie said. He had never been less concerned about STDs. "Not at all."

Gary smiled. "Then I'll just swab your penis, then," he said pleasantly.

"Fine," Archie said, relieved. He lifted his hands to his hips and looked over Gary's shoulder at the wall.

Gary put the penlight back in his mouth and lowered out of Archie's sight. Archie kept his eyes focused dead ahead, cringing as the dry fuzzy end of the Q-tip tickled lightly along the shaft and then around the tip of his penis. It was over quickly. Gary did it expertly, like he swabbed penises thirty times a day. Archie exhaled the breath he had been holding and Gary dropped the Q-tip into a plastic vial.

"Does it ever *not* work?" Archie asked.

"What?" Gary asked, looking up.

"You threatened to jam the stick up my dick so I'd agree to the swab," Archie said.

Gary lowered his head, but Archie could see he was smiling. "You could have refused."

"But I didn't," Archie said.

"But you didn't," Gary said, still smiling. He picked up his pen and started writing something on the label of the plastic vial. "You can put on your pants now," he said, not looking up.

Archie stepped off the plastic sheeting, picked up his underwear off the bed and pulled them on, and did the same with his pants. He was starting to put on his shirt when Gary stopped him.

"Not so fast," Gary said. "I still need a blood draw."

Archie tossed the button-down aside and sat on the edge of the bed, his bare feet on the floor.

Gary took a seat next to him and crossed Archie's forearm over his knees. He tied a urine-yellow rubber tourniquet around Archie's upper arm, letting it snap tightly into place, and then wiped the inside of Archie's elbow with iodine. "You have nice veins," Gary said.

"I've been told that before," Archie said.

Gary tossed the used cotton ball in a small orange biohazard bag and then produced a hypodermic syringe from his kit. He took the cap off the needle.

"What will they test for?" Archie asked.

"I expect they'll run a general tox screen as well as some tests for more specific drugs along the line of what she's used in the past," Gary said.

Gary slid the needle into Archie's vein. Archie watched as his blood filled the hypodermic's barrel. Opiates would show up on any basic tox screen, and Archie knew he'd started last night with plenty of pills. "I took some Vicodin last night," Archie told Gary. Then there were the two he'd chewed when he'd come to on the riverbank. "And this morning," Archie added

"Okay," Gary said.

"I just thought I should mention it," Archie said.

Gary withdrew the needle and pressed a cotton ball in the crook of Archie's elbow and bent the arm closed around it. "You better spend some time thinking about what you're going to tell them when they ask about it," he said. He gave Archie a meaningful look and then glanced toward the closed door. "We're done," he called.

Archie was still buttoning his shirt when he walked into the living room. Everyone stopped what they were doing and looked at him. Raul Sanchez sat on Archie's sofa with Bob Eaton, the chief of police. Martin Ngyun had Susan's laptop on his knees on a stool at the kitchen bar, and Claire was standing close to Henry by the window. Susan had the refrigerator door open. She was the only one who didn't look up. She was pulling bread and peanut butter out of the fridge, clearly intent on making a sandwich.

Archie forced himself to look around the room, to meet all of their eyes, until, one by one, the heads turned back to what they had been doing.

There had been more, at first. Archie had counted seventeen cops in his small apartment when Gary had escorted him into the bedroom. Then Henry had explained the sensitive nature of the video, and all nonessential personnel had been asked to leave. Archie imagined them all home posting status updates on Facebook, publicly wondering what new humiliation Archie Sheridan had suffered now.

"How are you doing?" Eaton asked from the couch. Archie couldn't remember the last time he'd seen the chief out of uniform, but tonight he was in street clothes—a blue Columbia Sportswear jacket, jeans that looked ironed, and a button-down shirt that was open at the collar. One of his hiking boots had come unlaced.

"I've just had my penis swabbed, Bob, how are you doing?" Archie said.

Eaton coughed uncomfortably. His hair was entirely white, but the light reflecting off his jacket tinted it with blue. "This is . . ." Eaton flailed helplessly. "This is . . ." He looked around the room, but nobody came to his aid. What was there to say? Archie could think of a few things: *This is . . . humiliating, demeaning, degrading, denigrating, mortifying.* But Eaton wasn't really a word man. He squinted at Archie and Archie almost felt sorry for him. "Do you need to talk to someone about this?" Eaton asked.

They were all looking at Archie again, except for Susan, who was spreading peanut butter on a piece of wheat bread. Archie could smell the peanut butter from across the room.

"Am I supposed to be traumatized?" Archie asked. This was exactly what he'd wanted to avoid, all of those eyes brimming with concern, as if he'd survived some ordeal. "You know what's traumatizing?" Archie lifted his shirt, exposing the thick scar that ran up his midsection. "Having your spleen forcibly removed without anesthesia. *That's* traumatizing." He directed his chin toward his laptop, which still sat open on the kitchen bar. "That, right there, is cuddling."

He had already decided that he was going to tell them. Now he swallowed hard and made himself go through with it. "Look," he said. "Some of you know this." He glanced across the room at Susan, who peeked up from her sandwich. "The rest of you have at least heard rumors, so I'll just be clear." He shut his eyes. It was the only way he could say it. "I had an affair with her."

"Archie," Henry said sharply, "stop."

Archie could feel the weight of everyone's attention; it made his neck burn. *An affair? Was that even the right word?* Archie opened his eyes. "Gretchen Lowell and I had a sexual relationship during the period she infiltrated the investigation," he said. The words tumbled out now. He lifted his hand, the one without the ring. "You'll notice that I'm no longer married." The apartment was completely silent. Claire threaded her hand through Henry's, but Archie could tell from her expression that his confession hadn't been news to her. He wondered what, if anything, Henry had told her and what she'd figured out on her own. "That's what she's doing on the tape," he said. "Reliving old times."

He'd done it.

He stole a glance at Susan. She was on the other side of the kitchen bar, facing him, eyebrows raised, frozen, with a piece of bread in one hand and a butter knife in the other.

Ngyun was facing Susan's laptop screen, his features bathed in its blue light. But his hands weren't moving over the keys, and his mouth was open.

Sanchez cleared his throat. He had his palms together, his fingertips touching his lip. "Well, shit," he said quietly.

But Eaton was the only one who looked truly, utterly surprised. He was looking at Archie with abject astonishment. Apparently not everyone had heard the rumors after all.

"You slept with her?" Eaton sputtered. "With Gretchen Lowell?"

Archie met his eye. There was no going back now. "We had sex, yes," he said. "Many times."

"When did it end?" Eaton asked.

"She locked me in a basement and tortured me," Archie said, deflecting the question. "What do you think?"

Eaton turned to Henry, who was shaking his head at the floor. "You knew about this?" Eaton asked him.

"Not at the time," Archie said quickly before Henry could answer.

"She seduced him, Bob," Henry said, crossing the living room to take the chair nearest Eaton. "He was under a lot of pressure, remember?" Henry scratched the back of his head. The chair creaked. "Overworked. Exhausted. He was vulnerable. She knew that." He touched his mustache. "She did it to fuck with all of us," he said.

"It hasn't been easy for Archie," Claire said. She walked over and stood behind Henry. "It was a mistake," she said, giving Archie a supportive smile. "He's been punished enough for it."

Archie didn't deserve their support, but he was grateful for it.

Eaton hunched forward and studied his hands. Sanchez zipped up his FBI windbreaker and then unzipped it, and then zipped it up again. The room was so quiet Archie could hear the fridge humming. Susan perched cross-legged with her shoes on his counter, holding her sandwich with both hands, her eyes doing her own survey of the room and studiously avoiding his.

"Is that why she let you live?" Eaton asked.

"I honestly have no idea why she let me live," Archie said.

Sanchez leaned back against the couch and stuffed his hands in his jacket pockets. "Why make this confession now?"

Archie shrugged. "I don't care who knows anymore."

"Like any one of you wouldn't have fucked her given half the chance," Claire said with a snort. Henry shot her a look. "What?" she said with a shrug. "It's true."

"They want to keep a lid on it," Susan said from the kitchen, a biteful of sandwich in her cheek. "That's what they've been talking about while you were in there. They think warning people she's back will cause a panic."

The lightness in Archie's arms vanished. He looked around the room, stunned, waiting for someone to contradict her. Keep a lid on the fact that the Beauty Killer was back? They had to warn people—if not for the public's protection, then to help apprehend Gretchen. Someone might spot her.

"Good to see you're feeling better," Sanchez said to Susan, narrowing his eyes.

"Thanks," she said, coloring slightly. "The Midol really helped."

"You can't keep a lid on this," Archie said to Eaton. Gretchen had designed this scenario after all, of that Archie was certain. And if Gretchen expected them to stay tight-lipped, the only proper response was to shout her presence from the rooftops. "You're going to issue a statement, right, Bob?"

"Do you know what tomorrow is?" Eaton asked. The lines in his face seemed to deepen. "It's Halloween."

Halloween. Archie shook his head and smiled. She couldn't have planned it better. "Of course it is," Archie said. He moved around to the chair across from Henry and sat down.

Sanchez looked like he was waiting for him to say something.

"What's so funny?" Sanchez asked.

"You think this is a coincidence?" Archie asked him. "Her coming back now?"

"You have to warn people," Susan said from the kitchen. "You have to make an announcement."

"She's right," Archie said.

"So, what?" Sanchez asked. "So they can lock their doors?"

Archie looked across the coffee table at Henry, who was sitting quite still. He'd been noticeably silent on the subject.

"Henry's with us on this," Sanchez said.

Henry's pale eyes looked tired. He spread his palms plaintively. "People will keep their kids home from trick-or-treating," he said to Archie. "There will be people in costume. People dressed up like Gretchen, for Christ's sake. It's a recipe for panic. You know that there will be drunk jackasses who take a shot at the first girl in a blond wig they see."

Claire offered Archie an apologetic shrug. "If she doesn't know we know she's in the area, it gives us an edge," she said. "We can catch her."

Archie looked around. These people were all smart, all dedicated. How could they all be so wrong?

"She knows," Archie said, exasperated. He lifted his hand toward his laptop. "Look at her. She knows she's being filmed."

"She doesn't know you've even seen the tape," Sanchez said. "She doesn't know you've shared it with us."

Susan was still on his counter, eating her sandwich. She paused and shook some crumbs off her orange T-shirt, and then brushed them off her purse, which sat gaping open next to her. She was being uncharacteristically calm about all this, Archie noticed. She'd offered a few pronouncements, sure, but there'd been no bitter pleading, no dramatics.

Her purse hadn't been on the counter earlier.

Archie raised an eyebrow at her.

Susan shrugged.

"It's moot," Archie announced to the group.

"What the fuck is that supposed to mean?" Sanchez asked.

Susan took a bite of her sandwich and chewed.

"It's already done, isn't it?" Archie asked Susan. "Who'd you go to?"

Susan swallowed. "The *Herald*," she said. "It'll be up on their Web site as soon as they can confirm some of the details."

Henry put his head back and closed his eyes. Claire said, "Oops." Eaton and Sanchez turned the same shade of purple, and Sanchez shot Archie an accusatory look.

"Hey," Archie said, putting up his hands. "I'm not the one who didn't take away her phone."

Archie's bedroom door opened and they all looked as

Gary emerged, carrying a metal case. He stopped short, took in the scene, and then glanced back at the bedroom door, like he might turn around and go back through it.

"You done?" Sanchez asked him.

Gary held up the case and tapped it. "Got everything I need," he said.

"Okay, go," Sanchez said. "And Gary," he added, picking at something in the corner of his eye. "Use a pseudonym instead of Detective Sheridan's name, okay?"

Gary nodded. He stood there for a moment in uncomfortable silence and then said, "Well . . ." The word tapered off. He looked around the room and then cleared his throat and made a beeline for his coat. He was still pulling it on as he went through the front door.

They all swiveled to look at Susan now. She was chewing. The room smelled like peanut butter. "What did you tell them exactly?" Henry asked.

Susan made them wait until she swallowed. "That there was security footage of Gretchen in Lake Oswego last night," she said. "I left Archie out of it."

"Good," Henry said. He turned back to the room. "We keep the content to ourselves. As far as anyone else is concerned, the footage shows Gretchen Lowell alone."

"We have to respond," Sanchez said. "Roadblocks. Helicopters. We should send out a statement advising the public to remain calm. Get all the patrol units on the roads. What's the reward at?"

"Half a million," Archie said.

Sanchez raised an eyebrow at him.

"I saw a billboard," Archie said.

"Anything you need, you let me know," Eaton told Sanchez. "The mayor has your back." He jabbed a finger at Susan. "You, lady, are banned from all my press conferences."

"Oh," Susan said, drawing her face into a frown. "I'm heartbroken." She winked at Archie.

Archie couldn't quite believe it, but Susan had done it. She had forced the issue. If he'd been standing next to her, he would have actually kissed her. He moved his eyes away from her. *On the forehead.*

Henry scratched his neck. "What about that thing earlier?" he asked Sanchez.

"About Casanova, here?" Sanchez said with a glance at Archie. "Obviously Gretchen's got a hard-on for him. She let him live, which was certainly a romantic gesture. So he fucked her," he said with a shrug. "She's a world-class piece of ass. I think that Claire made a good point."

"Men are ruled by their dicks," Claire said.

"That's another way of putting it," Sanchez said. "What I mean is, it doesn't change anything as far as I'm concerned." He looked at Archie. "You remember any pillow talk that might help us locate her?"

"No," Archie said.

Sanchez sat back and stretched one arm along the back of the couch. "Then it stays in this room," he announced.

Archie couldn't quite believe what he was hearing. Was Sanchez really going to let this go?

"Good," Henry said. "So, we're all agreed?" His eyes landed on Eaton.

Eaton's head was down. He was looking at his hands, twisting the gold band on his ring finger. He glanced over at Archie and nodded.

"I'm in," Claire said, laying a hand on Henry's shoulder.

"Me, too," Susan said from the counter with her mouth full.

Only Ngyun was left. He was still on the stool by the kitchen bar, bent over Susan's laptop. Archie could hear the sounds of his fingers on the keyboard.

"Ngyun?" Henry said loudly.

Ngyun looked up from Susan's laptop, startled. "Sorry," he said. "I wasn't listening."

Henry smiled and scratched at the corner of his mouth. "Archie's personal life stays in this room," he said.

"Yeah, sure, whatever," Ngyun said, eyes returning to the keyboard.

Archie didn't know what to say. He heard the sound of an incoming text and saw Henry go for his pocket. Archie was still composing a speech a moment later when Henry stood up quickly. He held his phone out, showing an incoming text.

"The warrants just got signed," Henry announced, grinning. "We've got teams mobilized around the island."

"I'm going to pee," Claire said, darting for the bathroom. The island? They were going to storm the island?

"She's not still on the fucking island," Archie groaned.

But they were all standing, checking their phones, putting on their jackets.

Archie started to get up but Sanchez leaned forward and put a hand on his arm. "You're staying here," Sanchez said. "The first thing I did after watching your little sex tape was to station a unit downstairs, one in front of your family's building, and one at Ms. Ward's house."

Archie could tell by his demeanor that there was no arguing. Sanchez was running the show.

"Where's your weapon?" Sanchez asked.

"Desk drawer," Archie said.

Sanchez walked to Archie's desk, opened the drawer, and withdrew the gun. He checked the magazine for bullets and then walked it back and laid it on the coffee table in front of Archie.

Ngyun appeared next to Sanchez, carrying Susan's open laptop. Stickers and decals plastered the back of the screen. HELLO KITTY. MARY'S CLUB. FOOD FIGHT. PEACE, LOVE, AND CUPCAKES. The ubiquitous outline of the state of Oregon with a green heart at its center.

"I'm going to need to keep this overnight," Ngyun said to Sanchez. "There's malware on it, all right, a RAP. That's a remote administration tool. They can embed these Trojan horses in all sorts of things. It was probably attached to something Susan downloaded, a game, maybe."

"I told you I haven't downloaded anything weird from the Internet," Susan called from the kitchen.

"You also haven't updated your operating system in four years," Ngyun called back. He looked down at Archie. "I should check all your computers," he added. "I can start with your laptop tonight."

"Don't bother," Archie said. If he was going to be stuck there all night, he at least wanted to be able to sort through some of the island's security footage. "I'll bring it into the office tomorrow. I hardly even use it. I never download anything onto it." Archie's mind went to his work machine and his stomach turned. That computer had all sorts of sensitive files on it. If she'd managed to hack into that, she'd have access to all his e-mails, investigation files, and gateways to other law enforcement databases. "Start with my desktop," he told Ngyun.

Henry stepped next to Ngyun and Sanchez and handed Ngyun the flash drive from Leo. "Take this," Henry said. "You can check it for malware. And we're going to need all the footage reviewed. Look for anything relating to Gretchen or Lisa Watson or"—he looked at Archie—"anything else."

Archie glanced back at his laptop on the kitchen bar. It had gone to screen saver, a black universe filled with stars. He'd never actually downloaded any of the security footage. There went his plan for the evening.

Susan crawled across the bar and pulled her hooded sweatshirt off the stool she'd draped it over, nearly knocking Archie's computer off the counter in the process. "Be careful with that," she called as Ngyun walked by carrying her laptop in his shoulder bag. "I've got, like, eight unfinished novels on that thing."

There was an anticipatory energy in the room. Ginger scampered around from person to person, sure that one of these people putting on hats and jackets would be taking her for a walk. Claire walked back from the bathroom, pulling on her dark blue watch cap, touching Henry's arm as she swept past on her way to retrieve her coat from the coat rack. It was taking all of Archie's control to stay sitting in that chair. He knew they wouldn't find anything, but he still itched to be going along.

"I'll call you," Henry said.

Archie took a breath and nodded.

Susan bounced up next to Henry. She had her hood up and her purse strap across her chest. The R in WORST on her orange T-shirt had a glob of peanut butter on it.

"Where do you think you're going?" Henry asked her.

"With you?" she said brightly.

Archie coughed.

Henry crossed his arms. He'd lost weight since his hospital stay, but he was still broad and he could still look scary.

"Home?" Susan guessed again.

"Straight home," Archie said.

Henry looked at Susan and then at Archie. "It won't be so bad," he said. "Watch TV or something,"

Susan and Archie eyed each other warily. Her hair had dried and looked curlier than usual. It made her face look softer. She reached up and scratched at a tiny pimple on her forehead. Archie put his hand out and wiped the peanut butter off Susan's T-shirt with his finger. She gave him a half smile.

"Walk her to her car," Archie said to Henry.

"You heard the man," Henry said to Susan, giving her a push toward the door.

Archie watched as they all gathered.

Sanchez held back, engaged in an e-mail or text. When he finished, instead of heading for the others, he came over and squatted next to the arm of Archie's chair. He pulled out his tin of mints and offered it to Archie. Archie shook his head. Sanchez put a mint in his mouth, closed the tin, and stowed it.

"Tell me something," Sanchez said. "You ever step out on Debbie before?"

"No," Archie said. "Not before Gretchen."

"And the one time you do, it's with a serial killer?" Sanchez said, his face glowing. "You poor fuck."

"Yeah," Archie said.

Sanchez was shaking his head, amazed, the white mint clenched between his teeth.

"Thanks," Archie said. "For earlier."

Sanchez scooted forward and the bill of his FBI cap

grazed Archie's forehead. "Leo told you I'm dirty, didn't he?" he said.

"Let's go," Henry called from the door.

Archie kept his face neutral, barely daring to breathe.

Sanchez nodded, reading Archie's reaction as affirmation. "Hm," he said.

The others were talking by the door, immersed in their own discussion.

Sanchez's eyebrows knitted. "We've known each other, what, fifteen years?" he said quietly. "You really believe for a second I'd do something like that?" Archie didn't know what to say. Sanchez exhaled slowly. His breath was warm peppermint. "I'd tell you I'm not," he said. Then he shrugged with a laugh. "But I guess I'd tell you that either way, right?" He laid a hand on Archie's shoulder as he stood up. Then he turned and headed for the door to catch up with the others. Archie watched them all leave. Then the door closed, and he was alone. The smell of Sanchez's mint hung in the air.

Archie got up and walked over to his empty kitchen. Susan had left four pieces of sandwich crust sitting out on his counter. He picked up a piece of crust and put in his mouth. The sky was dark. Dead leaves stuck to the factory windowpanes. He couldn't figure out where those dead leaves came from—there weren't any trees around. Flashes of red and blue light bounced off the glass as the patrol cars down below pulled away from the curb. Archie ate the rest of Susan's crust. The bread was stale and stuck in his throat.

It was going to start again. Once the story broke it would be Gretchen Lowell 24–7 as far as the media was concerned. Every cop in the city would be looking for her. Archie knew how this worked. The press would get on board with the idea that Gretchen had murdered Lisa Watson. They would run with it. And in the distraction of a citywide manhunt, Lisa Watson's real killer would go free.

Archie couldn't allow that to happen.

He punched a number into his phone.

Robbins picked up right away. "Morgue," he said.

"It's me," Archie said. "Have you started the Lisa Watson autopsy yet?"

"First thing tomorrow morning," Robbins said. "I've had a shooting, a house fire, a bat attack, a jumper off the Fremont Bridge, and two car accidents today."

"A bat attack?" Archie said. He heard the familiar wet slurp of a latex-clad hand removing an organ from an open abdomen. Most people were in bed and Robbins was in the middle of an autopsy.

"Two kids found an injured bat, took it home, and then died of rabies," Robbins said. Archie recognized the spring of a metal scale as Robbins laid an organ on it to be weighed.

"Well, call me as soon as you're done tomorrow, okay?" Archie said. "It's important."

"It's always important," Robbins said, sounding unimpressed. "But sure, you got it."

Archie heard the organ slide into a plastic bag. "This time, it really is important," Archie said. He might not be able to go after Gretchen, but he could make sure that Lisa Watson's murder didn't get lost in the shuffle. He could do that.

Robbins sighed. "Okay," he said.

Archie hung up and went and sat down wearily on the couch. A piece of the red thread stuck to the seat cushion next to him, a casualty of Susan's attack on his throw pillow. Archie brushed the thread into his hand and transferred it carefully to the coffee table and stared at it. Ginger came out from under the coffee table, hopped up on the couch, set her chin on his lap, and started licking the peanut butter off his fingers.

Archie knew what he had to do. He studied his phone, and mentally rehearsed what he was going to say.

The next call was going to be harder, but he wanted Debbie to hear it from him, before she heard it from the *Herald*.

CHAPTER

33

Susan sat in her Saab watching as the police cars parked around her pulled away and headed south toward Lake Oswego. With its wide streets and half-empty warehouses, the produce district always looked particularly empty at night. She cranked up the heat. The radio was reporting that a young woman had been found dead in Lake Oswego and that police were investigating. Susan listened intently. The story was oblique—they didn't name Lisa Watson, and there was no reference to Gretchen. They described the death as a "suspicious drowning." The radio announcer went on to another story, some remains had been found up river—they thought it might be a flood victim. Susan stared at the car radio, a flutter of excitement in her chest. Any minute now, the *Herald* would go live with the story that Gretchen Lowell was back in the area, and then the around-the-clock coverage would begin. There would be no time for any other story then.

A knock on Susan's car window made her jump.

Henry's hulking figure loomed outside. He had delivered her to her car by the elbow, deposited her inside, and then closed the driver's-side door. She'd thought he'd continued to his own car. Now she wondered if he'd been standing there this whole time.

He probably had.

She turned down the radio and rolled down the window. The knob had come off the window crank, so this took a lot of effort.

Henry pointed at the LOADING ONLY sign adjacent to the hood of her car.

"I know," she said quickly. She had parked in the loading zone because it was the closest spot to the door and she'd been rattled enough when she got there that she didn't want to walk half a block in the dark by herself. "Sorry. I was in a hurry."

A gray sedan stopped in the street behind Henry, its headlights slicing through the darkness. "Henry," Sanchez's voice called, "you're riding with Claire, right?"

Henry looked over his shoulder. "Yeah," he said. "See you there." Sanchez peeled away and Henry turned back to Susan. "Straight home," Henry said. He hesitated. "You want me to follow you?"

Susan glanced around at the desolate surroundings. Maybe it wasn't so insane to let Henry give her an escort, just for his peace of mind.

"Say the word," Henry said. "They can do this without me."

Claire's Ford Fiesta pulled up behind Henry and stopped where Sanchez had just been. Claire idled there, waiting.

Henry raised his eyebrows questioningly at Susan.

She was being an idiot. It was only a few miles. And there were cops at the other end. "I'm fine," Susan said. She gave Henry a small salute. "Straight home. Promise."

"Okay," Henry said. He looked up, over her car, at Archie's building for a moment, and then he tapped the hood of her car with his hand. "Go," he said.

Susan nodded and pulled away from the curb, turning the radio up as she did. Sam Cooke's husky croon came over the speakers. As she drove away she watched in the rearview mirror as Henry climbed into Claire's Fiesta and the tail-lights disappeared into the night.

Archie had warned Henry about Sanchez, right?

Susan bobbed her head along to the Sam Cooke song.

Something glinted on the dashboard as she passed a streetlight. Susan swiped her finger along the spot and then brought it close to her face and peered at it. Her finger was dark with dust —she really had to buy some Armor All—and in the middle of the dirt was a single speck of gold glitter. That was the thing with glitter; it got everywhere. But she still couldn't figure out where this bit had come from. She rubbed the dust and the glitter off on her pants and sucked in her breath as she glanced up.

Susan slammed on her brakes and the car jolted to a stop, jerking Susan against her seat belt. She heard a mountain of crap from her backseat slide onto the floor behind her.

Princess Leia was pulling a *Star Wars* stormtrooper across Water Avenue. Susan had nearly hit them, but neither was acknowledging that fact. The stormtrooper was drunk. He was carrying a can of beer. Princess Leia had a cigarette in one hand. It was Halloween Eve, Susan reminded herself. They were probably on their way to a party. Her pounding heart was slowing now. The businesses along that stretch—industrial buildings housing microbrew tasting rooms and restaurants and kayak shops—were closed, and the street-lights were placed far apart and left much of the street dark-ened. But there could be a party in one of the warehouses.

Princess Leia and the stormtrooper continued stumbling up a side street and Susan continued along Water Avenue, white-knuckling the wheel, keeping her eye out for costumed revelers who might decide to dart in front of traffic.

Susan could just make out the giant red neon OMSI sign up ahead, and the sight of it made her relax a bit. The Ore-gon Museum of Science and Industry was closed, but its brick façade was a reassuring landmark. The road home was just past it.

She had never really noticed before how empty this route

was at night. A sea of empty museum parking lots stretched alongside the street. You could never find parking at OMSI when you needed it. Now Susan wished the parking lots weren't so big. Sam Cooke was still singing. It was a long song.

FRANKIE REACHED DOWN IN HER POCKETBOOK
AND UP WITH A LONG FORTY-FOUR
SHE SHOT ONCE, TWICE, THREE TIMES AND
JOHNNY FELL TO THE HARD WOOD FLOOR
AW, HE WAS A MAN ALRIGHT
BUT FRANKIE SHOT HIM BECAUSE
HE WAS DOING HER WRONG.

Something else slid off the backseat onto the floor.

Susan was used to that. When you kept as much crap in your car as she did, you got accustomed to some shifting. Half-empty Snapple bottles rolled under the seat. Books and glossy magazines slid around. Plastic water bottles knocked together. She had rubber boots in her car, extra jackets, two canvas camp chairs, about twenty reusable grocery store bags, old notebooks, pens and pencils, used paper coffee cups, tubes of lipstick in a rainbow of colors, and probably a hundred dollars in change.

BUT THE LAST THING HE TOLD HER WAS
FRANKIE, YOU KNOW I LOVE YOU
WHY? HONEY WHY DID YOU —

The music stopped.

"Breaking news," an announcer cut in briskly. "The *Oregon Herald* is reporting that escaped serial killer Gretchen Lowell was spotted in Lake Oswego late last night. Police officials say they are investigating but do not have any public comment at this time."

The car jerked and then let out a slow, mournful whine.

"No," Susan said out loud. "No, no, no."

A red light was blinking on the dash readout. That light

had never come on before. She didn't know what it meant. What did it mean?

The car was coughing to a stop, the radio announcer's voice coming in and out. "Dangerous." "Escaped." "Precautions." Susan steered it to the side of the street, just as the Saab's engine gave one last death rattle and died. As it did, all the lights—dash lights, headlights—went off, too, and the radio went deathly silent. It was suddenly very dark and very quiet.

She pulled her purse onto her lap and started digging for her phone. Her hand found a box of gum, a compact, a notebook. Why did she have so much stuff that was the same size as a cell phone? Then her hand tightened around her iPhone. She pulled it out. It lit up under her touch, and she wanted to cry at the sight of that comforting retina display glow. She touched the telephone icon and the number keys appeared. She touched one key.

There was a knock on her window.

Susan looked up, and a paralyzing terror gripped her by the throat.

CHAPTER

34

Henry stood in Jack Reynolds's front yard, his weight mostly on his good leg. The other leg bothered him more than he let on most days, but he thought he did a pretty good job of hiding it. He squinted as the police choppers overhead sent another blizzard of fall leaves swirling up in their searchlight beams. He'd already gotten leaf debris in his eye. The air settled and the noise and light passed. Two choppers were circling the little island; a third searched the perimeter of the lake. Judging by the residential lights on around the lake, no one was asleep. Once the news got out about Gretchen, cops from every surrounding county had started showing up. Flashing lights stretched along the island's private road as far as Henry could see. State cops. City cops. FBI vehicles. Henry lifted a hand to shield his eyes from another passing chopper. The searchlight blazed around him for a moment, and a gust of wind flattened the grass at his feet. Then the chopper continued onward, passing over four crime scene investigators who were hauling equipment across the grounds in the direction of the boathouse. The churned-up air from the chopper blades made their white Tyvek suits flap like plastic bags in the wind. The grass rippled. Then it fell dark again. The earsplitting chug of the chopper engine faded. Henry glanced back at the Tudor manse, which was lit up like Christmas. Patrol cops ran in and out of the house, one hand on their hats every time a chopper passed overhead. Henry shook his head. It looked like the invasion of Grenada.

Jack Reynolds chuckled.

Henry looked over at him. Jack was still in the Thurston Howell getup, but had added a plaid wool scarf that made him look even more ridiculous. He had come out of the house a few minutes before, drinking something fancy out of a crystal lowball glass and smoking a cigar.

"What's so funny?" Henry asked. Landscape lighting peppered the grounds, but the part of the yard they were in was dark except for a light planted in the grass at their feet that lit Jack from below, so that he was all cheekbones and jaw. Henry knew he was probably similarly lit, but he was pretty sure he looked less like Dracula.

"She's not here," Jack said. "I'm not sure what they think they're going to find."

"You sent Leo to Archie with the footage," Henry said. He knew it was a reckless play, saying it outright. But Henry wanted to see how Jack would react. "You had to know this was coming," Henry added.

Jack's grin spread. "I had my people review all the security footage after the two of you left this afternoon," he said. He lifted his glass to his lips. "Being the responsible citizen that I am." He savored the alcohol in his mouth and then swallowed it. It was whiskey, Henry could smell it. "I didn't want to be harboring evidence of a murder," Jack said with a shrug. "Plus, I can't have someone slaughtering my party guests—even the ones who aren't officially invited. It doesn't look good. I don't want to get a reputation as a bad host." He bent his head and looked down into his glass, swirling it absentmindedly. "Plus, I wanted to see what Archie would do."

It was Henry's turn to chuckle. Of course Jack wouldn't

turn over any sort of evidence to the cops unless there was something in it for him. "You thought he'd bury it," Henry said.

"Shit, yes," Jack said with a sharp laugh. "I thought he'd throw that flash drive in the river. That's what I would have done. How about you? Most people wouldn't want that kind of thing getting out. You see the video? I got a hard-on just watching it."

Jack was goading him, but Henry wasn't going to take the bait. "So Archie was supposed to destroy the footage," Henry said, "and then you'd have had a nice piece of blackmail material in your back pocket."

Jack put his hand over his heart. "Of course I would hope I'd never need to use it," he said.

"Of course," Henry said.

Another chopper went by overhead, and the air was briefly full of shredded leaves. Jack's scarf whipped in the wind.

"But it turns out that Archie Sheridan is actually the Boy Scout everyone says he is," Jack said. He had to shout to be heard over the chopper engine.

"We both know that's not true, don't we, Jack?" Henry shouted back.

"I find that I hear conflicting reports on that topic," Jack said.

The chopper passed and the wind stopped. Jack picked a piece of dead leaf out of his glass and flicked it away.

"You're a ball of contradictions yourself," Henry said. "This afternoon you refused to turn over the security footage we politely asked for without a warrant. Now look at us. You've turned over the tapes. You've got half the cops in the county crawling all over your property. And as far as I can tell, you don't seem that unnerved by it."

Jack leaned slightly forward and the yellow light from the landscaping fixture carved deeper into his face. His eyes, though, were still shadowed in black. "She murdered my daughter," he said. "I want her caught."

"Not half as bad as I do," Henry said.

Jack lifted his cigar to his face and his mouth turned up into a sinister smile. "He means something to her," Jack said. "Doesn't he?"

Henry flinched, and then quickly composed his face into what he hoped looked like dismissive disbelief. "Because of the tape?" he asked. "She wanted to humiliate him."

"You see it, too," Jack said with a certainty that raised the hackles on Henry's neck. Jack puffed on his cigar, and the air filled with the woody smell of it. "This business I'm in, it's not just sales," Jack said. "It's politics. It's manipulation. It's dogs pissing on each other." He puffed on the cigar again. A patrol cop jogged by, holding his hat on. "Everyone has a weakness," Jack said. He looked down toward Henry's bad leg as if to demonstrate. Henry shifted his weight uncomfortably. "When you can find what that is, you can exploit it," Jack continued. "That's power. You think you know what I do? You don't know half of it. This island?" He waved the cigar in front of them. "I could buy ten of these. I could pay cash for them tomorrow. I am very good at this. I see people's vulnerabilities. And Archie Sheridan means something to her. And it's going to get her caught." Jack lowered the cigar and his face shadowed. "I wonder what he'll do then," he said.

Henry waved his hand in front of his face, clearing away the cigar smoke. "What do you want him to do, Jack?" Henry asked.

"Same as you, my friend," Jack said. "I want him to kill her." He lifted his cigar to his mouth again and his eyes sparkled. "Think he will?"

Henry didn't like the direction this conversation was heading. "I don't know," he said. He scanned the grounds, looking for Claire, and was pleased to see her silhouette coming across the yard from the direction of the boathouse, a flashlight bouncing in her hand. The pregnancy had changed her walk, but Henry would still know her anywhere.

"I can help," Jack said, stepping close to Henry. "I can get you an unmarked weapon. Clean things up."

Henry turned slowly and looked at Jack. He was perfectly

still, the cigar burning in one hand, the drink in the other. Henry rubbed his eyes. "Where's your lawyer, Jack?"

Jack shrugged, but Henry could tell the gesture was forced. "Leo? He's at the club," Jack said.

"Well, you might want to get advice from counsel before you conspire to commit murder," Henry said. "You know, for next time."

Claire had almost reached them.

"I'll keep that in mind," Jack said.

Claire angled the flashlight to Henry's right, and he stepped away from Jack and walked over so that they could speak privately.

"You make a new friend?" she asked.

"Yeah," Henry said. "Terrific guy. I've asked him to be the godfather."

Claire sniffed the air. "You smell like a cigar bar," she said.

"It's all right," Henry said. "It's Cuban. What's the story?"

"There's nothing," Claire said. "Landscapers worked all day, cleaning up after the party. They used a leaf blower on the beach. If there was any evidence, it's gone now. And of course there's no sign of Gretchen."

"What about in the house?"

The warrant specified that they were looking for Gretchen Lowell. That meant they could only look for Gretchen Lowell. Anything hinky in plain sight was fair game, but they couldn't open any drawers that Gretchen couldn't fit in.

"She's not hiding in the house," Claire said. "And your friend didn't leave a pound of heroin and some cash sitting out."

Henry looked back at Jack. Jack raised his glass in a toast. Behind him, another pair of cops exited the Tudor. No wonder Jack seemed so relaxed. There was nothing to incriminate him. Was the house always this tidy, or had Sanchez given Jack a heads-up while they were waiting for the warrant to go through?

Claire leaned forward and laid her head against Henry's shoulder. "I actually like the smell of cigars," she said.

Jack turned and started walking back toward the house. Henry didn't know what Jack was up to. He didn't know what Gretchen was up to. The one person who might be able to help wasn't there. But if this involved Archie, Henry wasn't going to rest until he got some answers.

"Want to go to a strip club with me?" Henry asked Claire.

Claire lifted her face to look up at him. "I thought you'd never ask," she said.

CHAPTER

35

It was almost midnight and Archie had untucked his shirt and was sitting on the couch with Ginger, his shoes off and his socked feet on the coffee table. The remnants of his own peanut butter sandwich were on a paper towel in front of him, along with an empty beer bottle, his service revolver, and the bloodstained Band-Aid he'd recently peeled off the crook of his elbow. He was considering having another beer when he heard someone knock.

Archie reached for his gun and followed Ginger to the door.

He expected it to be a cop—maybe someone from the unit Sanchez had stationed out front, or some other member of Sanchez's team sent to grill Archie again. He just hoped it wasn't Gary coming back for more pubic hair.

"Who is it?" Archie called through the door.

"It's me," Rachel answered.

Archie looked for a place to put his gun down, settled on the mail table, and opened the door.

A smile spread across his face. Rachel stood in the hallway with a hand on her hip. Her poppy-red coat was tied tight at the waist and showed a lot of cleavage and leg. It was short enough that he could see that the black stockings she was wearing came only to her upper thighs. The black pumps she wore had four-inch heels, raising her to his height and lengthening her legs. Her long blond hair was loose and tousled. Her eyelashes looked thicker than usual. She smiled back at him and batted her eyes. She clearly hadn't seen the news. Archie thought about telling her; she'd find out sooner or later and wonder why he hadn't. But the prospect of having one last ordinary night without the albatross of Gretchen Lowell around his neck was too attractive for Archie to resist. Once Rachel knew that Gretchen was back, she would look at him the way the others did.

"Is that your costume?" Archie asked.

She stepped forward and touched one of his shirt buttons. "Part of it," she said. "You know, it will be Halloween in a few minutes."

Archie moved his hand to her thigh, feeling the smooth stockings give way to warm bare flesh. His detective skills were leading him to believe that whatever she was wearing under that coat, it wasn't much. He had a feeling he was going to find out for sure. "Well, you better come in, then," he said.

She swept past him, her hips swinging, and the red coat lifted to expose the backs of her thighs above the stockings.

Archie glanced down the hall as he closed the door, wondering if the unit Sanchez had charged with protecting Archie from a beautiful blond had noticed this particular beautiful blond. But if Rachel had been in all evening, and just come upstairs, there'd be no way for his protection detail to spot her. They were monitoring traffic into his building, not people already here.

When Archie turned back to the room, Rachel was standing in front of his laptop, typing something on the keyboard. Archie felt a flash of panic, before he remembered that Ngyun had taken the flash drive with the boathouse footage. Rachel's eyes were on the screen. She typed something into an open field.

"What are you doing?" Archie asked Rachel.

Rachel looked at him and winked. "Putting some music on," she said. She hit another button and music started playing through his laptop speakers. It was some sort of seventies-era funk, which only served to remind Archie that the song had been recorded before Rachel was born.

Ginger threw an annoyed glance at the laptop and then put her ears back and trotted over to the couch.

Rachel walked to Archie's desk and wheeled his desk chair to the middle of the room.

Archie stood with his hands in his pockets, watching as she adjusted the position of the chair slightly and then twirled to face him. He could feel the beat of the funk through the floor.

Rachel unbuttoned the top button of her coat and pulled at the collar, exposing more of her breasts, and then she started to parade toward him, hips swaying in time to the music. She glowed. She was Technicolor.

Archie felt a pressure in his groin.

The high heels enhanced the sway of her hips. She led with her pelvis as she walked to him, as if it were pulling her to him. The bottom of the coat flapped open, exposing a garter over bare thigh. He could physically feel her getting closer, the pressure building with each step. He imagined her arms around his neck, her fingers unbuttoning his shirt, her mouth on his.

But when she was just an arm's length away, she stopped. Archie's body clenched with thwarted desire. He wanted to touch her. He needed to touch her. His skin felt prickly with heat. He took his hands out of his pockets and stepped toward her.

A coy smile played across Rachel's lips. She reached for his wrist and led him to the chair she had positioned in the center of the room.

God, she was beautiful. But it wasn't just her features and curves. She was lit up from within; she glowed with youth and health. It was still unbelievable to Archie that she wanted him.

Rachel sat Archie down and then opened his legs and

stepped between his knees. "Don't move," she said. And she leaned in and kissed him on the mouth. Her hands traveled through his hair as her tongue moved around his mouth. Her fingers traced his earlobes, his jaw, the back of his neck, then she curled her fingers and drew her fingernails over his scalp. It felt good. She increased the pressure, digging her nails into his skin, and it felt even better, waves of pain heightening the pleasure. Archie's head swam. He was trembling. He lifted his hands to her hips.

She withdrew as soon as he'd touched her. She pulled away and stepped back, leaving him helpless with longing, his mouth open dumbly.

Rachel laughed. Her cheeks were rosy, a sheen of sweat sparkled on her collarbone. Archie wondered when she was going to take off that coat. Rachel wagged a finger at him and then reached into one of her pockets. Her grin widened as she pulled out a pair of handcuffs. "Don't worry," she said, dangling the cuffs in front of him. "I brought backup in case you couldn't control yourself."

The cuffs were police-issue nickel handcuffs with a double lock. Smith & Wesson. Archie recognized them right away. "Those are my handcuffs," he said.

She pressed her knee against the inside of his thigh and gave him another wink. "I found them in your bedside table," she said.

She said it like it was something naughty, but that's just where he kept them. He'd never given it a second thought. It was a drawer. He also kept his gun in there sometimes.

Archie was trying not to ruin the mood, but it was tough. "Did you happen to find the key that was with them?" he asked.

Rachel reached back into the coat pocket and came up with a small silver key. "I'll put it somewhere safe," she said. She unbuttoned her coat and slipped the key into what Archie could only presume was the cup of her bra. "There," she said. Her eyes were bright. She opened her mouth slightly and knelt between his legs.

Archie wanted more than anything to unzip his pants. He

looked at the ceiling. He didn't know what to do. What was he supposed to do?

Rachel put her hand on his wrist and started to guide it behind his back.

Archie was trying to be a good sport about this. But as the cold metal brushed against his skin, he twisted his hand and wrapped his fingers around her wrist. "Hold on," he said.

She looked up at him, her face inches below his. He could see the tops of her breasts, the black lace of a bra strap. "It's a lap dance, Archie," she said. "Hands-free. This keeps you honest. It will be worth it. I promise."

Archie didn't let go of her wrist. This was a line he didn't want to cross. He knew where it headed. But his body ached for her and he didn't feel strong.

"Trust me," Rachel said.

Trust her? He barely knew her. But he felt his grip loosen and then Rachel took his hand again and pulled it behind the chair.

"Wait . . . ," Archie said. She looked up. The tip of her pink tongue pushed against the inside of her lower lip. It was a birthday present. It would be rude to refuse it. Besides, Archie really wanted to see what was under that coat. "Close the blinds first," Archie said.

Rachel's smile widened and she stood up and walked quickly to the window. Archie exhaled slowly. He heard the sound of the blinds closing, but he didn't turn his head. He stared straight ahead, trying to gather his wits. He heard another blind close. The music was loud, but there was no one to complain—Rachel was his only neighbor. He glanced around for Ginger, and saw only her nose poking out from under the coffee table. The third blind closed. Then the fourth. Rachel's stilettos clicked against the wood floor as she came up behind him. Archie took a long, slow breath and tried to relax. He caught a whiff of vanilla again as she leaned over his shoulder, her cheek against his, and reached down his chest with her hands. Her touch was full of promise and the pleasure it brought dissolved the last willpower he had. He let her take each of his hands and pull them around behind the chair.

Her head slid away from his, and she sank onto her knees behind him. Archie flinched as the metal handcuffs snapped around one wrist, and then the other.

When Rachel appeared in front of him again, she'd dropped the coat. Archie's breathing was audible now and he could feel sweat forming on his upper lip. The black bra and thong were lace; the corset she wore over them was black satin with a row of tiny metal hooks and eyes up the front. The corset nipped her waist and accentuated her hips, exaggerating her hourglass shape. The shoulder straps of the corset pushed her breasts together and forward. Her pink nipples, visible under the black lace, hardened under Archie's gaze.

Archie had always thought women looked best naturally, in the comfort of their own skin and nothing else. All the extraneous bedroom garments seemed too constrictive, too contrived. Now he realized that he'd been completely wrong.

Rachel pivoted one of her knees to the side. Her black thigh-high stockings were attached with garters to the corset, leaving the tan flesh of her upper thigh bare. Archie's scalp itched with sweat. The inside of Rachel's thigh hollowed slightly where it met her pelvis. Without thinking, Archie moved to touch her there, his hands straining uselessly against the cuffs.

"There's more," Rachel said. "Don't look." She picked up her purse from the floor behind him. He could hear her digging around for something, and then pulling something out of her purse, and he caught a whiff of latex. He heard the sound of rubber against skin.

Then Rachel walked back around and stood in front of him.

Archie was so startled by what he saw that it took him a moment to process it.

Rachel was wearing a latex Halloween mask. It was the kind of mask you pull over your entire head, with eyes cut out and a slit at the mouth and two holes at the nostrils. The hair was molded onto the rubber and painted yellow. The skin of the rubber face was painted light peach, and the thing had a smirking red mouth and painted-on movie star eyebrows and eyelashes.

But Archie knew who it was supposed to be. It was supposed to be Gretchen Lowell.

The arousal Archie had felt a moment before evaporated, replaced by revulsion.

"Take it off," Archie spat.

Rachel just stood there, head cocked, the horrible Halloween mask obscuring her features. Archie could hear her breathing under the rubber. "Why?" she asked, sounding hurt. Her stance shifted. She dropped her hands from her hips.

She'd done this for him, Archie realized. It hadn't been some bad joke. She'd thought he'd *like* it. "It's not funny," Archie said. The mask was grotesque. His eyes went to the floor, his knees, anywhere else. "It doesn't even look like her," Archie said. "You look more like her without it."

She always liked it when he told her that she looked like Gretchen. He knew she took it as a compliment.

Rachel lifted her hands and peeled the mask up over her head. Her hair was messy, her face pink. Her lipstick had smudged. "You think I look like her?" she asked hopefully. She tossed the mask on the floor. Her eyebrows lifted. "Tell me how I look like her," she said.

Archie looked at where the mask lay on the floor, inside out, pink and glistening, like something fetal, then back at Rachel.

She bit her lip, looking at him with anticipation, waiting. She had resumed her provocative stance, a hand on each hip, one leg turned out slightly.

Archie would never understand women.

"You have similar hair," he said flatly. He looked her up and down. "Your breasts are a similar shape and size." He reconsidered that. "But your areolas are smaller," he said. "You're roughly the same height. She's a little taller." He knew exactly by how much. "Two inches taller," he said.

"Your face shape is the same. Her nose is slightly longer. You have similar mouths. But you have capped teeth. Her teeth are natural. You both have blue eyes, but Gretchen's are lighter, with a darker blue ring at the edge of the iris. Her eyes are a little larger and farther apart than yours. You have beautiful skin, like she does. But you're tanner. Her skin is very pale, almost translucent. It feels smoother than your skin does. And you smell different. She always smells flowery to me."

He looked up at Rachel defiantly. He expected her to be offended. He wanted her to be offended.

Her mouth was slightly open. "You did it," she said softly. "You slept with her."

The room felt very close and hot. "Maybe I just have an eye for detail," Archie said.

Another song started playing. It had a disco beat and lyrics Archie couldn't understand.

Rachel closed her eyes, and stood very still for a long moment. Her breasts lifted as she breathed. Her hands were at her sides and she slowly slid a finger along the edge of one of her stockings. And then she opened her eyes and started to dance.

Archie sat quietly, unsure how to react.

Rachel's eyes remained trained on him as she moved, her hips undulating. She ran her hands over her breasts and down her belly and moaned. Her fingers moved over her pelvis and she gyrated under her touch, and Archie felt blood rush back to his groin. Rachel's mouth was open. Her tongue flicked over her bottom lip. All the while her hips kept swinging. Archie's breath felt hot in his mouth. He didn't know a lot about lap dances, but it was clear that Rachel was good at them. He didn't know how she managed not to fall in those heels.

Rachel smiled as she put a hand on each of his knees and then pushed them apart. She stepped between his legs so that her breasts were at his face and Archie strained against the handcuffs, breathing hard. Rachel turned around and, hips moving in circles, lowered herself slowly onto his crotch.

She made him wait, moving in exquisite slow motion, so that by the time she made contact he was so hard that every muscle in his body felt coiled.

Her blond hair was in his face as she writhed against him. Archie could barely breathe. Every movement of her body sent a shudder through his solar plexus. His legs felt weak. His head was light.

She lifted off him and slowly turned to face him. One of her bra straps had slipped over her shoulder and hung loose around her upper arm. She unhooked one of the hook-and-eye closures of her black corset. Archie licked his lips, which suddenly felt chapped. Rachel unhooked another. The corset started to spread open. Archie curled his toes. His pelvis was on fire. Rachel unhooked the last hook and the corset split open around her and dropped to the floor.

The skin of her abdomen bore faint red seams where the wires of the corset had pressed against her flesh. Her nipples were hard pink pebbles under the black lace. The small silver key was visible, pressed against the flesh of her left breast under the lace.

The heat in his groin was almost unbearable. Archie dug his wrists against the cuffs, to distract himself from the discomfort.

This was its own kind of torture, not being able to move his hands, not being able to touch her.

His scalp itched.

She squatted and placed a hand on each of his knees and then scooted forward, her thumbs tracing the insides of his thighs. When she was entirely between his legs she started unbuttoning his shirt. She did it deliberately, starting at the bottom and working her way up. When she was done, she moved the shirt open and unbuttoned his pants.

He made a grateful, hopeful noise and she looked up and smiled. Then she unzipped his pants and reached inside and lifted him out and Archie exhaled with relief. She kept her eyes on him as she put her mouth around his cock. The heat of her mouth, the firm slickness of her throat, made his whole body tremble. He could smell her, them, the sweat and sex.

He was overcome. He lifted his hips so she would take him in more deeply and she closed her eyes, her brow knitted in concentration, as she opened her throat to him another inch. She held her hair back with one hand and began to pump her head up and down, and Archie could hear the smack of saliva and skin over the music. Each time she opened her throat to him, taking him deep inside her, his eyes fell on the black heart tattoo above the curve of her ass. He kept his eyes on it as it rose and fell. His body hummed with endorphins. Sweat ran down his chest. She took him again and again, hot and wet and tight, until he couldn't stand it any longer. His breath caught in his throat.

"I'm going to come," he said.

He had thought she'd move off him, but instead her fingers tightened on his thigh, her nails stinging his skin, and she kept her mouth tight around the base of his cock.

He put his head back, opened his throat, and groaned as he released into her mouth.

Her fingernails dug into his thighs as she clung to him, pumping her head in the rhythm of his ejaculations, swallowing his cum.

When he was done, she slid her mouth off him and sat back on the floor at his feet. Her chin glistened with saliva and semen.

Archie's head swooned. His heart was pounding in his chest. Sweat dampened his shirt.

Rachel wiped her mouth with the back of her hand and grinned. "Happy birthday," she said.

He should have been grateful. That was what Archie usually felt after a sexual encounter. But as the reality of what had just happened hit him, Archie felt increasingly uncomfortable. "Uncuff me," he said.

Rachel's blue eyes studied him for a moment. Then she raised an eyebrow, shrugged, put her hands on his knees, and stood up. She worked her fingers inside her bra, removed the silver key, and walked behind him.

Her hair brushed against his elbow as she bent to unlock the cuffs. Handcuffs could be tricky. Unlocking them was sometimes a bitch. But Rachel didn't seem to have any trouble with it. He heard the key turn in the lock and then felt the cuffs fall away. He immediately brought his hands around to his lap and looked at them. Tender red welts circled his wrists.

Rachel stepped next to him and stood on one foot so she could unbuckle a shoe, and then kicked it off and did the same with the other foot. She picked up the shoes. She was a good four inches shorter now, her body transformed without the tilt. She ran her fingers through his sweaty hair and then bent down and kissed him on the cheek. Her skin felt cool. "Next time you handcuff me," she whispered.

She stepped away then and he turned to watch her as she moved toward the bathroom, already unhooking her bra behind her back. The heart-shaped tattoo sat above the waistline of her thong. It rocked back and forth as she walked.

The bathroom door closed and the shower started.

Archie sat in the chair he'd been cuffed to, rubbing his sore wrists, as stomach acid burned his throat.

Ordinarily he would have joined her for a shower—he certainly needed one—but he didn't feel like it now. He rubbed his face, and then stood up, reordered himself, and zipped and buttoned his pants. The music was still blaring through his laptop speakers. Shirt flapping open, he walked over to the laptop and closed the music-streaming Web site that Rachel had running. The room went silent except for the sound of the shower running in the bathroom.

There was a beer in the fridge, and Archie went and got it out and opened it and took a long pull off the bottle before he'd even pushed the fridge door closed. Then he headed toward the living room, glancing again at the laptop as he passed. He froze, his eyes on the computer's built-in camera. It was just a small black square, smaller than an eraser at the end of a pencil, centered above the screen. He'd never used it. He didn't use Skype or take pictures with it. In fact, until now, he had forgotten it was there.

A prickly sensation spread across his shoulders, like dozens of sharp pins settling on his flesh.

He pivoted slowly to his left. The chair he had been cuffed to was in direct line of sight of the camera.

If Gretchen could take over control of a computer, she could control the computer's camera.

Breathing quickly, Archie turned back to the laptop. He threaded his hand through his hair, trying to think. He hadn't downloaded anything. He never downloaded anything. He hardly ever used that computer. He had viewed the surveillance footage from the island on it. Could there have been malware in that? He had no idea. What else was there? He stepped up to the laptop, put his beer down on the counter beside it, and opened up his documents folder, consciously averting his gaze from the camera. He scanned through the list of his computer documents, looking for anything that might jar his memory, something that would click. It didn't take long. As soon as he saw the document names, his spine went rigid. They were titled *Ryan Motley 1–7*. Each a different news story about a missing child, all victims of a serial killer named Ryan Motley. He'd downloaded those documents onto his computer from a flash drive almost three months ago. Susan had used the same flash drive to download the same documents onto her laptop. The flash drive had come from Gretchen. She'd given it to Archie over a year ago. Archie had kept it in a desk drawer while he tried to figure out what to do with it. Susan had finally forced the issue when she'd stolen it from his desk. Could Gretchen have masterminded such an elaborate plan that long ago?

The tingling sensation now burned down his arms. The small hairs on the back of his neck lifted. He recognized the feeling. It was the sensation of being watched.

Archie squinted at the tiny camera lens. It was like a small dark eye.

His lungs were heavy, like they were full of sand.

He wiped the sweat off his palms and then moved his fingers to the keyboard and clumsily opened a Word document. He could feel heat coming from the computer, hear its fan blowing. He blinked at the screen, ran his hand over his face, and told himself to stop right now, to call Ngyun, to call Henry, to slap the computer closed and turn around and walk away and wait. But he didn't do any of those things. Instead, keeping his eyes set on the camera, he typed a single sentence:

ARE YOU THERE?

CHAPTER

36

Archie's eyes stung from staring at the screen. Minutes passed. He had the feeling that Gretchen was poised with her fingers over a keyboard the entire time, and that she just wanted to make him wait. Then a letter appeared, and another. He was watching, live, as she typed her response below his question in the document he had opened. A word appeared, then a second and a third. Three words, but it was enough to make Archie feel that the floor had gone out from under him.

I
HAVE
SUSAN.

His body betrayed him. That's what panic does—it takes over. Blood flow was rerouted. Pupils dilated. The heart and lungs accelerated. Saliva and tears dried up. Archie tried to think about this now, to abstract what he was feeling so he could put it aside and function. He looked at his hands. They were trembling. *Don't be weak,* he told himself. *Stay in control.* He stared at his fingers, forcing them to steady, and then returned his eyes to the screen as a new sentence appeared one letter at a time until they formed three more words. This time, it was an instruction.

WAIT
FOR
ME.

Archie went to the mail table by the door, got his gun, and returned to the counter. He made sure there was a cartridge in the chamber and then tucked the gun back in the holster and clipped the holster to the waist of his pants, leaving it unsnapped.

He had to make himself breathe. He had to place his hands on the bar in front of him and stare at them, willing them to stop trembling. He had to collect himself. After a few moments, he could feel the panic begin to bleed away, replaced by a stillness and a chilling calm.

His bedroom door opened behind him and he composed his expression and turned around to face Rachel. Her hair was wet and combed back flat against her head and her face was clean of makeup. She had put on a pair of gray yoga pants and a white tank top that she kept in a drawer in his bedroom, and she was carrying his handcuffs.

He was certain now that she had adjusted the laptop when she'd turned on the music, angling it so that it provided the camera with the perfect view. She'd known exactly what she was doing. She had set him up.

Now she moved toward him, smiling, her bare feet soundless on the wood floor. He could see her black bra under the ribbed white fabric of the tank, the black thong under the yoga pants. As she got close he smelled the familiar scent of his own shampoo. When she reached him, she laid the handcuffs gently in his hand.

Archie's fingers tightened around them. "You're good with these," he said. "A lot of people get tripped up by the locking mechanism."

She winked at him. "Thanks."

"Good, for an amateur," he said. He reached behind her and easily snapped a cuff around one of her wrists. She looked startled, and he moved quickly, walking her backward to the chair and sitting her down before she had time to process what was happening. Then he threaded the cuffs under the bottom slat of the chair back and snapped the other cuff around her free wrist. "You always want to anchor the cuffs if you can," he said. "That way the suspect can't move."

He thought he saw a flash of fear behind her eyes, but then it was gone. She settled back in the chair and looked at him with a smile. Then she opened her knees. "Are we playing again so soon?" she said.

Archie put his foot on the chair between her legs, his toe at her crotch, and leaned close to her, so she could see his eyes and know how serious he was. "I'm not playing," he said.

She was afraid now. She tried to hide it, but the color vanished from her cheeks, and she pressed her back against the chair, pulling away from him. "How do you know what I like?" he asked her.

Rachel met his gaze. Her nostrils flared as she breathed. "You have a lot of responsibility in your job," she said. "A lot of power. Sometimes it feels good to give up that power for a little while. To be bound." She tilted her head at him, and her eyebrows lifted. "But you like it the other way, too, don't you? You like seeing me tied up." Archie's body went rigid. Rachel was appraising him now. She leaned forward slightly. "Did Gretchen Lowell use to let you tie her up?" she asked.

Archie backed away a few steps from the chair.

Any trace of fear he'd read in Rachel's face was gone. She regarded him without emotion. She didn't look much like Gretchen at all, he realized. The coloring was similar; the build was close. They had a similar genetic makeup. They both had large blue eyes and symmetrical features, wide cheekbones and plump lips. But really, Gretchen was much prettier.

Archie lowered his eyes and concentrated on buttoning

his shirt. His wrists didn't hurt anymore. He felt numb. "Are you my birthday present, Rachel?" he asked.

"Don't give me that sad look," Rachel said. "You knew what I was. The tattoo. All the questions I wouldn't answer. The way I came on to you. You suspected from the beginning."

"I just thought you were really into scar tissue," Archie said with a mirthless laugh. She was right, though. He had known she was hiding something. It was one of the things that allowed him to be with her. She didn't ask his secrets and he didn't ask hers. It had seemed sort of ideal at the time.

"You never gave me Henry's number," Rachel said.

Archie glanced up from his shirt.

"Earlier today," she said, "when I told you about last night. I said that I didn't have Henry's number, so I couldn't call to make sure you were okay. You could have given it to me then, but you didn't."

She'd noticed that.

"I was really worried for you," Rachel said, voice catching. "I thought she'd killed you."

Archie studied her face, trying to find any truth in it. She smiled.

He didn't know what was real anymore. It didn't matter anyway. He looked out the window at the dark sky. Gretchen would be here soon. He finished buttoning his shirt and tucked it in. "How much did she pay you?" Archie asked.

Rachel grinned. "A *lot*."

"Thanks," Archie said dryly.

"I'm expensive," she said.

"And worth every penny."

Rachel's expression softened. "It was fun," she said.

"I'm glad," Archie said. "How was it arranged?"

"She contacted me via e-mail. She paid through an offshore account. Our contact has been limited to that."

She said it so casually. Like it was any other business arrangement. Like she'd been hired as a nanny. Archie didn't know if she was naïve or just deluded. "You know that she's a serial killer, right?" Archie asked. "You caught that part?"

"She used a different name," Rachel said defensively. "I didn't know who she was when I agreed to the booking, I swear. She was still at the state hospital at the time. She must have used an intermediary."

"When did you figure it out?" Archie asked.

Rachel hesitated. "It didn't take long once I'd gotten here. Once I'd met you. You say her name in your sleep. You told me yourself how much I look like her. But I didn't see anything wrong with it. She was paying me to give you pleasure. And it seemed like you could do with some."

"How charitable of you," Archie said. He picked his beer off the counter and took a long pull, trying to settle his nerves. It was warm and flat.

"She means something to you," Rachel observed.

Archie let that idea sink in. "I chase her," he said. "She chases me. We've been doing it since you were in middle school." He considered his beer. Then took another sip. "We have our ups and downs, like any other couple."

"You've slept with her," Rachel said.

Archie could lie. But why? To protect his reputation? His family? Rachel had been hired to fuck him. She didn't have a lot of leverage in the morality department. "Yes," he said. He could have left it at that. But he couldn't say it, without trying to explain. "Before I knew who she was. She had infiltrated the investigation as a psychologist. We thought the Beauty Killer was a man back then. There was a consensus that a woman couldn't be capable of that kind of sadism"—he shook his head and laughed—"which I find fucking hysterical in retrospect." He shrugged. "I'm not making excuses. Because I slept with her after I knew who she was, too, right before she gave me this." Archie traced his fingers over the scar on his neck. "But I would put that in the category of breakup sex. Are you really from San Diego?"

"Yes," Rachel said.

Archie walked over to his jacket, which was slung over the back of one of the living room chairs, and Rachel twisted around to look at him. "I mean, originally," she continued. "I travel the world now. My job takes me a lot of places.

Dubai. London. New York. Vegas. I specialize in the girl-friend experience."

He got the bottle of Oxycodone out of his jacket pocket, snapped it open, and tapped three pills into his palm. His back was to Rachel. "She told you what I'd like," he said. The pills were tiny. Vicodin were chalky white oblongs the size of bullets, but these were delicate round dots, as small as an *O* on a keyboard. They had no weight. He couldn't even feel them in his hand.

"No," Rachel said. "Not until tonight. I'm a professional. I like to think I don't need that much instruction. If it makes you feel better, she knew you'd figure it out. She told me that once you did I could tell you everything you wanted to know."

Archie tossed the three tiny pills down the back of his throat and washed them down with the last swig of his beer. If he was going to pull this off, he was going to need to care less, and he could always count on the pills for that. "Well, I'm glad she doesn't think I'm a *total* fucking idiot," he said.

He set the empty beer bottle on the coffee table and pulled on his jacket and thought about what else he might need. He walked over to his desk, opened a drawer, and got an extra round of ammo from the box and put it in his jacket pocket. Then he returned to the kitchen bar and leaned back against it and looked at Rachel.

She had stopped trying to work the cuffs loose and sat stiffly in the chair. Her knees were pressed modestly together, and one leg was bouncing restlessly. Her toes pressed against the floor.

"What are we doing?" Rachel asked.

"We're waiting," Archie said.

Rachel's eyes went very slowly to the door. Archie could see her shoulders begin to move again as she went back to work trying to squirm out of the cuffs.

"Are you afraid?" he asked. "You took the job. You should meet your employer."

Rachel snapped her eyes back at him. "You think she's coming here?" she asked. Her voice was strained with fear. This time Archie was convinced it was authentic.

"She went through a lot of trouble to make sure everyone else would go to that island," Archie said.

Rachel looked at him blankly and Archie realized that she had no idea what he was talking about. He didn't talk about his work with her. She didn't know anything about the island. It was possible that she didn't even know that Gretchen was back in the area. "Never mind," he said. "This little show tonight, that was her idea?"

"I got an e-mail," Rachel said. "And a ten-grand bonus." Rachel glanced at the laptop at Archie's elbow and her mouth tightened. "You know, she's watching us," Rachel said. "Probably right now."

Archie turned and put his face in front of the laptop and waved for a moment and then turned back to Rachel, who was looking at him like he had gone crazy. "She can see us," Archie explained. "She can't hear us."

Rachel looked at the door again, her face frantic. "What's your plan?" she asked.

"Oh, I have no fucking idea," Archie said brightly. "I'm feeling a little exposed here, pretty epically mind-fucked, so you'll have to excuse me if I just play this by ear."

"Maybe you should call for backup?" Rachel suggested.

"Then she won't come," Archie said. He leaned back against the counter on his elbows. "I want her to come. I want to see what she does." He glanced out the window again. The sky was black, like someone had rubbed out the stars with their thumb. "I don't think she's very far away."

"Uncuff me," Rachel pleaded.

"I don't want you to leave," Archie said.

Rachel lifted her chin. "Am I in trouble?" she asked.

"For what?" Archie asked. "The prostitution? Or the aiding and abetting an escaped killer?"

"You don't get to judge me," Rachel said, eyes hardening. "You're the one who fucked her. What happened, Archie? Did you like it when she was cutting into you in that basement? When she'd drag that scalpel across your chest, did it make you hard? Did you beg her to push it in deeper?"

"Something like that," Archie said. He walked to the

window and gazed out. He didn't see any sign of the patrol unit that Sanchez had mentioned. "She didn't even have to seduce me," Archie said. "I went to her house one night. I knocked on her door, knowing what I wanted to happen." He could see Gretchen even now, opening her door in a white satin robe, her smile when she'd seen it was him, and his relief when she'd asked him inside. Gretchen had a beautiful smile. It lit up a room.

"You're a fool," Rachel said gently.

Archie glanced back at her. "News flash," he said dryly.

"No," Rachel said. She shook her head and sighed. "She let you think you seduced her. Women know how to do that. Believe me, she was in control the entire time. You didn't make a move that she didn't manipulate. Men are simple that way. No offense."

"Bullshit," Archie said. "I'm an adult. I was married with a family and I made the choice to betray them." The thought of it still made him feel an almost physical pain. "I went there of my own free will. And I went back over and over again. Even when things got weird." He shook his head bitterly. Who was he kidding? "Especially then," he said. "I liked it. All of it." He rubbed his eyes with his hand. "I liked it a lot. It must have been there, in me, all along, right? But it turns out I'm capable of a lot of things that I didn't know I was capable of a few years ago."

Someone opened the front door. Archie heard the knob turn and the faint creak as the hinges rotated. The door was just out of his line of sight, blocked by the refrigerator. But he saw Rachel's eyes widen in terror and she began to squirm wildly on the chair. Everything slowed. He lifted his weapon and aimed it at the empty place where Gretchen would move through when she came through the door.

He heard a shuffling as Ginger worked her way out from under the coffee table, trotted to the center of the room, her nails clicking on the wood floor. But she didn't go all the way to the door. The sound of her steps stopped suddenly somewhere in the center of the room. She didn't bark. She just stood there.

Rachel gulped back sobs.

Archie took a step toward the door, with his weapon raised. He could feel the Oxycodone warming his blood.

He waited for Gretchen to step inside where he could see her, but she didn't appear.

"Are you waiting for an invitation?" Archie called.

No one answered.

Sweat thickened on Archie's upper lip.

Rachel was still squirming on the chair, making tiny gulping sounds. "Rachel?" Archie hissed. "What can you see?" Her eyes remained fixed on the doorway. He couldn't tell if she didn't hear him or was just too frightened to respond.

Archie couldn't stand this anymore. He slid along the kitchen bar, the gun raised in front of him.

He saw her foot first, a white pump planted on his threshold. Then each step revealed more of her, like a curtain pulling back on a stage.

Gretchen Lowell, in his doorway.

Archie felt a rush of feeling—seeing her in person—that made his throat go dry. Or maybe it was just the pills kicking in.

She was wearing an old-fashioned white nurse's uniform, white stockings, and low white pumps. Her blond hair was pulled back neatly and a nurse's cap sat on top of her head. Over the dress she was wearing a dark blue thigh-length cape with four brass buttons that fastened at the neck. She tossed one side of the cape back over her shoulder, revealing its red lining and also the fact that her white dress was splattered with blood.

Archie aimed his weapon at the center of her face. "There you are," he said.

She gave him a ravishing smile and sauntered forward toward him, hips swinging. Archie fought to keep his weapon trained at her head, even as he darted his eyes from the sights to take in what was coming at him. She was covered in blood. Arcs of arterial spray decorated the dress from the hem to the collar. As she got closer, he saw a fine spray of red on her neck, chest, and cheek. Archie's mind went to his protection detail outside and his stomach clenched. He had been a fool to tell Henry that she only killed when she had to. She had killed again. And she had done it with relish.

"Don't worry," Gretchen said, waving a French-manicured hand at the blood. Her eyes were bright. "It's fake."

Archie lowered the gun from her head down her neck to her chest, where the white dress was spattered with red. Now that he looked more closely, the color of the blood was a bit too orange, a bit too shiny.

Gretchen tossed one corner of her cape over her shoulder jauntily, showing off the red lining. "Happy Halloween," she said.

Ginger put her ears back and trotted over next to Archie.

"You're in costume," Archie said slowly, flabbergasted.

"Tell me the truth," Gretchen said, frowning and holding her arms out at her sides to display her ensemble. "Too slutty?"

Sometimes Archie was certain that she actually was quite insane. "Your sense of humor escapes me," he said.

Gretchen bit her lip and stepped toward him and Archie raised his weapon and braced it with both hands. She didn't stop. He didn't lower the weapon. Ginger growled. Gretchen snapped her fingers, and Ginger's ears flattened and she darted off toward the couch. Gretchen's eyes never wavered from Archie. She kept coming. When she stopped, her forehead was directly in front of the barrel of the gun. Archie released the safety and curled the first joint of his finger around the trigger. They were both perfectly still. He could hear Rachel breathing. His trigger arm ached. If he flinched or coughed, the gun would fire. Gretchen tilted her head slightly, her large blue eyes on him. Then she leaned forward and pressed her forehead against the barrel of the gun. Archie could feel her pushing, the pressure of the grip against his palm. His finger was stiff around the trigger. He felt his elbow weaken. Gretchen smiled at him. His elbows ached. She leaned her skull harder against the barrel, lifting her heels off the floor, putting her weight behind it. He could see the tendons in her pale neck tense. Archie was backed against the bar; there was nowhere to go. He wasn't going to shoot her. They both knew that. If he did, Susan would be lost.

Archie bent his elbow and drew it back to his waist. Gretchen stumbled forward, catching herself by putting her palms on his chest. A bright red ring, like a target, lingered on her forehead where the barrel of his gun had been. Archie's weapon was at his side, now directed at Gretchen's midsection. She kept her hands on him. They were so close that he could feel her breath on his face. The gun was the only thing between them. Archie's cramped trigger finger was still on the trigger. Gretchen inhaled and closed her eyes, like she was remembering some long-forgotten smell. Then she opened her eyes and fixed them on him, those blue eyes with the dark blue rings around the irises. "It's good to see you," she said gently.

Archie could feel a layer of sweat between the grip of the gun and his hand. "It hasn't been that long," he said. "Apparently."

Gretchen's eyes traveled over his face. Then she reached up and threaded her fingers through his hair. "Look at all this gray hair," she said.

Despite himself, Archie felt his body relax under her touch. A gentle tingling sensation spread across his skin. His muscles loosened. "You've aged me," he said, and he took his finger off the trigger of the gun. She knew the moment he'd done it. Maybe he'd glanced down or relaxed his shoulder or she felt his hand shift between their bodies. But she knew. And her free hand was there, between them, moving the gun out of his hand. He let her take it. He didn't care. He wasn't going to shoot her, not now, not today.

She set the gun on the bar behind him. "You need to take better care of yourself," she said.

Rachel was still sobbing softly. Gretchen gave an irritated sigh and rolled her eyes. "I find that sound irksome," she said. She pivoted to Archie's side, and leaned back against the bar next to him, facing Rachel.

Rachel cowed under Gretchen's gaze, eyes on the floor, her body twisted away from them.

"I know emotions can be tough for you psychopaths," Archie said. "So I'll help you out with this one." He indicated Rachel. "That's called fear."

"I know what that's called," Gretchen said, eyeing Rachel like she was a particularly unappealing piece of meat. She turned to Archie. "Are you going to introduce me?" Gretchen asked.

"I was under the impression that you'd met," Archie said.

"Not formally," Gretchen said with a smirk.

"Gretchen, this is Rachel," Archie said flatly. "Rachel, this is your employer."

Rachel was shaking, the handcuffs rattling against the wood of the chair. Her cheeks were wet with tears. "Don't kill me," she pleaded.

"She's not going to kill you," Archie said with a pointed look at Gretchen. "Because if she does, I'm not going with her."

Gretchen raised an eyebrow.

Archie held his ground.

Then Gretchen inhaled deeply and her eyelids fluttered. "I can smell you in here," she said. "The room reeks of sex."

Archie's gut twisted, but he tried not to show it on his face. "Did you like watching?" he asked.

"Mmm," she said. "It was almost like being here."

Her eyes grazed the floor, landing on the rubber mask, and she walked to it and picked it up. She turned it right side out and held it aloft on one hand, so that she was facing her own profile. Then she laughed.

"It doesn't do you justice," Archie said. His body was feeling calmer, looser. He was no less afraid, but the Oxycodone made his body forget that a little.

Gretchen tossed the mask back on the floor. "No," she said. "It doesn't, does it?" She cocked her head and examined Rachel some more. "Do you like her?" she asked Archie.

Archie searched for the correct answer, the one that would ensure that Rachel made it out of here alive. "I liked having sex with her, because she reminded me of you," he said.

Gretchen gave him an approving smile. "Very good," she said. Then she walked to Rachel and put her arm around her. Rachel shrank from her touch, but Gretchen just kept patting her shoulder, comforting her, until Rachel's wracked breathing had slowed. "It was a fine effort, little one," Gretchen said to her. "But restraining him isn't enough." Gretchen looked up at Archie, her eyes blazing. "You have to hurt him," Gretchen said. "He likes to be hurt." She squeezed Rachel's shoulder. "I told you that."

Rachel was shaking her head. "I couldn't . . ."

"That's okay," Archie said quickly. "I soured on those games about the time I woke up strapped to a gurney in your basement," he added to Gretchen.

But Gretchen's attention was now firmly on Rachel. She stroked Rachel's hair like she was calming a lamb she was readying to slaughter. Archie knew that look in Gretchen's eyes—that heated anticipation—it might as well have been a rattle on a snake. Archie moved to Gretchen's side and laid his hand on her shoulder blade. He could feel the muscles of her back contract under his touch. She turned from Rachel and faced him.

"What do you want, Gretchen?" Archie asked.

Her eyebrows lifted slightly. "Aren't you happy to see me?" she asked. She sighed, leaned her cheek against his shoulder, and lifted a hand to his chest. Archie swallowed hard. Up close, her skin always amazed him. It was smooth, without lines or pores, like a doll's. He moved his hand down to the small of her back.

"Is she still alive?" he asked softly.

Gretchen took a few breaths, nuzzling against his shirt. "I know how much you care about her," she said, fingers drumming against the cloth of his shirt. "I know you want to keep her safe. But I also know that you are little bit tempted to put a bullet through my brain. So I want you to know this." She was drawing on his chest with her finger. The same shape, over and over. A heart. "She is someplace where no one will find her, so if you kill me, she will die."

Archie fought to keep his pulse steady. Her ear was over his heart, so that she would notice any nervous system change. He was grateful for the pills in his system. He did not want to betray Susan by caring too much.

Gretchen gazed up at him. Her eyes were like a doll's, too, he realized—they reflected back what the viewer wanted to see. "Do you understand?" Gretchen asked.

Archie nodded. He tried not to think about Susan. He concentrated instead on Gretchen, on that famous beauty. He let himself feel Gretchen's breasts against his body, the firmness of her thigh placed against his pelvis. He let himself want her, let his adrenaline ebb, embraced the soft warmth coursing through his body. It was always there—that reserve of repressed sexual desire—it was just a matter of surrendering to it. Susan's life depended on it. He put his lips on Gretchen's forehead and gently kissed her hairline. The fake blood tasted like peppermint. "I want your word that you'll let her go after we're done," he said carefully.

Gretchen smiled magnanimously. "If I wanted her dead, she'd be dead," she said.

"Then let's go," Archie said.

Gretchen stepped away from him and looked down at Rachel with a disappointed frown. "It's a shame," she said. "I would have had fun slaughtering you."

Rachel was trembling, snot dripping from her nose, her face wet with tears.

Archie stepped in front of Gretchen and leaned close to Rachel with his hands on his knees. He wanted to offer her some comfort, to touch her, to rub her arms, to put his hands on her face, anything to calm her. But he didn't want to give Gretchen any more reasons to kill her. Rachel's eyes were desperate. "They'll figure this out soon," Archie told her in as confident a tone as he could muster. "Henry will come.

Tell him everything." He lifted his eyebrows at her. "You hear me, Rachel?" he said. "*Everything*. Make sure he looks at my computer." Rachel nodded. "Are the cops outside alive?" Archie asked Gretchen.

"They'll recover," Gretchen said with a dismissive wave. "I know how it disappoints you when I slaughter lawmen. Where's your phone?"

"On the coffee table," Archie said.

Gretchen swept over to the coffee table and picked up his phone. "You've got a text from Henry," she said, her eyes on the screen. "Looks like I'm not on the island." She took the battery out of the phone, closed it back up, and then tossed the phone to Archie. He caught it and placed the dead phone next to his gun. He removed the extra ammo from his pocket and laid it next to the phone. Gretchen was standing by the door, waiting for him.

Ginger was hiding under the coffee table. Archie went around to the kitchen counter and got a treat. Usually Ginger came scrambling over at the sound of the lid coming off the treat jar, but this time Archie had to call her. He gave her the treat and she took it and carried it back under the coffee table. Archie stood up. "Make sure someone takes care of my dog," he said to Rachel.

"She's gained weight," Gretchen said from the door. "You're feeding her too much."

"I find it hard to say no to her," Archie said. He came around the bar again, and found his shoes on the floor where he'd taken them off hours before.

"Remember, she only gets the sensitive-stomach Science Diet," he said to Rachel.

"Enough chitchat," Gretchen said. "Time to go, darling."

Archie bent over to pull on his shoes, momentarily blocking Gretchen's view of him. "Rachel," he whispered immediately. Her eyes moved to him. "Tell Henry Susan is the priority," he whispered. "Not me. If they have to shoot me to put a bullet in Gretchen, tell him I said that was okay," he said. Her eyes widened almost imperceptibly. Archie knot-

ted his shoes and stood up. "By the way," he added, no longer whispering, "I think we should split up."

He turned to Gretchen. "I'm ready," he announced. "Let's
get this over with."

CHAPTER

37

The vinyl banner hanging outside the Dancin' Bare said that tonight was the HALLOWEEN EVE STRIPTASTICA. Claire already had to pee. Her fingers were swollen from being on her feet so much today. And she was hungry enough that she was seriously considering the two plates of fried onion rings for the price of one advertised on the banner. "You take me to the nicest places," she said to Henry as they approached the door.

"Wait until you get inside," Henry said.

"Oh, I've been inside," Claire said, grabbing him playfully on the ass of his black jeans.

Henry jumped and turned back to her, eyebrows raised, just as the bouncer stepped out the front door with his hand on the back of a patron he was in the process of eighty-sixing. Claire and Henry both stopped short as the bouncer gave the man a gentle push and he staggered past them. The expelled patron was dressed in some sort of psycho clown costume, which in Claire's book would have been reason enough to kick him out of the club. The rubber clown mask had a frizz of neon-orange hair, a red ball nose, and a black-lipped, yellow-toothed maniacal grin. He had several one-dollar bills clutched in his white-gloved fist. They watched as he stumbled drunkenly over his size-thirty shoes and disappeared around the corner. Claire heard the sound of retching a few moments later, and had to swallow hard to keep from following suit.

"I hate Halloween," the bouncer grumbled.

Henry and Claire both flashed their badges.

"So, what?" the bouncer said, narrowing his eyes at them. "You're dressed as cops?"

Henry started to open his mouth to explain, but Claire cut him off. Henry would take too long. She wanted to get home to bed. "We *are* cops, Einstein," Claire said, lifting her chin to stare up into the bouncer's broad, bearded face. "Now step aside. I feel like my unborn child is getting crabs just standing here."

"Sorry, ma'am," the bouncer said. He held the door for Claire and she walked through, with Henry following her.

Claire had been telling the truth. She had been to the Dancin' Bare before. But that had been five years ago, when she'd been the only woman at Greg Fremont's bachelor party. They'd gone to two other clubs before this one, and two more after it, and her memory got a little hazy. But now she remembered this place. Three stages. A full bar. Dim lighting. An aroma like a frat boy's armpit. She looked around at the orange and black streamers that twisted overhead and the orange and black balloons that bounced against the ceiling, vibrating to the dance music blasting over the club speakers. One balloon popped and dropped, unnoticed, into the crowd. Claire couldn't even see the strippers. There were too many people standing between the door and the stages. The clientele was mostly male, but there were women, too. Everyone was in costume. There were a lot of bees, Claire noticed, and a shirtless Easter Bunny dirty dancing with what appeared to be a sexy pirate wench ghost. Henry took her hand—Henry almost never took her hand—and held her fingers tight as he led her through the mingled devils, aliens, ninjas, cowboys, and superheroes. They found Leo Reynolds nursing a drink at a table in front of the third stage, where a dancer in a witch hat and nothing else was writhing around a brass pole that looked like it needed cleaning.

Leo glanced up at them blearily.

There were no empty chairs, but Henry whispered something to a zombie sitting nearby and he stood up quickly and left. Henry pulled the chair over and gestured for Claire to sit.

There was a time when Claire would have refused such an act of chivalry as sexist, but she now took the chair and sat down gratefully. Henry put his palms on the table and leaned over Leo. Claire had seen that move before. It was intended to intimidate. But Leo didn't look all that shaken. Leo lifted his glass, toasted each of them, and then drank.

"We just got done searching the island," Henry shouted at him over the music.

Leo Reynolds was a handsome guy—there was no denying it. But Claire had never understood why Archie hadn't done more to warn Susan off him. The guy was waist-deep in his father's business.

"I got a few messages about that," Leo shouted back. "I told Jack it wouldn't work. I knew Archie wouldn't bury that footage."

Claire perked up, not sure she'd heard right. Bury the footage? But Henry gave her an I'll-explain-later look and she settled back in her chair. She knew she was probably supposed to be playing good cop or bad cop or something, but she could barely hear and she had to pee.

"Any evidence of Gretchen killing that young woman on your island was obliterated by your landscape crew this morning," Henry shouted at Leo.

Claire crossed her legs tightly and tried to look tough.

"They clean the grounds after every event," Leo shouted back. "Jack would do a lot of things, but he would never do anything to intentionally protect Gretchen Lowell."

She really had to pee now. Claire clenched her knees together and jiggled her legs up and down.

Henry was asking Leo about the video footage, whether it had all been turned over, and Leo was saying he didn't know, and both of them were posturing. Men. At this rate, they'd be another half hour.

The naked witch writhed and gyrated onstage.

Claire stood up and Henry and Leo both looked at her with startled expressions.

Claire put her hand on Henry's shoulder. "I have to," she yelled, "you know."

Henry nodded, and Claire turned away from the table and started scanning for restroom signs. She came up with nothing. It was too crowded, and streamers hung everywhere, covering everything. The club had servers—she'd seen a few women in short shorts and Dancin' Bare tank tops, but she didn't see any of them now. So she decided to head for the bar to ask a bartender where the hell the toilets were. She walked sideways through the crowd, most of whom were watching a nun disrobe on the main stage. A man covered in blue body paint and naked except for what looked like a diaper stepped in front of her, blocking her path. He held out a clear plastic condiment to-go container filled with a neon-green gelatin.

"Jell-O shot?" he shouted.

Claire pointed down to her belly. "I'm pregnant, dickwad."

"They're lime!" he shouted.

Claire didn't have time for this. People didn't understand what it was like, having to pee like that. She stepped on the guy's bare blue foot and squeezed past him as he doubled up in pain. She was elbowing around a couple of dirty-dancing cowboys when she finally saw a sign on the wall with an arrow pointing to restrooms. She was sweating a little now—she had to pee so bad. She made her way hurriedly out of the crowd and followed the arrow down a hallway lit entirely with red light like a darkroom until she came to a door with a female silhouette sign on it. Someone had drawn boobs and pubic hair on the silhouette with a black Sharpie.

Claire threw open the door, relieved to find the room unoccupied. The bathroom was dimly lit, which was probably a blessing. The walls were painted black. A sink in a vanity faced two stalls. Claire scrambled into one of the stalls, and then saw what was in the toilet and backed out and into the other stall. She didn't have to pee *that* badly.

Sorry, Claire said silently to her belly, as she set her gun in its holster on the toilet paper dispenser, wiggled her pants down, and then balanced precariously over the toilet seat, determined not to allow her skin to make contact.

When she was done, she got her pants back up—maternity pants were really wonderful, that elastic waist—and pulled her sleeve down to cover her hand before she flushed. You couldn't be too careful.

She was still reattaching the holster to the elastic waist of her pants when she came out of the stall. There was a naked woman waiting there. Claire averted her eyes reflexively. In the bathroom, the music muffled by the walls, it felt like different rules. Claire secured the holster. The woman hadn't moved. She was still there, her ass perched on the edge of the counter in front of the sink where Claire needed to wash her hands. Claire lifted her eyes. The woman wasn't naked. She was wearing glitter, red devil horns, a red G-string, and sky-high pumps. Her body was lithe and toned. A small tattoo of a star peeked out above the matchbook-sized front panel of her G-string. She was either a stripper or someone very committed to pulling off a realistic stripper costume. Claire tugged at the waist of her maternity pants, feeling like a whale.

"All free," Claire said. She hoped she hadn't gotten too much pee on the seat.

The stripper still didn't move. They were the only two people in the bathroom. The other stall was still empty. The stripper hadn't been waiting to use a toilet, Claire realized. She'd been waiting for her, for Claire. Claire stepped to the sink and reached around the stripper's hip for the faucet. The stripper shifted slightly to make room for her. She was tall even before the heels. It was like meeting a slutty, naked Amazon. Claire held her hands under the faucet.

"You're here with him," the stripper said cautiously. "The cop."

"I'm a cop, too," Claire said, a little defensively. People were always surprised by that—like she didn't look cop-ish enough or something. It made Claire crazy.

The stripper didn't look surprised. She looked thoughtful.

Claire glanced around for the soap.

"There," the stripper said, pointing to a small soap dispenser.

Claire squirted the orange gel into her wet hands.

"The bald guy knows Archie," the stripper said. "Do you?"

Ha! The bald guy. Henry would love that.

"Yeah, I know Archie. He's my boss." Claire rinsed her hands in the sink. "Technically," she said. "I mean, more of a team leader." She looked up in the mirror at her own reflection and sighed. She didn't wear makeup when she was working, and she kept her hair short. It had been a strategy early on, to be one of the boys, to not be a distraction. But sometimes she longed for a nice red lipstick. The stripper met Claire's gaze in the mirror. Her lips were painted crimson and her eyes were expertly outlined with thick kohl eyeliner and affixed with heavy false eyelashes. The lashes looked uncomfortable. Claire reached for a paper towel, trying to figure out how the hell this woman knew Archie Sheridan. "So, how do you know Archie?" Claire asked, unable to help it.

"I heard about that girl they found near the island," the stripper said.

Claire tried to react casually. She dried her hands and tossed the wet towel into an overflowing trash can. Then she extended a hand. Claire's nails were unpolished and clipped short; the stripper's nails were long and the same fire-engine-red as her G-string. "Hi, I'm Claire," Claire said. "What's your name?"

The stripper held her hand out and Claire shook it. "Star," she said. "I'm Star."

"Okay, Star," Claire said. Even with her butt leaned against the counter, the stripper towered above her. "Is there anything you want to tell me about the girl we found dead at the lake?"

"The news says you think Gretchen Lowell killed her," Star said.

Claire was careful how she phrased it. "There's evidence that Gretchen Lowell was on the island last night," she said.

Star crossed her arms under her breasts. The glitter on her collarbone looked like gold dust. "I don't think she did it," she said.

"Why do you say that?" Claire asked.

Star hesitated. Then she leaned toward Claire slightly. Her lashes fluttered. She was probably having a hard time holding them up, Claire guessed.

"She wasn't the only dangerous person out there that night," Star said.

Something was dawning on Claire. "Were you at that party, Star?"

Star's lashes fluttered some more and she shrugged and looked at the floor. "I'm just saying, if someone else, someone at that house, if one of them did it, got rough, I just wouldn't be surprised."

"We searched it today," Claire said. "The crime scene had been cleaned up by the grounds crew."

Star looked back at Claire, the intensity of her gaze palpable. "Did you search all of it?" she asked.

"All of the island?" Claire asked, puzzled. "Yes." She was missing something, and she didn't like it when she missed things.

Star's eyes were still on Claire. "Do you know how it got its name?" she asked.

Claire didn't even know it had a name besides Jack Reynolds's island, though now that she thought of it, it probably did.

"I've gotta go," Star said. "I'm on in a minute and I still have to ice my nipples."

Star didn't have a watch—Claire wasn't sure how she

knew she was on in a minute—but she seemed certain. Star checked her makeup in the mirror and then stepped back from the sink and drew herself to her full height so that Claire was staring at her nipples, which were the size of raspberries, and looked like they didn't need any icing at all.

"Tell Archie Sheridan we're even," Star said, adjusting her devil horns. Then she unlocked the bathroom door and sashayed out, a red line indented on her ass from where she had perched it against the counter.

Claire was already digging her phone out of her pocket. She needed to find out what Jack Reynolds's island was called, and she knew just the person who'd have that sort of useless trivia floating around in her brain. The fact that it was the middle of the night made Claire only hesitate for a second before dialing. Susan wouldn't mind. Susan loved to be part of the action.

Henry had taken Claire's chair and now sat watching Leo across the table, trying to block out the electronic disco crap that was pounding through all the speakers. The bottle in front of Leo was almost empty. Henry watched as Leo poured the remainder into his glass and drank. Whatever sorrows he had, he was trying hard to drown them. Henry knew that Leo had to act the part, but this was getting dangerous. He leaned forward and put his hand on Leo's arm. "I think you've had enough," he said. Leo gave him a glassy-eyed smile and Henry shouted it again, to be sure Leo had heard him over the music.

Leo pulled his arm away, lifted his glass to his mouth, and drank.

Henry sat back and crossed his arms. He didn't know what he'd been thinking, coming here. Leo was no help at all. Henry looked around for Claire. Why did women take so long in the bathroom? What did they do in there, exactly?

Henry reached across the table, took the glass out of Leo's hand, and slugged back the contents. He was doing him a favor, really. Leo was staring forlornly at his now-empty hand

and Henry returned the glass to Leo's palm. The music made the table vibrate. "There's nothing you can tell me about Lisa Watson or Gretchen Lowell?" Henry asked, shouting. "No information?"

Leo studied his empty glass for a moment. Then he lifted a finger and one of the servers who'd ignored Henry's every effort to order a glass of water immediately materialized with another bottle of whiskey. Leo poured some whiskey into his glass, sloshing some onto the table, which seemed a real shame to Henry—it was good whiskey.

"You're drunk," Henry said. Leo didn't respond. His attention was on the stage, where a change in music indicated that a new show had started. Henry turned his head to look, and recognized the stripper with devil horns from the other night. A cheer went up when she walked on, a popular act, apparently. She put a hand around the pole and took flight around it, her brown hair lifting behind her as a version of "Frankie and Johnny" started up. It was Johnny Cash, off of *The Fabulous Johnny Cash*. Henry had it on vinyl.

FRANKIE AND JOHNNY WERE SWEETHEARTS
LORDY HOW THEY DID LOVE
THEY SWORE TO BE TRUE TO EACH OTHER
AS TRUE AS THE STARS ABOVE
HE WAS HER MAN
HE WOULDN'T DO HER WRONG

The stripper lifted one long leg and stretched it up along the pole until she was in a standing split. Then she leaned back into a backbend. Her breasts stayed perfectly upright, her nipples pointing skyward. You had to admire the athleticism. Johnny Cash! Wait until he told Archie about this. The stripper opened her knees and bent over. Henry felt a warm buzzing in his nuts. He shifted his position a little, and glanced around for Claire. The buzzing continued. *His phone.* Of course. He pulled the phone out of his front pocket and glanced at it wearily. The caller ID said it was coming from the morgue. Henry pushed his chair back from the table and stood up, lifting the phone to his ear. "Yeah?" he shouted, one eye still on the stage.

I AIN'T GONNA TELL YOU NO STORY
I AIN'T GONNA TELL YOU NO LIE
JOHNNY LEFT HERE 'BOUT AN HOUR AGO
WITH A GAL NAMED NELLIE BLY

A voice mumbled something on the other end of the phone. Henry put his finger in his other ear. "What?" he said loudly.

"It's Robbins," Robbins yelled. "Where are you?"

The stripper winked at Henry.

SHE SAID, "HE'S MY MAN. BUT HE'S DOIN' ME WRONG"

"Give me a minute," Henry shouted into the phone. He opened his wallet, glanced around for Claire, and then laid a twenty-dollar bill on the edge of the stage.

SHE'S TAKING HER MAN TO THE GRAVEYARD
BUT SHE AIN'T GONNA BRING HIM BACK
SHE SHOT HER MAN
BECAUSE HE WAS DOIN' HER WRONG

"Henry?" Robbins shouted.

Henry turned and headed for the door. He still didn't see Claire. The bar was shoulder-to-shoulder with half-aroused costumed yahoos, but Henry didn't have time for niceties. He straight-armed through the horde and nearly flattened a blue guy in a diaper who tried to force a Jell-O shot into Henry's hand.

THIS STORY HAS NO MORAL
THIS STORY HAS NO END
THIS STORY GOES TO SHOW
THAT YOU CAN'T PUT YOUR TRUST IN MEN

Henry cleared the bouncer and stepped outside, immediately feeling his blood pressure go down twenty points as the fresh air washed over him. The relative silence was deafening. He lifted the phone back to his ear. "Okay, go ahead," he said, walking into the parking lot.

"I thought you guys were champing at the bit for the Watson autopsy."

Henry stopped walking. "What?"

"Archie called," Robbins said, a note of impatience in his voice. "Said you guys wanted the Watson results. So I, being a dedicated public servant, decided to stay and do the autopsy despite the fact that it means working well past midnight. Then I call your partner, and what's he doing? He's asleep. And you're apparently at a party."

The back of Henry's neck itched vaguely. "What do you mean, Archie was asleep?" Henry asked.

"I tried him first," Robbins said. "He didn't pick up."

"Archie always picks up," Henry said. He checked his watch. It was just after one A.M.

"Well, maybe he took a sleeping pill or something," Robbins said. There was a pause. "I saw the news. The guy probably has a lot on his mind."

Henry was pacing now, his bad leg starting to throb. "Archie doesn't take sleeping pills."

"You're going to want to hear what I found," Robbins said.

Henry stopped moving. He had to get ahold of himself. He cleared his throat. Then he said, "Go ahead."

"Her killer put something inside her," Robbins said. "A playing card. It was rolled up and pushed up into her vagina, almost to her cervix."

"A playing card?"

"A suicide jack," Robbins said. "I went to a conference in Hawaii last spring. A colleague of mine from Miami told a story about a similar case. He said he was aware of four other cases. Young women. Sexually assaulted. Tortured. All found with cards inside them. I didn't find semen. I did manage to pull some skin from under her fingernails and I sent it to the

DNA lab with a rush request. But I'm telling you, Gretchen Lowell didn't do this."

A serial killer. Henry rubbed his forehead. *Another* serial killer. In any other instance, Henry would have questions for Robbins, follow-up. But not right now. Right now his head was somewhere else entirely. "Okay," Henry said.

"Okay?" Robbins repeated incredulously. "How about, 'Excellent work, thanks for staying—'"

Henry hung up. He punched in Archie's number. "Pick up," he muttered to himself, "pick up, goddamn you." It rang and rang. Then went to voice mail. Henry's mouth was dry. He hung up and immediately called the dispatcher and asked to be patched through to the patrol car assigned to Archie's security detail. He had to consciously relax his fist around the phone—worried he'd snap it in two. He wanted Archie to be drunk, high, passed out on the couch, in the shower, ignoring the phone, fast asleep, anything. But this felt wrong. This felt very wrong. The dispatcher came back after a minute. Her voice was tense. "We're not getting a response," she said.

Henry closed his eyes, anger flooding his body, expanding his chest, filling him. *Goddamn her.* The psycho bitch had done it again. "Send backup there," Henry spat into the phone. *"Now."*

The front door to the club swung open and Claire came jogging out, holding up her phone, face stricken. "There you are," she said, out of breath. "I can't get ahold of Susan. The patrol detail at her mother's house said they'd been told she was spending the night at Archie's."

"Told?" Henry sputtered. "Told by fucking whom?"

"Apparently the chief got a text from Susan's phone," Claire said, walking past him toward the car. "He relayed the message to her protection detail and to her mother. Everyone was so busy, no one thought to question it."

Henry jammed his phone in his pocket and ran after Claire. A string of expletives were at the tip of his tongue, but he reminded himself of the baby and gritted his teeth instead.

Claire climbed into the passenger side of the car, as Henry got behind the wheel.

"That fucking cunt," Claire said. "If she fucking hurts them, I swear to fuck I'll fucking shoot her my-goddamn-self."

CHAPTER

38

Susan sat in a circle of light, arms wrapped tightly around her knees. Beyond the perimeter of the light, there was only darkness. It was like being in a tiny vessel submerged in a deep, black vastness. She studied the dark, trying to make out images, but her brain played tricks on her, presenting connections and then taking them away. She could not see how big the room she was in was; she could not see the door she had come through, or the ceiling above her, or the walls on any side. She had a terrible, consuming feeling that there was something very bad in the darkness behind her. She didn't turn around to look. The darkness was her ally. It would protect her from seeing its secrets. She studied her hands in the lantern light, her palms raw from rubbing them against her pant legs. She was not here. She was somewhere else. She was in an airplane crossing over the polar ice cap at night. She was on a tiny submarine in the Mariana Trench.

But the cold concrete floor radiated through the seat of her pants and the thin soles of her shoes reminding her exactly where she was.

She held her palms over the Coleman, and pretended it was a campfire.

* * *

It had taken Susan twenty minutes to find the lantern. When Gretchen had closed the door behind Susan, she had found herself in complete darkness—thick and dangerous and absolute. She kept her back against the door, eyes aching, straining to see, both hands frantically working the doorknob. That's when Susan heard the first nail. She knew the sound, the head of a hammer driving a heavy nail into wood; then the sudden muted resonance as the nail cleared the wood and continued into concrete. Gretchen was sealing her inside.

Susan didn't pound on the door, didn't scream out for help. She knew there wasn't any point.

She had to help herself.

Gretchen had said there'd be a lantern.

The hammer hit another nail.

Susan stepped away from the door, and into the black. It felt like falling. The smell of urine and dirt made her stomach turn. She stumbled forward, groping blindly, until she tripped and fell to her knees, and her hands landed on something padded. She ran her fingers over it, a broad swath of damp woven polyester. In addition to urine and dirt, Susan could now detect a hint of mildew. She felt around the object's edge—it was as wide as the distance between her armpit and fingertips, and three times as long. Susan sat up, momentary distracted from her plight by her successful detective skills. It was a mattress. Just a few inches thick. The sort of thing they used at summer camps, or psych wards. Susan felt a hard knot in her throat as she swallowed. How long did Gretchen expect to keep her here?

The hammer striking another nail brought her mind back to the moment.

She scrambled to her feet and dived again into the darkness, getting to a crumbling concrete wall, feeling for another door, a light switch, anything—finding nothing, and then turning back and zigzagging in a new direction.

Her foot kicked something. It clattered on its side and rolled away on the floor and she fell to her knees and clamored after the sound. Her fingers connected with an object and she pulled it onto her lap. Plastic. The right size. She traced the hourglass shape with her hands, and moved a fingertip along the handle on top. Shaking with excitement, she moved her attention to the lantern's base, fumbling around until her fingers located the nickel-sized button. Then she pressed it.

She squinted as the white LED bulb flickered to life. Her eyes watered. She cradled the lantern protectively in her arms, like it was a child. She knew this lantern. The sense of familiarity gave her comfort. It was a Coleman camp lantern, and it was green. Not just any green. It was the color green of sleeping bags and the Green Bay Packers and the Coleman cooler her dad had had when she was a kid. Bliss had bought a Coleman camp lantern at a yard sale to match it. They had given that lantern to her father for his birthday.

The hammering had stopped.

Susan didn't move.

If she listened hard, she could hear the faint sound of some sort of fan and the distant thrum of water moving through pipes, though that might have just been the blood rushing through her head.

She was underground. She knew that much. She was someplace where no one would ever find her.

There was a mattress. Maybe there was water, too. Maybe Gretchen had left her a hot plate and a selection of Hungry Man soups. Susan lifted the Coleman by the handle to look around, but before she could even stand up, something made her stop. She pulled the lantern closer, to examine it. It could have been anything. It was dirty in there. She was dirty. The lantern was bound to be dirty, too.

The LED bulb illuminated every detail of the handprint on the lantern's clear plastic globe. The specks of dirt, the whorls of fingertips, laugh line, life line, and the blood that stained the palm and several fingers.

Susan gagged and coughed and lowered the lantern to the floor, and snapped her hand away. Then she extended both her hands, palms down, in front of her, and very slowly, held her shaking hand a few inches in front of the clearest print. They were the same size.

She turned her hands over and held them in the light, knowing, already, what she would find. They were caked with blood and dirt.

Her eyes roamed the perimeter of the light. She didn't even know what direction she'd stumbled from; she was completely turned around. What was it she had touched? Had it come from the mattress? The wall?

The lantern cast a ghostly flicker in a circle three feet around her. Beyond it, the dark made her eyes hurt. Was there a body in there with her, someone Gretchen had already murdered?

Susan rubbed her palms hard against her thighs, and then wrapped her arms around her knees and hugged herself. She could feel her heartbeat pounding in her chest so hard it felt like her rib cage might split. She made herself inhale a deep lungful of rank air, then exhaled and concentrated on slowing her heart.

Go to your calm blue ocean, Bliss would always say. Like it was easy. Like everyone loved the tropics. Calm blue oceans made Susan think of drowning. Susan had to find something else. She glanced up over her knees.

Susan held her palms over the Coleman lantern, and pretended it was a campfire. She was camping with her dad. They were in the Trinities, and they were looking up at the stars. Susan could feel the thrumming in her chest slow as she pictured the scene. She kept breathing. They were sitting outside of their tent, on the soft ground. The Coleman was their only source of light other than the stars. Her dad had a book open and he was reading to her by lantern light. Susan closed her eyes and pressed her forehead against her knee-caps. What book was it?

The Hitchhiker's Guide to the Galaxy.

Susan half laughed, half sobbed. She knew the first lines by heart.

*Far out in the uncharted backwaters of the unfash-
ionable end of the Western Spiral arm of the Galaxy
lies a small unregarded yellow sun. Orbiting this at a
distance of roughly ninety-eight million miles is an
utterly insignificant little blue-green planet whose ape-
descended life forms are so amazingly primitive that
they still think digital watches are a pretty neat idea.*

Susan opened her eyes. This wasn't right.

This lantern wasn't like her father's at all. What had she
been thinking? His had been similar, yes, but it had been tin,
and fueled by propane. This one was plastic, and . . .

Her pulse was throbbing again.

Susan leaned forward and flipped the lantern upside
down. The light shifted to the floor, illuminating a dirty gray
expanse of concrete, but she could still make out the battery
compartment on the underside of the lamp. She turned the
lamp upright, squinting in its direct light, and turned it in
her hands, searching for the answer. She found the sticker
near the bottom of the lamp's base, a few inches below the
Coleman logo. *Four D cell batteries,* it read. *Run time: 175
hours.*

Susan did the math. That was seven days. If the batteries
were fresh. If the bulbs were new. If the sticker was even
accurate.

A terrible notion occurred to her: What if she was down
here longer than that?

The darkness seemed to press in around her. Susan felt
goose bumps rise on her legs and arms.

It was clear what she had to do.

She would have to ration herself. She would have to save
the light.

She was in the Trinities, and she was in her tent, and her
father was there right beside her, and it was time for bed.
They had down sleeping bags. And books to read in the
morning. And Bliss had made them terrible trail mix with
flaxseeds and when they woke up they were going to feed it
to the birds.

"Good night, Dad," Susan said softly into the darkness, and she put her finger on the lantern's on/off button and pushed it.

The blackness was absolute. It was somehow darker than it had been before she had even found the Coleman. She had to blink to reassure herself that her eyes were still open. It was like death. It was like her consciousness and her body had been separated. This was what Gretchen did. She terrorized. She tortured. It wasn't enough that she was going to kill Susan, she was going to make her scared first.

Susan reached for the lantern and turned it back on.

Fuck it. She had never been very good at rationing anything. She pulled her T-shirt over her knees for warmth, scraped a bit of peanut butter off the front of the shirt, and ate it.

Anyway, she wasn't camping with her dad. Her dad was dead. She wasn't sure now that they had ever been camping. Maybe she had just seen that tin Coleman in the basement.

Susan hugged her knees and kept her eyes on the edge of the light.

She was on a submarine. She was on a submarine in the deep Pacific, exploring the Mariana Trench. And she was absolutely alone.

CHAPTER

39

The island was a dark shape in the distance. Archie stood next to Gretchen in the thick woods of an undeveloped lakeside property. The trees went right down to the lake's waterline and were dense enough to obscure the houses on either side of the two-acre lot. The ground was a soft bed of cedar needles and the branches of the hulking evergreens blotted out the stars. They had parked on the side of the road and then Gretchen had led him through the trees with only a small penlight to guide them. He'd tripped on tree roots and fallen twice, but she navigated the woods easily, as if she'd memorized the terrain. She also had the advantage of not being high.

The cold black water of the lake lapped gently at the muddy shore. The dead leaves that lined the bank were soft and fetid, and smelled of rot.

"Where are we going?" Archie asked.

"The one place the police know I'm not," Gretchen said.

Archie gazed back up at the island. It was a hundred yards away, and he had a feeling they weren't going to take the bridge. "Are we going to swim?" he asked.

She turned to him. The white of her nurse's uniform

seemed to glow faintly in the dark, making her look almost ghostly. She swung the penlight back into the woods and he followed her between the rough trunks until they came to a sort of clearing. Far above them, there was a shred of dark blue where the treetops didn't entirely cloak the sky. Gretchen aimed the light near the toes of her white pumps.

"Here," she said. "Clear it."

Archie looked at the ground she was indicating with the penlight. He could see in the light that the bed of cedar needles had been disturbed. The older, darker needles were mixed in with the lighter, dryer ones. He dropped to his knees and started sweeping the pungent needles aside with his hands, piling them to one side. A few inches below the surface, his palms touched wood. Archie used the forearm of his corduroy blazer to brush the rest of the needles aside, and then he sat back on his heels. The wooden slab that he had revealed was three feet by four feet. The air smelled thickly of cedar. Splinters stung his hands.

"There are two tunnels in," Gretchen said. "Jack Reynolds's island? Look on a map, darling. It's called Runner Island. The old man who built the house in the twenties was a bootlegger. Jack's interest in the island went beyond an enthusiasm for Tudor architecture. The other tunnel is newer, reinforced, well lit. I assume it's the one they use for their business. This one is a bit dodgy. I had to pry the door open from the inside. You're not afraid of spiders, are you?"

Archie looked behind them, through the trees, toward the dark water. "It goes under the lake?" he asked. It had been ten months since he'd pulled Susan's lifeless body from the floodwaters, but the dark water still gripped at something in his chest.

"You're not going to drown, darling," Gretchen said gently.

He believed her. She would not let him drown. He believed her because she had said it, and because he had long ago come to terms with the fact that when he did die, it would be on Gretchen Lowell's terms. "So how is it going to happen?" he asked her.

She paused. The small circle of light thrown by the penlight in her hand remained at her feet, unmoving. "I haven't decided yet."

"Well, that's comforting," Archie said.

Gretchen shifted the light to a blocky wooden handle and then bent over and pulled the tunnel door open with a rusty creak. The door slammed onto the ground, filling the air with dust and dirt. They both stood looking at the inky well at their feet. The light of the penlight was swallowed by the darkness. Archie could barely see where solid ground gave way to air, but he thought he saw a ladder descending into the pit.

"After you," Gretchen said.

Archie had the brief sensation that he was standing next to his own open grave, and then he thought of Susan, shook it off, and felt his way into the hole.

The wooden ladder went straight down. It was ancient and soft with dry rot and splintered under Archie's hands. He counted the rungs as he descended, each foothold giving slightly under his weight. After twenty, he hit solid ground. He stepped back into the blackness and brushed the splinters from his hands. Gretchen stepped off the ladder next to him. She had the penlight in her mouth and she dropped it into her hand and shone it around the dirt floor until she zeroed in on something and went to it. The space filled with white fluorescent light. Archie blinked for a moment, seeing spots. Then his eyes adjusted. Gretchen was standing in her blood-spattered nurse's costume holding the handle of a Coleman battery-powered camp lantern. The walls of the pit were rough-hewn rock and dirt, reinforced with decaying timber beams. The air was earthy and dank. A jagged tunnel headed horizontally into blackness.

Something dropped onto Archie's head and started crawling across his forehead. He flicked it away, without seeing what it was. "Happy Halloween," he said dryly.

"This way," Gretchen said, pointing the light to indicate that he should follow her.

The tunnel was just big enough that they could walk side by side, Archie occasionally ducking as his head brushed rotting timber beams. The walls were carved out of rock. The dirt floor was uneven and seemed to slope slightly downward, though Archie couldn't be sure. The sensation wasn't Oxycodone related. The temperature dropped the farther they went, until it felt a good fifteen degrees cooler down here than it had been up on the surface. Gretchen's white stockings and shoes gleamed. Rats scampered at the periphery of the lantern light. Archie could hear them squealing.

"You got to Susan between my house and her mother's," Archie said. He was hunched over, hands in his pockets, trying to stay in the light.

"I was watching you," Gretchen said. "I knew where she'd go once I put that question on her screen, and she showed right up, predictable little thing."

Archie ducked under another beam. Loose dirt sprinkled from the tunnel's ceiling, falling on them from overhead like rain. "You must have tampered with her car before everyone else showed up," he said.

"Even an old Saab has a computer," Gretchen said, brushing the dirt from her shoulders. "I hacked the electronic control system of her car, and then I was able to control the car's computer wirelessly from a laptop." She touched his elbow. "Watch this rock," she said, shining the lantern in front of him, to illuminate a rock in his path the size of a lunchbox. Archie stepped around it.

"The car's computer controls the radio," Gretchen continued. "The horn. The engine. It's really quite amazing. Susan doesn't vary her route from your house, you know. I didn't even have to follow her. I went ahead, and waited. And then I offered her a ride." She smiled. "I think I might have frightened her."

Another rat darted from the light. The ceiling spit more dirt in Archie's hair. "So you drove her somewhere," Archie said. He was trying to puzzle out what time Susan had left his apartment, how far Gretchen could have gotten with her in order to make it back to his house when she did. He thought that Susan had left between ten and ten-thirty. Gretchen had shown up just past one A.M.

"I'll save you the math, darling," Gretchen said. "I had almost three hours to take her somewhere and get back to you," she said. "And I'll give you a hint, I didn't drug her."

"You needed her mobile," Archie said. He searched the tunnel floor ahead of them for signs of footprints. Gretchen had been down here before—maybe Susan had been her first guest. But the uneven ground threw too many shadows for Archie to make out any trace of disturbed ground.

"No one comes down here anymore," Gretchen said idly. "Jack and his people don't use these parts of the tunnels."

"I wonder why," Archie said.

Archie ducked under another timber support beam that had disintegrated to cobwebs and splinters, and tried not to think about the ten thousand pounds of pressure from the lake pressing to get in.

They kept going, advancing in silence, Archie's mind busy trying to figure out if Susan was really somewhere down there, or if Gretchen just wanted him to think that Susan was down there somewhere so that he'd trudge along obediently beside her. Occasionally he glanced around at the darkness that filled in behind them. It was complete black, like the world was evaporating with each of their steps, disintegrating into nothingness. Archie remained close to Gretchen. He didn't want to risk stepping outside of the light.

"I have a surprise for you," Gretchen said.

Gretchen's surprises were never good. "Will it use up my health insurance deductible?" Archie asked.

"It's a gift," Gretchen said, picking up her pace. "You'll like it."

Archie hurried along beside her. "I don't want any more presents."

"Guess what it is," Gretchen said.

Was it an illusion, or was the tunnel getting smaller? "What *what* is?" he asked.

"The present," Gretchen said.

There was only black space up ahead, no way to see how far they had to go, if this tunnel ever ended. "I'm not really in the mood for games," Archie said. He was breathing hard. The tunnel air was light on oxygen.

"What do you like to do best of all?" Gretchen asked. She stopped and lifted the lantern, illuminating both of their faces.

Archie raised a hand to shade his eyes. "I give up," he said.

"Catch killers," she said brightly.

Archie dropped his hand and gazed at her in incomprehension. The light carved dark shadows into her face, sharpening each angle. "You're turning yourself in?" he asked.

"No," she said. She lowered the lantern. "Don't be silly, darling." She turned on her shiny white heel and started moving again, and Archie found himself instantly enveloped by darkness. Rocks crunched under his feet as he struggled to catch up with her.

They continued in silence again, so that the only sounds were the rats, the gravel under their feet, and the distant menacing whisper of the lake moving over their heads.

"There," Gretchen said finally.

She aimed the light straight ahead, where the tunnel ended at a thick wooden door set in a concrete wall. They had come to the end of the line.

"It sticks," Gretchen said. "We'll both have to push."

Archie didn't argue. Wherever that door led, he was confident he would like it more than the tunnel he was standing in. He put his shoulder against the warped wood and leaned into it as Gretchen turned the rusty knob. With the only other exit back the way they had come, Archie gave it his all, inhaling a century's worth of dust and cobwebs in the process. It took three body slams before the door gave way, and he tumbled through the doorway in a cloud of dirt, barely getting his hands out in front of him in time to break his fall as he toppled into darkness. The first thing he noticed was that the floor on the other side was hard. He got to his feet, palms stinging, shoulder aching, coughing up dust, as Gretchen came through the door behind him with the light. They were standing at the intersection of two concrete passageways. Archie shook the cobwebs off his blazer, thumbed the dust from his eyes, and glanced around. This wasn't like the pseudo-mine-shaft they'd just come through; this was a basement.

They were on the island, or under it.

It was not the first time Gretchen had taken him to a basement. The last time, Archie had nearly died. Archie rubbed his shoulder where he'd bashed it into the door for her. "Should I be worried?" he asked.

Without answering, Gretchen turned and moved swiftly away down the concrete hall, taking the lantern with her. Again, Archie found himself in the dark.

"Hey?" Archie said. "Wait."

He could see the faint outline of her silhouette, the glow of her stockings and cap, and then, in an instant, she was gone. Everything went black. Archie's senses were electrified, as he fought the dread that suddenly gripped him by the gut. He looked back in the direction of the door they had just come through, but it was too dark, he couldn't see if it was still open. His skin felt prickly and cold. Then he heard the creak of rusty hinges. *A door up ahead.* That's why Gretchen had vanished so suddenly—she had stepped behind an open door. Archie made his way tentatively forward, finding the wall with his hand to guide him, a cold sweat on his neck. Then he saw it—a ribbon of white outlined the door in the darkness. Archie's fingers grazed the chalky concrete wall as he felt his way closer. His hand found the doorknob and he turned it and pushed the door open.

Gretchen was standing with the lantern at her feet, waiting for him.

"Get the light switch, would you, darling?" she purred.

Archie hesitated, confused.

"Just inside the door to the right," she said.

Archie reached a hand to the wall just inside the door. Sure enough, after a little fumbling he came across a light switch. He flicked it. The room was instantly illuminated by the yellow glow of an incandescent overhead bulb. The bulb was bare and electrical wires ran across the ceiling and down the wall to the light switch. It looked old and sketchy, but it was electricity. Archie could see more than a few feet in front of him. He squinted as he took in the room. Cobwebs stretched across the corners of the concrete ceiling. Over the years the cement had decayed, and sprinkled the floor with concrete gravel. Pieces of broken brown glass glittered in the concrete dust like tiny flecks of gold. The larger shards of glass had been swept over to a corner, along with a half dozen brown growlers that would have been excellent for storing hooch about eighty-five years ago. A wooden table was pushed up against the far wall, its surface recently cleaned. A black laptop sat at its center.

"You could have hit the light on the way in," Archie pointed out.

Gretchen bent over and switched off the lantern. "I wanted to see which way you'd run," she said.

"I'm not letting you out of my sight," Archie said.

Gretchen took off her white nurse's cap and ran her hands over her blond hair. "How sweet," she said. She motioned for him to come closer. He walked a few steps and stopped, and she crossed the room to him. Bits of dust and cobwebs clung to her hair and the shoulders of her cape. But her face gleamed with excitement.

"How would you like to catch the man who killed Lisa Watson?" she asked him.

Archie looked at her uncertainly. There was no smirk, no sarcastic glint in her eye. "I'm not convinced that you *didn't* kill Lisa Watson," Archie said.

Gretchen lifted an eyebrow. "Please," she said. "Really?"

Archie had assumed she'd brought him here because she knew about the tunnels, and thought the police wouldn't return after serving the search warrant. But maybe that hadn't been it at all.

Gretchen's eyes were bright. "I saw him."

"You saw him?" Archie repeated. He had no idea what she was playing at.

Gretchen nodded. "That night, at the party, I saw him pick her out."

Archie rubbed at the concrete grit in his eyes. She was good. He had to hand it to her. She had him. He needed to know more. Even if there was only a tiny chance that she was telling the truth, he had to pursue it. "Tell me," Archie said with a sigh.

Gretchen moved a little closer to him, radiant in her delight. "I noticed the way he moved through the party," she said. "He was looking for someone. As soon as he saw her, he started following her. I was intrigued. I knew he was going to kill her."

"But you didn't try to stop it," Archie asked.

"It wasn't any of my business," Gretchen said. "But when he put her in the water, I fished her out for you." Her eyes were keen and penetrating, a teasing smile on her lips. "I know how you like dead girls."

Archie swallowed hard, uneasy with her closeness, feeling the itch of their proximity. He slid his hand in his pocket and folded his fingers around the pill bottle, his knuckles pressing against his thigh. "What did he look like?" Archie asked.

"Like you," Gretchen said. "Like everyone that night. He was wearing a tuxedo and a black mask. But I think I can limit the pool of suspects." She looked at him eagerly, waiting. But he didn't know where she was headed and could only meet her gaze with a blank look. "He killed her on the island," she said, leading him, "but there's no footage?"

No footage. Archie's hand was sweating; the plastic pill bottle slipped from his fist. There were cameras all over that island. Gretchen was right. If Lisa Watson had been killed on the island, then the killer had managed to avoid a blanket of surveillance. "He knew where the cameras were," Archie said. Gretchen was staring at him, nodding as Archie pieced it together. "It's someone who works here," he said.

Gretchen grinned widely, threaded a piece of hair behind her ear, and leaned forward to put her bare cheek next to his. The edge of her cape brushed against his leg. His fingers circled the round cap of the pill bottle. "There's more," she whispered.

Acid rose in Archie's throat. "You befriended her," he said, finally understanding. "When you saw her being stalked, you wanted to be close to her, to see what would happen." The girl in the bathroom. Ronin had been right. Lisa Watson had come alone. Gretchen had been on the other side of that door. "That was you."

Gretchen's face glowed with pleasure. "You almost spotted me," she said. "I saw you come inside the house and I only barely managed to dive into the bathroom in time." She shrugged. "When I came out, both you and Lisa were gone. I raced to the back door and I saw him leading her away. I followed them. He whispered in her ear the whole way. He stayed off the paths. Out of view of the cameras. I followed in his footsteps. He took her to the boathouse. Into this old tunnel system," she said. "She went willingly," she added. "Probably excited to see Al Capone's vault or something." Gretchen cocked her head and Archie thought he saw something like admiration in her eyes. "It was a good place to kill her. I didn't hear any screaming. He took his time with her. He didn't bring the body up until it was nearly dawn."

Archie stared at her, desperate for how to respond, his mind racing. He had spent half the night unconscious near the boathouse. Had he been twenty feet away while a girl had been murdered? Had he laid there with a hard-on while some girl was tortured to death? He rubbed his face with his hands, the idea of it almost too awful to contemplate. "At what point did you take me down there?" he asked Gretchen.

Her eyes widened in surprise. "I didn't take you there. You don't remember? You made it out of the house all on your own. He was already in the passage with the girl when you came wandering down the stairs bleeding. I helped you lie down so you wouldn't fall in the pool and drown." She touched a button on his shirt. "I was taking care of you, darling. I put you someplace where I knew he wouldn't see you."

But not just anywhere. "Somewhere on camera," Archie said.

Gretchen smiled. "Yes."

"You wanted me to see you," Archie said.

Her eyes smoldered. Archie wanted another pill.

"Did you like it?" she asked huskily. Her hand slithered down the front of his shirt. "Seeing me?"

Archie caught her by the wrist, just as her fingers began to plunge under the waistband of his pants. "You saw him bring the body out of the boathouse?" he asked.

Gretchen twisted her wrist out of his grip. "He brought her body up a half hour before dawn," she said, as Archie let her slowly walk her fingers back up his shirtfront. "He used a kayak from the boathouse to float her fifteen feet from shore, and then he dumped her." She drew a small circle over one of his shirt buttons with her finger. "I could tell from the sound of the body going in the water that he'd weighted her down. Once you woke up and stumbled off toward the house, I figured I'd better pull the girl out of the lake, and leave her where you might find her." She unbuttoned his shirt and moved her finger inside, stroking the scar tissue that pebbled his chest as Archie stiffened. "I borrowed the kayak, untethered her, and I towed her body across the lake to a neighbor's dock." Her touch felt electric. His skin prickled with heat. "Hauling silt-covered corpses through freezing water is not my favorite way to start the day, so I hope you appreciate it," Gretchen said. She worked loose a second button and smiled at him playfully. "Happy birthday," she said.

Gretchen's hand moved deeper under his shirt, her fingers sweeping lightly over his skin. Archie coughed. "You didn't kill her," he said. "But you let her die."

"I guess that makes me guilty of negligent homicide," Gretchen said, her fingertips tracing his heart-shaped scar. The scar had blocked his hair follicles and the skin there was smooth and sensitive. "Do be sure to add that to the list," she continued. She gave him an exasperated look. "Really, darling, you're nitpicking. I thought you'd be pleased to have a murder to solve."

Archie pulled away from her, wiped the sweat from his

lip, and started buttoning his shirt. "I'm never pleased to have a murder to solve," he said. His chest burned.

Gretchen glared at him, pouting.

"How did you think this was going to go?" he asked, unable to keep the anger from his voice. "Did you think you and I would do police work together?" Gretchen's psychopathic logic could be bewildering, but this was insane even by her standards. "We tried that, didn't we?" Archie added. "Back when you said you were a consulting psychologist." Back when she'd betrayed him, tortured him, left him in a medically induced coma for a month, destroyed his marriage. "Maybe no one ever made it official," Archie said, "but you're fired." He looked Gretchen in the eye. "You let that girl die. You disturbed evidence. You didn't do any of this as some deranged birthday present for me. You did it for fun, for your own satisfaction." He could tell he was right by the defiance in her face. "Tell me something," he said. "Back at the lake, when you were on top of me, what were you thinking about? Were you imagining him raping and murdering that girl?" Their faces were inches apart. "Did it excite you?"

Gretchen went rigid. For a moment Archie thought he had pushed her too far. But then the corner of her mouth turned up in a smile. She liked it when he could figure her out. She looked at him without blinking. Smirking like that, splattered with fake blood, she looked deranged.

"You'll catch him for me," she said with certainty. "You'll have to." Her eyes flashed with determination. "Remember, you're a hero. This is what heroes do. She wasn't his first kill. He knew what he was doing. He was organized. He knew what he wanted."

Archie turned away and rubbed his face with both hands, trying to think. She was right. If she was telling the truth. Targeting a stranger, luring her to a killing ground, and then disposing of the body—these all indicated the work of a serial killer. If Gretchen hadn't pulled Lisa Watson's corpse up, they wouldn't even know there'd been a murder. How many women had this man killed whose bodies hadn't surfaced, who were maybe in the lake right now? If Gretchen was telling the truth. If. *If.* "I want to see Susan," Archie said, turning back.

"Not yet," Gretchen said. She ran her finger along the collar of his shirt and looked up at him coyly. "Ask me how we're going to do it."

Of course. Archie had forgotten whom he was dealing with. Gretchen Lowell always had a plan. "How are we going to catch him?" Archie asked.

Gretchen straightened his collar. Then she turned smartly and walked to the table and opened the laptop. "I know where he buried the knife," she said over her shoulder. She threw Archie a smug smile. "A hundred cops just searched the island," she said. "What do you think the odds are he'll move it?"

Archie's mind was reeling. Had Gretchen really engineered a police search of the island in order to drive the killer back to where he'd stashed the weapon?

Gretchen's attention was back on the screen. She lifted a finger and beckoned him without looking. "Come, darling," she said.

He went to her, beads of broken glass crunching lightly under his feet. The light from the computer gave her white dress a gentian glow. As he stepped beside her he saw that the laptop screen showed another video feed with the same telltale time stamp at the bottom. More surveillance footage. It took Archie a moment to puzzle out what he was seeing— tree trunks, low bushes, rocky earth. An outdoor light nearby provided just enough illumination to make out grainy shapes, but no real clarity.

"I accessed the island's security cameras," Gretchen explained. "I had to adjust the angle of one of the cameras. This spot wasn't visible originally. Luckily it all looks the same, so I don't think anyone on Jack's crack security detail has noticed yet."

Archie studied the muddy black-and-white images on the screen. "Where is this?" he asked.

"Behind the boathouse," Gretchen said.

"You saw this man lead the victim into the boathouse, and then dispose of her body and bury the knife there?" Archie asked, making sure he understood. If she was right, then there would be evidence on the knife. If the killer had buried it right away, he wouldn't have had time to clean it up. It would have Lisa Watson's blood on it. It might even have the killer's prints. Archie needed to get to that knife. He needed to call Henry. He turned toward the door. But before he could move, Gretchen stepped in front of him.

For a moment, Archie had forgotten.

"Look," Archie said, trying to make her understand. "We can't ID him from the video," he explained. "It's too dark, and it certainly isn't admissible. If he does come back for the knife, I want to be there to witness it. We might not even need him, if I can recover the knife and get it to the lab."

She gave him a sympathetic frown. Then her blue cape fluttered.

Archie felt a flash of pain and a pressure in his abdomen. He looked down. Gretchen's fist was pressed against his belly, her fingers around the handle of a scalpel. The blade was inside him, below his left rib cage. The blade could be an inch long or six inches. However long it was, she'd driven it into him up to the hilt.

"Remember why you're here," she said fiercely. Her left eye twitched. "I'll kill your little pigeon if you're not nice to me."

Archie remained perfectly still. Gretchen knew where to put a blade in where it would hurt the worst without actually killing him. He didn't want to pull away and risk throwing off her aim. She directed the scalpel slightly upward, and Archie inhaled sharply. The pain was intense now, a worsening cramp. He made himself take a few long, slow breaths. *Use the pain. Let it do its work.* His senses sharpened. She smelled like lilacs. The back of his neck was on fire. "Pull it out," he said between gritted teeth.

She smiled at him and with a casual flick of her elbow slid the blade out of his flesh. It was three inches, Archie guessed, the surgical steel stained with his blood. He brought his hand to the wound. The slit in his shirt was already darkened with red.

"Does the blade feel the same going in," Gretchen asked, "with all that scar tissue?"

Blood oozed from the wound. Archie pulled up his shirt to look at the half-inch dark red notch in his flesh. "It still hurts, if that's what you mean," Archie said.

Gretchen smirked. "Good," she said. She slipped the blade into an envelope case in her dress pocket. His blood was on her hand. She withdrew a folded white handkerchief out of her other pocket, gave it a shake, and then started cleaning off her fingers. "You're not leaving me," she said, wiping his blood from the curve of her thumb. "When he comes for the knife, you'll have him on tape."

She refolded the handkerchief neatly and then pressed it on Archie's wound and held it there. The wound was tender, and the pressure hurt, but Archie didn't pull away. There was a new stain on the front of her dress, a red smear on her hip, about the size of a quarter. It saturated the fabric differently from the fake blood spatter around it, both uglier and more vivid. Real blood was messy that way.

The handkerchief was reddening.

Archie blamed himself. He'd let himself get distracted by Lisa Watson's killer. But that wasn't why he was here, despite Gretchen's intentions.

"I want to see her," Archie said.

Gretchen lifted the cloth and then pressed it back into place. "Patience, darling," she said.

Archie put his hand under her chin and lifted her face up to his. The tiny drops of fake blood along her jawline were sticky under his fingers. Her makeup was in place. Her coloring was even. Stabbing him had not even elevated her heart rate. He touched the side of her face. "Please," he said.

She met his gaze without emotion. He couldn't tell what she was thinking. After a long moment she took his hand in hers and lowered it from her face and pressed it to the hand-kerchief. "Since you've learned to ask nicely," she said.

She returned to the laptop. Archie followed her hesitantly, holding the handkerchief to his belly. He watched as her fingers glided over the keyboard and another window appeared onscreen next to the video feed from outside.

Like the security footage, the feed was in black-and-white and the resolution wasn't sharp, but Archie knew Susan immediately. She was a small figure, sitting with her arms around her knees in a ball of light surrounded by darkness. He recognized the shape of the lantern at her feet—a Coleman, like Gretchen's.

Susan was somewhere in the subbasement with them.

Archie's eyes traveled over the outline of the blade case in Gretchen's front pocket. His pulse throbbed in his ears. If Susan was in the basement, then Archie didn't need Gretchen. He could find her himself. He wondered if he could put his hands around Gretchen's neck and break it before she stabbed him somewhere that mattered. He didn't have a lot of practice breaking necks. It would probably be close.

"You think you can find her without me?" Gretchen asked. "Maybe she's down here. But there are dozens of rooms, old tunnels, secret passageways. Maybe she's in another basement. They do make such excellent cells." Gretchen leaned into him and nuzzled against his neck again, and Archie winced as her hip connected with his wound. "You need me," Gretchen said.

Archie kept his eyes fixed on the screen, on Susan, trying to make sense of all this. Three hours was enough time for Gretchen to have taken Susan, driven to the lake, and made it through the tunnels with Susan in tow, and then back to Archie's place. And adjusting the security camera behind the boathouse, installing the webcams—she'd had all day to do that.

Susan rocked back and forth on the screen, her arms squeezed tightly around her knees. It was hard to tell how big the room was, but Susan seemed especially small. It looked like she didn't want to take up much space, like she didn't want to touch anything around her. Her face, in the lantern light, was a blur of white and black static.

Why sit in the middle of the floor like that? Why not sit against a wall?

Archie had a sickening revelation. "You put her in his kill room, didn't you?" Archie said.

Gretchen lifted her head from his chest and gave him a wicked smile.

Archie looked back at the screen. Susan was still in a tight little ball, rocking back and forth. He needed to get her out of there. But Gretchen would never be convinced to move her, especially if Archie showed concern. He had to make it about something else. Archie injected a note of irritation into his voice. "Is there physical evidence in there?" he asked.

Gretchen's eyes flicked to the screen.

"I want to see it," Archie said firmly. "The longer she's in there, the more evidence she can corrupt. Blood samples, hair, fibers, prints—it's all useless to me if she steps on it."

Gretchen was looking at the screen, watching Susan.

"You won't let me recover the knife," Archie said. "If he comes back for it, the security footage isn't admissible. I assume you're not willing to testify. That leaves me with exactly nothing." He gave her an aggrieved look. "So that's my birthday present? A killer I can't catch?"

On the screen Susan looked up, as if she'd heard them, as if she knew they were watching, and for a moment the black-and-white static of her face came into focus, a shadow darkening her eyes. She extended her arm, and held up her middle finger.

That-a-girl.

Gretchen's gaze moved from the screen to Archie, and she regarded him with that cold, impenetrable expression he knew so well. Then something behind the mask fluctuated, and her lip quavered. "Do you really think I ruined your life?" she asked.

The scalpel wound barely hurt now. The handkerchief was soaked with blood. Archie peeled it from his flesh and tossed it on the table. "No," he said. "I did that all by myself."

CHAPTER

40

A dirty two-by-four barred the door to Susan's impromptu cell. Nails were driven through the wood, securing it in place.

"Were you planning on ever letting her out?" Archie asked Gretchen.

"I didn't have a key to the lock," Gretchen said with a shrug. She picked up a hammer that was on the floor in front of the door and handed it to him.

The head of the hammer was rusty. The wooden handle was blackened with dirt. It looked like something she had found in the tunnels. Archie jammed the hammer's claw between the piece of wood and the door and jimmied it. The effort strained his muscles, making his wound pulse with pain. But he stayed at it, until the two-by-four finally came loose and clattered to the concrete floor with a crack, sending up a cloud of concrete and wood dust.

Archie coughed and wiped the dust from his eyes.

Gretchen held her hand out for the hammer. "I'll take that," she said.

Archie looked down at the hammer. "I wasn't going to

bash your head in until I confirmed that she was inside," he said, handing it over.

He turned the knob and pushed the door open. Susan was on her feet now, near the lantern in the center of the room. Archie had never been so happy to see her in his life. But she appeared disoriented, backing away, terrified. She didn't know it was him—the light spilling from the hallway behind him must have blackened his features. Then Archie felt Gretchen reach around the door and slide her hand along the wall and an overhead incandescent bulb came on.

The room was filled with bright light.

Susan blinked and gazed up at the bulb over her head. "Shut the fuck up," Susan said.

Her hair was wild and her hands were balled into fists. She whipped her head toward the doorway, her body coiled like a feral cat's. Then he saw her take in his presence. Her defensive posturing crumpled with relief, and she cried out—a heartbreaking yelp of relief and elation. Then Gretchen stepped beside him, and Susan stiffened.

The room smelled like concrete and urine. The floor was fissured with cracks.

Susan looked cautiously from Archie to Gretchen. "Are you two back together?" she asked.

Archie moved toward her. He could feel Gretchen's eyes on his back. He didn't want to get too close. Any affection he showed for Susan would just give Gretchen another reason to kill her. "Are you all right?" Archie asked her.

Susan gave him an indignant look. "No, Archie. I'm not all right."

He tried to keep his body language composed. "You're going to be fine," he said. "She's not going to kill you." He raised his voice pointedly. "Are you, Gretchen?"

"Probably not," Gretchen said, after a pause.

Susan was shaking, whether from fright or fury Archie couldn't tell. She had been down here for hours, with no water or bathroom, knowing that Gretchen could return at any moment. She looked exhausted. Archie wanted to take his blazer off and drape it around her shoulders, to take her in his arms, but he knew that Gretchen wouldn't like it. He just had to keep Susan calm, and make sure she didn't do or say anything that would get her killed before he could get her out of here. "She's not going to hurt you," Archie said evenly. "She wanted my attention and now she has it. She just used you to get to me."

Susan wiped some snot from her nose and flailed her arm at the wall. "She's killed people here," she said, hiccupping.

Archie moved his eyes around the room, taking in the blood spatter on the walls, the bloodstains on the mattress.

"Not her," Archie said. "Someone else has."

"I'm helping Archie out with a case," Gretchen said breezily from behind him.

"What's she talking about?" Susan demanded from Archie.

How was he going to explain this one?

"The man who killed Lisa Watson the night of the party," Gretchen said before Archie could answer. "We think he works for Jack Reynolds, and that he's killed before."

Archie wished Gretchen would stop talking. He glanced back at her. She was still standing just inside the door. She blew him a kiss.

"*We?*" Susan said to Archie.

"Gretchen was here that night," Archie told Susan.

"No shit," Susan said.

Archie wondered if she would ever be able to look at him without seeing the images from the flash drive footage. "The woman found dead this morning," Archie continued. "Gretchen didn't kill her."

Susan looked skeptical.

"Gretchen saw it," Archie said. "She witnessed the killer lure Lisa Watson into the tunnels and then later bring up her body and dump it in the lake."

The lantern on the floor went out. Susan glared accusingly at Gretchen. "That wasn't even a hundred hours!" she sputtered.

"I didn't say the batteries were new," Gretchen said.

Archie tried to ignore them both, and began to scan the room clockwise as if it were any other crime scene, taking in the walls, ceiling, and floor. The mattress, Archie noticed, wasn't just soaked with blood. It was soaked with generations of blood. Stains overlapped one another, in various stages of oxygenation.

"You can't believe her story," Susan said. "She's a pathological liar." Susan hiccupped again. "What are you doing?"

Archie had inched closer to the mattress. "I'm looking for clues," he said.

"I thought you said Gretchen saw him," Susan said.

"He was wearing a mask," Gretchen said from the door.

"It must have been a big mask," Susan muttered.

"I only saw him from a distance, pigeon," Gretchen said.

Archie could hear the irritation in Gretchen's voice. If Susan kept goading her, it wouldn't matter what Archie said or did—Gretchen would kill her. "You were right," Archie announced to Gretchen. "There are varying ages of bloodstains here." Archie glanced over at Susan. "He's killed more than one person in this room."

"A serial killer, huh?" Susan said. "I know someone else like that." She pointed at Gretchen. *"Her."*

Archie willed Susan to understand what he was trying to do, that he had to go along with this, that he was doing it for her. "If I can stop this guy, I can save lives," he said.

Susan crossed her arms. "Your judgment hasn't been exactly stellar lately," she said. She pursed her lips and lifted her chin. "The stripper?" she said. "For instance?"

Archie cringed.

"What stripper?" Gretchen asked.

"I did not have sex with the stripper," Archie said to Susan. "Not that I have to explain that." He looked back at Gretchen. "To either of you." He turned back to Susan, remembering suddenly how infuriating she could be. "I had to talk to Leo. In private. And I wasn't drunk, by the way. It was nonalcoholic beer."

Susan scratched her ear. "Oh," she said.

Archie concentrated on what was in front of him. The

hole in his belly stung now every time he took a step. He kept his back to Gretchen and moved along the walls, studying the blood spatter. An open cardboard box in the corner was full of chains. They looked roughly the same size as the ligature marks on Lisa Watson's torso. Propped against the box were three unopened packages of five-pound scuba-diving weights and a neat stack of black mesh bags. The weights went in the bag, the chain threaded through the bag's handle, and you'd have a nice anchor for a corpse. The killer had stocked up. He had enough supplies to dispose of several more people before he'd have to go back to the dive store. A black nylon reusable grocery bag sat on the other side of the box. Archie nudged it open with his foot.

"What is it?" Susan asked.

"Lightbulbs," Archie said. He glanced up at the single bulb that illuminated the room overhead. It would be inconvenient if it burned out in the middle of a murder. The killer had thought of everything.

Archie surveyed the rest of the room.

When his eyes returned to Susan he saw that she was staring at the bloodstain on his shirt. "I'm fine," he said quickly.

"It's real?" Susan said. "I thought it was fake." She glanced at Gretchen. "From touching her."

Gretchen laughed. "Don't fret, pigeon," she said. "Archie doesn't feel like himself if he's not bleeding just a little bit."

The room went dark. It was sudden and complete, a blind, enveloping nothingness. Susan cried out.

"Gretchen?" Archie called, frozen.

She didn't respond. Susan hiccupped.

"Get on the floor," Archie said to Susan. He didn't know what was happening, but whatever it was, he wanted Susan out of the line of fire. The hinges on the door creaked. "Gretchen?" Archie called again into the black. "I'm coming toward the door," he said. He stumbled forward in the dark, hands groping the air in front of him. As he made his way to the door, he half expected to feel the plunge of a blade into his flesh.

But then his hand touched concrete. He'd made it across

the room. He fumbled along the wall until his fingers found the light switch.

He turned it on and light filled the room again. Archie glanced back at Susan, who was looking up at him from where she'd dropped to the floor. They didn't speak. The room was deathly quiet, but Archie could just make out something on the edge of the silence. He listened carefully, craning his head toward the door. The noise was growing louder, more distinct. It was the sound of footsteps approaching. Gretchen was coming back.

"Get behind me," he whispered to Susan. Susan had just started to get up as the doorknob turned. Archie backed up toward her to get between her and whatever was on the other side of the door. The door creaked opened. Karim and Cooper and two of the buzz cuts stood on the other side. Cooper had a gun leveled at them. Karim held a flashlight. They looked as surprised to see Archie as he was to see them.

"Well," Karim said in his clipped British accent. "What do we have here?"

"Oh, thank God!" Susan said, brushing whatever had been on the floor off her pants. "You don't even know what we've been through. We need to get out of here, now, before she comes back."

But Cooper didn't lower his gun.

Karim swept into the room, and the buzz cuts trotted in after him like trained Rottweilers.

Archie took a step backward, toward Susan. "I don't think they're here to rescue us," Archie said.

CHAPTER

41

Archie knew it would sound insane, but it was only now that he was realizing how truly insane it sounded.

"Gretchen Lowell is in my basement?" Jack repeated, delighted. He was leaning against the front edge of his office desk, his face flushed with amusement. He had been asleep. His usually neat hair was flattened on one side. The sweatpants, cashmere sweater, and leather slippers he was wearing looked like something that had been chosen hastily. The windows behind him looked out into darkness.

"Yes," Archie said. He looked at his watch. It was just past four A.M. Gretchen had probably made it off the island by now, and instead of going after her, he was sitting here trying to explain himself to a crime boss. He had cobwebs in his hair, dust and dirt and blood on his clothes, and a three-inch-deep penetrating wound in his abdomen. "We're wasting time," Archie said.

But no one moved.

Susan fidgeted in the chair next to him, chewing on her cuticles. Cooper was standing near the wall to Archie's left, his weapon held loosely at his side, his face impassive. Razor Burn was just behind Susan, arms crossed, his eyes on his boss. Archie twisted around to look at Karim, wincing as his wound stung. Karim was perched on the gold-striped settee in the center of the room, reading a copy of *Town & Country* magazine, seemingly unaware that Archie had spoken at all.

Archie gingerly turned back to Jack. The landline on Jack's desk was almost within reach. Archie could lunge for it, start dialing, maybe, but there was no way he would be able to get a call made before Cooper stopped him. He had to get Jack to understand. Jack was a businessman. He knew how to make informed decisions. Archie just had to make the argument sound reasonable. "We need to call in the task force," Archie said. "While she's still in the area. Get Leo, Jack. Please. He'll believe me. He'll tell you I'm not crazy. If we call for backup now, we might still be able to catch her." Jack's eyes were still bright, the grin still frozen on his face. Archie knew he had to go further. "She killed Isabel, Jack. And you're letting her get away."

Jack looked at him for a full minute. Archie could hear a clock ticking and the sound of Karim turning magazine pages. "Are you high?" Jack asked, finally.

Razor Burn laughed. It was a forced short bark, like a dog's.

Archie sighed and rubbed his face with his hands. *Fine.* They wanted him to go through it again, he would go through it again. He would go through it a thousand times. However many times it took to get them to understand. "Gretchen kidnapped Susan," he said. "She used her to get me to follow her down into the tunnels. She was in that room until moments before your men arrived." He indicated the bloody hole in his shirt. "She stabbed me with a scalpel. You need to let me call for backup before it's too late."

"With a scalpel," Jack said, his face a picture of merriment.

Archie shook his head. It did sound incredible. "It gets better," he said. "She's wearing a blood-spattered nurse costume."

Jack blinked at Archie.

"It's Halloween," Archie said.

A grin spread across Jack's lips and he punched a finger in Archie's direction. "You've finally cracked up, haven't you?"

"He's telling the truth," Susan groaned. "She brought us both here. You need to let Archie call for help. Or he'll arrest you for hindering the investigation. He needs a doctor."

"*Obstructing* the investigation," Archie said, correcting her. "But, yeah."

Razor Burn gave Susan a push on the back of her head. "You don't get to tell Jack what to do," he said.

Susan lifted a hand to her scalp and twisted around, her face crimson. "Don't touch me," she hissed. Razor Burn's iron-man façade wavered. Archie reached across and set a cautioning hand on Susan's elbow, but she jerked it away. Archie could see the color building on Razor Burn's cheeks, as his blood vessels filled with rage. His eyes were on Jack, clearly looking for a green light to teach Susan a lesson.

Archie's entire body tensed, his muscles coiled, ready to throw himself at Razor Burn. In that instant, his wound didn't hurt at all. Out of the corner of Archie's eye, he saw Cooper step forward from the wall.

The smile on Jack's face had finally faded. "Easy," he cautioned Razor Burn.

Archie heard another magazine page turn. "Did you know that Christie Brinkley remodeled her home in the Hamptons?" Karim called from the couch.

Razor Burn looked confused. Susan exhaled dramatically and crossed her arms. "I've had a really bad day," she said to Jack. "Your party sucked. I think my boyfriend and I are breaking up. I got taken hostage by a serial killer. I have spiders in my hair. And you're being a pigheaded asshole. I'm telling you," she added, with a glance over her shoulder at Razor Burn, "if someone points a gun at me again, or threatens me in any way, I'm going to lose it."

Archie couldn't help but smile. She was something else. Jack raised his eyebrows at Archie. Archie shrugged. Jack turned back to Susan. "A pigheaded asshole?" he said.

"Think about it, Jack," Archie said, seeing his opportunity. "Gretchen was here Saturday night. Why is it so hard to believe she'd come back?"

Jack frowned. He pulled at one of his earlobes. Then his eyes moved uncertainly to Cooper.

"We didn't see anyone else down there," Cooper said.

"She must have heard you coming and run down the opposite hall," Archie said.

Cooper frowned. "It's a labyrinth," he said to Jack. "There are tunnels no one's been down since the thirties."

Cooper had opened a door. Jack pulled at his ear some more, thinking.

Archie heard the magazine snap shut and looked around at Karim, who had stood up from the couch. Karim walked over to Archie and Susan and extended the *Town & Country* between them. "Would you like some reading material?" he asked.

"I've read it," Susan said.

Karim turned to Archie.

"No, thanks," Archie said.

"Well, then, since we won't be enjoying magazines, may I ask you a question?"

Jack looked on with interest.

Archie had a bad feeling about where this was headed.

Karim went for his jacket pocket. At first Archie thought he was going for his gun. The pocket of his gray suit was cut deep—custom—large enough to stow a couple of 45s if you didn't mind what the bulge did to the cut of the suit. But instead Karim withdrew some sort of camera. He held it between Susan and Archie. "What's this, then?" Karim asked.

Archie glanced at Susan. Her eyes were on the device.

The camera was the size of a pool ball and mounted on what looked like a pedal with an antenna on it. "I have no idea," Archie answered.

"It's a webcam," Susan said quietly.

"It's a webcam!" Karim said triumphantly. "Yes, that's right. Brilliant." Everyone leaned in to get a closer look. "It transmits footage wirelessly," Karim continued, now talking more to Jack than to Archie. "It was in the room where we found them."

Archie could feel the mood in the room blacken.

"Gretchen set that up so she could spy on me," Susan said. "She held me in that room, and she monitored me with that thing."

Karim was turning the webcam over in his hands, studying it.

"You're tampering with evidence," Archie pointed out.

Karim's face registered no emotion. He had stopped listening to Archie. This was entirely for Jack. "He was setting up surveillance," Karim explained to Jack. He handed Jack the webcam and then stood up fluidly and brushed the wrinkles from his slacks. "Sheridan is a cop," he added. "He wasn't down there chasing serial killers. He was down there installing surveillance as part of an ongoing investigation into your activities. We're all aware that you're being watched. We're aware that they're building a case. Obviously, Detective Sheridan is participating in that effort."

Jack was frowning at Archie, his knuckles white around the webcam in his hand. Archie tried to look trustworthy but his exasperation was making it difficult.

"Are we all familiar with the principle of Occam's razor?" Karim asked the room.

Razor Burn coughed.

Susan sighed. "When you have two competing theories that make exactly the same predictions, the simpler one is the better," Susan said.

"That's not helping us," Archie said to Susan.

"What?" she said. "I took philosophy."

Jack's face reddened and he hurled the webcam hard against the wall. It hit a framed photograph of a boat and then scattered on the floor in pieces.

Everyone flinched except Karim.

"I don't have my badge," Archie said emphatically, "or my gun or my phone or a walkie-talkie." He glanced at Susan. "I'm here with a civilian. Without backup. You don't use those tunnels. Why would I want to monitor them?" He pointed at the remnants of the webcam. "That's not mine."

Jack turned to Cooper, and for a moment Archie thought Jack might draw his finger across his throat and Cooper would shoot Archie in the back of the head.

"If I were here as a cop," Archie said, "I'd be asking you to explain the bloodstains in your basement."

Jack looked back at Archie. Archie had, for the first time, his full attention. The room was quiet.

"They didn't tell you?" Archie asked.

Karim and Cooper had spent ten minutes alone with Jack when they'd all first come up the stairs from the tunnels. Susan had insisted on peeing, and Razor Burn had insisted on standing outside the bathroom with a gun while she did, and Archie had insisted on staying with Razor Burn, to ensure Susan's safety. Then Susan had slurped down about fifteen cupped hands' worth of water from the bathroom sink, and had to pee again. It was enough time, Archie figured, to get Jack pretty up to date.

Judging by the perplexed expression on Jack's face, apparently not.

"What's he talking about?" Jack asked Cooper. Karim was standing next to Jack, but Jack didn't ask him.

"There were some stains on a mattress on the floor," Cooper said matter-of-factly. "And spatter on the walls. It could have been blood."

"Lisa Watson was murdered down there," Susan said. "And she's not the only one."

They all turned to look at her. She had her feet on the chair and her knees lifted to her chest with her WORST HALLOWEEN COSTUME EVER T-shirt pulled over them. Mud scarred the chair's upholstery from her dirty sneakers. She wasn't hiccupping anymore, Archie realized.

"The girl from the dock?" Jack said slowly.

Razor Burn rocked back nervously on his heels. "So the Beauty Killer's been taking people out down there?" he said. He looked questioningly at Karim. "We can't get in trouble for that, right?"

"Don't be a fool," Karim said.

Archie didn't think that Gretchen had killed anyone down there. But he kept that to himself. He was finally getting through to them. Jack was boring a hole in the floor, clearly deep in thought. Archie didn't want to risk confusing the issue. He exchanged a look with Susan. She gave him a little nod.

"Every second that we sit here talking," Susan said to Jack, "Gretchen gets that much farther away."

Jack lifted his eyes to Archie. There was something new in his face. Something hungry. "She's really down there?" Jack asked him.

Archie resisted the urge to scream, *Yes, that's what I've been saying,* and instead simply said, "Yes."

Jack seemed to contemplate that. He and Leo had the same pale penetrating eyes. His fondness for whiskey had left tiny red capillaries visible on his nose and cheeks. His mouth tightened. His nostrils flared. He was nodding to himself. Pumping himself up. His face looked hot to the touch. He grinned at Archie, like they shared a secret.

Archie had a terrible feeling that he knew what Jack was thinking. "She's dangerous," he said quickly. "You can't go after her. Let me call for a SWAT team."

But Jack was already up, already moving around his desk. "She's an intruder on my property," he said. He reached back and pulled open a desk drawer and lifted out a semiautomatic handgun. "I'm going to do what you should have done a long time ago, my friend." He pointed the gun at Archie. It was a SIG P226. No safety. A big gun. "I'm going to shoot her."

Jack laughed and lowered the SIG and then started going through more drawers. This was going very wrong. Archie looked around at Karim, Cooper, and Razor Burn. They had to know this was nuts, but none of them said anything. Susan looked over at Archie, eyes wide. Archie searched for something to say to Jack, some way to defuse this. "I'll go with you," he said, starting to stand.

Archie felt a hand on his shoulder before he'd even made

it to his feet, and then was shoved hard back into his chair. Pain radiated through Archie's abdomen and he winced and brought his hand to his wound.

"Sorry," Cooper said softly from behind him.

Archie shifted his weight in his seat, and concentrated on Jack. "She's armed," he told Jack. "She's got a scalpel."

Jack slid a box of ammo out of the drawer and put it in the pocket of his sweatpants. It bulged awkwardly from his hip as he came back around the desk. He stopped in front of Archie.

Cooper's hand seemed to get heavier on Archie's shoulder.

"Don't worry," Jack said with a lascivious smile. He nudged Archie with the barrel of his gun and the smile turned into a sneer. "You can fuck her dead body when I'm done with her."

"Don't do this, Jack," Archie said.

"Who cares?" Susan asked loudly. There was a pink spot on each of her cheeks. "Let them kill her," she said, and the viciousness in her voice made Archie cold. Her eyes dared him to disagree, to challenge her. "Unless you don't want her dead," she added accusingly.

There was nothing Archie could say that she wanted to hear. He didn't have time to explain that right now he was far more worried about Jack's prospects than Gretchen's. "Give me a gun," Archie urged Jack.

Jack rocked back and forth on the balls of his feet, delighted. "See?" he crowed to Susan. "He just wants to be the one to do it." He slapped Archie hard on the shoulder, and Archie winced in pain again. "Not a chance," Jack said.

"She'll kill you," Archie said quietly. Blood oozed from the wound under his palm.

"That's why I hire commandos," Jack said brightly. "For just this kind of thing." Jack jabbed a finger at Razor Burn. "Collins," he said. "You're with me. Get Ronin and the others up. I'll meet you all at the elevator."

Razor Burn responded with a clipped nod, executed a military turn, and headed for the door, already unholstering his Glock.

"Shoot her in the head," Susan called as the door closed behind him.

Jack was pulling on a windbreaker with a yacht race emblem on the chest.

Karim had picked up the *Town & Country* again and was paging through it.

Outside the window behind the desk, it was still dark. It would be an hour before dawn. "Don't go down there," Archie said. "I'm not going to warn you again."

"She killed my Isabel," Jack said, and for a moment Archie saw a trace of the man he'd visited more than a dozen years ago, the man who'd fallen to his knees after Archie told him that his daughter was dead. Maybe that man was always in there, under the surface.

Archie hesitated. "What if I told you she didn't?" he asked.

A shadow fell across Jack's face. "That would be a riot, coming from you. I heard about you this summer. Trying to convince everyone that she didn't kill all her victims."

"You know," Archie said, leaning back in his chair. "Do what you want."

Cooper's hand lifted from Archie's shoulder. "You want company?" Cooper asked Jack.

"I need you two to stay here," Jack said with a glance at Karim. Karim was engrossed in his magazine and barely seemed to hear. "Stay with them," Jack told Cooper. "Make sure they don't call anyone until I get back." He cocked his head at Susan. But she refused to meet his gaze. Jack's tongue flickered. He didn't like being ignored, which Archie knew was exactly why Susan was doing it. Jack moved directly in front of her, took her by her chin, and forced her to look at him. He smiled, satisfied, and released her. "If they're uncooperative, kill them," he instructed Cooper. Susan's chin had a mark where Jack had grabbed her. Archie kept his hands tight around the ends of the arms of his chair.

Jack started for the door.

"Good luck," Archie said darkly.

Jack hesitated and turned back around. "Give me your extra gun," he said to Cooper.

Cooper hesitated and then bent over and lifted a pant leg to reveal an ankle holster. He unholstered the weapon and handed it to Jack.

Jack put a gun in each pocket of his yachting jacket and then glanced back at Archie. "No one knows you're here, my friend," he said to Archie. "Don't test me."

Then Jack grinned madly. He drew each of the guns out of his pockets and, two-fisted, headed for the door to the hall. Halfway out, he caught Archie's eye one last time. Eyes bright, face ruddy, a spring in his step, he looked like a kid about to enter Disneyland. He looked happy.

For an instant, Archie was jealous.

"Help yourselves to a drink," Jack called merrily. And then the door closed and he was gone.

For a moment, no one said anything. Then Cooper reached into his pocket and tossed Susan a deck of cards. "Stay busy," he said. "It might be a while."

CHAPTER

42

Archie poured himself a double shot of Jack's forty-one-year-old single-malt scotch. There was a mirror in front of him at the bar, and he could see Cooper watching him, his gun still drawn. Susan had moved to the gold-striped settee, where she now sat playing hearts with Karim. She was staring at her cards intently. Karim's gaze was fixed on her, clearly waiting for her to make some sort of move.

"I can't do this with you glaring at me like that," Susan said.

Karim leaned forward on the settee and set his cards delicately on the table next to his gun. "Do you want me to refresh you on the rules?" he asked.

Susan narrowed her eyes at him over her cards.

Archie replaced the cap on the whiskey bottle and pushed it back in line with the other expensive liquor bottles. He'd blotted the scalpel wound with all the cocktail napkins on the bar and it appeared to have stopped bleeding. He could have thrown away the bloody napkins—each napkin was square with a drawing of a sailboat in one corner—but Archie left them in a stack next to the Tanqueray instead. He checked the reflection in the mirror again. Cooper was still watching him. Archie could see the silver glinting in his mouth. Anyone with teeth like that had done some hard living at some point.

"Do you want a drink?" Archie asked him.

"No," Cooper said.

"AA?" Archie asked.

"Ten years," Cooper said.

Archie lifted his glass and toasted Cooper in the mirror. "Congratulations," he said. The whiskey was bright and smooth in his throat and he savored it for a moment before he turned around to face the room. The house was quiet. They hadn't heard anything since Jack had left. No voices. No footsteps.

Cooper cracked his neck.

The clock ticked.

Susan pulled three cards from her hand and then made a face and picked one back up. "One more second," she said to Karim.

Karim hooked a finger under his yellow bow tie and loosened it slightly.

Archie walked over to where they were playing and sat down in one of the two black leather club chairs that faced the settee.

Cooper followed him, and sat down in the chair next to Archie's.

"He does that," Susan said, indicating Cooper as she glanced up from her cards. "He followed me around during the whole party. You get used to it after a while. It's like when a stray follows you on a walk. You know it's not your dog, but it's kind of nice to have him along."

"Clever T-shirt," Cooper said to Susan.

"Thanks," she said, looking down at her orange Halloween T-shirt. "Goodwill. Two-ninety-nine."

A distant thud echoed through the house. Archie and Susan jumped, and Cooper stood, gun raised toward the door.

Karim was the only one who hadn't flinched. He arched an eyebrow over his cards at Cooper. "A bit on edge, are we?" he asked.

A long moment passed and then Cooper exhaled slowly,

lowered his weapon, and sat down again, resting his gun on his knee.

Archie listened, but didn't hear the noise again.

Susan settled on a third card and laid it down with the other two she had discarded, and Karim picked them up and added them to his hand. "You don't believe this business about Gretchen Lowell, do you?" Karim asked Cooper, as he looked at his cards.

Cooper was still eyeballing the door.

"It's rubbish," Karim continued, laying down a card. "Creative. But total rubbish."

Susan laid down a card on top of Karim's. "You guys should get a cat," she said. "You know, a pet to ease up the tension around here."

"The bloody pythons would eat it," Karim said.

Susan made a little strangled sound of fright.

"Told you," Cooper said to her.

"There are no pythons on this island," Archie said.

Susan gave him a dubious look.

"Listen," Karim said to Archie. "Jack's not here. Why don't you tell us why you were really down there?" He played another card, and then Susan followed, and they traded like that back and forth until Susan smiled smugly and transferred the entire pile in front of Karim on the settee.

"I told you why we were down there," Archie said. He set his drink down on the *Town & Country magazine*. "Why were *you* down there?" Gretchen had said that the tunnels they were in weren't used anymore. They certainly appeared abandoned. Now the obvious question occurred to Archie. What reason would Jack's men have to search them?

Karim's expression didn't change. He brushed something off the knee of his gray slacks.

He was stalling.

Cooper cleared his throat and sat forward. "We monitor the traffic near the house," he said. "We're aware of the FBI surveillance, so we pay attention to unfamiliar cars. We noticed a black Audi parked near some undeveloped property Jack owns. As that property happens to be the location of one of the old tunnel entrances, we checked it out, and discovered that the area around the entrance had been disturbed. It appeared that someone had entered the property. So we put a team together to patrol the tunnels. We hadn't been down there long before we saw the light go on under the door of the room you were in."

Archie lifted his glass and took another sip of whiskey. His glass had left a wet ring on Christie Brinkley's forehead. "We?" he asked Cooper.

Cooper was quiet.

Archie looked at Susan, to see if she was listening, but she appeared to be studying her cards.

"That's right—*we,*" Karim said, sounding a little agitated. He pointed a finger at Cooper. "Trust me, mate. Jack's not going to find Gretchen Lowell in the tunnels."

"You're right," Archie said. "I don't think she's in the tunnels, either."

Cooper's shoulders heaved and he sat back heavily in his chair. "You think she's off the island by now?" he asked Archie.

"I didn't say that," Archie said softly.

Cooper's eyes moved from Archie to Karim. "What's he talking about?" he asked Karim.

Karim's face was impenetrable. "He's trying to fuck with you," he said.

Cooper hesitated and then turned to Archie. "Where do you think she is?" he asked.

Susan was still looking at her cards but a small frown line had appeared between her eyebrows.

Archie picked up his glass and turned it slowly in his hand, making them wait. He kept his eyes on Karim. "She has a funny idea that she can catch the man who killed that girl they found on the dock yesterday," Archie said.

"I thought she killed that girl herself," Cooper said.

"She says she didn't," Archie said. Karim had diverted his attention to the game now, his fingers pinching his cards. He reached a hand up and straightened his tie.

"She says she saw a man in a mask lead the girl from the

party into the tunnels and then bring a corpse up a few hours later," Archie said.

Archie watched as Karim studied the carefully fanned cards in his hand, his eyes roaming from one to the next, as if seeing each one for the first time. The back of the cards had been embossed with gold crests.

"She's curious who this man might be," Archie said.

Susan inhaled quickly and laid down a black queen.

"Fuck," Karim said, flinching at the sight of the card. He swept the pile of cards toward him, as Susan smiled.

"Fancy cards," Archie said to Cooper.

Cooper smirked. "Gift from the boss last Christmas," he said. "We all got them. Generous motherfu—"

Archie saw Cooper's eyes move to the door an instant before Cooper sprang to his feet. He had leapt up so quickly that Archie, startled, had nearly dropped his drink.

Cooper's body was rigid, muscles tense, gun trained at the door.

The door was closed. No one moved. The only sound was the clock ticking.

"Uhhh," Susan said. But Cooper lifted a hand and silenced her. Then, weapon raised, Cooper started walking toward the door.

Archie wasn't sure exactly what Cooper's job was, but he suspected that he wasn't given to hysteria. Whatever Cooper had heard, they had to take it seriously. Archie put his drink down, and got up and went after him.

For a big man, Cooper was light on his feet. He had a big stride. Archie had to take two steps for each of his. But Archie caught up, and as he neared the door on Cooper's heels, he could hear it, too—a muffled shuffling coming from the other side. Cold sweat tickled the back of his neck. He reflexively reached for his weapon, but his hand found only air. Cooper leaned a shoulder against the wall to the left of the door. The door opened in, and the doorknob was on the left-hand side. Cops learned to approach a closed door from whatever side the knob was on—that way you could avoid placing your body in front of the door, where you might get shot. Cooper was approaching the door like a cop. The next noise was louder. It was the sound of something or someone making contact with the other side of the door. Cooper lowered the elbow of his firing arm and moved his gun to his rib cage in a close-contact firing position.

Archie felt Susan come up behind him. "Get back," he hissed at her. Her freckled face was pale. Over her shoulder Archie could see Karim, now standing, back near his place at the settee.

Susan didn't move. Her eyes were fixed on something past Archie, something at the bottom of the door. He followed her gaze to the floor. The floor at the door's threshold was darker than it should have been. Archie inched forward. It wasn't a shadow. It wasn't the grain of the wood. Archie glanced at Cooper. Cooper's wild eyebrows lifted. Archie moved Susan against the wall behind him and then crouched as low as possible. Cooper was waiting, watching him, his hand poised to turn the doorknob. His breathing was slow and steady. There were no more sounds on the other side of the door. Archie reached and slid a finger along the crack where the door met the floor. His finger touched something wet. He knew by the feel of it that it was blood.

Archie heard Susan say something and felt Cooper shift, leaning closer. Something scraped against the other side of the door. The source of the noise was closer to the ground than the other sounds they'd heard—only a few inches above the floor. Cooper stepped back and aimed his weapon at the noise.

Archie looked at the blood on his finger and moved in front of the door directly into Cooper's line of fire. He pressed his ear against the door and listened. He closed his eyes. He could hear the scraping noise again, louder. And then a faint rattling. It grew louder and then faded, and then repeated the pattern. It was breathing.

Archie reached up and, ignoring Susan's and Cooper's protests, he turned the doorknob. He could immediately feel the weight of the body against the door, and had to get to his feet and use his shoulder to brace it so that he could open it slowly. Cooper stepped to Archie's left, and helped anchor the door with his foot as he aimed his weapon through the ten-inch opening, and Archie peered around to see what was on the other side.

Razor Burn was slumped on the hall floor, his back against the door, his chin on his chest. Cooper shifted his foot and Archie felt the full weight of Razor Burn's body again. He eased the door open as Cooper continued to scan the hallway with his weapon. When the door was at a wide enough angle, Archie was able to take Razor Burn by the armpits and drag him inside the room. As soon as Razor Burn's heels crossed the threshold, Cooper slammed the door shut.

"See anything out there?" Archie asked Cooper. Razor Burn was unresponsive, his breathing shallow, his shirt soaked in blood. Archie reached for his wrist to take a pulse. Susan hovered at his shoulder. Archie didn't see Karim.

"A lot of blood," Cooper said. "You think this was her?" he asked.

Archie's fingers touched something slippery and warm in Razor Burn's hand. He reflexively recoiled and Razor Burn's limp hand fell open and the glistening, lumpy, rope of flesh he had been holding slopped onto his shirt. Susan squealed. Razor Burn's abdomen gaped open, revealing subcutaneous fat and the red meat of muscle. He had been holding his own intestines.

Archie's mouth went dry. He swallowed hard. "It's her," he said.

Cooper was silent, but his eyes were vigilant. He lifted his chin and turned his gaze out the front window behind Jack's desk. He was listening, Archie realized. But all Archie could hear was Razor Burn's strained, rattled wheeze. His pulse was so weak it was almost undetectable. Archie knelt over him. His bulging intestinal tissue lay in a bloody heap across his belly.

"Sirens," Cooper said.

Archie heard them then. The familiar wail of emergency vehicles was so distant that it was almost imperceptible. Help was coming. If it got here fast, Razor Burn might even live. Archie wiped the sweat from his forehead with his sleeve and propped Razor Burn's knees up to keep as much blood as possible circulating in his heart.

"What can I do?" Susan asked.

"Find me a clean cloth or napkin," Archie said.

Susan scrambled toward the bar.

"I didn't call for the police," Karim said darkly. "Who did?"

Archie glanced at him. He was still standing over by the settee. Couldn't he see that they were trying to save his buddy's life?

Karim's eyes were icy. "You've set this whole thing up," he said. "This is all part of your investigation."

"What investigation?" Cooper asked.

Archie cradled Razor Burn's head, trying to comfort him. "The murder of Lisa Watson," Archie said.

"You're going to arrest me," Karim said, only a faint note of concern in his voice.

The darker, thicker hose of Razor Burn's large bowel bulged from his open wound. "Yep," Archie said.

"Found something," Susan said, and Archie's eyes lifted as she crossed back toward them from the bar, holding a white dishcloth.

Archie saw what Karim was going to do an instant before it happened. Karim's gaze shifted to Susan, and Archie saw his lip curl, and the menace in his eyes, and he knew then what Gretchen had meant about the murderous look she'd seen directed at Lisa Watson.

Karim moved for Susan. She was looking at Archie, pleased to have found what he needed—she didn't see Karim coming for her. Archie started to stand, but Karim was too quick. He snatched Susan from behind and Archie saw a flash of light as Karim snapped a knife to Susan's neck.

Archie and Cooper were both on their feet now. Cooper's gun was trained on Karim. Cooper and Archie exchanged a brief glance—just long enough for Cooper to give Archie an almost imperceptible nod. And just like that, they were on the same side.

Susan's eyes looked large and white, the irises straining to see the blade at her neck. Her lips were stretched in a grimace. Tears gleamed at the corners of her eyes. "You have got to be fucking kidding me," she said through gritted teeth.

The sirens were louder now, but Archie still couldn't tell how far away they were—sound could travel a long way over water.

Karim's eyes darted to the window. He was clearly trying to do the same math. Then Karim seemed to make a decision, and with a rough jerk, he began to drag Susan sideways toward the door. She stumbled and lost her footing and Karim wrenched her up. "You are a cow," he seethed. He pulled his elbow back until the sharp point of the blade was nestled just under her jaw. The viciousness of his words barely registered on his composed features. "And I will slaughter you like one."

Susan's face had gone bone-white.

Archie searched helplessly around for a weapon—something, anything—he could use against Karim. A broken bottle? He'd never make it to the bar in time.

Karim flicked the knife and Susan yelped as an arc of blood spat forward onto her shirt and the toes of her shoes. Archie heard his own voice cry out as she was hurt, a strangled sound of pain that might have been only in his mind. He waited, frantic and useless. There was no arterial spray. Susan was still standing. Her earlobe bore a dark red cleft where the knife had split it.

Susan was mewling, tears streaming down her cheeks. It killed Archie to witness her terror, to be so close and yet so worthless. She was looking at him, pleading with her eyes, and there was nothing he could do. If he lunged at them, Karim would surely cut her throat. The sirens seemed like they were getting closer, but for all Archie knew they could be responding to a fire on the other side of the lake. Susan was limp in Karim's grip now, surrendering to him completely. Satisfaction spread across Karim's face. Archie's stomach turned. Karim was feeding off her fear.

There was no fire. The sirens were coming for them. It occurred to Archie in a flash. *Karim's teaspoon*. No one had

called 911 from the island because no one had needed to—
the DNA must have matched trace evidence found on Lisa
Watson's body. Even if something happened to Archie, Henry
would have the evidence he needed to put Karim away.

Archie stepped in front of the door, grasping for something to say that would buy their reinforcements some time.
"You dug it up," Archie said.

Karim's mouth twitched. He lifted his elbow as if he might
drive the knife across Susan's throat.

Cooper hadn't blinked, his eyes fixed down the barrel of
his weapon, finger on the trigger.

Susan shut her eyes.

"The knife," Archie continued. "It's dirty."

"You're watching me," Karim said. His eyes traveled
around the room. "I knew you were watching me."

He was right at the cusp, like a flame near gas. Archie
thought he might combust before their eyes.

"I can't let you leave this room, Karim," Archie said.

"Archie," Cooper barked.

Archie swung his head around. Razor Burn had somehow
managed to prop himself up onto his elbows, his gut in a
slippery pink heap, a gun in his hand. Archie could see the
ankle holster he'd drawn the gun from between his pant leg
and his black sock. His face was pallid and waxen and blood
coated his mouth, but his eyes were trained on Archie and the
gun seemed steady enough.

"Shoot him," Karim said.

Razor Burn fired. The shot was an earsplitting crack and
Archie lurched and then caught himself, his ears ringing.
Immediately, another crack split the silence. When Archie
looked up, Razor Burn was on the floor, blood gurgling
from where Cooper had shot him in the neck. His intestines
were spread across his thigh. The smell of gunpowder hung
in the air. Cooper didn't bother to kick the weapon from
Razor Burn's hand. There was no question he was dead.

Archie spun around to check on Susan. Karim had used
the distraction to move past Archie, closer to the door. Susan's
arms were pinned at her sides as she shuffled backward, the

knife at her throat. She was crying, her wet eyes fixed on him, terrified.

Then he knew.

He followed her gaze down his chest.

The bullet had gone in just under his left rib cage, almost in the very spot where Gretchen had stabbed him. It didn't hurt. Archie studied the dime-sized bullet hole in his blazer. He could see the dark ring of lead that had wiped off the surface of the bullet as it passed through the corduroy. He opened the jacket. The bloodstain on his shirt from the scalpel had been completely obliterated by the dark red stain spreading from the fresh bullet hole. He could feel the warmth of his own blood pulse against his skin. His knees wobbled. The sirens wailed.

Archie sucked in a breath and straightened up.

Karim was almost to the door with Susan.

Archie cupped his hand over the wound and stumbled forward, just as Karim pulled Susan through the door and into the hall, kicking the door shut behind him. Karim knew the tunnel system. If he took Susan belowground, Archie wouldn't stand a chance of finding them.

"Archie," Cooper called sharply.

Archie didn't stop. He couldn't stop. Karim had Susan. He reached the door and threw it open, barely aware of Cooper coming up behind him. "Take this," Cooper said. Archie looked down. Cooper pressed his gun into Archie's hand and backed away.

The sirens. They were louder now. It sounded like dozens of vehicles. Archie knew where Cooper was headed—out through the large window in Jack's office. Cooper clearly didn't want to be here when the police arrived. Archie didn't stop him. He raised Cooper's weapon and turned down the hall. He could see Karim and Susan up ahead. Susan was dragging her feet, making herself heavier, and it had slowed Karim down some.

Blood streaked the white walls on either side of the hall, where Razor Burn had leaned as he'd tried to make it back to the office. The Oriental runner that ran down the center of the hall was darkened with blood where Razor Burn had fallen and crawled. A framed photograph had been knocked off the wall and now lay in pieces on the floor. Archie glanced down as he stepped over it and saw the face of fourteen-year-old Isabel Reynolds smiling up at him from under splintered glass.

When he looked up, Susan and Karim were out of sight. Archie plunged onward, Cooper's gun clutched in his right hand, his left still trying to slow the flow of blood seeping from his wound.

He saw the first body as he cleared the hallway and entered the main foyer. Ronin lay facedown in a dark pool of blood. His throat had been cut so savagely that Archie could see the white pulp of his partially severed spinal column.

Archie heard a noise on the stairs and spun around, ready to shoot. Leo was crouched halfway down the stairs, shirtless, in black pajama pants, gun drawn. Archie lowered his own weapon slightly, breathing hard.

"I heard shots," Leo said, scrambling barefoot down the rest of the stairs. The color drained from his face as he took in the carnage on the floor. His lips drew back and he physically recoiled, even as his shooting arm tensed.

Archie had never seen Leo Reynolds afraid before.

The sirens were loud now. Right outside. They reverberated inside the house, an insistent wail.

"What's happening?" Leo asked hoarsely.

Bloody footprints continued from the body to the left, toward the hall bathroom where Archie had met Lisa Watson, marking Karim's path. Archie motioned for Leo to follow him. There wasn't time to explain. "Gretchen's here," Archie said. "Karim has Susan."

Leo didn't ask any more questions. He looked Archie up and down, his face registering Archie's alarming condition, and then Leo nodded and raised his weapon. "Let's go," he said.

They followed the footprints. Archie limped forward, the sound of Susan's whimpering echoing in his head. He could feel the gunshot in his gut now. It burned every time he took a breath. Blood spread down his pant leg. But he kept moving.

The footprints continued through the foyer, into the smaller hall that led to the back of the house. This was where the real butchery had happened. Archie counted six bodies on the hall floor—all members of Jack's security detail, by the looks of them. Blood was everywhere—on the walls, the floor, dripping from the chandelier. The smell of fresh meat permeated the air.

Archie didn't think anyone was still alive, but he didn't have time to check. He could see Karim and Susan twenty feet up ahead, against the wall across from the bathroom that Gretchen had hid in. Susan's ear was red with blood. She was looking right at Archie, her face twisted in desperation. Karim adjusted the knife at her throat, his eyes on Archie and Leo as he repeatedly jabbed a button on the wall with his elbow.

The elevator.

Archie stepped over a body, his gun raised at Karim, not looking down, feeling his way with his foot, not stopping for anyone, not caring about anyone but Susan.

"Let her go, Karim," Leo ordered.

Karim made no sign of hearing him. As Archie got closer, he saw that the textile hanging on the wall had been moved aside like a curtain, revealing the hidden elevator's steel doors. The doors parted silently and Karim twisted Susan around to push her inside. But as he shoved Susan forward, she let out a scream and scrambled backward. Karim threw her against the wall next to the elevator, as a figure stumbled out between the steel doors, his hands at his throat. The figure took a step and then fell to his knees.

Archie recognized the yachting jacket.

"Jack?" Leo said.

The sirens had reached a fever pitch. They weren't getting louder anymore. They were here.

Karim looked around wildly, and then pulled Susan from the wall. She howled as he twisted her arm behind her, and Archie could see by the shape of her shoulder that it was dislocated. Karim threw her into the open elevator as both Archie and Leo ran for the steel doors. Jack was on the floor in front of the elevator, sputtering, spurting blood, and Leo dropped to his knees next to him. Archie dived for the elevator, but couldn't get his hand between the doors in time. In that last second, as the elevator doors closed, Archie caught a glimpse of Susan, at Karim's feet, doubled over and clutching her shoulder, her face contorted in pain. She didn't look up.

Archie punched the elevator button and it lit up. "Where does this go?" he demanded from Leo.

Leo had pulled the jacket off his father and was trying to press it against Jack's bloody, gaping throat. He seemed not to hear Archie.

Someone was pounding at the front door, shouting.

"Leo!" Archie said sharply.

Leo looked up. "The new tunnel system," he said. "It opens up in a large storage room. There's a hall off it that leads to some offices and some more storage rooms. The door at the end of that hall leads to the tunnel under the lake and comes up in the basement of a house on the other side of the road."

The elevator doors slid open.

"Do you want me to come with you?" Leo asked, his father unconscious in his arms.

"Stay here," Archie said, looking back toward the front door. "Tell them what's happened."

"What *has* happened?" Leo asked.

Leo's bare feet were wet with the blood they had walked through. His father was dying. Archie knew he was desperate for answers. But he didn't have time to elaborate. Archie stepped into the elevator. "Karim killed Lisa Watson," Archie told Leo. "The dead guy in the office was shot while he was shooting me. Gretchen killed everybody else."

An arc of blood spatter looked like a letter *C* on the back wall of the elevator. Jack's throat had been cut in here. There were two floor buttons inside the elevator. The top one had a 1 on it and the bottom one had a B on it. Archie pressed the B button.

Leo was rocking his father in his lap. But as the elevator doors started to close, he looked up. "Archie," he said. "Keys!"

He fumbled in his father's pocket and managed to toss a set of keys to Archie just as the steel doors closed. Archie caught the keys and put them in his jacket pocket.

The elevator began to descend, and the sensation made Archie's head swim.

"Going down," said a woman's crisp automated voice.

A red digital readout above the elevator doors showed a number 1 with a downward-facing arrow on either side of it. Archie kept his eyes on the readout. He waited for it to change, but the 1 stayed up despite the fact that he could feel the elevator moving. He had to remind himself that he wasn't just moving between floors—the elevator had to pass through the house's actual basement and then through dirt and shale to the subbasement. *Any minute now*, he told himself. Finally the digital readout disassembled and re-formed as the letter B. The elevator bounced slightly as it settled at the bottom of the shaft. Archie took a breath, stepped to the corner of the elevator just inside the doors, and raised his weapon.

"Lower level," the woman's voice announced pleasantly.

The doors opened.

Archie blocked the doors open with his foot and did a quick scan outside the elevator with his weapon. There was no sign of movement. He pivoted out of the elevator and backed against the wall, gun raised.

This was nothing like the tunnels Gretchen had led him through. It looked like an industrial-grade warehouse or some kind of secret government facility. The ceilings were low, but the room seemed to go on and on in every direction. Pallets were stacked almost to the ceiling in places, creating the illusion of walls. Panels of fluorescent lights radiated overhead along with what looked to be a state-of-the-art sprinkler system.

Archie checked the concrete floor for traces of blood and saw what looked like a partial footprint in front of one of the pallet stacks maybe twenty feet out. He heaved himself toward it, clutching his side, but when he reached the footprint, he didn't see another.

The low hum of the air recirculation system echoed off

the concrete walls. Archie listened for footsteps, anything, but he could feel his senses slipping from him. The periphery of his vision was blackening. His hands had gone numb.

Archie leaned against the tarp-covered stack of pallets next to him and groped in his pocket for the amber pill bottle Jack had given him. He popped the white cap off and shook some of the small white pills onto his palm and then brought them to his mouth. He was so thirsty that he could barely manage enough saliva to choke them down. His hand tasted like blood, and the pills coated his tongue with a bitter paste. He looked at the floor, willing the pills to take effect, to give him just enough relief to keep moving. *Don't think. Don't stop. Just move.* His eyes were still on the floor when the toe of a shiny white pump stepped into his sight line. He followed the white stockings—now threaded with runs and speckled with drops of blood—up her shapely leg, her face a picture of compassion.

She took the amber plastic pill bottle from his hand, snapped the childproof white cap back on, and tucked the bottle back into his jacket pocket. Her white dress was soaked with blood. The cape and the hat were gone. "You're looking peaked, darling," she said.

Archie struggled to find the strength to speak. He couldn't let Gretchen distract him. He didn't care if she went back to jail. He didn't care if she made a fool of him again. He just wanted to get Susan back alive. "Where are they?" he asked her.

Gretchen's eyes were jubilant. "I told you I'd find you a serial killer," she said. "It's really been quite a bit of fun."

Archie glowered at her. Karim might have a knife to Susan's throat, but Gretchen might as well have put it there. She owed him. "If he kills her," Archie said, "I'll make you pay."

Gretchen batted her lashes at him, looking hurt. "I think you're being rather mean."

"Tell me where they are," Archie said. It twisted his insides to talk, to breathe. Each word took so much effort he had to pause between them.

Gretchen cocked her head, studying him, her eyes landing

on the blood that had soaked through his shirt and pant leg. "You shouldn't be bleeding that much," she said, and Archie thought he detected a flicker of distress in her voice.

"Shot," Archie said with a cough.

Gretchen's bearing stiffened. She reached to open his blazer, but he pulled away. "No," he said. "Tell me." He'd lost too much blood. He was getting too weak too fast. "Hurry," he said.

Gretchen pointed across the room to a hallway.

It was sixty feet away. In Archie's condition it might as well have been the English-fucking-Channel.

He glanced back at the elevator.

"I disabled it," Gretchen said. "I found a maintenance panel. All I had to do was cut some wires. Looks like we're on our own for a little while longer."

He was out of time. Susan was out of time. He had to try. Archie pushed himself off the pallets and staggered toward the hallway that Gretchen had indicated. He couldn't stand upright. He had to walk bent over, or the pain would overwhelm him. His left leg had started to drag.

He hadn't made it more than a few steps when Gretchen caught up with him. "Do you want my help?" she asked, flitting at his elbow.

Archie set his sights on the next block of pallets. "No," he said. His pants were so blood-soaked that the fabric stuck to his thigh as he walked. His left hand was bloody up to the elbow. He could feel his body failing him, his breaths growing shorter, his muscles weakening. He was so thirsty. But he pushed on, the gun clenched in his hand. Ten steps. Fifteen. Thirty. Fifty. He had passed four stacks of pallets. When he got to the fifth, he had to stop and lean against it to gather his strength. The hallway was only ten feet away, almost within his grasp. But he wouldn't make it. He was too weak.

He had to hear Susan's voice.

Archie mustered all his strength, swallowed hard, pressed his wound with his hand, lifted his head, and hollered her name.

"Susan!"

His despairing voice bounced off the concrete walls, echoing through the room, reverberating down the hall.

"I'm here!" Susan yelled back. She was cut off abruptly, forcibly silenced. But it was enough. Even with the basement acoustics Archie was certain that her voice was coming from up ahead. It was the motivation he needed.

Adrenaline pulsed into his fists and he heaved himself off the pallets and hobbled, grimacing, toward the hallway's beckoning rectangle of light. His breaths came in pants now. He could still only move hunched over, hand pressed against his wound. Ten steps—each footfall a painful blur.

Then he was there. He had made it. He leaned up against the wall and lifted his gun. His shooting arm trembled as he pointed the weapon down the empty hall. The fluorescent lights cast a greenish glow. There were two doors about halfway down the left side of the hall, and a steel fire door at the end of the hall, thirty feet dead ahead.

"That door leads to the tunnel off the island," Gretchen said from behind him. She stepped next to him and pointed to the fire door. He didn't know where she'd come from, if she had caught up with him again or if she had been there all along. She smiled at him. "But Jack lent me a key."

Archie struggled to understand—*he* had Jack's keys. He grasped for them in his jacket pocket with his bloody hand. But Gretchen stopped him, holding up a brass key of her own.

"I took the master," she explained. "Jack was kind enough to point it out to me."

She'd slaughtered Jack for that key. But why? Then it hit him. "You locked the door," Archie said. She had sealed Karim's only escape off the island. They had him trapped.

She leaned across the doorway close to his ear. "The first door," she whispered in his ear. "That's where Karim has Susan." She directed him to look where she was pointing. "Can you see it?"

Archie peered down the hall at the first door. His vision

was spotty. But when he concentrated, the door came into focus and Archie saw that it was very slightly ajar.

He could do this.

He could get to her.

Karim was cornered.

Archie raised his gun again. He couldn't hold it very high—it was too heavy suddenly, too cumbersome—but he could get it up enough. He took a step forward. And another. The darkness at the corners of his vision swirled in and out of his sight line. He squeezed his eyes shut a few times, and rubbed them with his bloody hand. But he kept moving. Another step. His legs felt like jelly. The hallway seemed to tilt and stretch around him—he had to brace himself against the rough concrete wall. He checked the door. It was still a good dozen steps away. He had to summon another burst of energy. But he was too weak to call out to Susan again. A crushing pain cut through Archie's spine. He staggered a few more steps, supporting himself on the concrete wall, and then looked back at the trail of blood his palm had left on the wall's slick white paint. It was the same blood pattern that marked the fatal path Razor Burn had taken to Jack's office. The floor shifted suddenly. Archie tried to recover his balance, but the wall seemed to pull away and he sank to his knees on the floor. He was sweaty and cold, his heart pounding in his chest. He had lost too much blood. He wasn't going to make it. He was worthless. *Get up,* he said in his head. He looked at the first door: an arm's reach away, a light on inside, the shuffle of movement. Archie had found them. He was so close. *Get up,* he pleaded. He made a deal with himself. *I'll do anything.*

Gretchen's face materialized next to him. Her skin shimmered, bathed in a silvery slight. A golden glow framed her head like an aura. Her expression was serene, like a painting of a saint. This was all proof, he thought, that his brain was shutting down. "Do you want my help?" Gretchen asked again sweetly.

Archie pulled away from her and tried once more to stand, but he was so shaky and feeble it was no use. He sank back to the floor, useless and weak. He couldn't do it. But he had to get to Susan. No matter what it took.

"Yes," Archie said in a voice barely above a whisper.

"What's that, darling?" Gretchen asked.

"Yes," Archie said.

He groped for the wall, and his hand found it this time. He leaned into his palm, trying to get enough leverage to stand, and he managed to get a foot on the floor in front of him. The seams and eyelets of his brown leather shoe were caked with mud and blood. The shoe looked foreign to him, like it belonged to someone else's foot. Tiny drops of blood dotted the toe. He blinked and the dots swam before his eyes.

Gretchen was crouched next to him, her shoes even bloodier than his. She shifted the deadweight of his arm over her shoulder and Archie surrendered, letting her support his weight. She held his hand by his wrist against her breast. He could see the gun in his hand, the barrel pressed against her dress, but he couldn't feel his own fingers around the grip. His hands were too numb. Gretchen moved her other arm around his waist. Her blond hair brushed his forearm, and through everything, through all of the pain and the shakiness, he could still feel that—he could feel the gentle thrill of Gretchen's hair against his flesh. She tightened her hold on his wrist.

"This is going to hurt," she whispered.

He inhaled sharply as she lifted him to his feet. The pain from the gunshot felt like the crack of a whip. Even his tears stung. His vision blanched. His stomach turned. His legs felt bulky and anesthetized. But when his vision came back into focus, he was upright. The toe of her bloody white pump pressed against the outside curve of his shoe. She loosened her grip on his wrist and he lurched for the wall with his hand, to help stabilize himself. He was sweaty and fighting for breath, his body ringing with pain. They were standing, bodies still entangled. Gretchen's face was flushed from the effort of lifting him. She smelled like blood, like a slaughterhouse, or maybe, Archie thought, he was the one who smelled like that. Her expression was one of gentle patience, the devoted caretaker.

Archie's arm was still slung over her shoulder, his gun hand resting against her breast. He cleared his throat and lifted his chin, honing in on the open door that was now so close. He could feel a pulse where Gretchen held his wrist, but he couldn't tell if it was his heartbeat or hers.

As he focused on the pulse, he began to make out sounds coming from behind the door—drawers being opened, papers thrown, the sound of glass breaking on the concrete floor. Whatever Karim was doing in there, he was leaving a path of destruction.

Archie started toward the door. Gretchen held him up, taking all of his weight, their bodies moving together. Underneath the destructive ruckus, Archie could still feel the pulse that beat between them. It was louder than the shattering glass, louder than wood cracking. It was the beat that kept him moving. He could feel it in his body. The pulse was rapid and thready and he knew it must be his. Tachycardia. Hypovolemic shock. Gretchen knew it, too. He could feel her fingers pressing into the soft inside of his wrist, monitoring him.

They were four steps from the door. Karim was cursing on the other side, throwing objects against the wall. Gretchen paused. Archie's momentum was so committed to moving forward that he nearly fell over, but she caught him and then turned him and set him gently against the wall. Archie didn't understand. They were so close. He needed her help, the rhythm of their pulse.

But then she let go of his wrist, and the rhythm stopped. His body went quiet. He knew that the concrete behind his back was supposed to feel hard, but it felt doughy, formless, like he could sink right through it. Gretchen touched his ear. Her face took up all the space in his vision. There was no one and nothing but her. He could still hear the havoc behind the door, but inside—in his head—all was mute. It was like he was physically disassociating from himself. He wasn't going to make it through the door. He wasn't going to get to Susan. He was going to die, as he always knew he would, at Gretchen's feet. Archie smiled at the irony, as his head lolled back.

* * *

Gretchen is on top of him, straddling him, and he is deeper inside her than he has ever been in anyone. He gazes up at her, his senses painfully exquisite. Her hand is knotted in his hair, pulling so hard at the roots that she has bent his head backward into the pillow. He can barely breathe. Strands of her own sweat-soaked hair stick to the sides of her face, but she has never looked more beautiful to him. The bedroom window is open, and he can hear the wind moving through the dry leaves in the trees, the box spring moaning beneath them, each time Gretchen catches her breath. His skin prickles with heat. Pain blazes where her fist meets his scalp, blotting out his guilt and self-doubt. There is just the pain and her and sex and the black wall of bliss that slices through him like a blade. Her face comes in and out of view. Her hard nipples graze his chest as her breasts swing forward, then back. Her mouth is open, the upper lip twitching as her breathing quickens. Her skin glows. Her eyelids flutter. She grinds against him harder, knotting her fist tighter in his hair as she does, so that the pain and pleasure intermix until they are indistinguishable. He drives himself even harder and deeper inside her, desperate for relief. He can see her shoulder move as her other hand works her clitoris. She opens her mouth wider and moans and spots of color appear on her cheeks.

"Now," she says.

Archie flings an arm out, feels blindly for the Taser on the bedside table, and finds it. She is writhing on top of him, half mad, and his body is consumed by pleasure, her fist in his hair, his neck jammed back. He can hear the snapping sound of his hair severing from the roots. His head is twisted at an angle that allows him to look at her. He never let himself imagine he would be with someone who looked like Gretchen Lowell. Every part of her is perfect. He holds the Taser a few inches out, pointed at the dip of her waist. She makes another sound, a gentle mewling.

Archie's eyes move to the Taser. The gun-shaped grip, the yellow safety logo. The laser sight glows red on Gretchen's flesh.

She curls over him then, her eyelashes brushing his Adam's apple. Then she lets go of his hair.

The sudden absence of pain is almost disorienting.

"Do it," she pleads.

Archie pulls the trigger.

All of her muscles seize as the two darts make contact, sending fifty thousand volts of electrical current coursing through her body, incapacitating her. As her muscles contract, her pelvis and legs tighten around his cock. He comes instantly, and powerfully, inside her. She jerks and falls against him, and he pulls her into his arms, staying inside her as she twitches. He clings to her, counting down in his mind, waiting for the thirty-second energy burst to pass and her central nervous system to come back online. Slowly, her color returns and the rigidity of her body softens. When she lifts her head, she is out of breath and he can feel that her heart is beating as furiously as his. But she is grinning at him, a sheen of saliva on her chin, her eyes bright with pleasure.

He can never stop, he realizes. Everything has changed. It is like having sex for the first time.

He can never have enough of her.

He wants to snatch the moment back, to undo it.

Then, somewhere, far away, he hears something crash and break against a wall. He pulls away from Gretchen, sits up, and turns his head toward the sound.

"Archie?" Gretchen asks.

"Archie?" Gretchen's voice was a hoarse whisper. Archie blinked and his head jerked up, and she came into focus. Her blue eyes met his gaze and then moved over his face, a small frown line appearing between her eyebrows. He had passed out for a second. Now she was examining him, Archie realized, her eyes roving over him, finger on his pulse, medically assessing him to see how much time he had left. Not long, he figured. But his interest at this point was purely academic. He only needed long enough.

Gretchen took his hand in hers. The gun was somehow still in his fist. Gretchen peeled off his fingers one by one from the grip. He let her do it. It was like he was watching it happen to someone else. It didn't occur to him to resist. He couldn't have, even if he'd had the presence of mind to want to.

It was all so slow, so foreign. His fingers were stiff and sticky with blood. When she had the gun free she ejected the magazine and held it up in front of his face. "You've got two bullets," she told him. She caught his eye. "You hear me?" she asked. "Two." She waited for him to manage a nod and then she reinserted the magazine into the handgrip. It fell into place with a familiar metallic click. Then she disengaged the safety and handed it back to him. This time, as he folded his hand around it, he could feel the weight of the metal. He was no longer numb. The grip of the gun was electric against his flesh.

"You want to save her?" Gretchen whispered. She smiled encouragingly.

He *did* want to save her. He wanted Susan to stay alive. Right now, it was the most important thing in the world to him.

Gretchen stepped back. "Then save her," she said.

Something else crashed beyond the door. Archie felt the pulse of the impact through the wall. Then he heard Susan gasp loudly in pain.

"Wait," Archie whispered to Gretchen. His vision was too blurry. He blinked, trying to clear it. He cared too much. This wasn't going to work. He was going to fail. Gretchen stepped back in front of him and came into focus again, that beautiful face of hers. She raised an eyebrow. He was too weak. He needed some intensity, an internal switch to be thrown. He was desperate. There was no one else. Karim would kill Susan by the time the others found a way in. Susan was counting on him.

"Hit me," Archie said.

The corners of Gretchen's mouth twitched up in a smile. Then she raised a hand and slapped Archie hard across the face. He felt a dizzying slash of pain and the impact turned his head to the wall. His face stung. His head buzzed. His eyes teared. But a burst of endorphins cut through the fog in his brain like a knife. The heat on his cheek where she'd made contact burned. He took a few long breaths, his head still turned toward the wall, feeling lighter with each inhalation, as if he had been given more access to oxygen somehow. He was seeing things more lucidly, more surely. He was still alive. He turned back to face Gretchen. Her eyes were spirited. Her nostrils flared with anticipation. She liked to cause people pain. Now she looked at him, her eyes inviting him to hit her back. Archie's hand itched to do it, too. He could break her nose if he wanted to. He could shatter that exquisite bone structure, leaving her swollen and deformed, bleeding into her mouth. No one would blame him. He let that desire live in him for a moment, using it to nourish his strength. He summoned every bit of energy and nerve he had, and then, cheek still hot from her touch, he propelled himself off the wall. He staggered past her without looking back, raised his weapon, and pushed open the door.

CHAPTER

43

Susan's dislocated shoulder pulsed with pain. Her wrist ached from Karim's viselike grip. Every time he yanked her arm, jamming bone into the nerve tissue around her hollow shoulder socket, she gulped back a gasp of agony.

Karim kept one hand on her and one around the knife. She'd thought he'd have to put that knife down at some point, but he never did. The knife was like an extension of his hand. He pulled another drawer out of a desk, rifled through it, and tossed it against the wall. The wood split against the concrete and the drawer's contents bounced onto the floor—papers, a plastic calculator, thumbtacks, pens, an orange rubber Super Ball that bounced joyfully across the room before rolling under a copy machine. Susan flinched and Karim twisted her wrist to bring her to him. The pain made her knees buckle and hot tears well in her eyes. He pulled her close and brought the knife to her face. His breath was sour. His face smelled like pungent aftershave. She didn't want to look at him, so instead she kept her eyes fixed on the knife. She could see a sliver of her reflection in the blade, a wet, red eye.

"Are you scared?" Karim asked. His British accent made the inquiry sound almost genteel.

Susan knew better than to answer. Instead, she eyed the gun in Karim's waistband, inches away from her free hand. But she'd done this math before. If she went for the gun, he'd cut her throat; if she ran, he'd shoot her. With one arm hanging limp and useless, she didn't stand a chance at overpowering him.

"You're not scary," a voice said from the door.

Susan looked over, hardly daring to trust her ears. Archie stood in the doorway, with a gun in his hand pointed at Karim. But her elation deflated as she took in the rest. Archie's pallor was corpselike, and he was soaked with blood from his ribs to his knees. He was braced against the doorjamb as if he needed the support to stay standing.

Karim reacted instantly, moving her in front of him and lowering the blade to the center of her throat, wrenching Susan's shoulder in the process.

"You okay?" Archie asked her.

Susan took a few breaths as the pain subsided. "I think my shoulder's dislocated, but yeah," she said. He had lost a lot of blood. And he had still come after her. "How about you?"

"Fine," he said. He gave her a weak smile. "Why?"

"You've just come to chat, have you?" Karim asked, sounding irritated.

"Thanks for reminding me," Archie said, his eyes flicking from Susan to Karim. The instant Archie looked at Karim, Susan saw all the warmth in Archie's face evaporate. "You're under arrest," Archie told Karim. "You have the right to remain silent." He leaned a shoulder against the doorjamb. Susan could tell he had tried to do it casually, but he was clearly wobbly on his feet. Archie cleared his throat. "Anything you say or do can and will be held against you in a court of law. You have the right to an attorney. If you cannot afford an attorney one will be provided at no cost." Archie's gun started to drift toward the floor. Susan saw Archie notice it and jerk the weapon back up into the general range of Karim's head. "Do you understand these rights as I've explained them to you?" Archie asked Karim.

This wasn't good. Susan could see in Archie's eyes that this wasn't good. She glanced behind Archie, expecting Henry to appear, or Leo or Sanchez or . . . anyone. But there was no one else. Archie had come alone. What had happened to those sirens they had all heard approaching? Susan felt a knot of dread like a fist in her chest. Archie was bleeding badly. His face looked like her father's had in the hours before he'd died, like he knew, like half of him had already gone.

With a terrible sinking feeling, Susan realized that Archie couldn't save her. He couldn't even save himself.

"Can I ask," Karim inquired of Archie, "have you ever been shot before?"

Susan watched Archie, riveted. His hand was now clawed around the doorjamb, supporting his weight. He blinked slowly at Karim. "Interestingly enough, no," Archie said.

"You've lost half your blood, mate," Karim said. "You're in shock. You can barely walk. Your brain's not getting oxygen. Your organs are going to start shutting down. You think you can shoot straight? If you'd stayed immobile and received treatment you'd probably have made it. But now?" Karim made a show of checking his watch. "Your golden hour is almost up."

Susan swallowed a sob, and the blade stung at her neck. "Archie," she said. She tried to smile through her tears. "It's okay." She didn't want him to die, not because of her. "You can go," she said. Her voice cracked as she said it. "Go back and get help."

Archie gave her a small, sad smile, like he knew something she didn't. Then his eyes lifted back to Karim.

Karim tightened his grip on Susan's wrist, pulling painfully at her dislocated shoulder. Her eyes burned with tears but she didn't cry out, she didn't make a sound. She swallowed all of it.

"I have something that you want," Archie said to Karim. He took his hand off the doorjamb, put his full weight against his shoulder, and dug his hand into his pants pocket. He wavered slightly on his feet, like someone who is drunk but doesn't want anyone to catch on. Susan willed him to stay upright because if he fell she had the feeling he wasn't going to be able to get up.

Archie extended his hand and jingled a large set of keys.

Susan felt Karim lean forward.

"Jack's keys," Archie said. He indicated the damage-strewn room. "That's what you've been looking for, I assume? The key to the exit?"

Karim was breathing loudly through his nose. The keys glittered. Archie jangled them again like someone teasing a cat.

"Toss them to me," Karim said.

Archie opened his hand and let the keys fall. They landed a few feet from his toes. His eyes stayed on Karim. "Oops," Archie said.

Karim let go of Susan's wrist and she felt him reach behind her back and pull the gun from his waistband. The gunmetal scraped along her spine as he drew the weapon and pointed it at Archie. He kept it trained on Archie as he switched hands, exchanging the hilt of the knife to his off hand and the gun in his right. The blade itched at Susan's neck, and she tried not to swallow, her bad arm now hanging limply at her side.

Karim pressed behind her, forcing her forward, his body pushing her, the blade biting at her skin. Susan managed to take her bad arm by the wrist with her other hand to try to keep it steady, but she still winced each time they took a step. Her throat stung where the blade had nicked her flesh. She concentrated on Archie. Walking to Archie. If she made it, she told herself, she got to go home. She got to go home to Jefferson Starship and cherry incense and Bliss and her cara-mel apples. She got to sleep on her futon bed, and she'd take life more seriously, write a real book, and maybe she'd finally learn how to play guitar. She'd choose a direction, like Bliss had said. Susan didn't mind Jefferson Starship, really, she'd always secretly liked that band.

Archie nodded at her, coaxing her toward him. She wanted to believe that he had a plan—that he was stronger than he looked—but the closer she got, the direr his condition seemed.

Karim was right. Archie could barely stand. If she made it to him, Susan told herself, she'd hold him up. That was all he needed, someone to lean against. They would both get to go home. The knife nicked her flesh again, and Susan winced, feeling a thread of blood trickle down her neck. Karim pushed her forward another step. They were still a few feet shy of Archie when Karim jerked to a stop, wrenching Susan's shoulder again. She bit her lip from the pain.

"Get them," Karim said.

She looked at Archie. He gave her a slight nod. The ring of keys was on the floor. There were maybe forty keys affixed to a black horseshoe-shaped charm. Karim lowered Susan forward, the blade still at her neck, his gun still trained on Archie. Again, Archie gave Susan an encouraging nod. She extended her good arm, fingers straining for the keys. She recognized the horseshoe charm. It was Hermès. Jack had probably spent three hundred dollars on it. She told herself that if she could just touch it, she could keep it. It was a horseshoe. It would bring her luck.

She had to battle for every inch. Karim held her uncomfortably close, folding his body over hers as she leaned lower for the keys, his armpit at her ear, the knife at her throat. The smell of his aftershave had turned sour with sweat. As she bent over, her T-shirt and pants parted and she felt the bare flesh of her lower spine touch the buttons of his shirt and she flinched at the intimate sensation. She strained for that horseshoe. It was still beyond her fingertips and she stretched as far as she could, as Karim slowly extended the knife forward to allow her more movement. She sobbed, despite herself, and he laughed and pushed into her from behind, and she could feel the hardness of him pressing between her legs. She kept her head down, not wanting Archie to see her face. Her fingers touched the horseshoe. It was black rubber, with four little white squares along each side and a white squiggle at the top of the hump. It was the kind of squiggle that kids use to indicate a bird in a drawing. The white bird's wings were open. It was flying right at her. She just needed another millimeter and she'd have it. The blade pressed against her throat and she heard the chilling sound of the sharpened metal scraping against her own flesh. She felt something wet crawl down her collarbone under her T-shirt and into her bra, but she didn't know if it was blood or sweat. She had the keys in her hand. As her fingers closed around the horseshoe, she felt Karim's right arm brace against her shoulder. It was a tiny movement. Nothing anyone would have noticed. But their bodies were so close that Susan could actually feel him plant his stance, and adjust his shooting arm ever so slightly.

Susan didn't have time to think. She jammed her elbow back hard into Karim's solar plexus the instant before he fired. Karim grunted in pain and the knife dropped a fraction of a centimeter, but it was enough. Susan was able to duck out from under his arm. She lifted her head, to see if Archie had been hit. Archie was still in the doorway, gun raised. The moment she was out of Karim's reach, Archie fired. The gunshot reverberated off every concrete surface. Susan dropped to the floor. She was still on her hands and knees, her bad arm dragging on the floor, when Karim swooped behind her and wrenched her upward. She struggled to free herself but he took hold of her wrist and twisted her arm so hard she put her head back and yowled. She was still whimpering when Karim pushed her, face-first, into the wall next to the door, and held her there.

She glanced frantically to her left and saw Archie still in the doorway. He was even paler now, almost waxen. His gun was still trained on Karim—the end of the barrel close enough that Susan could have touched it—but Archie's arm had sunk from a ninety-degree angle to a seventy-degree angle. His eyes were anguished. Susan could see him straining to raise the weapon, but he didn't seem to have the strength.

"The gun's getting heavy, isn't it?" Karim asked Archie, his voice smug. "Your head's swimming. You don't have the strength to pull the trigger."

Archie fired again.

Susan closed her eyes and braced herself. Karim's body jerked. But the knife didn't leave her throat. Then she heard the sickening sound of Karim's laugh. She forced herself to open her eyes. Archie was sinking to the floor. He'd used the last of his strength to shoot Karim, and he'd hit him—Susan had felt the impact. She strained around to see Karim, and he rotated her roughly so that they were face-to-face. Karim lifted his arm and showed her the tear and streak of blood where Archie had managed to graze Karim's bicep. Susan hated him. She could feel the contempt form on her face and she didn't try to hide it. She looked toward Archie. He was trying to stand again, then stumbled sideways, and leaned back against the wall to the left of the door and started to slide to the floor. The gun fell from his hand onto the concrete.

Susan's throat felt swollen, like it might close entirely.

Archie tried once more to stand, failed, and came to a rest in a sitting position, legs akimbo in front of him, back against the wall. He looked up at Susan and his eyes filled with tears. His lips were colorless and his expression was puzzled. "Sorry," Archie muttered.

Susan was shaking uncontrollably now. Karim pulled her into the doorway and sandwiched her against the doorjamb and then, to Susan's horror, he pressed his gun against Archie's forehead.

"I could kill you," Karim snarled at Archie. Then he bent his elbow and lifted the gun. "But instead I'm going to leave you here to die." Karim's breathing came in halting rasps. He was pressed against her hard, worming his pelvis against her, trying to work her legs open, but Susan kept her thighs clamped shut. Karim holstered the knife into his waistband and socked her hard between her legs. Susan cried out and Karim forced his hand into the front of her pants. He grinned, his face glistening with sweat. But he wasn't even looking at Susan. This was for Archie. Karim clawed his hooked hand against her underpants, digging to get inside her even as she clenched her body tight to resist him.

He was going to hurt her badly, but what bothered Susan the most was that Archie would have to watch it.

"I want you to spend the next few minutes thinking about

what I'm going to do to her," Karim said in a low, nasty voice. "I'm going to take my time. We're going to have a lot of fun together."

He grabbed her flesh through the underwear and twisted it, and Susan wailed in anguish. He grinned cruelly. This was what turned him on, not sex, but pain. "I'll fuck her raw before I gut her," Karim said. Karim paused and cocked his head. Then he lifted a foot and gave Archie's arm a kick. "You still awake, mate?" he asked. Archie didn't respond.

This wasn't happening, Susan told herself. This was all a bad dream.

"I'll fuck her," Karim spat at Archie, "and I'll make her say your name." Susan felt his hand release her and then fumble with opening his own pants. She glanced down at Archie. She couldn't see his face anymore, but one hand was motionless, palm up on the floor, and one leg was splayed lifeless in front of him. Susan heard Karim unzip his pants and she sucked in a lungful of air, determined not to give him the satisfaction of crying. She looked up at the ceiling, bit her lip, and steeled herself against whatever was coming.

Karim pinned her against the doorjamb again. Archie was slumped on the floor just feet away. Karim lowered his face to Susan's shoulder and licked her. When he lifted his head, there was blood around his mouth. He scraped the knife down her throat, like he was giving her a shave.

"Say, 'Fuck me, Archie,' " Karim said.

Susan was so horrified she couldn't even speak. For a second she thought she might throw up.

Karim frowned at her, his dark eyes murderous. Then he stepped back and gave Archie a kick.

Susan couldn't see Archie well enough from her position to see Karim make contact, but when Karim brought his foot back the toe was covered in blood. He'd kicked Archie in his wound. Archie hadn't even whimpered.

"Say it, or I'll kill him now," Karim said.

Susan was sobbing. She didn't know what to do. But she knew that the sooner they got this over with, the sooner he'd kill her.

"Fuck me," she said weakly. She could see Archie's leg, his dirty brown shoe. She hoped he couldn't hear this. She hoped he was unconscious. She hoped he was dead. She looked at the ceiling. "Fuck me," she sobbed. The next word stuck in her throat, but she choked it out. "Archie."

"Since you asked for it," Karim said, and he jammed his hand in her pants again, his stiff fingers trying to penetrate her, his face a terrible snarl.

She heard herself moaning in pain.

She had to go limp. She had to force her body to relax. It wouldn't hurt as much that way. Not this part anyway. With a whimper of surrender, vomit rising in her throat, Susan made herself soft under his grip. She let her muscles uncoil. Karim saw it instantly. He grunted and started fumbling to get her pants down, as his erection pressed against her pelvic bone.

"Say it again," Karim said, panting.

Susan would win in the end. She would show Karim. She was going to ruin this for him. She was going to die quickly. "Fuck me, Archie," she said again.

There was a flash of light and something hot sprayed across Susan's face. It was in her eyes, her mouth. She blinked, speechless and immobile, as the red spray continued, spurting on her chin, her neck, her shoulders. Had Karim cut her? With a sharp enough blade it would take a minute before you'd feel the pain. Was she bleeding to death right now? She heard Karim's gun drop to the floor. He was looking right at her, his dark eyes boring into hers. Blood gurgled from a slice on his throat, a red slash like a smile. He leaned forward, his face folding toward hers, like he was going to kiss her. She turned her head sharply and squeezed her eyes shut. He stayed against her for a moment, his nose pressed against her cheek, radiating that sour smell. She could hear a sputtering sound that she realized was coming not from his lips, but from his throat. Then his head slid wetly down her body, her chest and belly, as he sank to the floor, his face finally coming to rest between her knees. Susan kicked him off her, and heard him fall backward, his skull hitting the floor with a thud. Then Susan opened her eyes. Standing where Karim had stood, her bloody scalpel gleaming in her hand, was Gretchen Lowell.

Susan's eyes automatically went to Archie. He was still slumped against the wall near her feet, eyes half-open, staring straight ahead.

Gretchen wiped her scalpel on her skirt. "Do I have to do everything myself?" she asked wearily.

Susan could barely breathe. She had to get to Archie, to see if he was okay. She inched around the doorjamb and lowered herself at Archie's side. His gun was on the floor by his thigh. Susan didn't give herself time to think or hesitate. She reached across him, picked up the gun with her good hand, spun around, and pointed it up at Gretchen.

Susan was breathing through snot and tears and she knew it sounded like crying. But she was not afraid. She was furious. She had fired a gun once at a range. She knew how to line up the sights. She knew to brace herself for recoil. Archie was dying and Gretchen had done it. Gretchen hadn't fired the gun, but she'd brought them both to that island. Susan was certain that Gretchen had orchestrated this whole thing somehow.

Gretchen arched an eyebrow. She didn't look scared or surprised or even mildly inconvenienced. It made Susan loathe her even more.

"You're not going to shoot me, pigeon," Gretchen said with a sigh. "I just saved your life."

Susan pulled the trigger. She braced herself but there was no recoil. No bang. Just a small hollow click. Gretchen didn't even blink. A sob was stuck in Susan's throat. She kept the gun aimed at Gretchen, but now her hands were shaking with frustration, making it even harder to steady the weapon.

"There were only two bullets," Gretchen said.

Susan squeezed the trigger again, and again, willing it to fire, but each time it just clicked uselessly. Gretchen crossed in front of Susan and knelt next to Archie. Susan kept the gun trained at her head, because even an empty gun was better than no gun at all. Gretchen placed two fingers on Archie's throat, and Susan squeezed the trigger again. This time she didn't hear the click. There was a noise coming from somewhere, a distant grinding hum that echoed off the concrete walls. It sounded like a dental drill. Or power tools. Susan inhaled quickly. That's what it was. The cops were trying to get to them through the locked tunnel door.

Gretchen must have heard the sound, too, but her face didn't register it. She was concentrating on Archie. She withdrew her fingers from his neck and lifted up one of Archie's eyelids. He didn't react. His eyes remained fixed and unfocused. His face was splotchy with varying shades of ash.

Susan's eyes burned. Help was so close. It couldn't be too late. She could barely bring herself to speak. "Is he alive?" she asked.

Gretchen didn't answer. She turned and seemed to scrutinize Susan. Even in this situation, Susan found herself fascinated by her. Even covered with blood, Gretchen looked like a movie star. Her hands were gloved with red. The white polyester dress was so stained it looked like it was patterned with roses. Gretchen reached over and plucked Archie's gun from Susan's hands and set it on the floor. They were so close that Susan could see the tiny earring holes in Gretchen's earlobes. Gretchen put one hand on Susan's upper arm and the other on top of Susan's bad shoulder.

Susan cringed from pain, afraid to move. "Don't touch me," she said.

Gretchen's grip tightened and she pressed Susan's shoulder to the wall, and simultaneously snapped Susan's arm forward. Susan howled. The pain bloomed outward from her shoulder, all the way to her scalp and toes. It made her hair stand up and the marrow in her bones dry up. Then, just as suddenly, it was over. The pain was gone. Susan, panting and sweating, tears streaming down her face, cautiously inspected her arm. She lifted it carefully and bent it back and forth at the elbow. She rotated her shoulder. The joint was back in the socket.

Gretchen had returned her attention to Archie. She held his bloodless face in her hands, a sad smile on her lips, her eyes glistening. Then she leaned forward and gently kissed him on the cheek. It was so tender that Susan nearly believed that Gretchen was actually experiencing an emotion.

Something deep in Susan's stomach twisted.

Was Archie dead?

Susan covered her mouth with her hand and shook her head, not wanting to believe it. Archie couldn't be dead. But there was so much blood. And he was so still and pale. She looked at Karim, who lay in a fetal position in the doorway. His eyes were also half open. His face was also waxen. A puddle of dark red blood encircled his head.

They were both dead.

Susan turned desperately back to Archie, only to find Gretchen was scrutinizing her again. Blood spatter spotted Gretchen's cheeks and neck like red freckles. The sadness Susan had thought she'd seen in her eyes was gone, if it had ever been there. Gretchen looked at Susan with the same mix of superiority and queenly detachment that she always did. Susan's lip trembled as she looked pleadingly at Gretchen, waiting for an answer, and at the same time not wanting to hear it.

Gretchen didn't offer any answers. Instead, she stood up and began adjusting the skirt of the bloodstained white dress.

Susan reached for Archie's hand, hoping it would be warm. It was cool to the touch and sticky with blood.

She could still hear the hum of power tools. And something else—the frantic beating of someone banging on a metal door.

"They'll be here soon," Gretchen said. "Best get him on his back on the floor and keep his knees up."

Susan gazed up at Gretchen, confused. A tiny pang of hope fluttered in her chest.

"It's just a little hypovolemic shock, dear," Gretchen said.

Archie was alive.

Susan made a sound somewhere between a giggle and a sob and hunched over Archie. His skin was clammy and mottled. His eyes were still half open and unseeing. How could someone bleed that much and survive? There were two red fingerprints on his neck where Gretchen had touched him. Susan pressed her own fingertips on top of the spots. Her heart was pounding so hard it was difficult to detect anything else. Then she felt it—a faint pulse. Susan started to cry.

"Keep him warm," Gretchen said, sweeping past Susan and plucking the ring of keys off the floor. She pocketed the keys, produced a nurse's cap, and began affixing the cap to the top of her blond head.

Gretchen was leaving. The thought flooded Susan with relief, followed by an immediate knot of dread. Gretchen was going to leave her here with Archie. But Susan didn't know what to do, how to take care of him. Keep him warm? With what?

"This was fun," Gretchen said gaily. She frowned a little. "I don't know what I'm going to do next year to top it." She gave Susan a curt smile, stood up a little straighter, and stepped through the door.

Susan looked helplessly at the empty space where Gretchen had been. "Wait," she said weakly. But the word was swallowed by the sound of the power tools.

For a moment, Susan couldn't move. She didn't know how to take care of someone. She couldn't even take care of herself. She couldn't lay him down—she'd hurt him, make it worse. She had told Jeff Heil he wouldn't die. She had said it again and again as he slipped away in her arms. She was supposed to take care of Pearl, and look what had happened to her.

Then Susan's eyes fell on a round metal object on the floor by Archie's hip, near her knee. It looked like it had fallen out of Archie's pocket. Reflexively, Susan snatched it up. She thought it was a pillbox. But when she pressed the little latch, the top popped up revealing the face of a compass. The hand was trembling, pointing north.

Don't worry about the direction. Just move.

Susan snapped the compass closed, stretched her arm around Archie's shoulders, and began to slowly ease him fully onto the floor. She anticipated him to groan or wince or cry out, but his face remained lifeless. When he was flat on his back, she crawled around his body and bent and lifted each of his legs. His hands were at his sides on the concrete. She reached for one to give it a squeeze. It felt cool and dead, like refrigerated meat. Susan lifted it and held it to her chest, trying to warm it. She glanced around the ransacked room. There was nothing to cover him with. She lifted the other hand, sticky with blood all the way to his elbow, and pressed it against her chest and neck. Three hikers had gotten lost once on Mount Hood and they'd kept each other alive through a snowstorm by staying pressed up against each other through the night. Susan stretched out next to Archie, wrapped her arms around his chest, and curled her body around his. The tiny hairs on her arms stood up and her skin goose-pimpled as a chill instantly radiated down to her toes. She felt something wet and she realized that the pool of Karim's blood was slowly spreading under them. Susan gripped Archie tighter. The compass was still in her hand, hard and smooth against her palm. "We'll be fine," she told him. Then she reached down and slid the compass back into Archie's pocket.

CHAPTER

44

Archie comes to consciousness gasping for air. Leo and Star are gone and he is alone in the guesthouse bedroom. His head is pounding, but he remembers everything. It unfolds in his mind like a Kinetoscope. Star coming down the stairs, Leo washing blood off in the sink, Leo putting his arm around Archie's neck.

Archie props himself up on his elbows.

Susan is in danger.

She is on the island.

"They're using her to control me," Leo had said. "You have to find her and get her out of here." The room spins. Archie grasps the bedpost and pulls himself into a seated position. Everything is undulating, throbbing along with his pulse. How long has he been out? Archie's eyes move to the bedroom window. He can see between the drapes that it's still dark. Maybe it's only been a few minutes. Maybe there's still time. He doesn't know. He doesn't even know why Leo did this to him, and right now he doesn't care. He knows that Susan needs him. That is enough. Using the bed for leverage, he hauls himself upright until he is bent over and dizzy, but standing. He glances around the room for a landline, but doesn't see one. He has to get downstairs. His head is already clearing. By the time he gets down the stairs, he is lucid. The guesthouse is quiet. The lights downstairs are low. Archie makes his way carefully through the living room and out the front door. The catering van is gone. He fumbles for the mask in his pocket and puts it on, and then moves briskly down a path leading through the grounds. The party is still going. He can hear the music coming from around the house. The lamplights and torches are like bright stars in the yard. But he doesn't see anyone else. No caterers or partygoers. It's like this part of the grounds has been closed to guests. The path in front of Archie forks in two. So many of the gravel garden paths split and meander and double back on themselves, that Archie has to glance around to get his bearings. He doesn't want to lose time. That's when he sees her.

He stops in his tracks.

She's not on a path. She's in the woods. But there is an accent spotlight angled up to illuminate a tree, and it catches her briefly in its glow. She is wearing a slinky red gown and a gold mask that glitters as she crosses the beam of light. Her hair is long and dark.

But Archie would know her anywhere.

It's Gretchen Lowell.

Archie knows every inch of her body; he recognizes the angle of her head, the contour of her shoulders, her carriage. But he knows she must be a hallucination, that he's gone too long without oxygen, that his eyes are playing tricks on him. Yet, there she is, right in front of him. She doesn't see him. He's sure of this. Her attention is focused elsewhere, up ahead. Archie follows her gaze and sees a flash of movement thirty feet in front of her, and he realizes that she's following somebody.

She looks so real.

He takes a step after her.

Then she's gone, out of the light, like she was never there. Archie panics, despite himself. He steps off the path and hurries across the grounds, toward the lake, toward the place where she had been. He scans the tree line, black foliage, the odd angles where accent lights cut through the darkness. He's not sure what he wants more—to see her and know he's not crazy, or to not see her and know he is.

He stays off the paths, stepping around plants, trying to stay in the dark.

As he gets closer to the empty spotlight, he sees a faint greenish glow through the trees and knows where he is. Two gargoyle lamps light the entrance down to the pool and boat-house. Archie stops. The music is muffled; the party seems distant. He peers around one of the lamps, but the stairs down the hillside are dark. The pool glows luminescent green. More gargoyle lamps light the path from the pool to the boat-house. Each throws a circle of light on the stone deck, leaving the gargoyle on top in shadow, a hunched silhouette, like a carrion bird waiting for meat.

Archie thinks he sees a shape dart past one of the lamps—a flash of red.

He steps back into the darkness, heart pounding.

Why would she be here, on the island?

But he knows she has come for him.

He is supposed to go down there. He is supposed to fol-low her.

And then, in a moment of clarity that surprises even him, Archie thinks, *no.*

He looks back in the direction of the house. The lights are just visible through the trees.

Susan is back there somewhere.

Along with a host of dangers: Razor Burn, who was prac-tically wearing a lanyard that said sexual predator; the Rus-sian, who looked like he knew how to kill someone with his kneecaps; and Jack, who had a billion-dollar drug business to protect. Then there was Leo. He had choked Archie un-conscious. Who knew what he was capable of?

Susan, Archie knows, will not be safe until she is off that island.

Archie starts walking, away from the stairs, away from phantom images at the edge of lamps. He doesn't know if Susan is somewhere on the grounds or in the house. He hopes they have her at the party, because if she's in the house, he won't stand a chance, especially without a weapon. He'll search the party, and if she's not there, he'll make a run for the bridge. So Archie follows the music. He can smell plants as he passes them, lavender and rosemary and lemon thyme. He focuses on Susan. A hundred feet ahead, Archie can see the torches and the shadows of partygoers moving in and out of their glow. Broadleaf plants tear under his feet. This part of the landscaping is lit with pink gel cans that make everything blush-colored. His mask itches. His shirt cuffs are pink.

If he can't find Susan quickly, he tells himself again, then he will go the bridge and hail the surveillance team, even if it costs Leo the operation.

A sound makes Archie stop short. Maybe it isn't a sound—maybe it's movement, a shuddering of leaves; but something sets off an alarm deep in Archie's lizard brain. The vegetation parts and Archie catches a glimpse of pink light reflected on the scales. A snake. Archie's spine goes rigid. The pink lights illuminate the ground just enough to reveal a creature as thick as Archie's arm. It's too big to be anything native. It has to have been intentionally released at some point on the island. Archie doesn't have an irrational fear of snakes. He has a rational fear of huge fucking snakes. He takes another step, but stops again as his foot hits a log of thick, coiled reptilian muscle. Archie feels the snake curl around his ankle. Archie lifts his leg off the ground and kicks it in the air like it's on fire. The snake has not managed to secure itself yet and Archie is able to shake it free.

As soon as it lets go, Archie pivots and lunges away. He manages to cover twenty feet in three steps before he loses his balance and falls. It takes him what feels like minutes to hit the ground. Even then he doesn't get his hands out in time. He expects to hit vegetation, soft ground. So he's surprised when his head smacks hard against something on the way down. He sees stars, but somehow manages to end up on his hands and knees in the dirt. He's lost his mask. He's no longer bathed in pink light, so he grapples with a hand for what he's hit, both to figure out what it is and to hold on to something. The information comes to him in fragments. A dog-sized figure. Cast in concrete. Batlike wings. Tucked among the plants like a garden gnome. Archie can just make out its silhouette through the thickening haze: a gargoyle—hunched and waiting for meat.

Archie feels blood dripping down the side of his face. He clings to the wing of the statue, trying to stay upright, but the garden is rotating around him, the inertia pulling him away. He loses hold and sinks backward into the foliage.

He knows the symptoms of a concussion.

But the ringing in his ears is making it hard to think. He can feel his consciousness fading.

Susan. He has to remember. He says her name again and again as the blackness takes him, until her name stops making sense, until he can't remember anymore where he was going or why.

The sky above him is like velvet.

Where was he going?

He can feel the plants under and around him, soft leaves and earth under his fingers. His eyes are closed. But he can still see an image. It's like a photograph on the inside of his eyelids: the gargoyle lamps on either side of the stairs leading down to the boathouse. He can smell the lake.

That's where he was going.

The boathouse.

He has to get down the stairs to the boathouse.

He doesn't remember why.

CHAPTER

45

Susan's ear hurt. It had taken fourteen stitches to close the skin over the cartilage where Karim had sliced her with the knife. Now she'd never be an earring model. They hadn't spared on bandages—the entire side of her head was enveloped in gauze and tape. Her left arm was in a sling. She looked like she'd just gotten back from World War I.

Susan ran a finger along the edge of the bandage on her head. The tape itched and she couldn't really hear out of that ear.

Her mother said something.

"What?" Susan asked, turning to peer at Bliss, who sat in a hospital armchair, knitting with neon-pink yarn.

"Don't pick at it," Bliss said.

Bliss's patchwork cargo pants were tucked into purple sheepskin boots and she was wearing a black OCCUPY WALL STREET T-shirt. She'd brought a plate of caramel apples, which sat on a tray one of the nurses had rolled in. Bliss's wooden knitting needles made a familiar clicking sound that Susan found comforting. Those first few hours, when they'd given Susan the good pain meds and she was drifting in and out, she liked hearing that sound every time she came to—it meant her mother was nearby.

"I thought they were coming to discharge me," Susan said. She was already dressed. Bliss had brought her clothes to change into—a blue and white batik blouse that Bliss had given Susan four years ago and that she'd never worn, green corduroy pedal pushers, and an ancient pair of Keens that Susan had bought at Goodwill to wear when she went beach-combing one summer for a story for the *Herald*. She looked ridiculous and the shoes smelled faintly of rotting seaweed. But Bliss didn't seem to notice.

"They said soon," Bliss said. She smiled approvingly. "Your sling matches the shirt."

They'd said "soon" an hour ago. Susan still had the IV port in her hand. A small bruise had formed where the needle pierced her skin. Archie's blood had taken a long time to come off her hands. They'd let Susan take a shower after she swore not to get the bandage wet and Susan had washed her hands raw under the hot water until every speck of blood was gone. But now she saw a faint line of red at the edge of her nail bed.

Susan curled her hand. "I smell like hospital soap," she said to her mother.

"How does your shoulder feel?" Bliss asked.

Susan rotated her shoulder gently. The doctors had done an MRI and seemed to think she'd be fine. She was lucky, they told her, that someone with medical training had per-formed what they called a "closed reduction" before long-term damage was done. "My shoulder's fine," she said, hopping off the bed. She walked to the window.

"And your vagina?" Bliss asked.

Susan blushed despite herself. "It kind of . . . throbs," Susan said. Karim had bruised her, but an examination had shown that he'd never gotten his vicious little hands inside her. "Luckily my vagina had titanium doors," she added.

"It's those Kegel exercises I taught you," Bliss said.

You could see almost all of the east side from her hospital

room up on the hill at OHSU. The complex loomed above the city at the top of a winding road. Serious cases, like Archie, arrived by helicopter. There were no mountains on the horizon today. The cloud cover blotted them off the landscape as if they had never existed.

"I want to see Archie," Susan said.

The clicking stopped. "I know," Bliss said.

Susan scratched at the fine scrape on her neck. It hadn't needed stitches. A fine crust of scab had already formed at the places where Karim's blade had nicked her flesh.

"Don't pick," her mother said, and the clicking started again.

Henry had stopped by with updates. Archie was out of surgery, in the recovery room. They knew that much. But Susan wouldn't feel right until she saw him.

In the distance, the OHSU aerial tram glided silently up the hill, over the houses of John's Landing. It carried hospital workers and patients from the medical buildings at the top of the hill to the medical buildings OHSU had at the South Waterfront. It had been controversial at first. No one in John's Landing wanted it built. But Susan thought the silver, egglike tram had a strange, graceful beauty.

"She's long gone by now," Susan said to her mother, and they both knew who she meant.

CHAPTER

46

Susan was still at the window when Leo Reynolds walked into her hospital room. She had been expecting some news about Archie, or the nurse with her discharge papers, and her face must have registered a flicker of disappointment because Leo stopped dead in his tracks.

He stood just inside the door, hands in the pockets of his smart-looking suit. There was an awkwardness to his bearing that Susan had never seen before. His easy confidence had an edge of nervousness to it.

"Come in," she said.

He glanced at Bliss.

Susan's mother made a humming sound and stood up. "Well, I think I'll go find a chai latte," she said. Then she left the room without her purse.

Susan stayed next to the window. Leo stayed where he was, just inside the door. The gap between their bodies felt like a canyon.

"Sorry about your dad," Susan said. She knew what it was to lose a father, even a nasty one like Jack Reynolds.

"Thanks," Leo said quietly. His hands were still in his pockets. He seemed drained. There were dark circles under his eyes. His shoulders hung. The jittery affect she'd noticed the last few times she'd seen him was gone. He was unusually still.

He'd lost everyone in his family, she realized—his mother when he was young, and now both his siblings and his father to violence. Her eyes went automatically to Bliss's purse, her knitting materials splayed out on the seat of her chair. She missed the sound of the wooden sticks.

"How are you?" Leo asked.

"Fine," Susan said. She forced a laugh and pointed to her bandaged head. "This is my Halloween costume. I'm going as a World War I vet just back from the Battle of Cantigny." Susan waited a beat, but Leo didn't smile. "All the nurses thought it was funny," she said.

"How are you, really?" Leo asked.

"I'm fine," Susan insisted. She shrugged and winced from a twinge in her shoulder. "I'll be fine." She tried to look nonchalant. "Only with a tiny bit less ear."

Leo nodded. "Good," he said. Then he cleared his throat. "I'm sorry," he said. "That you were brought into this. About what happened to you."

"You didn't bring me into it," Susan said. She knew where this was going, and was in no hurry to get there. She turned to look out the cold glass again.

Leo walked over to her and stood next to her and they both looked out the window for what seemed like a long time.

"Do you want me to do it?" he asked finally.

Susan felt her eyes well with tears and her throat constrict. She could barely look at him. But she made herself. She had told herself that she was going to do this like an adult. She knew what she was going to say. She'd already gone through it in her head. But now, faced with him, she couldn't find the words. She wanted to explain. She wanted an explanation.

His eyes remained steady on her, waiting, all of a sudden an attentive boyfriend. It just made Susan angrier.

"You didn't come after me," Susan blurted out. She could forgive Leo for abandoning her at the party. But not stepping up when she was being held hostage by a serial killer?

Leo nodded. He hadn't flinched at the accusation. He'd known it was coming.

"Archie did," Susan continued. "But you didn't." It sounded so selfish said out loud. "I understand," she added quickly. "Jack was bleeding right in front of you. The cops were coming. I understand all of it." She understood, but it didn't matter. "But you didn't come."

"The police arrived right after the elevator doors closed," Leo said softly, not looking at her. "They held me for questioning. They had to. It would have looked suspicious if they hadn't."

She could tell that he was explaining, not offering an excuse. But Archie had made it. Leo could have, too, if he'd wanted to. He could have gotten onto that elevator. And there was something else that didn't make sense. "Jack is dead," Susan said. "The investigation is over—why would your cover still need to be protected?"

Leo looked at her, and there was something in his eyes that made her uneasy. "I'm Jack's successor," he said. "I can take over the business. I'll have access to the international partners now." His neck was blotchy with color and his voice was low. "I can bring them all down."

Susan searched Leo's face. She couldn't tell if he was seething with ambition, or revenge. "But you're miserable," she said.

Leo shook his head. He looked fevered. "This makes it all worth it," he said. "Otherwise . . ." He sighed and his face changed. He looked out the window again and became circumspect.

Susan hated it when people became circumspect. It was always accompanied by silence, and she always felt compelled to fill that silence. But this time, Leo spoke first.

"Go ahead and say it," he said.

He was right. If she didn't say it, he would, and they both

knew that if he said it, she'd never be able to forgive him. Her face flushed with heat. "I think we should break up," Susan said.

Leo touched her cheek, and she gazed into his ice-blue eyes. She wanted to lean into his hand, to let him wrap his hand around her skull and pull her into him, but she didn't.

His hand lowered to her shoulder and he adjusted the strap of her sling. "Okay," he said.

Okay?

Just like that?

Leo leaned close to her and kissed her lightly on the cheek. His lips were cool and soft. She heard him mumble something, but the bandage on her ear muffled what he'd said.

"What?" she asked.

He took a step back and smiled.

"I didn't hear you," Susan said. She pointed at her ear. "The bandage."

"It's nothing," Leo said.

He turned and walked toward the door, leaving Susan standing by the window. She opened her mouth to say something, but nothing came out.

Leo was halfway across the room when he stopped.

Susan's heart leapt. He was having second thoughts. He was going to turn around and profess his love for her, offer to make it work whatever it took.

"Can I have a caramel apple?" Leo said, pointing at the rolling tray.

Susan's eyes went to the plate of caramel apples Bliss had laid out. "Help yourself," she said.

Leo picked up an apple by its Popsicle stick, leaving some caramel on the wax paper where the apple had been, and he left her.

CHAPTER

47

The first thing Archie saw when he opened his eyes was a beautiful angel. She was dressed all in white, her silvery wings spread out behind her, and a gold halo hovered over her chestnut hair. Her round, sweet face was peaceful, and a gentle smile played on her rosebud lips. Her eyes were on the word search book she had in her lap.

"Hey, kiddo," Archie whispered hoarsely to his daughter.

Sara's eyes brightened and as she hopped out of the chair, her halo bobbed up and down on the wire that attached it to her head of brown hair. "Daddy's awake!" she announced, as she scrambled to his bedside.

Archie's body felt like cold black water, like a lake. He lifted his hands to see the IV port taped there and the tangle of clear tubes. Images flashed in his mind as the night before pieced back together for him. Fresh white bandages covered his bare midsection.

Susan. Panic cleaved through Archie's chest. "Susan?" he asked, trying to lift his head, his voice cracking.

Ben and Debbie came into view. "She's fine," Debbie said with a reassuring smile, and relief washed over him.

"Henry's here," she added, though Archie couldn't see him. "He'll explain everything soon."

She was alive. Somehow, she was alive. Archie nodded. He blinked heavily at them, his eyes warm and full of grit. His body itched and his arms felt heavy.

"You're on the good stuff now," Debbie said. "Morphine. So don't worry if you fade in and out."

Archie fought to keep his eyes open, training his gaze on his son, who was wearing a black turtleneck, a black beret, sunglasses, and a fake goatee. "What are you supposed to be?" Archie asked weakly.

"I'm a beatnik," Ben said, glancing to a corner of the room Archie couldn't see. "Henry lent me his bongo drums."

Halloween. How could it still be Halloween?

"I promised I'd take them trick-or-treating after we leave," Debbie said.

Archie tried to do the math, to figure out how long he'd been in that room, to sort through the memory fragments. It was all so disorienting.

"You were brought here early this morning," Debbie said, reading his confusion. "You were in surgery for hours, but they say you'll make a full recovery." She had done this so many times now, the hospital vigil—she was an expert at it.

"Gretchen?" Archie asked, and the name seemed to float above his bed and hover there.

Debbie's pleasant features hardened. "Missing," she said. "I'm taking the kids trick-or-treating at the mall," she added pointedly. "They've told people to stay inside tonight."

The words condensed in Archie's brain like a clot. Gretchen had escaped. She was still out there. Somewhere. Archie could feel himself slipping away into oblivion again. He grasped for the angel's hand and touched her dress instead, the polyester smooth beneath his fingers.

"Susan?" Archie called out. He was groggy. Where was he? He tried to sit up and felt someone stop him.

"You're in the hospital." It was Henry's voice. "Easy."

He was in a blue room. The sky outside the window was a dingy slate. "Is Susan okay?" Archie asked.

Henry took his hands off Archie's shoulders. "Her ear's all stitched up," he said in an automatic tone that made Archie think they had had this conversation several times before. "Her arm's in a sling and she'll come see you as soon as she's discharged, I'm sure."

Archie relaxed a little, his eyes taking in his surroundings. He was in a long room with a pale blue couch, and a crowd of chairs, as if extra seating had been brought in from other rooms. He saw the word search book and remembered his children being there, and Debbie. He could hear muted hospital sounds—intercom announcements, snippets of hallway conversation. A plastic tray of half-eaten food sat near where Henry had been sitting, and the room smelled faintly of green beans and chicken.

Fragments of memories began to form in his brain, seizing him by the chest. "The uniforms outside my apartment?" Archie asked, trying to sit up again.

"They're okay," Henry said, gently pushing Archie back. "She drugged them."

"Did you get Karim?" Archie asked.

"Gretchen killed him," Henry said, pulling up a plastic chair and taking a seat next to Archie's IV pump. "We'll go through all the details when you're a little stronger." He paused, scratching at the white bristles on his chin. "One bit of business we do need to go over," he said. "Rachel's downtown. I had her held overnight as a material witness. You want her charged?"

Henry had gone to his apartment, just as Archie had known he would. He had found Rachel. She had told him everything. If Archie had had any shame left, he would have burned from the humiliation. But he was too tired, and Henry had witnessed his indiscretions before. "No," Archie said. Where Rachel had been involved, he had been a willing fool. "But tell her to lay low for a while," he said. "I don't think Gretchen would hurt her." He saw Gretchen in his mind, the nurse's costume splattered with blood. "But I don't know."

"Your dog is at my house, by the way," Henry said. "The kid next door is staying with her. Last time I checked in, he said that she had chewed the beads off my Minnetonka moccasins."

"Claire hates those shoes anyway," Archie said. He tried to smile, but it took too much strength. "How many dead at the house?" Archie asked.

"Ten, including Jack," Henry said grimly. "Eleven, if you count Lisa Watson. You're going to have to answer a lot of questions in the next few days."

Archie thought of the chaotic trail of blood, Razor Burn slashed by Gretchen and then shot by Cooper. It would take a diagram to figure it all out. "Did Cooper make it out?" he asked.

"Cooper?" Henry pulled out his notebook and flipped through it. A tiny fragment of green bean was stuck to his mustache. "We didn't find anyone by that name, alive or dead."

Archie smiled weakly. Razor Burn would have died anyway, but Cooper had saved Archie's life when he'd hastened the process.

"Should we be looking for him?" Henry asked. "Was it his gun you were using?"

Archie closed his eyes.

"Archie?" Henry asked from far away. "Should we be looking for him?"

Henry was in deep discussion with Sanchez. For a moment they didn't notice that Archie was awake. Archie tried to overhear what the two men were talking about, but their voices were hushed and urgent and Archie's senses were blurred by drugs. The plastic tray was gone. The sky was denser, emulsifying into dusk. The word search book was gone.

Sanchez noticed Archie first. "Look who's up," he said, and he and Henry both turned to Archie and headed to his bedside. Sanchez was in his FBI cap and bureau jacket, a badge on a lanyard around his neck, his weapon on his hip, and two BlackBerrys and a walkie-talkie clipped to his waistband.

"Nice costume," Archie said. "You look like a real G-man."

Sanchez looked down at his ensemble and grinned. "I was going to go as Hoover, but I couldn't find a feather boa."

Henry sat down in the plastic chair at Archie's bedside. "Sanchez was just updating me on the manhunt," he said. His eyebrows drew together. "Woman-hunt, whatever."

Sanchez stood next to Henry, arms crossed over his chest. "Your girl is pretty slick at avoiding capture, but we're working with our international partners to make it as hard as possible for her."

Archie was still trying to piece everything together. "How'd you get to us?" he asked Sanchez and Henry.

Sanchez rocked back on his heels. "The elevator was disabled right after you got down there," he said. "The thing was reinforced with steel, Kevlar, and bulletproof fiberglass. There was no way to get down the shaft. Leo was the one who showed us how to access the tunnel. He showed us the supply cabinet with tools to get through the door. If it hadn't been for him, you'd probably still be thirty feet under that island."

It appeared that Archie owed Sanchez an apology. "Sorry I thought you might be dirty," he said.

"Never said I wasn't," Sanchez said. "Leo thinks I am. Carl was worried about him, his allegiances. So he got my name on a list he knew would find its way into Leo's orbit. He wanted to see what the kid would do with it."

"He reported it," Archie said. "So he passed the test."

"He reported it to you," Sanchez said. "He was supposed to report it to Carl."

"Maybe he couldn't get his Ouija board to work," Archie said. It occurred to him that it had only been three days since Carl had been murdered. It seemed like longer. "What's the status of that investigation, anyway? Are there any suspects?"

Henry and Sanchez exchanged looks.

"What?" Archie asked.

Henry scratched his eyebrow. "It was Thor," he said.

Archie waited for the punch line. Henry leaned back in his chair and glanced up at Sanchez.

"As in the god of thunder?" Archie asked.

"He also goes by Ralph Huntley, when it's not Halloween," Sanchez said.

Henry shrugged. "Ralph thought Carl was flirting with his girl," he said.

"She was dressed up as the Enchantress," Sanchez added, "so, it's within the realm of possibility."

"Turns out Ralph has some anger management issues," Henry said. "The Enchantress dropped a dime on him—told detectives where to find the Beretta with his prints on it. He confessed this morning."

"You're saying that Carl's murder had nothing to do with Leo or Jack or any of it," Archie said.

"Doesn't look like it," Henry said.

Archie thought about all that Carl's murder had set in motion—it had sent Archie to Leo, and because they'd been seen together, Leo had been taken back to the island, Susan had been taken to keep Leo in line, which had drawn Archie to the island, which in turn had led Gretchen there. So many were dead. All due to a pass that may or may not have even happened. But at least one good thing had come of it. "I'm just glad that Leo is out of there," Archie said.

Henry made a coughing noise.

Sanchez looked at his fingernails.

"Leo's staying," Henry said.

It took a moment for Henry's words to register through Archie's morphine haze. "You're shitting me," Archie said, narrowing his eyes at Sanchez.

"Leo's idea," Sanchez said. "Not mine. He wants to take down the entire international syndicate," he added. "He might be able to do it, too."

"What about the whole underground narcotics warehouse thing?" Archie asked. They couldn't just pretend they hadn't seen it, not that kind of quantity.

"Oh, the DEA confiscated the dope," Sanchez said. "They're not crazy. But that shit's on Jack. And as you know, he's toes-up. So Leo takes over the old man's shop and the DEA has an agent in the catbird seat."

"What about you?" Archie asked.

"I'm done," Sanchez said. "That interagency cooperation business went out the window about the time I started protesting the decision to leave Leo in the game. The kid just lost his father. He's using drugs. I don't want him getting killed on my watch. Anyway, I think I have enough on my plate." He exhaled slowly. "I have the feeling that Gretchen Lowell is going to be keeping me very busy," he said. Sanchez glanced at his watch then and straightened up. "I'm supposed to be giving a press conference with the chief in fifteen minutes. We want to get the word out that you're still kicking." He nudged Henry's shoulder with his elbow. "You told him, right? How much worse it could have been?"

Henry's jaw tightened. "Not yet."

Sanchez beamed at Archie, apparently tickled to get to deliver the news. "Doctors said that if you'd had a spleen you would have definitely bled out," he said. "You'd be dead. The fact that she had already taken it out saved your life." Sanchez shook his head in disbelief.

Just perfect. "Lucky me," Archie said.

Sanchez eyeballed his watch again. "Either of you want to give me a statement to release to the media?" he asked Archie and Henry.

"Just make something up," Archie said. Then he remembered what Debbie had said. "Are they really telling everyone to stay indoors tonight?" Archie asked.

"The city is crawling with jokers wearing masks," Sanchez said. "She could be any one of them. The fewer people in costume, the better."

It was all so ridiculous, such a waste of time. Didn't they realize that? She had gotten what she came for. Archie looked from Sanchez to Henry. Why didn't they see it? "She's gone," Archie told them.

"Sure, she's gone," Sanchez said, extracting a small, neatly folded piece of paper from his jacket pocket with two fingers. "For now."

Sanchez held the paper out to Archie. "In the meantime, I know it's not much, but you'd appreciate it even more if you knew how much paperwork it took."

Archie took the piece of paper and unfolded it. It was a check made out to Archie from the FBI in the amount of $329.38.

"For the tuxedo," Sanchez explained. "It was the least we could do."

Archie laughed. It hurt, but it was the good kind of pain.

"Be seeing you," Sanchez said with a nod to both Henry and Archie, and he went out the door to Archie's room into the bright hospital hallway. As the door closed behind him, Archie noticed two uniformed patrol cops standing in the hall.

"It's a precaution," Henry said. "And not to change the subject, but I have a call." He pulled his phone from his pocket and showed it to Archie.

"Go ahead," Archie said.

Henry stood up and stepped away to the window to take the call. Archie watched him. He was wearing the black jeans and black cowboy boots he'd had on the day before. The pits of his black T-shirt were scalloped with sweat. The seams of his boots were edged with dirt, and the same pale yellow leaf still clung stubbornly to his heel. Henry's T-shirt was puckered with dried bloodstains. The black cotton camouflaged them, but Archie could see the hardened blood on the fabric, just as it struck him that the blood must be from him.

The anemic sky darkened behind Henry. Archie watched as his friend pulled his notebook from his pants again and held it against the wall to scribble a few notes. Then Henry thanked the person who had called, hung up, and put the phone back in his pocket.

Archie tried to sit up a little, immediately regretting it. "Who was that?" he asked, wincing.

"Lab," Henry said, walking back to Archie's bedside. "The DNA on Karim's teaspoon matched the DNA that Robbins found on Lisa Watson's body."

"And?" Archie asked.

"And what?"

Archie examined his friend's face, looking for some hints as to what was coming. But Henry wasn't giving him anything. "You're just learning this now?" Archie asked.

"Yep," Henry said. He sat on the edge of Archie's bed, folded his hands, and waited.

Archie struggled to understand. If Henry had only just now matched Karim's DNA, then what had led Henry and Sanchez to the island the night before? Henry would have had no way of tracing Archie to the island. Even once Henry had heard everything from Rachel—nothing would have led him to figure out where Gretchen had taken him.

"I thought . . ." Archie said.

"I called the number," Henry said.

Archie was still. He could feel the saline and the morphine dripping into his vein, the cold bright burn in his blood. He could feel Henry's girth on his bed, a heavy presence that seemed to anchor the bed to the floor. Archie watched as Henry wedged his hand into his pocket and pulled out a small folded piece of yellow paper: the Post-it note that Archie had given Henry before Jack Reynolds's party.

Henry unfolded the Post-it note and held it out to Archie. Archie didn't have to look. He knew what he'd written.

"It's a telephone number," Henry said.

Archie turned his eyes to the paper, a knot hardening in his throat. "I told you to look at that if I was gone for twenty-four hours," Archie said. "I came back."

"And then you disappeared again," Henry said evenly. "And there I am—you and Susan both missing, and I've got Rachel, or whatever the fuck her name is, with some hysterical, convoluted story, and I've got your computer infected with malware that Ngyun tells me has been on it since August, and I don't mind telling you, I'm getting mighty concerned at this point—and then"—he looked at Archie, incredulously—"I remember the number. Your Visa number, right? That was your joke. Only when I unfold it and look at it, I find this." Henry held the paper close to Archie's face. "Ten digits. A drop phone. Untraceable. A hotline I could call if you ever got in the kind of trouble I couldn't get you out of myself."

Archie didn't move.

"So I called it," Henry said.

He was looking at Archie intently—his skeptical blue eyes watching him, cataloging his reactions.

The shadows in the room seemed longer, the air thicker. Archie swallowed. "Did she pick up?" Archie asked hesitantly.

Henry shook his head, his face shining with amazement. "She did," he said. "She told me you were on the island, that Karim murdered Lisa Watson, among others, and that both you and Susan were in mortal danger. She even sounded a little concerned."

A sharp knock on the hospital room door made both men turn.

"You guys decent?" Claire's voice called.

Henry looked back at Archie and the gravity of his gaze made Archie's spine hurt. Then Henry crumpled the Post-it note in his hand and rolled the balled-up paper between his palms until it was the size of a marble. "Come in," he called at the door.

Claire walked in, gnawing at the side of a caramel apple.

"We're done," Henry said to her, standing up. "You ready to go home?"

"I have never been more ready to go home," Claire said, coming around Archie's bed and kissing Henry on the mouth. She gave Archie a supportive smile. "You look better. You should have seen yourself when we first found you two. You looked like you'd been dead for hours."

Archie didn't like to think of Susan having to see him like that. "She must have been terrified," he said.

"No," Claire said. "She was focused. She was holding you, to keep your body temp from tanking. She probably saved your life."

Archie tried to remember, but the last image he saw in his mind was Karim threatening Susan, Archie firing the gun. "I don't remember that," he said.

Claire frowned. "You always miss the good stuff, don't you?"

"Do I?" Archie asked.

Claire sighed and bent down and kissed Archie on the forehead. "Get some sleep," she said. "We'll come back in the morning once my ankles have returned to a semblance of their normal shape."

"I look forward to it," Archie said. "And remember, Ginger needs to sleep in the bed. It's what she's used to."

Henry hesitated. "You want me to stay?" he asked Archie. "I can sleep on the couch. So you have someone around. Between the cats and the corgi, it doesn't sound like there will be room for me in bed anyway."

Archie considered the offer—the truth was he wouldn't have minded the company and he still had a lot of questions. But Claire was giving him the evil eye. She needed Henry more than he did anyway. "You two go home together," Archie said. "I'll be okay."

Claire grinned widely, and tightened her arm around Henry's waist.

"Catch," Henry said, tossing Archie the balled-up Post-it note from his hand.

Archie caught it. "I never called the number," he said to Henry, his fist tightening around the small paper ball. "I didn't even know it worked. It was something she gave me a long time ago."

Henry put his arm around Claire, who Archie could tell was pretending not to understand their conversation. "Good thing, I guess," Henry said.

"Oh," Claire said to Archie, as if she'd just remembered something. "Star says you two are even, by the way."

"Star?" Archie said.

"Your stripper friend?" Claire said brightly. "She says hi, and that you're even."

Archie tried to think what that could mean and how it had come to pass that he even had a stripper friend. "Okay?" he said.

"I'll explain later," Henry told him.

Archie watched as they left the room, arm in arm. Archie was pretty sure he saw Claire give Henry's ass a squeeze as they went out.

* * *

A nurse in pink scrubs and a pair of white fuzzy rabbit ears on her head was checking Archie's vitals.

"Sorry I woke you," she whispered apologetically, her rabbit ears bobbing.

Archie blinked blearily. It was dark outside and the lights in his room had been adjusted to their dimmest setting, giving the space a faint golden glow, just enough light to find the bathroom, and not enough to read by. "What time is it?" he muttered.

"Eleven-thirty," she said. "Halloween's almost over."

She returned her gaze to the blood pressure cuff on his arm and Archie saw a figure curled on the love seat under the window over her shoulder. He thought it was Henry until he saw the black and white hair.

"She's been here for hours," the nurse whispered.

She removed the cuff, jotted down the blood pressure reading in his chart, and then stood. "I'll let you get back to sleep," she said with a mild smile. She walked to the door and paused. Her long ears threw a shadow on the blue wall. "Want the lights off?" she called softly.

"No," Archie said, his eyes still on Susan. "You can leave them how they are."

The rabbit nurse left noiselessly, leaving the lights on their muted setting. Archie used the remote on the side of his bed to adjust the mattress angle slightly so he could see Susan a little better. She was wearing clothes he'd never seen her in before—strange pants and a shirt that looked like something someone would bring back from an island vacation. The low light was just enough to illuminate the features of her face, serene with sleep, blemished only by the stark white bandage that covered her ear. Her knees were curled to her chest. Her head was resting on one hand like a child, and her other arm, the one in the sling, was draped across her belly. He could see her breathing, the slight rise and fall of her body against the baby-blue fabric of the couch. He watched her for a long time. Sometimes her bare feet would twitch or she would go to move her bad arm in her sleep and then her face would tense and her arm would settle back against her side.

Archie liked having her here.

He could have watched her all night.

He didn't even see her open her eyes. He was just watching her and after a while he became aware that she was watching him, too. Her breathing hadn't changed, her body was still, but her green eyes were wide and alert. Then she sat up and yawned.

"I guess I fell asleep," she said.

"I guess so," Archie said.

"What time is it?" Susan asked, looking around.

"Late," Archie said. "How are you?"

Susan put a hand on her shoulder. "My shoulder's okay. They said I might have had permanent damage if she hadn't fixed it when she did."

"She?" Archie asked. Then the implication hit him. "You mean Gretchen?"

"Yeah," Susan said, flustered. "Sorry. I forgot you were unconscious. She fixed it before she left."

Archie felt a prickling sensation creep up his arms. "Did she say anything?" he asked.

Susan rubbed her eyes with her good hand. "I've been through all this with Sanchez and the others," she said. She laid her head on the back of the couch, and her face fell into shadow. "She said it had been fun. And that help would be there soon. And that I should keep you warm. Then she left."

"Claire said by keeping me warm you saved my life."

Susan shrugged. "I just did what Gretchen told me." She paused. "Do you remember much?" she asked tentatively.

"Not really," Archie said. He tried to review the fragments of memory he had gathered, to put them in order. "I remember firing the gun, and then it all goes black."

Susan exhaled and he thought he saw relief in her body language.

"I can't see your face," Archie said.

Susan lifted her head. "What?"

"I want to see you," Archie said. "Come closer."

Susan looked confused, but she stood up and padded over to his bed in her bare feet. As she got closer, she moved from shades of gray and gold to full color, her face pink and freckled, her emerald eyes watching him intently. "Where's Rachel?" she asked.

Archie didn't even begin to know where to start. "She's . . ."—he searched for the right words—"gone," he said. "It didn't work out."

"I never liked her," Susan said. She shook her head and groaned, *"Blonds."*

She wavered slightly on her feet without seemingly noticing. "Leo and I broke up," she said.

Archie patted the edge of his bed with his hand and she sat down, facing him. "Do you want to talk about it?" he asked.

"Not really," she said. "Not yet. My mom brought caramel apples," she added. "If you want one."

"I'm not that hungry," Archie said.

"They don't have razor blades or anything," Susan said.

"I didn't think they did," Archie said.

Susan struggled to hold back a yawn and lost, her mouth widening as she closed her eyes and emitted a silent yowl. Then she gazed at him blearily. "I'm sorry I didn't get you a birthday present," she said.

"I think I've had enough presents this year," Archie said.

Susan scratched her arm. "I'm so tired," she said. "They gave me a pill. How do you take those things?"

"Come on," Archie said, moving over to make room for her in the narrow bed. Susan hesitated only for a moment before she folded herself on her side next to him. The bed was small, but there was room for both of them if Archie kept his legs straight and his arms at his sides, Susan on top of the covers, Archie underneath. Susan's face was at his shoulder, her nose and lips almost grazing his skin. Her knees pressed gently against his stitches, but he didn't move.

She closed her eyes and he watched her as her breathing slowed and equalized. Her foot twitched and Archie saw that a small yellow leaf was stuck there, on the bottom of her foot, clearly the same leaf that Henry had finally lost off his boot.

Archie smiled at that, and maybe it was the morphine, but he felt strangely happy. Lying there next to her, he thought that maybe he could remember what Claire had said about Susan warming him with her body. He had a memory of being very, very cold and then there being a warm presence beside him.

He glanced over at the bedside table where the balled-up piece of paper still lay. Then, very slowly, careful not to wake Susan, Archie reached over her and plucked the wad of paper from the table. He brought it to his chest, his hand trailing IV lines, and with a glance at Susan, he gingerly uncrumpled the square of yellow paper and flattened it out. He had a second copy at home, written in Gretchen's elegant handwriting, but Archie had a feeling that Henry had found it and destroyed it. The ten digits stared back at him from the wrinkled yellow paper. They were his connection to Gretchen. *"If you need me, darling,"* she'd said. Archie had looked at the telephone number so many times that he thought he knew it by heart, but now the digits looked unfamiliar to him, already reordering and fading in his memory.

Archie glanced at Susan. Then he closed his hand, crumpling the note in his fist. A plastic trash bin sat against the wall on the other side of his IV pole. Archie tossed the balled-up Post-it note at it overhand and it sailed through the air and into the trash.

Then he settled back into the bed with Susan. He was suddenly wide awake. Susan squirmed in her sleep, and Archie had to brace himself as her knee pressed again into his tender stitches, but he didn't care. He stayed very still, trying to be as small as possible, to give her enough room to be comfortable. Her mouth was open slightly, and her breath was hot against his shoulder, making the hair on the back of his neck bristle. His wound didn't hurt while he was still, and the morphine filled him with a woozy contentment. Susan moved in her sleep again and flopped a foot across his shin. He stayed awake for a long time, watching her like that, and then, finally, he slept.

ACKNOWLEDGMENTS

Thanks, as always, to my writing group: Chuck Palahniuk, Lidia Yuknavitch, Monica Drake, Erin Leonard, Mary Wysong, Suzy Vitello, Diana Jordan, and Cheryl Strayed. You could all write these books by now. My good friend and editor, Kelley Ragland, has unfailing instincts when it comes to my work, and has made this book better in a hundred ways. Joy Harris and Adam Reed, your awesomeness knows no bounds. Andy Martin and George Witte, you have always been my champions, and I will always be grateful to you. Hector DeJean, my publicist at Minotaur, thank you for being tall and able to talk comics, and thank you for all that publicity stuff, too. Everyone at St. Martin's Press/Minotaur is so classy and decent and smart. My husband and best friend, Marc Mohan, gave me a skull for Christmas. "I know you like dead things," he said. How lucky am I? Eliza Fantastic Mohan, this is the book I wrote when you were in first grade and finished when you were in second grade. If you are reading this, and you are under twenty-five, you are in big trouble, missy. A terrific bookstore here in Portland—Murder by the Book—will have gone out of business by the time this book is published. They have always been lovely to me and have hosted wonderful events, and they will be missed. Go buy a book at a local independent bookstore in their memory. Courtenay Hameister, Jason Rouse, and Sean McGrath, thank you for occasionally inviting me into the LiveWire writers' room. There is nothing like sketch comedy to cleanse the palate after a day of unapologetic heathenism and murder. Allison Frost and the gang at OPB's Think Out Loud, I do a little dance every time you invite me to be a Culture Club guest. Thank you, Bill and Mary, for the surveillance, and for the absinthe. And last, the world lost a good dog this year. Franklin, the Australian shepherd who finds the skeleton at the beginning of *The Night Season,* has died. He never did find a human corpse in real life, but he gave it one hell of a go and I think he got close a couple of times.

One Kick

Chelsea Cain

Kick Lannigan was kidnapped aged six and rescued aged twelve. In the early months following her freedom, Kick's parents put her through therapy and support groups but nothing helped. Then the detective who rescued her suggested Kick learn to fight; before she was thirteen she had mastered marksmanship, martial arts, boxing, archery and knife-throwing. She excelled at every one, vowing never again to be a victim.

But when two children in the Portland area go missing in the same month, Kick is approached with a proposition: use her past experiences and expertise to help investigators find these abductees. She has never forgotten what happened to her. And never forgiven those who did it . . .

'*One Kick* is superb! This novel will stay with you for a long time. And what a heroine . . .'
Jeffery Deaver

ISBN 978-1-47113-066-3